LINDA HOWARD

Trouble

HQN™

Recycling programs
for this product may
not exist in your area.

ISBN-13: 978-0-373-77569-9

TROUBLE

Copyright © 2011 by Harlequin Books S.A.

The publisher acknowledges the copyright holder
of the individual works as follows:

MIDNIGHT RAINBOW
Copyright © 1986 by Linda Howington

DIAMOND BAY
Copyright © 1987 by Linda Howington

CONTENTS

MIDNIGHT RAINBOW

CHAPTER ONE

HE WAS GETTING too old for this kind of crap, Grant Sullivan thought irritably. What the hell was he doing crouched here, when he'd promised himself he'd never set foot in a jungle again? He was supposed to rescue a bubble-brained society deb, but from what he'd seen in the two days he'd had this jungle fortress under surveillance, he thought she might not *want* to be rescued. She looked as if she was having the time of her life: laughing, flirting, lying by the pool in the heat of the day. She slept late; she drank champagne on the flagstone patio. Her father was almost out of his mind with worry about her, thinking that she was suffering unspeakable torture at the hands of her captors. Instead, she was lolling around as if she were vacationing on the Riviera. She certainly wasn't being tortured. If anyone was being tortured, Grant thought with growing ire, it was he himself. Mosquitoes were biting him, flies were stinging him, sweat was running off him in rivers, and his legs were aching from sitting still for so long. He'd been eating field rations again, and he'd forgotten how much he hated field rations. The humidity made all of his old wounds ache, and he had plenty of old wounds to ache. No doubt about it: he was definitely too old.

He was thirty-eight, and he'd spent over half his life involved in some war, somewhere. He was tired, tired enough that he'd opted out the year before, wanting nothing more than to wake up in the same bed every morning. He hadn't wanted company or advice or anything, except to be left the hell alone. When he had burned out, he'd burned to the core.

He hadn't quite retreated to the mountains to live in a cave, where he wouldn't have to see or speak to another human being, but he had definitely considered it. Instead, he'd bought a run-down farm in Tennessee, just in the shadow of the mountains, and let the green mists heal him. He'd dropped out, but apparently he hadn't dropped far enough: they had still known how to find him. He supposed wearily that his reputation made it necessary for certain people to know his whereabouts at all times. Whenever a job called for jungle experience and expertise, they called for Grant Sullivan.

A movement on the patio caught his attention, and he cautiously moved a broad leaf a fraction of an inch to clear his line of vision. There she was, dressed to the nines in a frothy sundress and heels, with an enormous pair of sunglasses shading her eyes. She carried a book and a tall glass of something that looked deliciously cool; she arranged herself artfully on one of the poolside deck chairs, and prepared to wile away the muggy afternoon. She waved to the guards who patrolled the plantation grounds and flashed them her dimpled smile.

Damn her pretty, useless little hide! Why couldn't she have stayed under Daddy's wing, instead of sashaying around the world to prove how "independent" she was? All she'd proved was that she had a remarkable talent for landing herself in hot water.

Poor dumb little twit, he thought. She probably didn't even realize that she was one of the central characters in a nasty little espionage caper that had at least three government and several other factions, all hostile, scrambling to find a missing microfilm. The only thing that had saved her life so far was that no one was sure how much she knew, or whether she knew anything at all. Had she been involved in George Persall's espionage activities, he wondered, or had she only been his mistress, his high-class "secretary"? Did she know where the microfilm was, or did Luis Marcel, who had disappeared, have it? The only thing anyone knew for certain was that George Persall had had the microfilm in his possession. But he'd died of a heart attack—in *her* bedroom—and the microfilm hadn't been found. Had Persall already passed it to Luis Marcel? Marcel had dropped out of sight two days before Persall died—if he had the microfilm, he certainly wasn't talking about it. The Americans wanted it, the Russians wanted it, the Sandinistas wanted it, and every rebel group in Central and South America wanted it. Hell, Sullivan thought, as far as he knew, even the Eskimos wanted it.

So where was the microfilm? What had George Persall done with it? If he had indeed passed it to Luis Marcel, who was his normal contact, then where was Luis? Had Luis decided to sell the microfilm to the highest bidder? That seemed unlikely. Grant knew Luis personally; they had been in some tight spots together and he trusted Luis at his back, which said a lot.

Government agents had been chasing this particular microfilm for about a month now. A high-level executive of a research firm in California had made a deal to sell the government-classified laser technology his firm had developed, technology that could place laser weaponry in space in the near future. The firm's own security people had become suspicious of the man and alerted the proper government authorities; together they had apprehended the executive in the middle of the sale. But the two buyers had escaped, taking the microfilm with them. Then one of the buyers double-crossed his partner and took himself and the microfilm to South America to strike his own deal. Agents all over Central and South America had been alerted, and an American agent in Costa Rica had made contact with the man, setting up a "sting" to buy the microfilm. Things became completely confused at that point. The deal had gone sour, and the agent had been wounded, but he had gotten away with the microfilm. The film should have been destroyed at that point, but it hadn't been. Somehow the agent had gotten it to George Persall, who could come and go freely in Costa Rica because of his business connections. Who would have suspected George Persall of being involved in espionage? He'd always seemed just a tame businessman, albeit with a passion for gorgeous "secretaries"—a weakness any Latin man would understand. Persall had been known to only a few agents, Luis Marcel among them, and that had made him extraordinarily effective. But in this case, George had been left in the dark; the agent had been feverish from his wound and hadn't told George to destroy the film.

Luis Marcel had been supposed to contact George, but instead Luis had disappeared. Then George, who had always seemed to be disgustingly healthy, had died of a heart attack...and no one knew where the microfilm was. The Americans wanted to be certain that the technology didn't fall into anyone else's hands; the Russians wanted the technology just as badly, and every revolutionary in the hemisphere wanted the microfilm in order to sell it to the highest bidder. An arsenal of weapons could be purchased, revolutions could be staged, with the amount of money that small piece of film would bring on the open market.

Manuel Turego, head of national security in Costa Rica, was a very smart man; he was a bastard, Grant thought, but a smart one. He'd promptly snatched up Ms. Priscilla Jane Hamilton Greer and carried her off to this heavily guarded inland "plantation." He'd probably told her that she was under protective custody, and she was probably stupid enough that she was very grateful to him for "protecting" her. Turego had played it cool; so far he hadn't harmed her. Evidently he knew that her father was a very wealthy, very influential man, and that it wasn't wise to enrage wealthy, influential men unless it was absolutely necessary. Turego was playing a waiting game; he was waiting for Luis Marcel to surface, waiting for the microfilm to surface, as it eventually had to. In the meantime, he had Priscilla; he could afford to wait. Whether she knew anything or not, she was valuable to him as a negotiating tool, if nothing else.

From the moment Priscilla had disappeared, her father had been frantic. He'd been calling in political favors with a heavy hand, but he'd found that none of the favors owed to him could get Priscilla away from Turego. Until Luis was found, the American government wasn't going to lift a hand to free the young woman. The confusion about whether or not she actually knew anything, the tantalizing possibility that she *could* know the location of the microfilm, seemed to have blunted the intensity of the search for Luis. Her captivity could give him the edge he needed by attracting attention away from him.

Finally, desperate with worry and enraged by the lack of response he'd been getting from the government, James Hamilton had decided to take matters into his own hands. He'd spent a small fortune ferreting out his daughter's location, and then had been stymied by the inaccessibility of the well-guarded plantation. If he sent in enough men to take over the plantation, he realized, there was a strong possibility that his daughter would be killed in the fight. Then someone had mentioned Grant Sullivan's name.

A man as wealthy as James Hamilton could find

someone who didn't want to be found, even a wary, burnt-out ex-government agent who had buried himself in the Tennessee mountains. Within twenty-four hours, Grant had been sitting across from Hamilton, in the library of a huge estate house that shouted of old money. Hamilton had made an offer that would pay off the mortgage on Grant's farm completely. All the man wanted was to have his daughter back, safe and sound. His face had been lined and taut with worry, and there had been a desperation about him that, even more than the money, made Grant reluctantly accept the job.

The difficulty of rescuing her had seemed enormous, perhaps even insurmountable; if he were able to penetrate the security of the plantation—something he didn't really doubt—getting her out would be something else entirely. Not only that, but Grant had his own personal experiences to remind him that, even if he found her, the odds were greatly against her being alive or recognizably human. He hadn't let himself think about what could have happened to her since the day she'd been kidnapped.

But getting to her had been made ridiculously easy; as soon as he left Hamilton's house, a new wrinkle had developed. Not a mile down the highway from Hamilton's estate, he'd glanced in the rearview mirror and found a plain blue sedan on his tail. He'd lifted one eyebrow sardonically and pulled over to the shoulder of the road.

He lit a cigarette and inhaled leisurely as he waited for the two men to approach his car. "Hiya, Curtis."

Ted Curtis leaned down and peered in the open window, grinning. "Guess who wants to see you?"

"Hell," Grant swore irritably. "All right, lead the way. I don't have to drive all the way to Virginia, do I?"

"Naw, just to the next town. He's waiting in a motel."

The fact that Sabin had felt it necessary to leave

headquarters at all told Grant a lot. He knew Kell Sabin from the old days; the man didn't have a nerve in his body, and ice water ran in his veins. He wasn't a comfortable man to be around, but Grant knew that the same had been said about himself. They were both men to whom no rules applied, men who had intimate knowledge of hell, who had lived and hunted in that gray jungle where no laws existed. The difference between them was that Sabin was comfortable in that cold grayness; it was his life—but Grant wanted no more of it. Things had gone too far; he had felt himself becoming less than human. He had begun to lose his sense of who he was and why he was there. Nothing seemed to matter any longer. The only time he'd felt alive was during the chase, when adrenaline pumped through his veins and fired all his senses into acute awareness. The bullet that had almost killed him had instead saved him, because it had stopped him long enough to let him begin thinking again. That was when he'd decided to get out.

Twenty-five minutes later, with his hand curled around a mug of strong, hot coffee, his booted feet propped comfortably on the genuine, wood-grained plastic coffee table that was standard issue for motels, Grant had murmured, "Well, I'm here. Talk."

Kell Sabin was an even six feet tall, an inch shorter than Grant, and the hard musculature of his frame revealed that he made it a point to stay in shape, even though he was no longer in the field. He was dark—black-haired, black-eyed, with an olive complexion—and the cold fire of his energy generated a force field around him. He was impossible to read, and was as canny as a stalking panther, but Grant trusted him. He couldn't say that he liked Sabin; Sabin wasn't a man to be friendly. Yet for twenty years their lives had been intertwined until they were virtually a part of each other. In his mind, Grant saw a red-orange flash of gunfire, and abruptly he felt the thick, moist heat of the jungle, smelled the rotting vegetation, saw the flash of weapons being discharged…and felt, at his back, so close that each had braced his shoulders against the other, the same man who sat across from him now. Things like that stayed in a man's memory.

A dangerous man, Kell Sabin. Hostile governments would gladly have paid a fortune to get to him, but Sabin was nothing more than a shadow slipping away from the sunshine, as he directed his troops from the gray mists.

Without a flicker of expression in his black eyes, Sabin studied the man who sat across from him in a lazy sprawl— a deceptively lazy sprawl, he knew. Grant was, if anything, even leaner and harder than he had been in the field. Hibernating for a year hadn't made him go soft. There was still something wild about Grant Sullivan, something dangerous and untamed. It was in the wary, restless glitter of his amber eyes, eyes that glowed as fierce and golden as an eagle's under the dark, level brows. His dark blond hair was shaggy, curling down over his collar in back, emphasizing that he wasn't quite civilized. He was darkly tanned; the small scar on his chin wasn't very noticeable, but the thin line that slashed across his left cheekbone was silver against his bronzed skin. They weren't disfiguring scars, but reminders of battles.

If Sabin had had to pick anyone to go after Hamilton's daughter, he'd have picked this man. In the jungle Sullivan was as stealthy as a cat; he could become part of the jungle, blending into it, using it. He'd been useful in the concrete jungles, too, but it was in the green hells of the world that no one could equal him.

"Are you going after her?" Sabin finally asked in a quiet tone.

"Yeah."

"Then let me fill you in." Totally disregarding the fact that Grant no longer had security clearance, Sabin told him about the missing microfilm. He told him about George Persall, Luis Marcel, the whole deadly cat-and-mouse game, and dumb little Priscilla sitting in the middle of it. She was being used as a smokescreen for Luis, but Kell was more than a little worried about Luis. It wasn't like the man to disappear, and Costa Rica wasn't the most tranquil place on earth. Anything could have happened to him. Yet, wherever he was, he wasn't in the hands of any government or political faction, because everyone was still searching for him, and everyone except Manuel Turego and the American government was searching for Priscilla. Not even the Costa Rican government knew that Turego had the woman; he was operating on his own.

"Persall was a dark horse," Kell admitted irritably. "He wasn't a professional. I don't even have a file on him."

If Sabin didn't have a file on him, Persall had been more than a dark horse; he'd been totally invisible. "How did this thing blow open?" Grant drawled, closing his eyes until they were little more than slits. He looked as if he were going to fall asleep, but Sabin knew differently.

"Our man was being followed. They were closing in on him. He was out of his mind with fever. He couldn't find Luis, but he remembered how to contact Persall. No one knew Persall's name, until then, or how to find him if they needed him. Our man just barely got the film to Persall before all hell broke loose. Persall got away."

"What about our man?"

"He's alive. We got him out, but not before Turego got his hands on him."

Grant grunted. "So Turego knows our guy didn't tell Persall to destroy the film."

Kell looked completely disgusted. "*Everyone* knows.

There's no security down there. Too many people will sell any scrap of information they can find. Turego has a leak in his organization, so by morning it was common knowledge. Also by morning, Persall had died of a heart attack, in Priscilla's room. Before we could move in, Turego took the girl."

Dark brown lashes veiled the golden glitter of Grant's eyes almost completely. He looked as if he would begin snoring at any minute. "Well? Does she know anything about the microfilm or not?"

"We don't know. My guess is that she doesn't. Persall had several hours to hide the microfilm before he went to her room."

"Why the hell couldn't she have stayed with Daddy, where she belongs?" Grant murmured.

"Hamilton has been raising hell for us to get her out of there, but they aren't really close. She's a party girl. Divorced, more interested in having a good time than in doing anything constructive. In fact, Hamilton cut her out of his will several years ago, and she's been wandering all around the globe since. She'd been with Persall for a couple of years. They weren't shy about their relationship. Persall liked to have a flashy woman on his arm, and he could afford her. He always seemed like an easygoing good-time guy, well-suited to her type. I sure as hell never figured him for a courier, especially one sharp enough to fool me."

"Why don't you go in and get the girl out?" Grant asked suddenly, and he opened his eyes, staring at Kell, his gaze cold and yellow.

"Two reasons. One, I don't think she knows anything about the film. I have to concentrate on finding the film, and I think that means finding Luis Marcel. Two, you're the best man for the job. I thought so when I…ah…arranged for you to be brought to Hamilton's attention."

So Kell was working to get the girl out, after all, but going about it in his own circuitous way. Well, staying behind the scenes was the only way he could be effective. "You won't have any trouble getting into Costa Rica," Kell said. "I've already arranged it. But if you can't get the girl out..."

Grant got to his feet, a tawny, graceful savage, silent and lethal. "I know," he said quietly. Neither of them had to say it, but both knew that a bullet in her head would be a great deal kinder than what would happen to her if Turego decided that she did know the location of the microfilm. She was being held only as a safety measure now, but if that microfilm didn't surface, she would eventually be the only remaining link to it. Then her life wouldn't be worth a plugged nickel.

So now he was in Costa Rica, deep in the rain forest and too damned near the Nicaraguan border for comfort. Roaming bands of rebels, soldiers, revolutionaries and just plain terrorists made life miserable for people who just wanted to live their simple lives in peace, but none of it touched Priscilla. She might have been a tropical princess, sipping daintily at her iced drink, ignoring the jungle that ate continuously at the boundaries of the plantation and had to be cut back regularly.

Well, he'd seen enough. Tonight was the night. He knew her schedule now, knew the routine of the guards, and had already found all the trip lines. He didn't like traveling through the jungle at night, but there wasn't any choice. He had to have several hours to get her away from here before anyone realized she was missing; luckily, she always slept late, until at least ten every morning. No one would really think anything of it if she didn't appear by eleven. By then, they'd be long gone. Pablo would pick them up by helicopter at the designated clearing tomorrow morning, not long after dawn.

Grant backed slowly away from the edge of the jungle, worming himself into the thick greenery until it formed a solid curtain separating him from the house. Only then did he rise to his feet, walking silently and with assurance, because he'd taken care of the trip lines and sensors as he'd found them. He'd been in the jungle for three days, moving cautiously around the perimeter of the plantation, carefully getting the layout of the house. He knew where the girl slept, and he knew how he was going to get in. It couldn't have been better; Turego wasn't in the house. He'd left the day before, and since he wasn't back by now, Grant knew that he wasn't coming. It was already twilight, and it wasn't safe to travel the river in the darkness.

Grant knew exactly how treacherous the river was; that was why he would take the girl through the jungle. Even given its dangers, the river would be the logical route for them to take. If by some chance her departure were discovered before Pablo picked them up, the search would be concentrated along the river, at least for a while. Long enough, he hoped, for them to reach the helicopter.

He'd have to wait several more hours before he could go into the house and get the girl out. That would give everyone time to get tired, bored and sleepy. He made his way to the small clearing where he'd stashed his supplies, and carefully checked it for snakes, especially the velvety brown fer-de-lance, which liked to lie in clearings and wait for its next meal. After satisfying himself that the clearing was safe, he sat down on a fallen tree to smoke a cigarette. He took a drink of water, but he wasn't hungry. He knew that he wouldn't be until sometime tomorrow. Once the action was going down he couldn't eat; he was too keyed up, all his senses enhanced so that even the smallest sound of the jungle crashed against his eardrums like thunder. Adrenaline was already pumping through his veins, making him so high that he could understand why the Vikings had gone berserk during battle. Waiting was almost unbearable, but that was what he had to do. He checked his watch again, the illuminated dial a strange bit of civilization in a jungle that swallowed men alive, and frowned when he saw that only a little over half an hour had passed.

To give himself something to do, to calm his tightly wound nerves, he began packing methodically, arranging everything so he would know exactly where it was. He checked his weapons and his ammunition, hoping he wouldn't have to use them. What he needed more than anything, if he was to get the girl out alive, was a totally silent operation. If he had to use his carbine or the automatic pistol, he'd give away their position. He preferred a knife, which was silent and deadly.

He felt sweat trickle down his spine. God, if only the girl would have sense enough to keep her mouth shut and not start squawking when he hauled her out of there. If he had to, he'd knock her out, but that would make her dead weight to carry through vegetation that reached out to wrap around his legs like living fingers.

He realized that he was fondling his knife, his long, lean fingers sliding over the deadly blade with a lover's touch, and he shoved it into its sheath. Damn her, he thought bitterly. Because of her, he was back in the thick of things, and he could feel it taking hold of him again. The rush of danger was as addictive as any drug, and it was in his veins again, burning him, eating at him like an acid—killing him and intensifying the feeling of life all at once. Damn her, damn her to hell. All this for a spoiled, silly society brat who liked to amuse herself in various beds. Still, her round heels might have kept her alive, because Turego fancied himself quite a lover.

The night sounds of the jungle began to build around him: the screams of the howler monkeys, the rustles and chirps and coughs of the night denizens as they went about their business. Somewhere down close to the river he heard a jaguar cough, but he never minded the normal jungle sounds. He was at home here. The peculiar combination of his genes and the skills he'd learned as a boy in the swamps of south Georgia made him as much a part of the jungle as the jaguar that prowled the river's edge. Though the thick canopy blocked out all light, he didn't light a lamp or switch on a flashlight; he wanted his eyes to be perfectly adjusted to the dark when he began moving. He relied on his ears and his instincts, knowing that there was no danger close to him. The danger would come from men, not from the shy jungle animals. As long as those reassuring noises surrounded him, he knew that no men were near.

At midnight he rose and began easing along the route he'd marked in his mind, and the animals and insects were so unalarmed by his presence that the din continued without pause. The only caution he felt was that a fer-de-lance or a bushmaster might be hunting along the path he'd chosen, but that was a chance he'd have to take. He carried a long stick that he swept silently across the ground before him. When he reached the edge of the plantation he put the stick aside and crouched down to survey the grounds, making certain everything was as expected, before he moved in.

From where he crouched, he could see that the guards were at their normal posts, probably asleep, except for the one who patrolled the perimeter, and he'd soon settle down for a nap, too. They were sloppy, he thought contemptuously. They obviously didn't expect any visitors in as remote a place as this upriver plantation. During the three

Who was his assailant? What was he doing here in the woman's bedroom? Had he been sent to kill her or was he, too, trying to steal her from Turego?

His opponent was probably in the black corner beside the wardrobe. Grant eased the knife out of its sheath, then pushed it in again; his hands would be as silent as the knife.

There…just for a moment, the slightest of movements, but enough to pinpoint the man's position. Grant crouched then moved forward in a blurred rush, catching the man low and flipping him. The stranger rolled as he landed and came to his feet with a lithe twist, a slim dark figure outlined against the white mosquito netting. He kicked out, and Grant dodged the blow, but he felt the breeze of the kick pass his chin. Moving in, he caught the man's arm with a numbing chop. He saw the arm fall uselessly to the man's side. Coldly, without emotion, not even breathing hard, Grant threw the slim figure to the floor and knelt with one knee on the good arm and his other knee pressed to the man's chest. Just as he raised his hand to strike the blow that would end their silent struggle, Grant became aware of something odd, something soft swelling beneath his knee. Then he understood. The too-still form on the bed was so still because it was a mound of covers, not a human being. The girl hadn't been in bed; she'd seen him come through the sliding doors and had hidden herself in the shadows. But why hadn't she screamed? Why had she attacked, knowing that she had no chance of overpowering him? He moved his knee off her breasts and quickly slid his hand to the soft mounds to make certain his weight hadn't cut off her breath. He felt the reassuring rise of her chest, heard the soft, startled gasp as she felt his touch, and he eased a little away from her.

"It's all right," he started to whisper, but she suddenly

twisted on the floor, wrenching away from him. Her knee slashed upward; he was unguarded, totally vulnerable, and her knee crashed into his groin with a force that sent agony through his whole body. Red lights danced before his eyes, and he sagged to one side, gagging at the bitter bile that rose in his throat, his hands automatically cupping his agonized flesh as he ground his teeth to contain the groan that fought for release.

She scrambled away from him, and he heard a low sob, perhaps of terror. Through pain-blurred eyes he saw her pick up something dark and bulky; then she slipped through the open glass door and was gone.

Pure fury propelled him to his feet. Damn it, she was escaping on her own. She was going to ruin the whole setup! Ignoring the pain in his loins, he started after her. He had a score to settle.

CHAPTER TWO

JANE HAD JUST reached for her bundle of supplies when some instinct left over from her cave-dwelling ancestors told her that someone was near. There hadn't been any sound to alert her, but suddenly she was aware of another presence. The fine hairs on the back of her neck and her forearms stood up, and she had frozen, turning terrified eyes toward the double glass doors. The doors had slid open noiselessly, and she had seen the darker shadow of a man briefly outlined against the night. He was a big man, but one who moved with total silence. It was the eerie soundlessness of his movements that had frightened her more than anything, sending chills of pure terror chasing over her skin. For days now she had lived by her nerves, holding the terror at bay while she walked a tightrope, trying to lull Turego's suspicions, yet always poised for an escape attempt. But nothing had frightened her as much as that dark shadow slipping into her room.

Any faint hope that she would be rescued had died when Turego had installed her here. She had assessed the situation realistically. The only person who would try to get her out would be her father, but it would be beyond his power. She could depend on only herself and her wits. To that end, she had flirted and flattered and downright lied, doing everything she could to convince Turego that she was both brainless and harmless. In that, she thought, she'd succeeded, but time was fast running out. When an aide had brought an urgent message to Turego the day before, Jane had eavesdropped; Luis Marcel's location had been discovered, and Turego wanted Luis, badly.

But by now Turego surely would have discovered that Luis had no knowledge of the missing microfilm, and that would leave her as the sole suspect. She had to escape, tonight, before Turego returned.

She hadn't been idle since she'd been here; she'd carefully memorized the routine of the guards, especially at night, when the terror brought on by the darkness made it impossible for her to sleep. She'd spent the nights standing at the double doors, watching the guards, clocking them, studying their habits. By keeping her mind busy, she'd been able to control the fear. When dawn would begin to lighten the sky, she had slept. She had been preparing since the first day she'd been here for the possibility that she might have to bolt into the jungle. She'd been sneaking food and supplies, hoarding them, and steeling herself for what lay ahead. Even now, only the raw fear of what awaited her at Turego's hands gave her the courage to brave the black jungle, where the night demons were waiting for her.

But none of that had been as sinister, as lethal, as the dark shape moving through her bedroom. She shrank back into the thick shadows, not even breathing in her acute terror. Oh, God, she prayed, what do I do now? Why was he there? To murder her in her bed? Was it one of the guards, tonight of all nights, come to rape her?

As he passed in front of her, moving in a slight crouch toward her bed, an odd rage suddenly filled Jane. After all she had endured, she was damned if she'd allow him to spoil her escape attempt! She'd talked herself into it, despite her horrible fear of the dark, and now he was ruining it!

Her jaw set, she clenched her fists as she'd been taught to do in her self-defense classes. She struck at the back

of his neck, but suddenly he was gone, a shadow twist-
..g away from the blow, and her fist struck his shoulder
instead. Instantly terrified again, she shrank back into the
shelter of the wardrobe, straining her eyes to see him, but
he'd disappeared. Had he been a wraith, a figment of her
imagination? No, her fist had struck a very solid shoulder,
and the faint rippling of the white curtains over the glass
doors testified that the doors were indeed open. He was in
the room, somewhere, but *where*? How could a man that
big disappear so completely?

Then, abruptly, his weight struck her in the side, bowling
her over, and she barely bit off the instinctive scream that
surged up from her throat. She didn't have a chance. She
tried automatically to kick him in the throat, but he moved
like lightning, blocking her attack. Then a hard blow to her
arm numbed it all the way to her elbow, and a split second
later she was thrown to the floor, a knee pressing into her
chest and making it impossible to breathe.

The man raised his arm and Jane tensed, willing now to
scream, but unable to make a sound. Then, suddenly, the
man paused, and for some reason lifted his weight from
her chest. Air rushed into her lungs, along with a dizzying
sense of relief, then she felt his hand moving boldly over
her breasts and realized why he'd shifted position. Both
terrified and angry that this should be happening to her,
she moved instinctively the split second she realized his
vulnerability, and slashed upward with her knee. He sagged
to the side, holding himself, and she felt an absurd sense of
pity. Then she realized that he hadn't even groaned aloud.
The man wasn't human! Choking back a sob of terror, she
struggled to her feet and grabbed her supplies, then darted
through the open door. At that point she wasn't escaping
from Turego so much as from that dark, silent demon in
her room.

Heedlessly, she flung herself across the plantation grounds; her heart was pounding so violently that the sound of her blood pumping through her veins made a roar in her ears. Her lungs hurt, and she realized that she was holding her breath. She tried to remind herself to be quiet, but the urge to flee was too strong for caution; she stumbled over a rough section of ground and sprawled on her hands and knees. As she began scrambling to her feet, she was suddenly overwhelmed by something big and warm, smashing her back to the ground. Cold, pure terror froze her blood in her veins, but before even an instinctive scream could find voice, his hand was on the back of her neck and everything went black.

Jane regained consciousness by degrees, confused by her upside-down position, the jouncing she was suffering, the discomfort of her arms. Strange noises assailed her ears, noises that she tried and failed to identify. Even when she opened her eyes she saw only blackness. It was one of the worst nightmares she'd ever had. She began kicking and struggling to wake up, to end the dream, and abruptly a sharp slap stung her bottom. "Settle down," an ill-tempered voice said from somewhere above and behind her. The voice was that of a stranger, but there was something in that laconic drawl that made her obey instantly.

Slowly things began to shift into a recognizable pattern, and her senses righted themselves. She was being carried over a man's shoulder through the jungle. Her wrists had been taped behind her, and her ankles were also secured. Another wide band of tape covered her mouth, preventing her from doing anything more than grunting or humming. She didn't feel like humming, so she used her limited voice to grunt out exactly what she thought of him, in language that would have left her elegant mother white with shock. A hard hand again made contact with the seat of her pants.

The man shifted uncomfortably, drawing her attention. "Look, honey, do you think you could loosen up on my pants? Or are you trying to finish the job you started on me with your knee?"

Jane felt the blood rush to her cheeks, and she hastily released her hold. "I'm sorry, I didn't realize," she whispered. She stood stiffly for a moment, her arms at her sides; then panic began to rise in her. She couldn't see him in the darkness, she couldn't hear him breathing, and now that she was no longer touching him, she couldn't be certain that he hadn't left her. Was he still there? What if she was alone? The air became thick and oppressive, and she struggled to breathe, to fight down the fear that she knew was unreasonable but that no amount of reason could conquer. Even knowing its source didn't help. She simply couldn't stand the darkness. She couldn't sleep without a light; she never went into a room without first reaching in and turning on the light switch, and she always left her lights on if she knew she would be late returning home. She, who always took extraordinary precautions against being left in the dark, was standing in the middle of a jungle in darkness so complete that it was like being blind.

Her fragile control broke and she reached out wildly, clawing for him, for reassurance that he was still there. Her outstretched fingers touched fabric, and she threw herself against him, gasping in mingled panic and relief. The next second steely fingers grasped her shirt and she was hurled through the air to land flat on her back in the smelly, rotting vegetation. Before she could move, before she could suck air back into her lungs, her hair was pulled back and she felt the suffocating pressure of his knee on her chest again. His breath was a low rasp above her, his voice little more than a snarl "Don't ever—*ever*—come at me from behind again."

Jane writhed, pushing at his knee. After a moment he lifted it, and eased the grip on her hair. Even being thrown over his shoulder had been better than being left alone in the darkness, and she grabbed for him again, catching him around the knees. Automatically he tried to step away from her entangling arms but she lunged for him. He uttered a startled curse, tried to regain his balance, then crashed to the ground.

He lay so still that Jane's heart plummeted. What would she do if he were hurt? She couldn't possibly carry him, but neither could she leave him lying there, injured and unable to protect himself. Feeling her way up his body, she scrambled to crouch by his shoulders. "Mister, are you all right?" she whispered, running her hands up his shoulders to his face, then searching his head for any cuts or lumps. There was an elasticized band around his head, and she followed it, her nervous fingers finding an odd type of glasses over his eyes. "Are you hurt?" she demanded again, her voice tight with fear. "Damn it, answer me!"

"Lady," the man said in a low, furious voice, "you're crazier than hell. If I was your daddy, I'd *pay* Turego to keep you!"

She didn't know him, but his words caused an odd little pain in her chest. She sat silently, shocked that he could hurt her feelings. She didn't know him, and he didn't know her—how could his opinion matter? But it did, somehow, and she felt strangely vulnerable.

He eased himself to a sitting position, and when she didn't say anything, he sighed. "Why did you jump me like that?" he asked in resignation.

"I'm afraid of the dark," she said with quiet dignity. "I couldn't hear you breathing, and I can't see a thing. I panicked. I'm sorry."

After a moment he said, "All right," and got to his feet.

her with real pain. She stood quietly, staring at the clearing herself, but she couldn't see anything wrong. Everything was quiet. The pilot was leaning against the outside of the helicopter, occupied with cleaning his nails; he certainly wasn't concerned with anything.

Long minutes dragged past. The pilot began to fidget, craning his neck and staring into the jungle, though anyone standing just a few feet behind the trees would be completely hidden from view. He looked at his watch, then scanned the jungle again, his gaze moving nervously from left to right.

Jane felt the tension in the man standing beside her, tension that was echoed in the hand that held her shoulder. What was wrong? What was he looking for, and why was he waiting? He was as motionless as a jaguar lying in wait for its prey to pass beneath its tree limb.

"This sucks," he muttered abruptly, easing deeper into the jungle and dragging her with him.

Jane sputtered at the inelegant expression. "It does? Why? What's wrong?"

"Stay here." He pushed her to the ground, deep in the green-black shadow of the buttressed roots of an enormous tree.

Startled, she took a moment to realize that she'd been abandoned. He had simply melted into the jungle, so silently and swiftly that she wasn't certain which way he'd gone. She twisted around but could see nothing that indicated his direction; no swaying vines or limbs.

She wrapped her arms around her drawn-up legs and propped her chin on her knees, staring thoughtfully at the ground. A green stick with legs was dragging a large spider off to be devoured. What if he didn't come back...whoever he was. Why hadn't she asked him his name? If something happened to him, she'd like to know his name, so she could tell someone—assuming that she could manage to get out of the jungle herself. Well, she wasn't any worse off now than she had been before. She was away from Turego, and that was what counted.

Wait here, he'd said. For how long? Until lunch? Sundown? Her next birthday? Men gave such inexact instructions! Of course, this particular man seemed a little limited in the conversation department. Shut up, Stay here and Stay put seemed to be the highlights of his repertoire.

This was quite a tree he'd parked her by. The bottom of the trunk flared into buttressed roots, forming enormous wings that wrapped around her almost like arms. If she sat back against the tree, the wings would shield her completely from the view of someone approaching at any angle except head on.

The straps of her backpack were irritating her shoulders, so she slid it off and stretched, feeling remarkably lighter. She hauled the pack around and opened it, then began digging for her hairbrush. Finding this backpack had been a stroke of luck, she thought, though Turego's soldiers really should be a little more careful with their belongings. Without it, she'd have had to wrap things up in a blanket, which would have been awkward.

Finally locating the hairbrush, she diligently worked through the mass of tangles that had accumulated in her long hair during the night. A small monkey with an indignant expression hung from a branch overhead. It scolded her throughout the operation, evidently angry that she had intruded on its territory. She waved at it.

Congratulating herself for her foresight, she pinned her hair up and pulled a black baseball cap out of the pack. She jammed the cap on and tugged the bill down low over her eyes, then shoved it back up. There wasn't any sun down here. Staring upward, she could see bright pinpoints of sun high in the trees, but only a muted green light filtered down to the floor. She'd have been better off with some of those fancy goggles that What's-his-name had.

How long had she been sitting there? Was he in trouble?

Her legs were going to sleep, so she stood and stomped around to get her blood flowing again. The longer she waited, the more uneasy she became, and she had the feeling that a time would come when she'd better be able to move fast. Jane was an instinctive creature, as sensitive to atmosphere as any finely tuned barometer. That trait had enabled her to hold Turego at bay for what seemed like an endless succession of days and nights, reading him, side-stepping him, keeping him constantly disarmed, and even charmed. Now the same instinct warned her of danger. There was some slight change in the very air that stroked her bare arms. Warily, she leaned down to pick up her backpack, slipping her arms through the straps and anchoring it this time by fastening the third strap around her middle.

The sudden thunderous burst of automatic weapon fire made her whirl, her heart jumping into her throat. Listening to the staccato blasts, she knew that several weapons were being fired, but at whom? Had her friend been detected or was this something else entirely? Was this the trouble he'd sensed that had made him shy away from the clearing? She wanted to think that he was safe, observing everything from an invisible vantage point in the jungle, but with a chill she realized that she couldn't take that for granted.

Her hands felt cold, and with a distant surprise she realized that she was trembling. What should she do? Wait, or run? What if he needed help? She realized that there was very little she could do, since she was unarmed, but she couldn't just run away if he needed help. He wasn't the most amiable man she'd ever met, and she still didn't exactly trust him, but he was the closest thing to a friend she had here.

Ignoring the unwillingness of her feet and the icy lump of fear in her stomach, Jane left the shelter of the giant tree and began cautiously inching through the forest, back toward the clearing. There were only sporadic bursts of gunfire now, still coming from the same general direction.

Suddenly she froze as the faint sound of voices filtered through the forest. In a cold panic she dove for the shelter of another large tree. What would she do if they were coming in this direction? The rough bark scratched her hands as she cautiously moved her head just enough to peer around the trunk.

A steely hand clamped over her mouth. As a scream rose in her throat, a deep, furious voice growled in her ear, "Damn it, I told you to stay put!"

CHAPTER THREE

JANE GLARED AT HIM over the hand that still covered her mouth, her fright turning into relieved anger. She didn't like this man. She didn't like him at all, and as soon as they were out of this mess, she was going to tell him about it!

He removed his hand and shoved her to the ground on her hands and knees. "Crawl!" he ordered in a harsh whisper, and pointed to their left.

Jane crawled, ignoring the scratches she incurred as she squirmed through the undergrowth, ignoring even the disgusting squishiness when she accidentally smashed something with her hand. Odd, but now that he was with her again, her panic had faded; it hadn't gone completely, but it wasn't the heart-pounding, nauseating variety, either. Whatever his faults, he knew his way around.

He was on her tail, literally, his hard shoulder against the back of her thighs, pushing her onward whenever he thought she wasn't moving fast enough. Once he halted her by the simple method of grabbing her ankle and jerking her flat, his urgent grip warning her to be quiet. She held her breath, listening to the faint rustle that betrayed the presence of someone, or something, nearby. She didn't dare turn her head, but she could detect movement with her peripheral vision. In a moment the man was close enough that she could see him plainly. He was obviously of Latin ancestry, and he was dressed in camouflage fatigues with a cap covering his head. He held an automatic rifle at the ready before him.

In only a moment she could no longer see or hear him, but they stayed motionless in the thick tangle of ferns for long, agonizing minutes. Then her ankle was released and a hand on her hip urged her forward.

They were moving away from the soldier at a right angle. Perhaps they were going to try to get behind their pursuers, then take off in the helicopter while the soldiers were still deep in the jungle. She wanted to know where they were going, what they would do, who the soldiers were and what they wanted—but the questions had to remain bottled up inside her. Now was definitely not the time for talking, not with this man—what *was* his name?—practically shoving her through the undergrowth.

Abruptly the forest cleared somewhat, allowing small patches of sunlight to filter through. Grasping her arm, he hauled her to her feet. "Run, but be as quiet as you can," he hissed in her ear.

Great. Run, but do it quietly. She threw him a dirty look, then ran, taking off like a startled deer. The most disgusting thing was that he was right behind her, and she couldn't hear him making a sound, while her own feet seemed to pound the earth like a drum. But her body seemed cheered by the small amount of sunlight, because she felt her energy level surge despite her sleepless night. The pack on her shoulders seemed lighter, and her steps became quick and effortless as adrenaline began pumping through her veins.

The brush became thicker, and they had to slow their pace. After about fifteen minutes he stopped her with a hand on her shoulder and pulled her behind the trunk of a tree. "Rest a minute," he whispered. "The humidity will wipe you out if you aren't used to it."

the slope steep enough that it was a miracle they hadn't crashed into the rocks at the streambed.

"I see it." He swarmed up the slope, lithe and sure-footed. He snatched the cap from a broken branch and in only a moment was back beside her. Jamming the cap on her head, he said, "Can you make it up the other side?"

There was no way, she thought. Her body refused to function any longer. She looked at him and lifted her chin. "Of course."

He didn't smile, but there was a faint softening of his expression, as if he knew how desperately tired she was. "We have to keep moving," he said, taking her arm and urging her across the stream. She didn't care that her boots were getting wet; she just sloshed through the water, moving downstream while he scanned the bank for an easy place to climb up. On this side of the stream, the bank wasn't sloped; it was almost vertical and covered with what looked like an impenetrable tangle of vines and bushes. The stream created a break in the foliage that allowed more sunlight to pour down, letting the plants grow much more thickly.

"Okay, let's go up this way," he finally said, pointing. Jane lifted her head and stared at the bank, but she didn't see any break in the wild tangle.

"Let's talk about this," she hedged.

He gave an exasperated sigh. "Look, Pris, I know you're tired, but—"

Something snapped inside Jane, and she whirled on him, catching him by the shirt front and drawing back her fist. "If you call me 'Pris' just one more time, I'm going to feed you a knuckle sandwich!" she roared, unreasonably angry at his continued use of that hated name. No one, but no one, had ever been allowed to call her Priscilla, Pris, or even Cilla, more than once. This damned commando had been rubbing her face in it from the beginning. She'd kept quiet about it, figuring she owed him for kicking him in the groin, but she was tired and hungry and scared and enough was enough!

He moved so quickly that she didn't even have time to blink. His hand snaked out and caught her drawn-back fist, while the fingers of his other hand laced around her wrist, removing her grip from his shirt. "Damn it, can't you keep quiet? *I* didn't name you Priscilla, your parents did, so if you don't like it take it up with them. But until then, climb!"

Jane climbed, even though she was certain at every moment that she was going to collapse on her face. Grabbing vines for handholds, using roots and rocks and bushes and small trees, she squirmed and wiggled her way through the foliage. It was so thick that it could have been swarming with jaguars and she wouldn't have been able to see one until she stuck her hand in its mouth. She remembered that jaguars liked water, spending most of their time resting comfortably near a river or stream, and she swore vengeance on Grant Sullivan for making her do this.

Finally she scrambled over the top, and after pushing forward several yards found that the foliage had once again thinned, and walking was much easier. She adjusted the pack on her back, wincing as she found new bruises. "Are we heading for the helicopter?"

"No," he said curtly. "The helicopter is being watched."

"Who are those men?"

He shrugged. "Who knows? Sandinistas, maybe; we're only a few klicks from the Nicaraguan border. They could be any guerrilla faction. That damned Pablo sold us out."

Jane didn't waste time worrying about Pablo's duplicity; she was too tired to really care. "Where are we going?"

"South."

testified to Costa Rica's volcanic origin. After taking his knife from his belt, he cut small limbs and lashed them together with vines, then propped one end of his contraption up by wedging sturdier limbs under the corners. Producing a rolled-up tarp from his backpack like a magician, he tied the tarp over the crude lean-to, making it waterproof. "Well, crawl in and get comfortable," he growled when Jane simply stood there, staring in astonishment at the shelter he'd constructed in just a few minutes.

Obediently she crawled in, groaning with relief as she shrugged out of her backpack and relaxed her aching muscles. Her ears caught the first distant rumble of thunder; whatever he did for a living, the man certainly knew his way around the jungle.

Grant ducked under the shelter, too, relieving his shoulders of the weight of his own backpack. He had apparently decided that while they were waiting out the rain they might as well eat, because he dug out a couple of cans of field rations.

Jane sat up straight and leaned closer, staring at the cans. "What's that?"

"Food."

"What kind of food?"

He shrugged. "I've never looked at it long enough to identify it. Take my advice: don't think about it. Just eat it."

She put her hand on his as he started to open the cans. "Wait. Why don't we save those for have-to situations?"

"This *is* a have-to situation," he grunted. "We *have* to eat."

"Yes, but we don't have to eat *that*!"

Exasperation tightened his hard features. "Honey, we either eat this, or two more cans exactly like them!"

"Oh, ye of little faith," she scoffed, dragging her own

backpack closer. She began delving around in it, and in a moment produced a small packet wrapped in a purloined towel. With an air of triumph she unwrapped it to expose two badly smashed but still edible sandwiches, then returned to the backpack to dig around again. Her face flushed with success, she pulled out two cans of orange juice. "Here!" she said cheerfully, handing him one of the cans. "A peanut butter and jelly sandwich, and a can of orange juice. Protein, carbohydrates and vitamin C. What more could we ask for?"

Grant took the sandwich and the pop-top can she offered him, staring at them in disbelief. He blinked once, then an amazing thing happened: he laughed. It wasn't much of a laugh. It was rather rusty sounding, but it revealed his straight white teeth and made his amber eyes crinkle at the corners. The rough texture of that laugh gave her a funny little feeling in her chest. It was obvious that he rarely laughed, that life didn't hold much humor for him, and she felt both happy that she'd made him laugh and sad that he'd had so little to laugh about. Without laughter she would never have kept her sanity, so she knew how precious it was.

Chewing on his sandwich, Grant relished the gooiness of the peanut butter and the sweetness of the jelly. So what if the bread was a little stale? The unexpected treat made such a detail unimportant. He leaned back and propped himself against his backpack, stretching his long legs out before him. The first drops of rain began to patter against the upper canopy. It would be impossible for anyone to track them through the downpour that was coming, even if those guerrillas had an Indian tracker with them, which he doubted. For the first time since he'd seen the helicopter that morning, he relaxed, his highly developed sense of danger no longer nagging him.

He finished the sandwich and poured the rest of the orange juice down his throat, then glanced over at Jane to see her daintily licking the last bit of jelly from her fingers. She looked up, caught his gaze, and gave him a cheerful smile that made her dimples flash, then returned to the task of cleaning her fingers.

Against his will, Grant felt his body tighten with a surge of lust that surprised him with its strength. She was a charmer, all right, but not at all what he'd expected. He'd expected a spoiled, helpless, petulant debutante, and instead she had had the spirit, the pure guts, to hurl herself into the jungle with two peanut butter sandwiches and some orange juice as provisions. She'd also dressed in common-sense clothing, with good sturdy boots and green khaki pants, and a short-sleeved black blouse. Not right out of the fashion pages, but he'd had a few distracting moments crawling behind her, seeing those pants molded to her shapely bottom. He hadn't been able to prevent a deep masculine appreciation for the soft roundness of her buttocks.

She was a mass of contradictions. She was a jet-setter, so wild that her father had disinherited her, and she'd been George Persall's mistress, yet he couldn't detect any signs of hard living in her face. If anything, her face was as open and innocent as a child's, with a child's enthusiasm for life shining out of her dark brown eyes. She had a look of perpetual mischievousness on her face, yet it was a face of honest sensuality. Her long hair was so dark a brown that it was almost black, and it hung around her shoulders in snarls and tangles. She had pushed it away from her face with total unconcern. Her dark brown eyes were long and a little narrow, slanting in her high-cheekboned face in a way that made him think she might have a little Indian blood. A smattering of small freckles danced across those elegant cheekbones and the dainty bridge of her nose. Her mouth was soft and full, with the upper lip fuller than the lower one, which gave her an astonishingly sensual look. All in all, she was far from beautiful, but there was a freshness and zest about her that made all the other women he'd known suddenly seem bland.

Certainly he'd never been as intimate with any other woman's knee.

Even now, the thought of it made him angry. Part of it was chagrin that he'd left himself open to the blow; he'd been bested by a lightweight! But another part of it was an instinctive, purely male anger, sexually based. He'd watch her knee now whenever she was within striking distance. Still, the fact that she'd defended herself, and the moves she'd made, told him that she'd had professional training, and that was another contradiction. She wasn't an expert, but she knew what to do. Why would a wild, spoiled playgirl know anything about self-defense? Some of the pieces didn't fit, and Grant was always uneasy when he sensed details that didn't jibe.

He felt pretty grim about the entire operation. Their situation right now was little short of desperate, regardless of the fact that they were, for the moment, rather secure. They had probably managed to shake the soldiers, whoever they worked for, but Turego was a different story. The microfilm wasn't the only issue now. Turego had been operating without the sanction of the government, and if Pris made it back and filed a complaint against him, the repercussions would cost him his position, and possibly his freedom.

It was Grant's responsibility to get her out, but it was no longer the simple in-and-out situation he'd planned. From the moment he'd seen Pablo leaning so negligently against the helicopter, waiting for them, he'd known that the deal had gone sour. Pablo wasn't the type to be waiting for them so casually; in all the time Grant had know him, Pablo had been tense, ready to move, always staying in the helicopter with the rotors turning. The elaborate pose of relaxation had tipped Grant off as clearly as if Pablo had hung a sign around his neck. Perhaps Pablo had been trying to warn him. There was no way he'd ever know for certain.

Now he had to get her through the jungle, out of the mountains, and south through a swamp, with Turego in hot pursuit. With luck, in a day or so, they'd find a village and be able to hitch a ride, but even that depended on how close behind Turego was.

And on top of that, he couldn't trust her. She'd disarmed that soldier far too casually, and hadn't turned a hair at anything that had happened. She was far too matter-of-fact about the whole situation. She wasn't what she seemed, and that made her dangerous.

He was wary of her, but at the same time he found that he was unable to stop watching her. She was too damned sexy, as lush and exotic as a jungle orchid. What would it be like to lie with her? Did she use the rich curves of her body to make a man forget who he was? How many men had been taken in by that fresh, open expression? Had Turego found himself off balance with her, wanting her, knowing that he could force her at any time—but being eaten alive by the challenge of trying to win her, of making her give herself freely? How else had she managed to control him? None of it added up to what she should have been, unless she played with men as some sort of ego trip, where the more dangerous the man, the greater the thrill at controlling him.

Grant didn't want her to have that much influence over him; she wasn't worth it. No matter how beguiling the expression in her dark, slanted eyes, she simply wasn't worth it. He didn't need the sort of complication she offered; he just wanted to get her out, collect his money from her father, and get back to the solitude of the farm. Already he'd felt the jungle pulling at him, the heated, almost sexual excitement of danger. The rifle felt like an extension of his body, and the knife fit his palm as if he'd never put it down. All the old moves, the old instincts, were still there, and blackness rose in him as he wondered bitterly if he'd ever really be able to put this life behind him. The blood lust had been there in him, and perhaps he'd have killed that soldier if she hadn't kicked the rifle up when she had.

Was it part of the intoxication of battle that made him want to pull her beneath him and drive himself into her body, until he was mindless with intolerable pleasure? Part of it was, and yet part of it had been born hours ago, on the floor of her bedroom, when he'd felt the soft, velvety roundness of her breasts in his hands. Remembering that, he wanted to know what her breasts looked like, if they thrust out conically or had a full lower slope, if her nipples were small or large, pink or brown. Desire made him harden, and he reminded himself caustically that it had been a while since he'd had a woman, so it was only natural that he would be turned on. If nothing else, he should be glad of the evidence that he could still function!

She yawned, and blinked her dark eyes at him like a sleepy cat. "I'm going to take a nap," she announced, and curled up on the ground. She rested her head on her arm, closed her eyes and yawned again. He watched her, his eyes narrowed. This utter adaptability she displayed was another piece of the puzzle that didn't fit. She should have been moaning and bitching about how uncomfortable she was, rather than calmly curling up on the ground for a nap. But a nap sounded pretty damned good right now, he thought.

Grant looked around. The rain had become a full-fledged downpour, pounding through the canopy and turning the

ungle floor into a river. The constant, torrential rains
eeched the nutrients out of the soil, making the jungle
nto a contradiction, where the world's greatest variety of
animal and plant life existed on some of the poorest soil.
Right now the rain also made it almost impossible for them
o be found. They were safe for the time being, and for the
first time he allowed himself to feel the weariness in his
muscles. He might as well take a nap, too; he'd wake when
he rain stopped, alerted by the total cessation of noise.

Reaching out, he shook her shoulder, and she roused to
stare at him sleepily. "Get against the back of the lean-to,"
he ordered. "Give me a little room to stretch out, too."

She crawled around as he'd instructed and stretched out
full length, sighing in ecstasy. He pushed their backpacks
o one side, then lay down beside her, his big body between
her and the rain. He lay on his back, one brawny arm
thrown behind his head. There was no twitching around,
no yawning or sighing, for him. He simply lay down, closed
his eyes and went to sleep. Jane watched him sleepily, her
gaze lingering on the hawklike line of his profile, noting
he scar that ran along his left cheekbone. How had he
gotten it? His jaw was blurred with several days' growth
of beard, and she noticed that his beard was much darker
than his hair. His eyebrows and lashes were dark, too, and
that made his amber eyes seem even brighter, almost as
yellow as an eagle's.

The rain made her feel a little chilled after the intense
heat of the day; instinctively she inched closer to the heat
he could feel emanating from his body. He was so warm…
and she felt so safe…safer than she'd felt since she was nine
years old. With one more little sigh, she slept.

Sometime later the rain ceased abruptly, and Grant
voke immediately, like a light switch being flipped on.
His senses were instantly alert, wary. He started to surge to

his feet, only to realize that she was lying curled against his side, with her head pillowed on his arm and her hand lying on his chest. Disbelief made him rigid. How could she have gotten that close to him without waking him? He'd always slept like a cat, alert to the smallest noise or movement—but this damned woman had practically crawled all over him and he hadn't even stirred. She must've been disappointed, he thought furiously. The fury was directed as much at himself as at her, because the incident told him how slack he had become in the past year. That slackness might cost them their lives.

He lay still, aware of the fullness of her breasts against his side. She was soft and lush, and one of her legs was thrown up over his thigh. All he had to do was roll over and he'd be between her legs. The mental image made moisture break out on his forehead. God! She'd be hot and tight, and he clenched his teeth at the heavy surge in his loins. She was no lady, but she was all woman, and he wanted her naked and writhing beneath him with an intensity that tied his guts into knots.

He had to move, or he'd be taking her right there on the rocky ground. Disgusted at himself for letting her get to him the way she had, he eased his arm from beneath her head, then shook her shoulder. "Let's get moving," he said curtly.

She muttered something, her forehead puckering, but she didn't open her eyes, and in a moment her forehead smoothed as she lapsed back into deep sleep. Impatiently Grant shook her again. "Hey, wake up."

She rolled over on her stomach and sighed deeply, burrowing her head against her folded arm as she sought a more comfortable position. "Come on, we've got to get going," he said, shaking her more vigorously. "Wake up!"

She aimed a drowsy swat at him, as if he were a pesk

ly, brushing his hand aside. Exasperated, Grant caught
her shoulders and pulled her to a sitting position, shaking
her once again. "Damn it, would you get up? On your feet,
honey; we've got some walking to do." Her eyes finally
opened, and she blinked at him groggily, but she made no
move to get up.

Swearing under his breath, Grant hauled her to her feet.
"Just stand over there, out of the way," he said, turning
her around and starting her on her way with a swat on her
bottom before he turned his attention to taking down their
shelter.

CHAPTER FOUR

JANE STOPPED, her hand going to her bottom. Awakened now, and irritated by his light, casual slap, she turned. "You didn't have to do that!"

"Do what?" he asked with total disinterest, already busy removing the tarp from the top of the lean-to and rolling it up to replace it in his backpack.

"Hit me! A simple 'wake-up' would have sufficed!"

Grant looked at her in disbelief. "Well, pardon me all to hell," he drawled in a sarcastic tone that made her want to strangle him. "Let me start over. Excuse me, Priscilla, but nappy time is over, and we really do have to—hey! Damn it!" He ducked in time, throwing his arm up to catch the force of her fist. Swiftly he twisted his arm to lock his fingers around her wrist, then caught her other arm before she could swing at him with it. She'd exploded into fury, hurling herself at him like a cat pouncing. Her fist had hit his arm with enough strength that she might have broken his nose if the blow had landed on target. "Woman, what in *hell* is wrong with you?"

"I told you not to call me that!" Jane raged at him, spitting the words out in her fury. She struggled wildly, trying to free her arm so she could hit him again.

Panting, Grant wrestled her to the ground and sat astride her, holding her hands above her head, and this time making damned certain that her knee wouldn't come anywhere near him. She kept wriggling and heaving, and he felt as if he were trying to hold an octopus, but finally he had her subdued.

Glaring at her, he said, "You told me not to call you Pris."

"Well, don't call me Priscilla, either!" she fumed, glaring right back.

"Look, I'm not a mind reader! What am I supposed to call you?"

"Jane!" she shouted at him. "My name is Jane! *Nobody* has *ever* called me Priscilla!"

"All right! All you had to do was tell me! I'm getting damned tired of you snapping at my ankles, understand? I may hurt you before I can stop myself, so you'd better think twice before you attack again. Now, if I let you up, are you going to behave?"

Jane still glared at him, but the weight of his knees on her bruised arms was excruciating. "All right," she said sullenly, and he slowly got up, then surprised her by offering his hand to help her up. She surprised herself by taking it.

A sudden twinkle lit the dark gold of his eyes. "Jane, huh?" he asked reflectively, looking at the surrounding jungle.

She gave him a threatening look. "No 'Me Tarzan, you Jane' stuff," she warned. "I've heard it since grade school." She paused, then said grudgingly, "But it's still better than Priscilla."

He grunted in agreement and turned away to finish dismantling their shelter, and after a moment Jane began helping. He glanced at her, but said nothing. He wasn't much of a talker, she'd noticed, and he didn't improve any on closer acquaintance. But he'd risked his own life to help her, and he hadn't left her behind, even though Jane knew he could have moved a lot faster, and with a lot less risk to himself, on his own. And there was something in his eyes, an expression that was weary and cynical and a little empty, as if he'd seen far too much to have any faith or trust left. That made Jane want to put her arms around him and shield him. Lowering her head so he wouldn't be able to read her expression, she chided herself for feeling protective of a man who was so obviously capable of handling himself. There had been a time in her own life when she had been afraid to trust anyone except her parents, and it had been a horrible, lonely time. She knew what fear was, and loneliness, and she ached for him.

All signs of their shelter obliterated, he swung his backpack up and buckled it on, then slung the rifle over his shoulder, while Jane stuffed her hair up under her cap. He leaned down to pick up her pack for her, and a look of astonishment crossed his face; then his dark brows snapped together. "What the—" he muttered. "What all do you have in this damned thing? It weighs a good twenty pounds more than my pack!"

"Whatever I thought I'd need," Jane replied, taking the pack from him and hooking her arm through the one good shoulder strap, then buckling the waist strap to secure it as well as she could.

"Like what?"

"Things," she said stubbornly. Maybe her provisions weren't exactly proper by military standards, but she'd take her peanut butter sandwiches over his canned whatever any time. She thought he would order her to dump the pack on the ground for him to sort through and decide what to keep, and she was determined not to allow it. She set her jaw and looked at him.

He put his hands on his hips and surveyed her funny, exotic face, her lower lip pouting out in a mutinous expression, her delicate jaw set. She looked ready to light into him again, and he sighed in resignation. Damned if she wasn't the stubbornest, scrappiest woman he'd ever met. "Take it off," he growled, unbuckling his own pack. "I'll carry yours, and you can carry mine."

If anything, the jaw went higher. "I'm doing okay with my own."

"Stop wasting time arguing. That extra weight will slow you down, and you're already tired. Hand it over, and I'll fix that strap before we start out."

Reluctantly she slipped the straps off and gave him the pack, ready to jump him if he showed any sign of dumping it. But he took a small folder from his own pack, opened it to extract a needle and thread, and deftly began to sew the two ends of the broken strap together.

Astounded, Jane watched his lean, calloused hands wielding the small needle with a dexterity that she had to envy. Reattaching a button was the limit of her sewing skill, and she usually managed to prick her finger doing that. "Do they teach sewing in the military now?" she asked, crowding in to get a better look.

He gave her another one of his glances of dismissal. "I'm not in the military."

"Maybe not now," she conceded. "But you were, weren't you?"

"A long time ago."

"Where did you learn how to sew?"

"I just picked it up. It comes in handy." He bit the thread off, then replaced the needle in its package. "Let's get moving; we've wasted too much time as it is."

Jane took his backpack and fell into step behind him; all she had to do was follow him. Her gaze drifted over the width of his shoulders, then eased downward. Had she ever known anyone as physically strong as this man? She didn't think so. He seemed to be immune to weariness, and he ignored the steamy humidity that drained her strength and drenched her clothes in perspiration. His long, powerful legs moved in an effortless stride, the flexing of his thigh muscles pulling the fabric of his pants tight across them. Jane found herself watching his legs and matching her own stride to his. He took a step, and she took a step automatically. It was easier that way; she could separate her mind from her body, and in doing so ignore her protesting muscles.

He stopped once and took a long drink from the canteen, then passed it to Jane without comment. Also without comment, and without wiping the mouth of the canteen, she tipped it up and drank thirstily. Why worry about drinking after him? Catching cold was the least of her concerns. After capping the canteen, she handed it back to him, and they began walking again.

There was madness to his method, or so it seemed to her. If there was a choice between two paths, he invariably chose the more difficult one. The route he took was through the roughest terrain, the thickest vegetation, up the highest, most rugged slope. Jane tore her pants sliding down a bluff, that looked like pure suicide from the top, and not much better than that from the bottom, but she followed without complaining. It wasn't that she didn't think of plenty of complaints, but that she was too tired to voice them. The benefits of her short nap had long since been dissipated. Her legs ached, her back ached, her bruised arms were so painful she could barely move them, and her eyes felt as if they were burning out of their sockets. But she didn't ask him to stop. Even if the pace killed her, she wasn't going to slow him down any more than she already had, because she had no doubt that he could travel much faster without her. The easy movements of his long legs told her that his stamina was far greater than hers; he could probably

walk all night long again without a noticeable slowing of
his stride. She felt a quiet awe of that sort of strength and
conditioning, something that had been completely outside
her experience before she'd met him. He wasn't like other
men; it was evident in his superb body, in the awesome
competence with which he handled everything, in the piercing gold of his eyes.

As if alerted by her thoughts, he stopped and looked
back at her, assessing her condition with that sharp gaze
that missed nothing. "Can you make it for another mile or
so?"

On her own, she couldn't have, but when she met his
eyes she knew there was no way she'd admit to that. Her
chin lifted, and she ignored the increasingly heavy ache
in her legs as she said, "Yes."

A flicker of expression crossed his face so swiftly that
she couldn't read it. "Let me have that pack," he growled,
coming back to her and jerking the straps free of the buckles, then slipping the pack from her shoulders.

"I'm handling it okay," she protested fiercely, grabbing
for the pack and wrapping both arms around it. "I haven't
complained, have I?"

His level dark brows drawing together in a frown, he
forcefully removed the pack from her grasp. "Use your
head," he snapped. "If you collapse from exhaustion, then
I'll have to carry you, too."

The logic of that silenced her. Without another word he
turned and started walking again. She was better able to
keep up with him without the weight of the pack, but she
felt frustrated with herself for not being in better shape,
for being a burden to him. Jane had fought fiercely for her
independence, knowing that her very life depended on it.
She'd never been one to sit and wait for someone else to
do things for her. She'd charged at life head-on, relishing

the challenges that came her way because they reaffirmed her acute sense of the wonder of life. She'd shared the joys, but handled the problems on her own, and it unsettled her now to have to rely on someone else.

They came to another stream, no wider than the first one they had crossed, but deeper. It might rise to her knees in places. The water rushing over the rocks sounded cool, and she thought of how heavenly it would be to refresh her sweaty body in the stream. Looking longingly at it, she stumbled over a root and reached out to catch her balance. Her palm came down hard against a tree trunk, and something squished beneath her fingers.

"Oh, yuk!" she moaned, trying to wipe the dead insect off with a leaf.

Grant stopped. "What is it?"

"I smashed a bug with my hand." The leaf didn't clean too well; a smear still stained her hand, and she looked at Grant with disgust showing plainly on her face. "Is it all right if I wash my hand in the stream?"

He looked around, his amber eyes examining both sides of the stream. "Okay. Come over here."

"I can get down here," she said. The bank was only a few feet high, and the underbrush wasn't that thick. She carefully picked her way over the roots of an enormous tree, bracing her hand against its trunk to steady herself as she started to descend to the stream.

"Watch out!" Grant said sharply, and Jane froze in her tracks, turning her head to look askance at him.

Suddenly something incredibly heavy dropped onto her shoulders, something long and thick and alive, and she gave a stifled scream as it began to coil around her body. She was more startled than frightened, thinking a big vine had fallen; then she saw the movement of a large triangular head and she gave another gasping cry. "Grant! Grant, *help me*!"

Terror clutched at her throat, choking her, and she began to claw at the snake, trying to get it off. It was a calm monster, working its body around her, slowly tightening the lethal muscles that would crush her bones. It twined around her legs and she fell, rolling on the ground. Dimly she could hear Grant cursing, and she could hear her own cries of terror, but they sounded curiously distant. Everything was tumbling in a mad kaleidoscope of brown earth and green trees, of Grant's taut, furious face. He was shouting something at her, but she couldn't understand him; all she could do was struggle against the living bonds that coiled around her. She had one shoulder and arm free, but the boa was tightening itself around her rib cage, and the big head was coming toward her face, its mouth open. Jane screamed, trying to catch its head with her free hand, but the snake was crushing the breath out of her and the scream was almost soundless. A big hand, not hers, caught the snake's head, and she dimly saw a flash of silver.

The snake's coils loosened about her as it turned to meet this new prey, seeking to draw Grant into its deadly embrace, too. She saw the flash of silver again, and something wet splashed into her face. Vaguely she realized that it was his knife she'd seen. He was swearing viciously as he wrestled with the snake, mostly astride her as she writhed on the ground, struggling to free herself. "Damn it, hold still!" he roared. "You'll make me cut you!"

It was impossible to be still; she was wrapped in the snake, and it was writhing with her in its coils. She was too crazed by fear to realize that the snake was in its death throes, not even when she saw Grant throw something aside and begin forcibly removing the thick coils from around her body. It wasn't until she actually felt herself coming free of the constrictor's horrible grasp that she understood it was over, that Grant had killed the snake. She stopped fighting and lay limply on the ground. Her face was utterly white except for the few freckles across her nose and cheekbones; her eyes were fixed on Grant's face.

"It's over," he said roughly, running his hands over her arms and rib cage. "How do you feel? Anything broken?"

Jane couldn't say anything; her throat was frozen, her voice totally gone. All she could do was lie there and stare at him with the remnants of terror in her dark eyes. Her lips trembled like a child's, and there was something pleading in her gaze. He automatically started to gather her into his arms, the way one would a frightened child, but before he could do more than lift his hand, she dragged her gaze away from his with a visible effort. He could see what it cost her in willpower, but somehow she found the inner strength to still the trembling of her lips, and then her chin lifted in that characteristic gesture.

"I'm all right," she managed to say. Her voice was jerky, but she said the words, and in saying them, believed it. She slowly sat up and pushed her hair away from her face. "I feel a little bruised, but there's nothing bro—"

She stopped abruptly, staring at her bloody hand and arm. "I'm all bloody," she said in a bewildered tone, and her voice shook. She looked back at Grant, as if for confirmation. "I'm all bloody," she said again, extending her wildly trembling hand for him to see. "Grant, there's blood all over me!"

"It's the snake's blood," he said, thinking to reassure her, but she stared at him with uncontrolled revulsion.

"Oh, *God*!" she said in a thin, high voice, scrambling to her feet and staring down at herself. Her black blouse was wet and sticky, and big reddish splotches stained her khaki pants. Both her arms had blood smeared down them. Bile rose in her throat as she remembered the wetness that had splashed her face. She raised exploring fingers and found the horrible stickiness on her cheeks, as well as smeared in her hair.

She began to shake even harder, and tears dripped down her cheeks. "Get it off," she said, still in that high, wavering voice of utter hysteria. "I have to get it off. There's blood all over me, and it isn't mine. It's all over me; it's even in my hair... It's in my *hair*!" she sobbed, plunging for the stream.

Cursing, Grant grabbed for her, but in her mad urgency to wash the blood away she jerked free of him, stumbling over the body of the snake and crashing to the ground. Before she could scramble away again, Grant pounced on her, holding her in an almost painful grip while she fought and sobbed, pleading and swearing at him all at once.

"Jane, stop it!" he said sharply. "I'll get the blood off you. Just hold still and let me get our boots off, okay?"

He had to hold her still with one arm and pull her boots off with his free hand, but by the time he started to remove his own boots she was crying so hard that she lay limply on the ground. His face was grim as he looked at her. She'd stood up to so much without turning a hair that he hadn't expected her to fall apart like this. She'd been pulling herself together until she'd seen the blood on herself, and that had evidently been more than she could bear. He jerked his boots off, then turned to her and roughly undid her pants and pulled them off. Lifting her into his arms as easily as he would have lifted a child, he climbed down the bank and waded out into the stream, disregarding the fact that his own pants were being soaked.

When the water reached the middle of his calves, he stood her in the stream and bent to begin splashing water on her legs, rubbing the blood stains from her flesh. Next, cupping water in his palms, he washed her arms and hands clean, dripping the cooling water over her and soaking her blouse. All the while he tended to her, she stood docile, with silent tears still running down her face and making tracks in the blood smeared across her cheeks.

"Everything's all right, honey," he crooned soothingly to her, coaxing her to sit down in the stream so he could wash the blood from her hair. She let him splash water on her head and face, blinking her eyes to protect them from the stinging water, but otherwise keeping her gaze fixed on his hard, intent features. He took a handkerchief from his back pocket and wet it, then gently cleaned her face. She was calmer now, no longer crying in that silent, gut-wrenching way, and he helped her to her feet.

"There, you're all cleaned up," he started to say, then noticed the pink rivulets of water running down her legs. Her blouse was so bloody that he'd have to take it off to get her clean. Without hesitation, he began to unbutton it. "Let's get this off so we can wash it," he said, keeping his voice calm and soothing. She didn't even glance down as he unbuttoned her blouse and pulled it off her shoulders, then tossed it to the bank. She kept her eyes on his face, as if he were her lifeline to sanity and to look away meant a return to madness.

Grant looked down, and his mouth went dry as he stared at her naked breasts. He'd wondered how she looked and now he knew, and it was like being punched in the stomach. Her breasts were round and a little heavier than he'd expected, tipped by small brown nipples, and he wanted to bend down and put his mouth to them, taste them. She might as well have been naked; all she had on was a pair of gossamer panties that had turned transparent in the water. He could see the dark curls of hair beneath the wisp of fabric, and he felt his loins tighten and swell. She was beautifully made, long-legged and slim-hipped, with the sleek muscles of a dancer. Her shoulders were straight, her arms slim but strong, her breasts rich; he wanted to spread her legs and take her right there, driving deeply into her body until he went out of his mind with pleasure. He couldn't remember ever wanting a woman so badly. He'd wanted sex, but that had been simply a physical pleasure, and any willing female body had been acceptable. Now he wanted Jane, the essence of her; it was her legs he wanted wrapped around him, her breasts in his hands, her mouth under his, her body sheathing him.

He jerked his gaze away from her, bending to dip the handkerchief in the water again. That was even worse; his eyes were level with the top of her thighs, and he straightened abruptly. He washed her breasts with a gentle touch, but every moment of it was torture to him, feeling her silky flesh under his fingers, watching her nipples tighten into reddened little nubs as he touched them.

"You're clean," he said hoarsely, tossing the handkerchief to the bank to join her blouse.

"Thank you," she whispered, then fresh tears glittered in her eyes, and with a little whimper she flung herself against him. Her arms went around him and clung to his back. She buried her face against his chest, feeling reassured by the steady beat of his heart and the warmth of his body. His very presence drove the fear away; with him, she was safe. She wanted to rest in his arms and forget everything.

His hands moved slowly over her bare back, his calloused palms stroking her skin as if he relished the texture of it. Her eyes slid shut, and she nestled closer to him, inhaling the distinctly male scent of his strong body. She felt oddly drunk, disoriented; she wanted to cling to him as the only steady presence in the world. Her body was awash in strange sensations, from the rushing water swirling about her feet to the faint breeze that fanned her wet, naked skin, while he was so hard and warm. An unfamiliar heat swept along her flesh in the path of his hands as they moved from her back to her shoulders. Then one hand stroked up her throat to cup her jaw, his thumb under her chin and his fingers in her hair, and he turned her face up to him.

Taking his time about it, he bent and fitted his mouth to hers, slanting his head to make the contact deep and firm. His tongue moved leisurely into her mouth, touching hers and demanding a response, and Jane found herself helplessly giving him what he wanted. She'd never been kissed like that before, with such complete confidence and expertise, as if she were his for the taking, as if they had reverted to more primitive times when the dominant male had his pick of the women. Vaguely alarmed, she made a small effort to free herself from his grasp. He subdued her with gentle force and kissed her again, holding her head still for the pressure of his mouth. Once again Jane found herself opening her mouth for him, forgetting why she'd struggled to begin with. Since her divorce a lot of men had kissed her and tried to make her respond. They'd left her cold. Why should this rough…mercenary, or whatever he was, make shivers of pleasure chase over her body, when some of the most sophisticated men in the world had only bored her with their passion? His lips were warm and hard, the taste of his mouth heady, his tongue bold in its exploration, and his kisses caused an unfamiliar ache to tighten within her body.

A mindless little whimper of delight escaped her throat, the soft female sound making his arms tighten around her. Her hands slid up to his shoulders, then locked around his neck, hanging on to him for support. She couldn't get close enough to him, though he was crushing her against him.

The buttons of his shirt dug into her bare breasts, but she wasn't aware of any pain. His mouth was wild, hungry with a basic need that had flared out of control, bruising her lips with the force of his kisses, and she didn't care. Instead she gloried in it, clinging to him. Her body was suddenly alive with sensations and needs that she didn't recognize, never having felt them before. Her skin actually ached for his touch, yet every stroke of his hard fingers made the ache intensify.

Boldly cupping her breast in his palm, he rubbed the rough pad of his thumb across her tightly puckered nipple, and Jane almost cried aloud at the surge of heat that washed through her. It had never been like this for her before; the urgency of the pure, brazen sensuality of her own body took her by surprise. She'd long ago decided that she simply wasn't a very physical person, then forgotten about it. Sex hadn't been something that interested her very much. The way Grant was making her feel completely shattered her concept of herself. She was a female animal in his arms, grinding against him, feeling and glorying in the swollen response of his body, and hurting with the emptiness deep inside her.

Time disappeared as they stood in the water, the late afternoon sun dappling them with the shifting patterns of light created by the sheltering trees. His hands freely roamed her body. She never even thought of resisting him. It was as if he had every right to her flesh, as if she were his to touch and taste. He bent her back over his arm, making her breasts jut enticingly, and his lips traveled hotly down her throat to the warm, quivering mounds. He took her nipple into his mouth and sucked strongly, and she surged against him like a wild creature, on fire and dying and wanting more.

His hand swept downward, his fingers curving between

her legs to caress her through the silk of her panties. The boldness of his touch shocked her out of her sensual frenzy; automatically she stiffened in his grasp and brought her arms down from around his neck to wedge them between their bodies and push against him. A low, gutteral sound rattled in his throat, and for a brief, terrified moment she thought there wouldn't be any stopping him. Then, with a curse, he thrust her away from him.

Jane staggered a little, and his hand shot out to catch her, hauling her back to face him. "Damn you, is this how you get your kicks?" he asked, infuriated. "Do you like seeing how far you can push a man?"

Her chin came up, and she swallowed. "No, that's not it at all. I'm sorry. I know I shouldn't have thrown myself at you like that—"

"Damned right, you shouldn't," he interrupted savagely. He *looked* savage; his eyes were narrowed and bright with rage, his nostrils flared, and his mouth a thin, grim line. "Next time, you'd better make sure you want what you're asking for, because I'm damned sure going to give it to you. Is that clear?"

He turned and began wading to the bank, leaving her standing in the middle of the stream. Jane crossed her arms over her bare breasts, suddenly and acutely aware of her nakedness. She hadn't meant to tease him, but she'd been so frightened, and he'd been so strong and calm that it had seemed the most natural thing in the world to cling to him. Those frenzied kisses and caresses had taken her by surprise, shaken her off balance. Still, she wasn't about to have sex with a man she barely knew, especially when she didn't quite know if she liked what little she did know about him.

He reached the bank and turned to look at her. "Are you

coming or not?" he snapped, so Jane waded toward him, still keeping her arms over her breasts.

"Don't bother," he advised in a curt voice. "I've already seen, and touched. Why pretend to be modest?" He gestured to her blouse lying on the ground. "You might want to wash the blood out of that, since you're so squeamish about it."

Jane looked at the blood-stained blouse, and she went a little pale again, but she was under control now. "Yes, I will," she said in a low voice. "Will you…will you get my pants and boots for me, please?"

He snorted, but climbed up the bank and tossed her pants and boots down to her. Keeping her back turned to him, Jane pulled on her pants, shuddering at the blood that stained them, too, but at least they weren't soaked the way her blouse was. Her panties were wet, but there wasn't anything she could do about that now, so she ignored the clammy discomfort. When she was partially clad again, she squatted on the gravel at the edge of the stream and began trying to wash her blouse. Red clouds drifted out of the fabric, staining the water before being swept downstream. She scrubbed and scrubbed before she was satisfied, then wrung out as much water as possible and shook the blouse. As she started to put the blouse on, he said irritably, "Here," and held his shirt in front of her. "Wear this until yours gets dry."

She wanted to refuse, but she knew false pride wouldn't gain her anything. She accepted the shirt silently and put it on. It was far too big, but it was dry and warm and not too dirty, and it smelled of sweat, and the musky odor of his skin. The scent was vaguely comforting. There were rust-colored stains on it, too, reminding her that he'd saved her life. She tied the tails in a knot at her waist and sat down on the gravel to put on her boots.

When she turned, she found him standing right behind her, his face still grim and angry. He helped her up the bank, then lifted their packs to his shoulders. "We're not going much farther. Follow me, and for God's sake don't touch anything that I don't touch, or step anywhere except in my footprints. If another boa wants you, I just may let him have you, so don't push your luck."

Jane pushed her wet hair behind her ears and followed obediently, walking where he walked. For a while, she stared nervously at every tree limb they passed under, then made herself stop thinking about the snake. It was over; there was no use dwelling on it.

Instead she stared at his broad back, wondering how her father had found a man like Grant Sullivan. They obviously lived in two different worlds, so how had they met?

Then something clicked in her mind, and a chill went down her spine. *Had* they met? She couldn't imagine her father knowing anyone like Sullivan. She also knew what her own position was. Everyone wanted to get their hands on her, and she had no way of knowing whose side Grant Sullivan was on. He'd called her Priscilla, which was her first name. If her father had sent him, wouldn't he have known that she was never called Priscilla, that she'd been called Jane from birth? *He hadn't known her name!*

Before he died, George had warned her not to trust anyone. She didn't want to think that she was alone in the middle of the jungle with a man who would casually cut her throat when he had no further use for her. Still, the fact remained that she had no proof that her father had sent him. He'd simply knocked her out, put her over his shoulder and hauled her off into the jungle.

Then she realized that she had to trust this man; she had no alternative. He was all she had. It was dangerous, trusting him, but not as dangerous as trying to make it out of the jungle on her own. He had shown flashes of kindness. She felt a funny constriction in her chest as she remembered the way he'd cared for her after he'd killed the snake. Not just cared for her, kissed her—she was still shaken by the way he'd kissed her. Mercenary or not, enemy or not, he made her want him. Her mind wasn't certain about him, but her body was.

She would have found it funny, if she hadn't been so frightened.

CHAPTER FIVE

THEY MOVED DIRECTLY away from the stream at a forty-five-degree angle, and it wasn't long before he stopped, looked around and unslung the packs from his shoulders. "We'll camp here."

Jane stood in silence, feeling awkward and useless, watching as he opened his pack and took out a small, rolled bundle. Under his skilled hands, the bundle was rapidly transformed into a small tent, complete with a polyethylene floor and a flap that could be zipped shut. When the tent was up he began stripping vines and limbs from the nearby trees to cover it, making it virtually invisible. He hadn't so much as glanced in her direction, but after a moment she moved to help him. He did look at her then, and allowed her to gather more limbs while he positioned them over the tent.

When the job was completed, he said, "We can't risk a fire, so we'll just eat and turn in. After today, I'm ready for some sleep."

Jane was, too, but she dreaded the thought of the night to come. The light was rapidly fading, and she knew that it would soon be completely dark. She remembered the total blackness of the night before and felt a cold finger of fear trace up her backbone. Well, there was nothing she could do about it; she'd have to tough it out.

She crouched beside her pack and dug out two more cans of orange juice, tossing one to him; he caught it deftly, and eyed her pack with growing irritation. "How many more cans of this do you have in that traveling supermarket?" he asked sarcastically.

"That's it. We'll have to drink water from now on. How about a granola bar?" She handed it to him, refusing to let herself respond to the irritation in his voice. She was tired, she ached, and she was faced with a long night in total darkness. Given that, his irritation didn't seem very important. He'd get over it.

She ate her own granola bar, but was still hungry, so she rummaged for something else to eat. "Want some cheese and crackers?" she offered, dragging the items out of the depths of the pack.

She looked up to find him watching her with an expression of raw disbelief on his face. He held out his hand, and she divided the cheese and crackers between them. He looked at her again, shook his head and silently ate his share.

Jane saved a little of her orange juice, and when she finished eating she took a small bottle from the pack. Opening it, she shook a pill into the palm of her hand, glanced at Grant, then shook out another one. "Here," she said.

He looked at it, but made no move to take it. "What the hell's that?"

"It's a yeast pill."

"Why should I want to take a yeast pill?"

"So the mosquitoes and things won't bite you."

"Sure they won't."

"They won't! Look at me. I don't have any insect bites, and it's because I take yeast pills. It does something to your skin chemistry. Come on, take it. It won't hurt you."

He took the pill from her hand and held it with a pained expression on his face while she took her own, washing it down with a sip of the orange juice she'd saved. She passed the can to him, and he muttered something obscene before he tossed the pill into his mouth and slugged down the rest of the juice.

"Okay, bedtime," he said, rising to his feet. He jerked his head toward a tree. "There's your bathroom, if you want to go before we turn in."

Jane stepped behind the tree. He was crude, he was rude, he was a little cruel—and he had saved her life. She didn't know what to expect from him. No matter how rough he was, he would eventually disarm her with an unexpected act of kindness. On the other hand, when things were going smoothly between them, he would say things that stung, as if deliberately trying to start a quarrel.

He was waiting for her by the opening of the tent. "I've already put the blanket down. Crawl in."

She knelt down and crawled into the small tent. He had spread the blanket over the floor, and she sat on it. He shoved their packs inside. "Put these out of the way," he instructed. "I'm going to take a quick look around."

She shoved the packs into the far corners of the tent, then lay down on her back and stared tensely at the thin walls. The light was almost gone; only a glimmer entered through the translucent fabric. It wasn't quite as dark outside yet, but the limbs he'd used as camouflage made it darker inside. The flap parted, and he crawled in, then zipped the opening shut.

"Take your boots off and put them in the corner next to your feet."

Sitting up, she did as he said, then lay down again. Her eyes strained open so widely that they burned. Her body stiff with dread, she listened to him stretch and yawn and make himself comfortable.

Moments later the silence became nearly as unbearable

as the darkness. "A collapsible tent comes in handy, doesn't it?" she blurted nervously. "What is it made out of?"

"Nylon," he replied, yawning again. "It's nearly indestructible."

"How much does it weigh?"

"Three pounds and eight ounces."

"Is it waterproof?"

"Yes, it's waterproof."

"And bug proof?"

"Bug proof, too," he muttered.

"Do you think a jaguar could—"

"Look, it's *jaguar* proof, *mildew* proof, *fire* proof and *snake* proof. I personally guarantee you that it's proof against everything except elephants, and I don't think we're going to be stomped on by an elephant in Costa Rica! Is there any other damned thing you're worried about?" he exploded. "If not, why don't you be quiet and let me get some sleep?"

Jane lay tensely, and silence fell again. She clenched her fists in an effort to control her nervousness, listening to the growing cacophony of the jungle night. Monkeys howled and chattered; insects squeaked their calls; underbrush rustled. She was exhausted but she had no real hope of sleeping, at least not until dawn, and at dawn this devil beside her would want to start another day of marathon travel.

He was totally silent in that unnerving way of his. She couldn't even hear him breathe. The old fear began to rise in her chest, making her own breathing difficult. She might as well be alone, and that was the one thing she absolutely couldn't bear.

"Where are you from?"

He heaved a sigh. "Georgia."

That explained his drawl. She swallowed, trying to ease

the constriction of her dry throat. If she could just keep him talking, then she wouldn't feel so alone. She'd know he was there.

"What part of Georgia?"

"South. Ever hear of the Okefenokee?"

"Yes. It's a swamp."

"I grew up in it. My folks own a farm just on the edge of it." It had been a normal boyhood, except for the skills he'd learned automatically in the swamp, those skills, which had eventually changed his life by shaping him into something not quite human. He willed the memories away, pulling a mental shade down over them, isolating himself. There was no use in thinking about what had been.

"Are you an only child?"

"Why all the questions?" he snapped, edgy at revealing any information about himself.

"I'm just interested, that's all."

He paused, suddenly alert. There was something in her voice, a tone that he couldn't quite place. It was dark, so he couldn't see her face; he had to go entirely by what his ears told him. If he kept her talking, he might be able to figure it out.

"I've got a sister," he finally said reluctantly.

"I'll bet she's younger. You're so bossy, you must be an older brother."

He let the dig pass and said only, "She's four years younger."

"I'm an only child," she volunteered.

"I know."

She searched frantically for something else to say, but the darkness was making her panic. She felt herself move to grab for him, then remembered what he'd said about startling him, and about not making offers she didn't mean. She ground her teeth together and stilled her reaching hands, the effort so intense that tears actually welled in her eyes. She blinked them away. "Grant," she said in a shaking voice.

"What?" he growled.

"I don't want you to think I'm throwing myself at you again because I'm really not, but would you mind very much if I…just held your hand?" she whispered. "I'm sorry, but I'm afraid of the dark, and it helps if I know I'm not alone."

He was still for a moment; then she heard his clothing rustle as he rolled onto his side. "You're really that afraid of the dark?"

Jane tried for a laugh, but the sound was so shaky that it was close to a sob. "The word 'terrified' only begins to describe how afraid I am. I can't sleep in the dark. All the time I was at that wretched plantation I was awake all night long, never sleeping until dawn. But at least I could use that time to watch the guards and figure out their routine. Besides, it wasn't as totally dark there as it is here."

"If you're so all-fired scared of the dark, why were you getting ready to hit the jungle on your own?"

A dark, handsome, incredibly cruel face swam before her mind's eye. "Because even dying in the jungle would be better than Turego," she said quietly.

Grant grunted. He could understand that choice, but the fact that she had so correctly summed up the situation illustrated once again that she was more than what she seemed. Then again, perhaps she already had reason to know just how vile Turego could be. Had Turego raped her, or would it have been rape? With this woman, who knew? "Did you have sex with him?"

The blunt question made her shudder. "No. I'd been holding him off, but when he left yesterday…it *was* just yesterday, wasn't it? It seems like a year ago. Anyway, I knew that, when he came back, I wouldn't be able to stop him any longer. My time had run out."

"What makes you so certain of that?"

Jane paused, wondering just how much to tell him, wondering how much he already knew. If he was involved, he would be familiar with Luis's name; if he wasn't, the name would mean nothing to him. She wanted to tell him; she didn't want to be alone in this nightmare any longer. But she remembered George telling her once that secrecy was synonymous with security, and she quelled the need to turn into Grant's arms and tell him how afraid and alone she had been. If he wasn't involved already, he was safer not knowing anything about it. On the other hand, if he was involved, *she* might be safer if he didn't realize how deeply she was a part of things. Finally, to answer his question, she said, "I wasn't certain. I was just afraid to stay, afraid of Turego."

He grunted, and that seemed to be the end of the conversation. Jane clenched her jaw against the sudden chattering of her teeth. It was hot and steamy inside the dark tent, but chills were running up and down her body. Why didn't he say something else, anything, rather than lying there so quietly? She might as well have been alone. It was unnatural for anyone to be that soundless, that utterly controlled.

"How was Dad?"

"Why?"

"I just wondered." Was he being deliberately evasive? Why didn't he want to talk about her father? Perhaps he hadn't been hired by her father at all and didn't want to be drawn into a conversation about someone he was supposed to have met, but hadn't.

After a measured silence, as if he had carefully considered his answer, he said, "He was worried sick about you. Surprised?"

"No, of course not," she said, startled. "I'd be surprised if he weren't."

"It doesn't surprise you that he'd pay a small fortune to get you out of Turego's hands, even though you don't get along with him?"

He was confusing her; she felt left out of the conversation, as if he were talking about someone else entirely. "What are you talking about? We get along perfectly, always have."

She couldn't see him, couldn't hear him, but suddenly there was something different about him, as if the very air had become electrically charged. A powerful sense of danger made the fine hairs on her body stand up. The danger was coming from him. Without knowing why, she shrank back from him as far as she could in the confines of the small tent, but there was no escape. With the suddenness of a snake striking, he rolled and pinned her down, forcing her hands over her head and holding them shackled there in a grip that hurt her wrists. "All right, Jane, or Priscilla, or whoever you are, we're going to talk. I'm going to ask the questions and you're going to answer them, and you'd better have the right answers or you're in trouble, sugar. Who are you?"

Had he gone mad? Jane struggled briefly against the grip on her wrists, but there was no breaking it. His weight bore down heavily on her, controlling her completely. His muscled legs clasped hers, preventing her from even kicking. "W-what...?" she stammered. "Grant, you're hurting me!"

"Answer me, damn you! Who are you?"

"Jane Greer!" Desperately, she tried to put some humor in her voice, but it wasn't a very successful effort.

"I don't like being lied to, sugar." His voice was velvety soft, and the sound of it chilled her to her marrow. Not even Turego had affected her like this; Turego was a dangerous, vicious man, but the man who held her now was the most lethal person she'd ever seen. He didn't have to reach for a weapon to kill her; he could kill her with his bare hands. She was totally helpless against him.

"I'm not lying!" she protested desperately. "I'm Priscilla Jane Hamilton Greer."

"If you were, you'd know that James Hamilton cut you out of his will several years ago. So you get along with him just perfectly, do you?"

"Yes, I do!" She strained against him, and he deliberately let her feel more of his weight, making it difficult for her to breathe. "He did it to protect me!"

For a long, silent moment in which she could hear the roaring of her blood in her ears, she waited for his reaction. His silence scraped along her nerves. Why didn't he say something? His warm breath was on her cheek, telling her how close he was to her, but she couldn't see him at all in that suffocating darkness. "That's a good one," he finally responded, and she flinched at the icy sarcasm of his tone. "Too bad I don't buy it. Try again."

"I'm telling you the truth! He did it to make me a less attractive kidnap target. It was my idea, damn it!"

"Sure it was," he crooned, and that low, silky sound made her shudder convulsively. "Come on, you can do better than that."

Jane closed her eyes, searching desperately for some way of convincing him of her identity. None came to mind, and she had no identification with her. Turego had taken her passport, so she didn't have even that. "Well, what about you?" she blurted in sudden fury. She'd taken a lot from him, endured without complaining, and now he'd frightened her half out of her mind. She'd had her back to the wall before, and had learned to strike back. "Who are you? How do I know that Dad hired you? If he did why didn't you know that no one ever calls me Priscilla? You were sloppy with your homework!"

"In case you haven't noticed, honey, I'm the one on top. *You* answer *my* questions."

"I did, and you didn't believe me," she snapped. "Sorry, but I don't have my American Express card with me. For God's sake, do I look like a terrorist? You nearly broke my arm; then you knocked me out. You've bounced me on the ground like a rubber ball, and you've got the utter gall to act like *I'm* dangerous? My goodness, you'd better search me, too, so you'll be able to sleep tonight. Who knows? I might have a bazooka strapped to my leg, since I'm such a dangerous character!" Her voice had risen furiously, and he cut her off by resting all his weight on her ribcage. When she gasped, he eased up again.

"No, you're unarmed. I've already had your clothes off, remember?" Even in the darkness, Jane blushed at the memory, thinking of the way he'd kissed her and touched her, and how his hands on her body had made her feel. He moved slowly against her, stopping her breath this time with the suggestive intimacy of his movements. His warm breath stirred her hair as he dipped his head closer to her. "But I wouldn't want to disappoint a lady. If you want to be searched, I'll oblige you. I wouldn't mind giving you a body search."

Fuming, Jane tried again to free her hands, but finally fell back in disgust at the futile action. Raw frustration finally cleared her mind, giving her an idea, and she said harshly, "Did you go in the house when Dad hired you?"

He was still, and she sensed his sudden increase of interest. "Yes."

"Did you go in the study?"

"Yes."

"Then a hotshot like you would have noticed the portrait over the mantle. You're trained to notice things, aren't you? The portrait is of my grandmother, Dad's mother. She was painted sitting down, with a single rose on her lap. Now, you tell me what color her gown was," she challenged.

"Black," he said slowly. "And the rose was blood red."

Thick silence fell between them; then he released her hands and eased his weight from her. "All right," he said finally. "I'll give you the benefit of the doubt—"

"Well, gee, thanks!" Huffily she rubbed her wrists, trying to keep her anger alive in the face of the enormous relief that filled her. Evidently her father had hired him, for otherwise how could he have seen the portrait in the study? She wanted to remain mad at him, but she knew she would forgive him because it was still dark. In spite of everything she was terribly glad he was there. Besides, she told herself cautiously, it was definitely better to stay on this man's good side.

"Don't thank me," he said tiredly. "Just be quiet and go to sleep."

Sleep! If only she could! Consciously, she knew she wasn't alone, but her subconscious mind required additional affirmation from her senses. She needed to see him, hear him, or touch him. Seeing him was out of the question; she doubted he'd leave a flashlight burning all night, even assuming he had one. Nor would he stay awake all night talking to her. Perhaps, if she just barely touched him, he'd think it was an accident and not make a big deal out of it. Stealthily she moved her right hand until the backs of her fingers just barely brushed his hairy forearm—and immediately her wrist was seized in that bruising grip again.

"Ouch!" she yelped, and his fingers loosened.

"Okay, what is it this time?" His tone showed plainly that he was at the end of his patience.

"I just wanted to touch you," Jane admitted, too tired now to care what he thought, "so I'll know I'm not alone."

He grunted. "All right. It looks like that's the only way I'm going to get any sleep." He moved his hand, sliding his rough palm against hers, and twined their fingers together. "*Now* will you go to sleep?"

"Yes," she whispered. "Thank you."

She lay there, enormously and inexplicably comforted by the touch of that hard hand, so warm and strong. Her eyes slowly closed, and she gradually relaxed. The night terrors didn't come. He kept them firmly at bay with the strong, steady clasp of his hand around hers. Everything was going to be all right. Another wave of exhaustion swept over her, and she was asleep with the suddenness of a light turning off.

Grant woke before dawn, his senses instantly alert. He knew where he was, and he knew what time it was; his uncanny sixth sense could pinpoint the time within a few minutes. The normal night sounds of the jungle told him that they were safe, that there was no other human nearby. He knew immediately the identity of the other person in the tent with him. He knew that he couldn't move, and he even knew why: Jane was asleep on top of him.

He really didn't mind being used as a bed. She was soft and warm, and there was a female smell to her that made his nostrils flare in appreciation. The softness of her breasts against him felt good. That special, unmistakable softness never left a man's mind, hovering forever in his memory once he'd felt the fullness of a woman against him. It had been a long time since he'd slept with a woman, and he'd forgotten how good it could feel. He'd had sex—finding an available woman was no problem—but those encounters had been casual, just for the sake of the physical act. Once it was finished, he hadn't been inclined to linger. This past year, especially, he'd been disinclined to tolerate anyone else's presence. He'd spent a lot of time alone, like an injured animal licking its wounds; his mind and his soul had been filled with death. He'd spent so much time in the shadows that he didn't know if he'd ever find the sunlight again, but he'd been trying. The sweet, hot Tennessee sun had healed his body, but there was still an icy darkness in his mind.

Given that, given his acute awareness of his surroundings, even in sleep, how had Jane gotten on top of him without waking him? This was the second time she'd gotten close to him without disturbing him, and he didn't like it. A year ago, she couldn't have twitched without alerting him.

She moved then, sighing a little in her sleep. One of her arms was around his neck, her face pressed into his chest, her warm breath stirring the curls of hair in the low neckline of his undershirt. She lay on him as bonelessly as a cat, her soft body conforming to the hard contours of his. Her legs were tangled with his, her hair draped across his bare shoulder and arm. His body hardened despite his almost savage irritation with himself, and slowly his arms came up to hold her, his hands sliding over her supple back. He could have her if he wanted her. The highly specialized training he'd received had taught him how to deal excruciating pain to another human being, but a side benefit to that knowledge was that he also knew how to give pleasure. He knew all the tender, sensitive places of her body, knew how to excite nerves that she probably didn't even know she had. Beyond that, he knew how to control his own responses, how to prolong a sensual encounter until his partner had been completely satisfied.

The sure knowledge that he could have her ate at him, filling his mind with images and sensations. Within ten minutes he could have her begging him for it, and he'd be inside her, clasped by those long, sleek, dancer's legs. The only thing that stopped him was the almost childlike trust with which she slept curled on top of him. She slept as if she felt utterly safe, as if he could protect her from anything. Trust. His life had been short on trust for so many years that it startled him to find someone who could trust so easily and completely. He was uncomfortable with it, but at the same time it felt good, almost as good as her body in his arms. So he lay there staring into the darkness, holding her as she slept, the bitter blackness of his thoughts contrasting with the warm, elusive sweetness of two bodies pressed together in quiet rest.

When the first faint light began to filter through the trees, he shifted his hand to her shoulder and shook her lightly. "Jane, wake up."

She muttered something unintelligible and burrowed against him, hiding her face against his neck. He shifted gently to his side, easing her onto the blanket. Her arms still hung around his neck, and she tightened her grip as if afraid of falling. "Wait! Don't go," she said urgently, and the sound of her own voice woke her. She opened her eyes, blinking owlishly at him. "Oh. Is it morning?"

"Yes, it's morning. Do you think you could let me up?"

Confused, she stared at him, then seemed to realize that she was still clinging around his neck. She dropped her arms as if scalded, and though the light was too dim for him to be certain, he thought that her cheeks darkened with a blush. "I'm sorry," she apologized.

He was free, yet oddly reluctant to leave the small enclosure of the tent. His left arm was still under her neck, pillowing her head. The need to touch her was overwhelming, guiding his hand under the fabric of her shirt, which was actually his. He flattened his hand against her bare stomach. His fingers and palm luxuriated in the warm silkiness of her skin, tantalized by the knowledge that even richer tactile pleasures waited both above and below where his hand now rested.

Jane felt her breathing hasten in rhythm, and her heartbeat lurched from the slow, even tempo of sleep to an almost frantic pace. "Grant?" she asked hesitantly. His hand simply rested on her stomach, but she could feel her breasts tightening in anticipation, her nipples puckering. A restless ache stirred to life inside her. It was the same empty need that she'd felt when she'd stood almost naked in his arms, in the middle of the stream, and let him touch her with a raw sensuality that she'd never before experienced. She was a little afraid of that need, and a little afraid of the man who created it with his touch, who leaned over her so intently.

Her only sexual experience had been with her husband. The lack of success in that area of their marriage had severely limited what she knew, leaving her almost completely unawakened, even disinterested. Chris had given her no useful standard, for there was no comparison at all between her ex-husband—a kind, cheerful man, slender and only a few inches taller than she was—and this big, rough, muscular warrior. Chris was totally civilized; Grant wasn't civilized at all. If he took her, would he control his fearsome strength, or would he dominate her completely? Perhaps that was what frightened her most of all, because the greatest struggle of her life had been for independence: for freedom from fear, and from the overprotectiveness of her parents. She'd fought so hard and so long for control of her life that it was scary now to realize that she was totally at Grant's mercy. None of the training she'd had in self-defense was of any use against him; she had no defense at all. All she could do was trust him.

"Don't be afraid," he said evenly. "I'm not a rapist."

"I know." A killer, perhaps, but not a rapist. "I trust you," she whispered, and laid her hand against his stubbled jaw.

He gave a small, cynical laugh. "Don't trust me too much, honey. I want you pretty badly, and waking up with you in my arms is straining my good intentions to the limit." But he turned his head and pressed a quick kiss into the tender palm of the hand that caressed his cheek. "Come on, let's get moving. I feel like a sitting duck in this tent, now that it's daylight."

He heaved himself into a sitting position and reached for his boots, tugging them on and lacing them up with quick, expert movements. Jane was slower to sit up, her entire body protesting. She yawned and shoved her tangled hair back from her face, then put on her own boots. Grant had already left the tent by the time she finished, and she crawled after him. Once on her feet, she stretched her aching muscles, then touched her toes several times to limber up. While she was doing that, Grant swiftly dismantled the tent. He accomplished that in so short a time that she could only blink at him in amazement. In only a moment the tent was once more folded into an impossibly small bundle and stored in his backpack, with the thin blanket rolled up beside it.

"Any more goodies in that bottomless pack of yours?" he asked. "If not, we eat field rations."

"That yukky stuff you have?"

"That's right."

"Well, let's see. I know I don't have any more orange juice…." She opened the pack and peered into it, then thrust her hand into its depths. "Ah! Two more granola bars. Do you mind if I have the one with coconut? I'm not that crazy about raisins."

"Sure," he agreed lazily. "After all, they're yours."

She gave him an irritated glance. "They're *ours*. Wait—here's a can of..." She pulled the can out and read the label, then grinned triumphantly. "Smoked salmon! And some crackers. Please take a seat, sir, and we'll have breakfast."

He obediently sat, then took his knife from his belt and reached for the can of salmon. Jane drew it back, her brows lifted haughtily. "I'll have you know that this is a high-class eating establishment. We do not open our cans with knives!"

"We don't? What do we use, our teeth?"

She lifted her chin at him and searched in the back-pack again, finally extracting a can opener. "Listen," she said, giving the opener to him, "when I escape, I do it in style."

Taking the opener, he began to open the can of salmon. "So I see. How did you manage to get all of this stuff? I can just see you putting in an order with Turego, collecting what you wanted for an escape."

Jane chuckled, a rich, husky sound that made him lift his dark gold head from his task. Those piercing yellow eyes lit on her face, watching her as if examining a treasure. She was busy fishing crackers out of the backpack, so she missed the fleeting expression. "It was almost like that. I kept getting these 'cravings,' though I seldom mentioned them to Turego. I'd just have a word with the cook, and he generally came up with what I wanted. I raided the kitchen or the soldiers' quarters for a little something almost every night."

"Like that pack?" he queried, eyeing the object in question.

She patted it fondly. "Nice one, isn't it?"

He didn't reply, but there was a faint crinkling at the corners of his eyes, as if he were thinking of smiling. They ate the salmon and crackers in companionable silence, with the food washed down by water from Grant's canteen. He ate his granola bar, but Jane decided to save hers for later.

Squatting beside the pack, she took her brush and restored order to her tangled mane of hair, then cleaned her face and hands with a premoistened towelette. "Would you like one?" she asked Grant politely, offering him one of the small packets.

He had been watching her with a stunned sort of amazement, but he took the packet from her hand and tore it open. The small, wet paper had a crisp smell to it, and he felt fresher, cooler, after cleaning his face with it. To his surprise, some of the face black he'd put on before going in after Jane had remained on his skin; he'd probably looked like a devil out of hell, with those streaks on his face.

A familiar sound caught his attention and he turned to look at Jane. A tube of toothpaste lay on the ground beside her, and she was industriously brushing her teeth. As he watched, she spat out the toothpaste, then took a small bottle and tilted it to her mouth, swishing the liquid around, then spitting it out, too. His stunned gaze identified the bottle. For five whole seconds he could only gape at her; then he sat back and began to laugh helplessly. Jane was rinsing her mouth with Perrier water.

CHAPTER SIX

JANE POUTED FOR A MOMENT, but it was so good to hear him laugh that after a few seconds she sat back on her heels and simply watched him, smiling a little herself. When he laughed that harsh, scarred face became younger, even beautiful, as the shadows left his eyes. Something caught in her chest, something that hurt and made a curious melting feeling. She wanted to go over and hold him, to make sure that the shadows never touched him again. She scoffed at herself for her absurd sense of protectiveness. If anyone could take care of himself, it was Grant Sullivan. Nor would he welcome any gesture of caring; he'd probably take it as a sexual invitation.

To hide the way she felt, she put her things back into her pack, then turned to eye him questioningly. "Unless you want to use the toothpaste?" she offered.

He was still chuckling. "Thanks, honey, but I have tooth powder and I'll use the water in the canteen. God! Perrier water!"

"Well, I had to have water, but I wasn't able to snitch a canteen," she explained reasonably. "Believe me, I'd much rather have had a canteen. I had to wrap all the bottles in cloth so they wouldn't clink against each other or break."

It seemed completely logical to her, but it set him off again. He sat with his shoulders hunched and shaking, holding his head between his hands and laughing until tears streamed down his face. After he had stopped, he brushed his own teeth, but he kept making little choking noises that told Jane he was still finding the situation extremely funny. She was lighthearted, happy that she had made him laugh.

She felt her blouse and found it stiff, but dry. "You can have your shirt back," she told him, turning her back to take it off. "Thanks for the loan."

"Is yours dry?"

"Completely." She pulled his shirt off and dropped it on her backpack, and hurriedly began to put her blouse on. She had one arm in a sleeve when he swore violently. She jumped, startled, and looked over her shoulder at him.

His face was grim as he strode rapidly over to her. His expression had been bright with laughter only a moment before, but now he looked like a thundercloud. "What happened to your arm?" he snapped, catching her elbow and holding her bruised arm out for his inspection. "Why didn't you tell me you'd hurt yourself?"

Jane tried to grab the blouse and hold it over her bare breasts with her free arm, feeling horribly vulnerable and exposed. She had been trying for a nonchalant manner while changing, but her fragile poise was shattered by his closeness and his utter disregard for her modesty. Her cheeks reddened, and in self-defense she looked down at her badly bruised arm.

"Stop being so modest," he growled irritably when she fumbled with the blouse. "I told you, I've already seen you without any clothes." That was embarrassingly true, but it didn't help. She stood very still, her face burning, while he gently examined her arm.

"That's a hell of a bruise, honey. How does your arm feel?"

"It hurts, but I can use it," she said stiffly.

"How did it happen?"

"In a variety of ways," she said, trying to hide her embarrassment behind a bright manner. "This bruise right here is where you hit me on the arm after sneaking into my bedroom and scaring me half to death. The big, multicolored one is from falling down that bluff yesterday morning. This little interesting welt is where a limb swung back and caught me—"

"Okay, I get the idea." He thrust his fingers through his hair. "I'm sorry I bruised you, but I didn't know who you were. I'd say we were more than even on that score, anyway, after that kick you gave me."

Jane's dark chocolate eyes widened with remorse. "I didn't mean to, not really. It was just a reflex. I'd done it before I thought. Are you okay? I mean, I didn't do any permanent damage, did I?"

A small, unwilling grin tugged at his lips as he remembered the torment of arousal he'd been enduring on her account. "No, everything's in working order," he assured her. His gaze dropped to where she clutched her blouse to her chest, and his clear amber eyes darkened to a color like melted gold. "Couldn't you tell that when we were standing in the stream kissing?"

Jane looked down automatically, then jerked her gaze back up in consternation when she realized where she was looking. "Oh," she said blankly.

Grant slowly shook his head, staring at her. She was a constant paradox, an unpredictable blend of innocence and contrariness, of surprising prudery and amazing boldness. In no way was she what he'd expected. He was beginning to enjoy every moment he spent with her, but acknowledging that made him wary. It was his responsibility to get her out of Costa Rica, but he would compromise his own effectiveness if he allowed himself to become involved with her. Worrying over her could cloud his judgment. But, damn, how much could a man stand? He wanted her, and he wanting increased with every moment. In some curious way he felt lighter, happier. She certainly kept him on his toes! He was either laughing at her or contemplating beating her, but he was never bored or impatient in her company. Funny, but he couldn't remember ever laughing with a woman before. Laughter, especially during the past few years, had been in short supply in his life.

A chattering monkey caught his attention, and he looked up. The spots of sunlight darting through the shifting layers of trees reminded him that they were losing traveling time. "Get your blouse on," he said tersely, swinging away from her to sling his backpack on. He buckled it into place, then swung her pack onto his right shoulder. The rifle was slung over his left shoulder. By that time, Jane had jerked her blouse on and buttoned it up. Rather than stuffing it in her pants, she tied the tails in a knot at her waist as she had with Grant's shirt. He was already starting off through the jungle.

"Grant! Wait!" she called to his back, hurrying after him.

"You'll have to stay with me," he said unfeelingly, not slackening his pace.

Well, did he think she couldn't? Jane fumed, panting along in his path. She'd show him! And he could darn well act macho and carry both packs if he wanted; she wasn't going to offer to help! But he wasn't acting macho, she realized, and that deflated some of her indignation. He actually was that strong and indefatigable.

Compared to the harrowing day before, the hours passed quietly, without sight of another human being. She followed right on his heels, never complaining about the punishing pace he set, though the heat and humidity were even worse than the day before, if that were possible. There wasn't any hint of a breeze under the thick, smothering canopy. The air was still and heavy, steamy with an almost palpable thickness. She perspired freely, soaking her clothes and making her long for a real bath. That dousing in the stream the day before had felt refreshing, but didn't really qualify as bathing. Her nose wrinkled. She probably smelled like a goat.

Well, so what, she told herself. If she did, then so did he. In the jungle it was probably required to sweat.

They stopped about midmorning for a break, and Jane tiredly accepted the canteen from him. "Do you have any salt tablets?" she asked. "I think I need one."

"You don't need salt, honey, you need water. Drink up."

She drank, then passed the canteen back to him. "It's nearly empty. Let's pour the Perrier into it and chuck the empty bottles."

He nodded, and they were able to discard three bottles. As he got ready to start out again, Jane asked, "Why are you in such a hurry? Do you think we're being followed?"

"Not followed," he said tersely. "But they're looking for us, and the slower we move, the better chance they have of finding us."

"In this?" Jane joked, waving her hand to indicate the enclosing forest. It was difficult to see ten feet in any direction.

"We can't stay in here forever. Don't underrate Turego; he can mobilize a small army to search for us. The minute we show our faces, he'll know it."

"Something should be done about him," Jane said strongly. "Surely he's not operating with the sanction of the government?"

"No. Extortion and terrorism are his own little sidelines.

We've known about him, of course, and occasionally fed him what we wanted him to know."

"We?" Jane asked casually.

His face was immediately shuttered, as cold and blank as a wall. "A figure of speech." Mentally, he swore at himself for being so careless. She was too sharp to miss anything. Before she could ask any more questions, he began walking again. He didn't want to talk about his past, about what he had been. He wanted to forget it all, even in his dreams.

ABOUT NOON THEY STOPPED to eat, and this time they had to resort to the field rations. After a quick glance at what she was eating, Jane didn't look at it at all, just put it in her mouth and swallowed without allowing herself to taste it too much. It wasn't really that bad; it was just so awfully bland. They each drank a bottle of Perrier, and Jane insisted that they take another yeast pill. A roll of thunder announced the daily downpour, so Grant quickly found them shelter under a rocky outcropping. The opening was partially blocked by bushes, making it a snug little haven.

They sat watching the deluge for a few minutes; then Grant stretched out his long legs, leaning back to prop himself on his elbow. "Explain this business of how your father disinherited you as a form of protection."

Jane watched a small brown spider pick its way across the ground. "It's very simple," she said absently. "I wouldn't live with around-the-clock protection the way he wanted, so the next best thing was to remove the incentive for any kidnappers."

"That sounds a little paranoid, seeing kidnappers behind every tree."

"Yes," she agreed, still watching the spider. It finally minced into a crevice in the rock, out of sight, and she sighed. "He *is* paranoid about it, because he's afraid that next time he wouldn't get me back alive again."

"Again?" Grant asked sharply, seizing on the implication of her words. "You've been kidnapped before?"

She nodded. "When I was nine years old."

She made no other comment and he sensed that she wasn't going to elaborate, if given a choice. He wasn't going to allow her that choice. He wanted to know more about her, learn what went on in that unconventional brain. It was new to him, this overwhelming curiosity about a woman; it was almost a compulsion. Despite his relaxed position, tension had tightened his muscles. She was being very matter-of-fact about it, but instinct told him that the kidnapping had played a large part in the formation of the woman she was now. He was on the verge of discovering the hidden layers of her psyche.

"What happened?" he probed, keeping his voice casual.

"Two men kidnapped me after school, took me to an abandoned house and locked me in a closet until Dad paid the ransom."

The explanation was so brief as to be ridiculous; how could something as traumatic as a kidnapping be condensed into one sentence? She was staring at the rain now, her expression pensive and withdrawn.

Grant knew too much about the tactics of kidnappers, the means they used to force anxious relatives into paying the required ransom. Looking at her delicate profile, with the lush provocativeness of her mouth, he felt something savage well up in him at the thought that she might have been abused.

"Did they rape you?" He was no longer concerned about maintaining a casual pose. The harshness of his tone made her glance at him, vague surprise in her exotically slanted eyes.

"No, they didn't do anything like that," she assured him. "They just left me in that closet...alone. It was dark."

And to this day she was afraid of the dark, of being alone in it. So that was the basis for her fear. "Tell me about it," he urged softly.

She shrugged. "There isn't a lot more to tell. I don't know how long I was in the closet. There were no other houses close by, so no one heard me scream. The two men just left me there and went to some other location to negotiate with my parents. After awhile I became convinced that they were never coming back, that I was going to die there in that dark closet, and that no one would ever know what had happened to me."

"Your father paid the ransom?"

"Yes. Dad's not stupid, though. He knew that he wasn't likely to get me back alive if he just trusted the kidnappers, so he brought the police in on it. It's lucky he did. When the kidnappers came back for me, I overheard them making their plans. They were just going to kill me and dump my body somewhere, because I'd seen them and could identify them." She bent her head, studying the ground with great concentration, as if to somehow divorce herself from what she was telling him. "But there were police sharpshooters surrounding the house. When the two men realized that they were trapped, they decided to use me as a hostage. One of them grabbed my arm and held his pistol to my head, forcing me to walk in front of them when they left the house. They were going to take me with them, until it was safe to kill me."

Jane shrugged, then took a deep breath. "I didn't plan it, I swear. I don't remember if I tripped, or just fainted for a second. Anyway, I fell, and the guy had to let go of me or be jerked off balance. For a second the pistol wasn't pointed at me, and the policemen fired. They killed both men.

The…the man who had held me was shot in the chest and the head, and he fell over on me. His blood splattered all over me, on my face, my hair…." Her voice trailed away.

For a moment there was something naked in her face, the stark terror and revulsion she'd felt as a child; then, as he had seen her do when he'd rescued her from the snake, she gathered herself together. He watched as she defeated the fear, pushed the shadows away. She smoothed her expression and even managed a glint of humor in her eyes as she turned to look at him. "Okay, it's your turn. Tell me something that happened to you."

Once he'd felt nothing much at all; he'd accepted the chilled, shadowed brutality of his life without thought. He still didn't flinch from the memories. They were part of him, as ingrained in his flesh and blood, in his very being, as the color of his eyes and the shape of his body. But when he looked into the uncommon innocence of Jane's eyes, he knew that he couldn't brutalize her mind with even the mildest tale of the life he'd known. Somehow she had kept a part of herself as pure and crystalline as a mountain stream, a part of childhood forever unsullied. Nothing that had happened to her had touched the inner woman, except to increase the courage and gallantry that he'd seen twice now in her determined efforts to pull herself together and face forward again.

"I don't have anything to tell," he said mildly.

"Oh, sure!" she hooted, shifting herself on the ground until she was sitting facing him, her legs folded in a boneless sort of knot that made him blink. She rested her chin in her palm and surveyed him, so big and controlled and capable. If this man had led a normal life, she'd eat her boots, she told herself, then quickly glanced down at the boots in question. Right now they had something green and squishy on them. Yuk. They'd have to be cleaned before even a goat would eat them. She returned her dark gaze to Grant and studied him with the seriousness of a scientist bent over a microscope. His scarred face was hard, a study of planes and angles, of bronzed skin pulled tautly over the fierce sculpture of his bones. His eyes were those of an eagle, or a lion; she couldn't quite decide which. The clear amber color was brighter, paler, than topaz, almost like a yellow diamond, and like an eagle's, the eyes saw everything. They were guarded, expressionless; they hid an almost unbearable burden of experience and weary cynicism.

"Are you an agent?" she asked, probing curiously. Somehow, in those few moments, she had discarded the idea that he was a mercenary. Same field she thought, but a different division.

His mouth quirked. "No."

"Okay, let's try it from another angle. *Were* you an agent?"

"What sort of agent?"

"Stop evading my questions! The cloak-and-dagger sort of agent. You know, the men in overcoats who have forty sets of identification."

"No. Your imagination is running wild. I'm too easily identifiable to be any good undercover."

That was true. He stood out like a warrior at a tea party. Something went quiet within her, and she knew. "Are you retired?"

He was quiet for so long that she thought he wasn't going to answer her. He seemed to be thinking of something else entirely. Then he said flatly, "Yeah, I'm retired. For a year now."

His set, blank face hurt her, on the inside. "You were a…weapon, weren't you?"

There was a terrible clarity in his eyes as he slowly

shifted his gaze to her. "Yes," he said harshly. "I was a weapon."

They had aimed him, fired him, and watched him destroy. He would be matchless, she realized. Before she'd even known him, when she'd seen him gliding into her darkened bedroom like a shadow, she'd realized how lethal he could be. And there was something else, something she could see now. He had retired himself, turned his back and walked away from that grim, shadowed life. Certainly his superiors wouldn't have wanted to lose his talents.

She reached out and placed her hand on his, her fingers slim and soft, curling around the awesome strength of his. Her hand was much smaller made with a delicacy that he could crush with a careless movement of his fingers, but implicit in her touch was the trust that he wouldn't turn that strength against her. A deep breath swelled the muscled planes of his chest. He wanted to take her right then, in the dirt. He wanted to stretch her out and pull her clothes off, bury himself in her. He wanted more of her touch, all of her touch, inside and out. But the need for her satiny female flesh was a compulsion that he couldn't satisfy with a quick possession, and there wasn't time for more. The rain was slowing and would stop entirely at any moment. There was a vague feeling marching up and down his spine that told him they couldn't afford to linger any longer.

But it was time she knew. He removed his hand from hers, lifting it to cup her chin. His thumb rubbed lightly over her lips. "Soon," he said, his voice guttural with need, "you're going to lie down for me. Before I take you back to your daddy, I'm going to have you, and the way I feel now, I figure it's going to take a long time before I'm finished with you."

Jane sat frozen, her eyes those of a startled woodland animal. She couldn't even protest, because the harsh desire in his voice flooded her mind and her skin with memories. The day before, standing in the stream, he'd kissed her and touched her with such raw sexuality that, for the first time in her life, she'd felt the coiling, writhing tension of desire in herself. For the first time she'd wanted a man, and she'd been shocked by the unfamiliarity of her own body. Now he was doing it to her again, but this time he was using words. He'd stated his intentions bluntly, and images began forming in her mind of the two of them lying twined together, of his naked, magnificent body surging against her.

He watched the shifting expressions that flitted across her face. She looked surprised, even a little shocked, but she wasn't angry. He'd have understood anger, or even amusement; that blank astonishment puzzled him. It was as if no man had ever told her that he wanted her. Well, she'd get used to the idea.

The rain had stopped, and he picked up the packs and the rifle, settling them on his shoulders. Jane followed him without a word when he stepped out from beneath the rocky outcropping into the already increasing heat. Steam rose in wavering clouds from the forest floor, immediately wrapping them in a stifling, humid blanket.

She was silent for the rest of the afternoon, lost in her thoughts. He stopped at a stream, much smaller than the one they'd seen the day before, and glanced at her. "Care for a bath? You can't soak, but you can splash."

Her eyes lit up, and for the first time that afternoon a smile danced on her full lips. He didn't need an answer to know how she felt about the idea. Grinning, he searched out a small bar of soap from his pack and held it out to her. "I'll keep watch, then you can do the same for me. I'll be up there."

Jane looked up the steep bank that he'd indicated. That was the best vantage point around; he'd have a clear view

of the stream and the surrounding area. She started to ask
if he was going to watch her, too, but bit back the question.
As he'd already pointed out, it was too late for modesty.
Besides, she felt infinitely safer knowing that he'd be close
by.

He went up the bank as sure-footedly as a cat, and Jane
turned to face the stream. It was only about seven feet wide,
and wasn't much more than ankle-deep. Still, it looked
like heaven. She hunted her lone change of underwear out
of her pack, then sat down to pull off her boots. Glancing
nervously over her shoulder to where Grant sat, she saw
that he was in profile to her, but she knew that he would
keep her in his peripheral vision. She resolutely undid her
pants and stepped out of them. Nothing was going to keep
her from having her bath…except maybe another snake,
or a jaguar, she amended.

Naked, she gingerly picked her way over the stony
bottom to a large flat rock and sat down in the few inches
of water. It was deliciously cool, having run down from a
higher altitude, but even tepid water would have felt good
on her over-heated skin. She splashed it on her face and
head until her hair was soaked. Gradually she felt the
sweaty stickiness leave her hair, until the strands were once
more silky beneath her fingers. Then she took the small
bar of soap out from under her leg, where she'd put it for
safekeeping, and rubbed it over her body. The small luxury
made her feel like a new woman, and a sense of peace crept
into her. It was only a simple pleasure, to bathe in a clear,
cool stream, but added to it was her sense of nakedness,
of being totally without restrictions. She knew that he was
there, knew that he was watching her, and felt her breasts
grow tight.

What would it be like if he came down from that bank
and splashed into the water with her? If he took the blanket

from his pack and laid her down on it? She closed her eyes, shivering in reaction, thinking of his hard body pressing down on her, thrusting into her. It had been so many years, and the few experiences she'd had with Chris hadn't taught her that she could be a creature of wanting, but with Grant she wasn't the same woman.

Her heart beat heavily in her breast as she rinsed herself by cupping water in her palms and pouring it over her. Standing up, she twisted the water out of her hair, then waded out. She was trembling as she pulled on her clean underwear, then dressed distastefully in her stained pants and shirt. "I'm finished," she called, lacing up her boots.

He appeared soundlessly beside her. "Sit in the same place where I sat," he instructed, placing the rifle in her hands. "Do you know how to use this?"

The weapon was heavy, but her slim hands looked capable as she handled it. "Yes. I'm a fairly good shot." A wry smile curved her lips. "With paper targets and clay pigeons, anyway."

"That's good enough." He began unbuttoning his shirt, and she stood there in a daze, her eyes on his hands. He paused. "Are you going to guard me from down here?"

She blushed. "No. Sorry." Quickly she turned and scrambled up the bank, then took a seat in the exact spot where he'd sat. She could see both banks, but at the same time there was a fair amount of cover that she could use if the need arose. He'd probably picked this out as the best vantage point without even thinking about it, just automatically sifting through the choices and arriving at the correct one. He might be retired, but his training was ingrained.

A movement, a flash of bronze, detected out of the corner of her eye, told her that he was wading into the stream. She shifted her gaze a fraction so she wouldn't be able to see him at all, but just the knowledge that he was

as naked as she had been kept her heart pounding erratically. She swallowed, then licked her lips, forcing herself to
concentrate on the surrounding jungle, but the compulsion
to look at him continued.

She heard splashing and pictured him standing there
like a savage, bare and completely at home.

She closed her eyes, but the image remained before her.
Slowly, totally unable to control herself, she opened her
eyes and turned her head to look at him. It was only a
small movement, a fraction of an inch, until she was able
to see him, but that wasn't enough. Stolen glances weren't
enough. She wanted to study every inch of him, drink in
the sight of his powerful body. Shifting around, she looked
fully at him, and froze. He was beautiful, so beautiful
that she forgot to breathe. Without being handsome, he
had the raw power and grace of a predator, all the terrible
beauty of a hunter. He was bronzed all over, his tan a deep,
even brown. Unlike her, he didn't keep his back turned in
case she looked; he had a complete disregard for modesty.
He was taking a bath; she could look or not look, as she
wished.

His skin was sleek and shiny with water, and the drop-
lets caught in the hair on his chest glittered like captured
diamonds. His body hair was dark, despite the sun-streaked
blondness of his head. It shadowed his chest, ran in a thin
line down his flat, muscled stomach, and bloomed again
at the juncture of his legs. His legs were as solid as tree
trunks, long and roped with muscle; every movement he
made set off ripples beneath his skin. It was like watching
a painting by one of the old masters come to life.

He soaped himself all over, then squatted in the water
to rinse in the same manner she had, cupping his palms to
scoop up the water. When he was rinsed clean, he stood
and looked up at her, probably to check on her, and met

her gaze head-on. Jane couldn't look away, couldn't pretend that she hadn't been staring at him with an almost painful appreciation. He stood very still in the stream, watching her as she watched him, letting her take in every detail of his body. Under her searching gaze, his body began to stir, harden, growing to full, heavy arousal.

"Jane," he said softly, but still she heard him. She was so attuned to him, so painfully sensitive to every move and sound he made, that she would have heard him if he'd whispered. "Do you want to come down here?"

Yes. Oh, God, yes, more than she'd ever wanted anything. But she was still a little afraid of her own feelings, so she held back. This was a part of herself that she didn't know, wasn't certain she could control.

"I can't," she replied, just as softly. "Not yet."

"Then turn around, honey, while you still have a choice."

She quivered, almost unable to make the required movement, but at last her muscles responded and she turned away from him, listening as he waded out of the water. In less than a minute he appeared noiselessly at her side and took the rifle from her hands. He had both packs with him. Typically, he made no further comment on what had just happened. "We'll get away from the water and set up camp. It'll be night pretty soon."

Night. Long hours in the dark tent, lying next to him. Jane followed him, and when he stopped she helped him do the work they had done the night before, setting up the tent and hiding it. She didn't protest at the cold field rations, but ate without really tasting anything. Soon she was crawling into the tent and taking off her boots, waiting for him to join her.

When he did, they lay quietly side by side, watching as the remaining light dimmed, then abruptly vanished.

Tension hummed through her, making her muscles tight. The darkness pressed in on her, an unseen monster that sucked her breath away. No list of compulsive questions leaped to her lips tonight; she felt oddly timid, and it had been years since she'd allowed herself to be timid about anything. She no longer knew herself.

"Are you afraid of me?" he asked, his voice gentle.

Just the sound of his voice enabled her to relax a little. "No," she whispered.

"Then come here and let me keep the dark away from you."

She felt his hand on her arm, urging her closer, then she was enfolded in arms so strong that nothing could ever make her afraid while they held her. He cradled her against his side, tucking her head into the hollow of his shoulder. With a touch so light that it could have been the brush of a butterfly's wings, he kissed the top of her head. "Good night, honey," he whispered.

"Good night," she said in return.

Long after he was asleep, Jane lay in his arms with her eyes open, though she could see nothing. Her heart was pounding in her chest with a slow, heavy rhythm, and her insides felt jittery. It wasn't fear that kept her awake, but a churning emotion that shifted everything inside her. She knew exactly what was wrong with her. For the first time in too many years, everything was right with her.

She'd learned to live her life with a shortage of trust. No matter that she'd learned to enjoy herself and her freedom; there had always been that residual caution that kept her from letting a man get too close. Until now she'd never been strongly enough attracted to a man for the attraction to conquer the caution.... Until now. Until Grant. And now the attraction had become something much stronger. The truth stunned her, yet she had to accept it: she loved him.

She hadn't expected it, though for two days she had felt it tugging at her. He was harsh and controlled, badtempered, and his sense of humor was severely underdeveloped, but he had gently washed the snake's blood from her, held her hand during the night, and had gone out of his way to make their trek easier for her. He wanted her, but he hadn't taken her because she wasn't ready. She was afraid of the dark, so he held her in his arms. Loving him was at once the easiest and most difficult thing she'd ever done.

CHAPTER SEVEN

ONCE AGAIN HE AWOKE to find her cuddled on top of him, but this time it didn't bother him that he had slept peacefully through the night. Sliding his hands up her back, he accepted that his normally keen instincts weren't alarmed by her because there was absolutely no danger in her except perhaps the danger of her driving him crazy. She managed to do that with every little sway of her behind. Reveling in the touch of her all along his body, he moved his hands down, feeling her slenderness, the small ribs, the delicate spine, the enticing little hollow at the small of her back, then the full, soft mounds of her buttocks. He cupped his palms over them, kneading her with his fingers. She muttered and shifted against him, brushing at a lock of hair that had fallen into her face. Her eyelashes fluttered, then closed completely once more.

He smiled, enjoying the way she woke up. She did it by slow degrees, moaning and grousing while still more asleep than awake, frowning and pouting, and moving against him as if trying to sink herself deeper into him so she wouldn't have to wake up at all. Then her eyes opened, and she blinked several times, and as quickly as that the pout faded from her lips and she gave him a slow smile that would have melted stone.

"Good morning," she said, and yawned. She stretched, then abruptly froze in place. Her head came up, and she stared at him in stupefaction. "I'm on top of you," she said blankly.

"Again," he confirmed.

"Again?"

"You slept on top of me the night before last, too. Evidently my holding you while you sleep isn't enough; you think you have to hold me down."

She slithered off him, sitting up in the tent and straightening her twisted, wrinkled clothing. Color burned in her face. "I'm sorry. I know it can't have been very comfortable for you."

"Don't apologize. I've enjoyed it," he drawled. "If you really want to make it up to me, though, we'll reverse positions tonight."

Her breath caught and she stared at him in the dim light, her eyes soft and melting. Yes. Everything in her agreed. She wanted to belong to him; she wanted to know everything about his body and let him know everything about hers. She wanted to tell him, but she didn't know how to put it into words. A crooked smile crossed his face; then he sat up and reached for his boots, thrusting his feet into them and lacing them up. Evidently he took her silence for a refusal, because he dropped the subject and began the task of breaking camp.

"We have enough food for one more meal," he said as they finished eating. "Then I'll have to start hunting."

She didn't like that idea. Hunting meant that he'd leave her alone for long stretches of time. "I don't mind a vegetarian diet," she said hopefully.

"Maybe it won't come to that. We've been gradually working our way out of the mountains, and unless I miss my guess we're close to the edge of the forest. We'll probably see fields and roads today. But we're going to avoid people until I'm certain it's safe, okay?"

She nodded in agreement.

Just as he'd predicted, at midmorning they came abruptly to the end of the jungle. They stood high on a steep cliff, and stretched out below them was a valley with cultivated fields, a small network of roads, and a cozy village situated at the southern end. Jane blinked at the suddenly brilliant sunlight. It was like stepping out of one century into another. The valley looked neat and prosperous, reminding her that Costa Rica was the most highly developed country in Central America, despite the thick tangle of virgin rain forest at her back.

"Oh," she breathed. "Wouldn't it be nice to sleep in a bed again?"

He grunted an absent reply, his narrowed eyes sweeping the valley for any sign of abnormal activity. Jane stood beside him, waiting for him to make his decision.

It was made for them. Abruptly he grabbed her arm and jerked her back into the sheltering foliage, dragging her to the ground behind a huge bush just as a helicopter suddenly roared over their heads. It was flying close to the ground, following the tree line; she had only a glimpse of it before it was gone, hidden by the trees. It was a gunship, and had camouflage paint.

"Did you see any markings?" she asked sharply, her nails digging into his skin.

"No. There weren't any." He rubbed his stubbled jaw. "There's no way of telling who it belonged to, but we can't take any chances. Now we know that we can't just walk across the valley. We'll work our way down, and try to find more cover."

If anything, the terrain was even more difficult now. They were at the edge of a volcanic mountain range, and the land had been carved with a violent hand. It seemed to be either straight up, or straight down. Their pace was agonizingly slow as they worked their way down rocky bluffs and up steep gorges. When they stopped to eat, they had covered less than one-fourth the length of the valley, and Jane's legs ached as they hadn't since the wild run through the jungle the first day.

Right on schedule, just as they finished eating, they heard the boom of thunder. Grant looked around for shelter, considering every outcropping of rock. Then he pointed. "I think that's a cave up there. If it is we'll be in high cotton."

"What?" Jane asked, frowning.

"Sitting pretty," he explained. "Luxurious accommodations, in comparison to what we've had."

"Unless it's already occupied."

"That's why you're going to wait down here while I check it out." He moved up the fern-covered wall of the gorge, using bushes and vines and any other toehold he could find. The gorge itself was narrow and steep, enclosing them on all four sides. Its shape gave a curious clarity to the calls of the innumerable birds that flitted among the trees like living Christmas decorations, all decked out in their iridescent plumage. Directly overhead was a streak of sky, but it consisted of rolling black clouds instead of the clear blue that she'd seen only moments before.

Grant reached the cave, then immediately turned and waved to her. "Come on up; it's clear! Can you make it?"

"Have I failed yet?" she quipped, starting the climb, but she'd had to force the humor. The desolation had been growing in her since they'd seen the valley. Knowing that they were so close to civilization made her realize that their time together was limited. While they had been in the forest, the only two people locked in a more primitive time, she'd had no sense of time running out. Now she couldn't ignore the fact that soon, in a few days or less, their time together would end. She felt as if she'd already wasted so much time, as if the golden sand had been trickling through her fingers and she'd only just realized what she held. She felt panic-stricken at the thought of discovering love only to lose it, because there wasn't enough time to let it grow.

He reached his hand down and caught hers, effortlessly lifting her the last few feet. "Make yourself comfortable; we could be here a while. This looks like the granddaddy of all storms."

Jane surveyed their shelter. It wasn't really a cave; it was little more than an indentation in the face of the rock, about eight feet deep. It had a steeply slanting ceiling that soared to ten or eleven feet at the opening of the cave, but was only about five feet high at the back. The floor was rocky, and one big rock, as large as a love seat and shaped like a peanut, lay close to the mouth of the cave. But it was dry, and because of its shallowness it wasn't dark, so Jane wasn't inclined to find fault with it.

Given Grant's eerie sense of timing, she wasn't surprised to hear the first enormous raindrops begin filtering through the trees just as he spread out the tarp at the back of the cave. He placed it behind the big rock, using its bulk to shelter them. She sat down on the tarp and drew her legs up, wrapping her arms around them and resting her chin on her knees, listening to the sound of the rain as it increased in volume.

Soon it was a din and the solid sheets of water that obscured their vision heightened the impression that they were under a waterfall. She could hear the crack of lightning, feel the earth beneath her shake from the enormous claps of thunder. It was dark now, as the rain blotted out what light came through the thick canopy. She could barely see Grant, who was standing just inside the mouth of the cave with his shoulder propped against the wall, occasionally puffing on a cigarette.

Chills raced over her body as the rain cooled the air. Hugging her legs even tighter for warmth, Jane stared through the dimness at the broad, powerful shoulders outlined against the gray curtain of rain. He wasn't an easy man to get to know. His personality was as shadowy as the jungle, yet just the sight of that muscular back made her feel safe and protected. She knew that he stood between her and any danger. He had already risked his life for her on more than one occasion, and was as matter-of-fact about it as if being shot at were an everyday occurrence. Perhaps it was for him, but Jane didn't take it so lightly.

He finished his cigarette and field-stripped it. Jane doubted that anyone would track them here through the rain, but it was second nature to him to be cautious. He went back to his calm perusal of the storm, standing guard while she rested.

Something shifted inside her and coiled painfully in her chest. He was so alone. He was a hard, lonely man, but everything about him drew her like a magnet, pulling at her heart and body.

Her eyes clouded as she watched him. When this was over he'd walk away from her as if these days in the jungle had never existed. This was all routine for him. What she could have of him, all that she could ever have of him, was the present, too few days before this was over. And that just wasn't enough.

She was cold now, chilled to her bones. The unceasing, impenetrable curtain of rain carried a damp coldness with it, and her own spirits chilled her from the inside. Instinctively, like a sinuous cat seeking heat, she uncoiled from the tarp and went up to him, gravitating to his certain warmth and comfort. Silently she slid her arms around his taut waist and pressed her face into the marvelous heat of his chest. Glancing down at her, he lifted an eyebrow in mild inquiry. "I'm cold," she muttered, leaning her head on him and staring pensively at the rain.

He looped his arm around her shoulder, holding her closer to him and sharing his warmth with her. A shiver ran over her; he rubbed his free hand up her bare arm, feeling the coolness of her skin. Of its own accord his hand continued upward, stroking her satiny jaw, smoothing the dark tangle of hair away from her face. She was in a melancholy mood, this funny little cat, staring at the rain as if it would never stop, her eyes shadowed and that full, passionate mouth sad.

Cupping her chin in his hand, he tilted her face up so he could study her quiet expression. A small smile curved the corners of his hard mouth. "What's wrong, honey? Rain making you feel blue?" Before she could answer, he bent his head and kissed her, using his own cure.

Jane's hands went to his shoulders, clinging to him for support. His mouth was hard and demanding and oh so sweet. The taste of him, the feel of him, was just what she wanted. Her teeth parted, allowing the slow probing of his tongue. Deep inside her, fire began to curl, and she curled too, twining against him in an unconscious movement that he read immediately.

Lifting his mouth from hers just a little, he muttered, "Honey, this feels like an offer to me."

Her dark eyes were a little dazed as she looked up at him. "I think it is," she whispered.

He dropped his arms to her waist and wrapped them around her, lifting her off her feet, bringing her level with him. She wound her arms around his neck and kissed him fervently, lost in the taste and feel of his mouth, not even aware he'd moved until he set her down to stand on the tarp.

The dimness at the back of the cave hid any expression that was in his eyes, but she could feel his intent amber gaze on her as he began calmly unbuttoning her shirt. Jane's mouth went dry, but her own shaking fingers moved to his chest and began opening his shirt in turn.

When both garments were hanging open, he shrugged out of his and tossed it on the tarp, never taking his eyes from her. Tugging his undershirt free of his pants, he caught the bottom of it and peeled it off over his head. He tossed it aside, too, completely baring his broad, hairy chest. As it had the day before, the sight of his half-naked body mesmerized her. Her chest hurt; breathing was incredibly difficult. Then his hard, hot fingers were inside her shirt, on her breasts, molding them to fit his palms. The contrast of his heated hands on her cool skin made her gasp in shocked pleasure. Closing her eyes, she leaned into his hands, rubbing her nipples against his calloused palms. His chest lifted on a deep, shuddering breath.

She could feel the sexual tension emanating from him in waves. Like no other man she'd known, he made her acutely aware of his sexuality, and equally aware of her own body and its uses. Between her legs, an empty throb began to torment her, and she instinctively pressed her thighs together in an effort to ease the ache.

As slight as it was, he felt her movement. One of his hands left her breast and drifted downward, over her stomach and hips to her tightly clenched thighs. "That won't help," he murmured. "You'll have to open your legs, not close them." His fingers rubbed insistently at her and pleasure exploded along her nerves. A low moan escaped from her lips; then she swayed toward him. She felt her legs parting, allowing him access to her tender body. He explored her through her pants, creating such shock waves of physical pleasure that her knees finally buckled and she fell against him, her bare breasts flattening against the raspy, hair-covered expanse of his chest.

Quickly he set her down on the tarp and knelt over her, unzipping her pants and pulling them down her legs, his hands rough and urgent. He had to pause to remove her boots, but in only moments she was naked except for the shirt that still hung around her shoulders. The damp air made her shiver, and she reached for him. "I'm cold," she complained softly. "Get me warm."

She offered herself to him so openly and honestly that he wanted to thrust into her immediately, but he also wanted more. He'd had her nearly naked in his arms before. In the stream, that wisp of wet silk had offered no protection, but he hadn't had the time to explore her as he'd wanted. Her body was still a mystery to him; he wanted to touch every inch of her, taste her and enjoy the varying textures of her skin.

Jane's eyes were wide and shadowed as he knelt over her, holding himself away from her outstretched arms. "Not just yet, honey," he said in a low, gravelly voice. "Let me look at you first." Gently he caught her wrists and pressed them down to the tarp above her head, making her round, pretty breasts arch as if they begged for his mouth. Anchoring her wrists with one hand, he slid his free hand to those tempting, gently quivering mounds.

A small, gasping sound escaped from Jane's throat. Why was he holding her hands like that? It made her feel incredibly helpless and exposed, spread out for his delectation, yet she also felt unutterably safe. She could sense him savoring her with his eyes, watching intently as her nipples puckered in response to the rasp of his fingertips. He was so close to her that she could feel the heat of his body, smell the hot, musky maleness of his skin. She arched, trying to turn her body into that warmth and scent, but he forced her flat again.

Then his mouth was on her, sliding up the slope of her breast and closing hotly on her nipple. He sucked strongly at her, making waves of burning pleasure sweep from her breast to her loins. Jane whimpered, then bit her lip to hold back the sound. She hadn't known, had never realized, what a man's mouth on her breasts could do to her. She was on fire, her skin burning with an acute sensitivity that was both ecstatic and unbearable. She squirmed, clenching her legs together, trying to control the ache that threatened to master her.

His mouth went to her other breast, the rasp of his tongue on her nipple intensifying an already unbearable sensation. He swept his hand down to her thighs, his touch demanding that she open herself to him. Her muscles slowly relaxed for him, and he spread her legs gently. His fingers combed through the dark curls that had so enticed him before, making her body jerk in anticipation; then he covered her with his palm and thoroughly explored the soft, vulnerable flesh between her legs. Beneath his touch, Jane began to tremble wildly. "Grant," she moaned, her voice a shaking, helpless plea.

"Easy," he soothed, blowing his warm breath across her flesh. He wanted her so badly that he felt he would explode, but at the same time he couldn't get enough of touching her, of watching her arch higher and higher as he aroused her. He was drunk on her flesh, and still trying to satiate himself. He took her nipple in his mouth and began sucking again, wringing another cry from her.

Between her legs a finger suddenly penetrated, searching out the depths of her readiness, and shock waves battered her body. Something went wild inside her, and she could no longer hold her body still. It writhed and bucked against his hand, and his mouth was turning her breasts into pure flame. Then his thumb brushed insistently over her straining, aching flesh, and she exploded in his arms, blind with the colossal upheaval of her senses, crying out unconsciously. Nothing had ever prepared her for this, for the total, mind-shattering pleasure of her own body.

When it was over, she lay sprawled limply on the tarp. He undid his pants and shoved them off, his eyes glittering and wild. Jane's eyes slowly opened and she stared up at him dazedly. Grasping her legs, he lifted them high and spread them; then he braced himself over her and slowly sank his flesh into hers.

Jane's hands clenched on the tarp, and she bit her lips to keep from crying out as her body was inexorably stretched and filled. He paused, his big body shuddering, allowing her the time to accept him. Then suddenly it was she who couldn't bear any distance at all between them, and she surged upward, taking all of him, reaching up her arms to pull him close.

She never noticed the tears that ran in silvered streaks down her temples, but Grant gently wiped them away with his rough thumbs. Supporting his weight on his arms, sliding his entire body over her in a subtle caress, he began moving with slow, measured strokes. He was so close to the edge that he could feel the feathery sensation along his spine, but he wanted to make it last. He wanted to entice her again to that satisfying explosion, watch her go crazy in his arms.

"Are you all right?" he asked in a raw, husky tone, catching another tear with his tongue as it left the corner of her eye. If he were hurting her, he wouldn't prolong the loving, though he felt it would tear him apart to stop.

"Yes, I'm fine," she breathed, stroking her hands up the moving, surging muscles of his back. Fine... What a word for the wild magnificence of belonging to him. She'd never dreamed it could feel like this. It was as if she'd found a half of herself that she hadn't even known was missing. She'd never dreamed that *she* could feel like this. Her fingers clutched mindlessly at his back as his long, slow movements began to heat her body.

He felt her response and fiercely buried his mouth against the sensitive little hollow between her throat and collarbone, biting her just enough to let her feel his teeth, then licking where he'd bitten. She whimpered, that soft, uncontrollable little sound that drove him crazy, and he lost control. He began driving into her with increasing power, pulling her legs higher around him so he could have more of her, all of her, deeper and harder, hearing her little cries and going still crazier. There was no longer any sense of time, or of danger, only the feel of the woman beneath him and around him. While he was in her arms he could no longer feel the dark, icy edges of the shadows in his mind and soul.

In the aftermath, like that after a storm of unbelievable violence, they lay in exhausted silence, each reluctant to speak for fear it would shatter the fragile peace. His massive shoulders crushed her, making it difficult for her to breathe, but she would gladly have spent the rest of her life lying there. Her fingers slowly stroked the sweat-darkened gold of his hair, threading through the heavy, live silk. Their bodies were reluctant to leave each other, too. He hadn't withdrawn from her; instead, after easing his weight down onto her, he'd nestled closer and now seemed to be lightly dozing.

Perhaps it had happened too quickly between them, but she couldn't regret it. She was fiercely happy that she'd given herself to him. She'd never been in love before, never wanted to explore the physical mysteries of a man and a woman. She'd even convinced herself that she just wasn't a physical person, and had decided to enjoy her solitary life. Now her entire concept of herself had been changed, and it was as if she'd discovered a treasure within herself. After the kidnapping she had withdrawn from people, except for the trusted precious few who she had loved before: her parents, Chris, a couple of other friends. And even though she had married Chris, she had remained essentially alone, emotionally withdrawn. Perhaps that was why their marriage had failed, because she hadn't been willing to let him come close enough to be a real husband. Oh, they had been physically intimate, but she had been unresponsive, and eventually he had stopped bothering her. That was exactly what it had been for her: a bother. Chris had deserved better. He was her best friend, but only a friend, not a lover. He was much better off with the warm, responsive, adoring woman he'd married after their divorce.

She was too honest with herself to even pretend that any blame for their failed marriage belonged to Chris. It had been entirely her fault, and she knew it. She'd thought it was a lack in herself. Now she realized that she did have the warm, passionate instincts of a woman in love—because she was in love for the first time. She hadn't been able to respond to Chris, simply because she hadn't loved him as a woman should love the man she marries.

She was twenty-nine. She wasn't going to pretend to a shyness she didn't feel for the sake of appearance. She loved the man who lay in her arms, and she was going to enjoy to the fullest whatever time she had with him. She hoped to have a lifetime; but if fate weren't that kind, she would not let timidity cheat her out of one minute of the time they did have. Her life had been almost snuffed out twenty years ago, before it had really begun. She knew that life and time were too precious to waste.

Perhaps it didn't mean to Grant what it did to her, to be able to hold and love like this. She knew intuitively that his life had been much harder than hers, that he'd seen things that had changed him, that had stolen the laughter from his eyes. His experiences had hardened him, had left him extraordinarily cautious. But even if he were only taking the shallowest form of comfort from her, that of sexual release, she loved him enough to give him whatever he needed from her, without question. Jane loved as she did everything else, completely and courageously.

He stirred, lifting his weight onto his forearms and staring down at her. His golden eyes were shadowed, but there was something in them that made her heart beat faster, for he was looking at her the way a man looks at the woman who belongs to him. "I've got to be too heavy for you."

"Yes, but I don't care." Jane tightened her arms about his neck and tried to pull him back down, but his strength was so much greater than hers that she couldn't budge him.

He gave her a swift, hard kiss. "It's stopped raining. We have to go."

"Why can't we stay the night here? Aren't we safe?"

He didn't answer, just gently disengaged their bodies and sat up, reaching for his clothes, and that was answer enough. She sighed, but sat up to reach for her own clothes. The sigh became a wince as she became aware of the various aches she'd acquired by making love on the ground.

She could have sworn that he wasn't looking at her, but his awareness of his surroundings was awesome. His head jerked around, and a slight frown pulled his dark brows together. "Did I hurt you?" he asked abruptly.

"No, I'm all right." He didn't look convinced by her reassurance. When they descended the steep slope to the floor of the gorge, he kept himself positioned directly in front of her. He carried her down the last twenty feet, hoisting her over his shoulder despite her startled, then indignant, protests.

It was a waste of time for her to protest, though; he simply ignored her. When he put her down silently and started walking, she had no choice but to follow.

Twice that afternoon they heard a helicopter, and both times he pulled her into the thickest cover, waiting until the sound had completely faded away before emerging. The grim line of his mouth told her that he didn't consider it just a coincidence. They were being hunted, and only the dense cover of the forest kept them from being caught. Jane's nerves twisted at the thought of leaving that cover; she wasn't afraid for just herself now, but for Grant, too. He put himself in jeopardy just by being with her. Turego wanted her alive, but Grant was of no use to him at all.

If it came to a choice between Grant's life and giving Turego what he wanted, Jane knew that she would give in. She'd have to take her chances with Turego, though it would be impossible now to catch him off guard the way she had the first time. He knew now that she wasn't a rich man's flirtatious, charming plaything. She'd made a fool of him, and he wouldn't forget.

Grant stepped over a large fallen tree and turned back to catch her around the waist and lift her over it with that effortless strength of his. Pausing, he pushed her tangled hair back from her face, his touch surprisingly gentle. She knew how lethal those hands could be. "You're too quiet," he muttered. "It makes me think you're up to something, and that makes me nervous."

"I was just thinking," she defended herself.

"That's what I was afraid of."

"If Turego catches us..."

"He won't," Grant said flatly. Staring down at her, he saw more now than just an appealing, sloe-eyed woman. He knew her now, knew her courage and strength, her secret fears and her sunny nature. He also knew her temper, which could flare or fade in an instant. Sabin's advice had been to kill her quickly rather than let Turego get his hands on her; Grant had seen enough death to accept that as a realistic option at the time. But that was before he had known her, tasted her and felt the silky texture of her skin, watched her go wild beneath him. Things had changed now. He had changed—in ways that he neither welcomed nor trusted, but had to acknowledge. Jane had become important to him. He couldn't allow that, but for the time being he had to accept it. Until she was safe, she could be his, but no longer. There wasn't any room in his life for permanency, for roots, because he still wasn't certain that he'd ever live in the sunshine again. Like Sabin, he'd been in the shadows too long. There were still dark spots on his soul that were revealed in the lack of emotion in his eyes. There was still the terrible, calm acceptance of things that were too terrible to be accepted.

If things had gone as originally planned, they would have gotten on that helicopter and she would be safely home by now. He would never have really known her; he would have delivered her to her father and walked away. But instead, they had been forced to spend days with only each other for company. They had slept side by side, eaten together, shared moments of danger and of humor. Perhaps the laughter was the more intimate, to him; he'd known danger many times with many people, but humor was rare in his life. She had made him laugh, and in doing so had captured a part of him.

Damn her for being the woman she was, for being lively and good-natured and desirable, when he'd expected a spoiled, sulky bitch. Damn her for making men want her, for making *him* want her. For the first time in his life he felt a savage jealousy swelling in his heart. He knew that he would have to leave her, but until then he wanted her to be his and only his. Remembering the feel of her body under his, he knew that he would have to have her again. His golden eyes narrowed at the feeling of intense possessiveness that gripped him. An expression of controlled violence crossed his face, an expression that the people who knew him had learned to avoid provoking. Grant Sullivan was dangerous enough in the normal way of things; angered, he was deadly. She was his now, and her life was being threatened. He'd lost too much already: his youth, his laughter, his trust in others, even part of his own humanity. He couldn't afford to lose anything else. He was a desperate man trying to recapture his soul. He needed to find again even a small part of the boy from Georgia who had walked barefoot in the warm dirt of plowed fields, who had learned survival in the mysterious depths of the great swamp. What Vietnam had begun, the years of working in intelligence and operations had almost completed, coming close to destroying him as a man.

Jane and her screwball brand of gallantry were the source of the only warmth he'd felt in years.

He reached out and caught her by the nape of her neck, his strong fingers halting her. Surprised, she turned an inquiring glance at him, and the small smile that had begun forming on her lips faded at the fierce expression he couldn't hide.

"Grant? Is something wrong?"

Without thinking, he used the grip he had on her neck to pull her to him, and kissed her full lips, still faintly swollen from the lovemaking they'd shared in the cave. He took his time about it, kissing her with slow, deep movements of his tongue. With a small sound of pleasure she wound her arms around his neck and lifted herself on tiptoe to press more fully against him. He felt the soft juncture of her thighs and ground himself against her, his body jolting with desire at the way she automatically adjusted herself to his hardness.

She was his, as she'd never belonged to any other man.

Her safety hinged on how swiftly he could get her out of the country, for he sensed Turego closing in on them. That man would never give up, not while the microfilm was still missing. There was no way in hell, Grant vowed, that he would allow Turego ever to touch Jane again. Lifting his mouth from hers, he muttered in a harsh tone, "You're mine now. I'll take care of you."

Jane rested her head against his chest. "I know," she whispered.

CHAPTER EIGHT

THAT NIGHT CHANGED forever the way Jane thought of the darkness. The fear of being alone in the dark would probably always remain with her, but when Grant reached out for her, it stopped being an enemy to be held at bay. It became instead a warm blanket of safety that wrapped around them, isolating them from the world. She felt his hands on her and forgot about the night.

He kissed her until she was clinging to him, begging him wordlessly for release from the need he'd created in her. Then he gently stripped her and himself, then rolled to his back, lifting her astride him. "I hurt you this morning," he said, his voice low and rough. "You control it this time; take only as much as you're comfortable with."

Comfort didn't matter; making love with him was a primitive glory, and she couldn't place any limits on it. She lost control, moving wildly on him, and her uninhibited delight snapped the thin thread of control he was trying to maintain. He made a rough sound deep in his throat and clasped her to him, rolling once again until she was beneath him. The wildly soaring pleasure they gave each other wiped her mind clear of everything but him and the love that swelled inside of her. There was no darkness. With his passion, with the driving need of his body, he took her out of the darkness. When she fell asleep in his arms, it was without once having thought of the impenetrable darkness that surrounded them.

The next morning, as always, she awoke slowly, moving and murmuring to herself, snuggling against the wonderfully warm, hard body beneath her, knowing even in her sleep that it was Grant's. His hands moved down her back to cup and knead her buttocks, awakening her fully. Then he shifted gently onto his side, holding her in his arms and depositing her on her back. Her eyes fluttered open, but it was still dark, so she closed them again and turned to press her face against his neck.

"It's almost dawn, honey," he said against her hair, but he couldn't force himself to stop touching her, to sit up and put on his clothing. His hands slipped over her bare, silky skin, discovering anew all the places he'd touched and kissed during the night. Her response still overwhelmed him. She was so open and generous, wanting him and offering herself with a simplicity that took his breath away.

She groaned, and he eased her into a sitting position, then reached out to unzip the flap of the tent and let in a faint glimmer of light. "Are you awake?"

"No," she grumbled, leaning against him and yawning.

"We have to go."

"I know." Muttering something under her breath, she found what she presumed to be her shirt and began trying to untangle it. There was too much cloth, so she stopped in frustration and handed it to him. "I think this is yours. It's too big to be mine."

He took the shirt, and Jane scrambled around until she found her own under the blanket they'd been lying on. "Can't you steal a truck or something?" she asked, not wanting even to think about another day of walking.

He didn't laugh, but she could almost feel the way the corners of his lips twitched. "That's against the law, you know."

"Stop laughing at me! You've had a lot of specialized training, haven't you? Don't you know how to hot-wire an ignition?"

He sighed. "I guess I can hot-wire anything we'd be likely to find, but stealing a vehicle would be like advertising our position to Turego."

"How far can we be from Limon? Surely we could get there before Turego would be able to search every village between here and there?"

"It'd be too risky, honey. Our safest bet is still to cut across to the east coast swamps, then work our way down the coast. We can't be tracked in the swamp." He paused. "I'll have to go into the village for food but you're going to stay hidden in the trees."

Jane drew back. "Like hell."

"Damn it, don't you realize that it's too dangerous for you to show your face?"

"What about *your* face? At least I have dark hair and eyes like everyone else. Don't forget, that soldier saw you, and your pilot friend no doubt told them all about you, so they know we're together. That long blond mane of yours is pretty unusual around here."

He ran his hand through his shaggy hair, faintly surprised at how long it was. "It can't be helped."

She folded her arms stubbornly. "You're not going anywhere without me."

Silence lay between them for a moment. She was beginning to think she'd won a surprisingly easy victory when he spoke, and the even, almost mild tone of his voice made chills go up her spine, because it was the most implacable voice she'd ever heard. "You'll do what I say, or I'll tie and gag you and leave you here in the tent."

Now it was her turn to fall silent. The intimacy that had been forged between them had made her forget that he was a warrior first, and her lover second. Despite the gentle passion with which he made love to her, he was still the same man who had knocked her out and thrown her over his shoulder, carrying her away into the jungle. She hadn't held a grudge against him for that, after the reception she'd given him, but this was something else entirely. She felt as if he were forcibly reminding her of the original basis of their relationship, making her acknowledge that their physical intimacy had not made her an equal in his eyes. It was as if he'd used her body, since she had so willingly offered it, but saw no reason to let that give her any influence over him.

Jane turned away from him, fumbling with her shirt and finally getting it straight. She wouldn't let him see any hint of hurt in her eyes; she'd known that the love she felt was completely one-sided.

His hand shot out and pulled the shirt away from her. Startled, she looked at him. "I have to get dressed. You said we need to—"

"I know what I said," he growled, easing her down onto the blanket. The lure of her soft body, the knowledge that he'd hurt her and her characteristic chin-up attempt to keep him from seeing it, all made it impossible for him to remember the importance of moving on. The core of ice deep inside his chest kept him from whispering to her how much she meant to him. The remoteness bred into him by years of living on the edge of death hadn't yet been overcome; perhaps it never would be. It was still vital to him to keep some small significant part of himself sealed away, aloof and cold. Still, he couldn't let her draw away from him with that carefully blank expression on her face. She was his, and it was time she came to terms with the fact.

Putting his hands on her thighs, he spread them apart and mounted her. Jane caught her breath, her hands going up to grab at his back. He slowly pushed into her, filling her with a powerful movement that had her body arching on the blanket.

He went deep inside her, holding her tightly to him. Her inner tightness made him almost groan aloud as wild shivers of pleasure ran up his spine. Shoving his hand into her hair, he turned her head until her mouth was under his, then kissed her with a violence that only hinted at the inferno inside him. She responded to him immediately. Her mouth molded to his and her body rose to meet his thrusts in increasingly ecstatic undulations. He wanted to immerse himself in her, go deeper and deeper until they were bonded together, their flesh fused. He held her beneath him, their bodies locked together in total intimacy. He reveled in the waves of intensifying pleasure that made them clutch at each other, straining together in an effort to reach the peak of their passion. When he was inside her, he no longer felt the need to isolate himself. She was taking a part of him that he hadn't meant to offer, but he couldn't stop it. It was as if he'd gotten on a roller coaster and there was no way to get off until it reached the end of the line. He'd just have to go along for the ride, and he meant to wring every moment of pleasure he could from the short time that he had her all to himself.

Jane clung to his shoulders, driven out of her senses by the pounding of his body. He seemed to have lost all control; he was wild, almost violent, his flesh so heated that his skin burned her palms. She was caught up in the depth of his passion, writhing against him and begging for more. Then, abruptly, her pleasure crested, and he ground his mouth against hers to catch her mindless cries. Her hot flare of ecstasy caught him in its explosion, and he began shuddering as the final shock waves jolted through his body. Now it was she who held him, and when it was over he collapsed on her, his eyes closed and his chest heaving, his body glistening with sweat.

Her fingers gently touched the shaggy, dark gold threads of his hair, pushing them away from his forehead. She didn't know what had triggered his sudden, violent possession, but it didn't matter. What mattered was that, despite everything, he needed her in a basic way that he didn't welcome, but couldn't deny. That wasn't what she wanted, but it was a start. Slowly she trailed her hand down his back, feeling the powerful muscles that lay under his supple bronzed skin. The muscles twitched then relaxed under her touch, and he grew heavier as the tension left him.

"Now we *really* have to go," he murmured against her breast.

"Ummm." She didn't want to stir; her limbs were heavy, totally relaxed. She could happily have lain there for the rest of the day, dozing with him and waking to make love again. She knew that the peace wouldn't last; in a moment he stirred and eased their bodies apart.

They dressed in silence, except for the rustling of their clothing, until she began lacing her boots on her feet. He reached out and tilted her chin then, his thumb rubbing over her bottom lip. "Promise me," he demanded, making her look at him. "Tell me that you're going to do what I say, without an argument. Don't make me tie you up."

Was he asking for obedience, or trust? Jane hesitated, then went with her instincts. "All right," she whispered. "I promise."

His pupils dilated, and his thumb probed at the corner of her lips. "I'll take care of you," he said, and it was more than a promise.

They took down the tent; then Jane got out the meager supply of remaining food. She emptied the last of the Perrier into his canteen, disposed of the bottles, and broke in two the granola bar that she'd been saving. That and a small can of grapefruit was their breakfast, and the last of their food.

The morning was almost gone, and the heat and humidity had risen to almost unbearable levels, when Grant stopped and looked around. He wiped his forehead on his sleeve. "We're almost even with the village. Stay here, and I'll be back in an hour or so."

"How long is 'or so'?" she asked politely, but the sound of her teeth snapping together made him grin.

"Until I get back." He took the pistol out of its holster and extended it to her. "I take it you know how to use this, too?"

Jane took the weapon from his hand, a grim expression on her mouth. "Yes. After I was kidnapped, Dad insisted that I learn how to protect myself. That included a course in firearms, as well as self-defense classes." Her slim hand handled the gun with respect, and reluctant expertise. "I've never seen one quite like this. What is it?"

"A Bren 10 millimeter," he grunted.

Her eyebrows lifted. "Isn't it still considered experimental?"

He shrugged. "By some people. I've used it for a while; it does what I want." He watched her for a moment, then a frown drew his brows together. "Could you use it, if you had to?"

"I don't know." A smile wobbled on her mouth. "Let's hope it doesn't come to that."

He touched her hair, hoping fervently that she never had to find the answer to his question. He didn't want anything ever to dim the gaiety of her smile. Bending, he kissed her roughly, thoroughly, then without a word blended into the forest in that silent, unnerving way of his. Jane stared at the gun in her hand for a long moment, then walked over to a fallen tree and carefully inspected it for animal life before sitting down.

She couldn't relax. Her nerves were jumpy, and though she didn't jerk around at every raucous bird call or chattering monkey, or even the alarming rustles in the underbrush, her senses were acutely, painfully attuned to the noises. She had become used to having Grant close by, his mere presence making her feel protected. Without him, she felt vulnerable and more alone than she had ever felt before.

Fear ate at her, but it was fear for Grant, not herself. She had walked into this with her eyes open, accepting the danger as the price to be paid, but Grant was involved solely because of her. If anything happened to him, she knew she wouldn't be able to bear it, and she was afraid. How could he expect to walk calmly into a small village and not be noticed? Everything about him drew attention, from his stature to his shaggy blond hair and those wild, golden eyes. She *knew* how single-mindedly Turego would search for her, and since Grant had been seen with her, his life was on the line now just as much as hers.

By now Turego must know that she had the microfilm. He'd be both furious and desperate; furious because she'd played him for a fool, and desperate because she could destroy his government career. Jane twisted her fingers together, her dark eyes intent. She thought of destroying the microfilm, to ensure that it would never fall into the hands of Turego or any hostile group or government—but she didn't know what was on it, only that it was supremely important. She didn't want to destroy information that her own country might need. Not only that, but she might need it as a negotiating tool. George had taught her well, steeped her in his cautious, quicksilver tactics, the tactics that had made him so shadowy that few people had known of his existence. If she had her back to the wall, she would use every advantage she had, do whatever she had to—but she hoped it wouldn't come to that kind of desperation. The best scenario would be that Grant would be able to smuggle her out of the country. Once she was safe in the States, she'd make contact and turn the microfilm over to the people who should have it. Then she could concentrate on chasing Grant until he realized that he couldn't live without her. The worst scenario she could imagine would be for something to happen to Grant. Everything in her shied away even from the thought.

He'd been hurt too much already. He was a rough, hardened warrior, but he bore scars, invisible ones inside as well as the ones that scored his body. He'd retired, trying to pull himself away, but the wasteland mirrored in his eyes told her that he still lived partially in the shadows, where sunlight and warmth couldn't penetrate.

A fierce protectiveness welled up inside her. She was strong; she'd already lived through so much, overcome a childhood horror that could have crippled her emotionally. She hadn't allowed that to clip her wings, had learned instead to soar even higher, reveling in her freedom. But she wasn't strong enough to survive a world without Grant. She had to know that he was alive and well, or there would be no more sunshine for her. If anyone dared harm him…

Perspiration curled the hair at her temples and trickled between her breasts. Sighing, she wondered how long she had been waiting. She wiped her face and twisted her hair into a knot on top of her head to relieve herself of its hot weight on the back of her neck. It was so hot! The air was steamy, lying on her skin like a wet, warm blanket, making it difficult to breathe. It had to rain soon; it was nearing the time of day when the storms usually came.

She watched a line of ants for a time, then tried to amuse herself by counting the different types of birds that flitted

and chirped in the leafy terraces above her head. The jungle
teemed with life, and she'd come to learn that, with caution,
it was safe to walk through it—not that she wanted to try
it without Grant. The knowledge and the experience were
his. But she was no longer certain that death awaited her
behind every bush. The animal life that flourished in the
green depths was generally shy, and skittered away from
the approach of man. It was true that the most dangerous
animal in the jungle was man himself.

Well over an hour had passed, and a sense of unease was
prickling her spine. She sat very still, her green and black
clothing mingling well with the surrounding foliage, her
senses alert.

She saw nothing, heard nothing out of the ordinary, but
the prickling sensation along her spine increased. Jane sat
still for a moment longer, then gave in to the screaming
of her instincts. Danger was near, very near. Slowly she
moved, taking care not to rustle even a leaf, and crawled
behind the shelter of the fallen tree's roots. They were
draped in vines and bushes that had sprung to life already,
feeding off the death of the great plant. The heaviness of
the pistol she held reminded her that Grant had had a reason
for leaving it with her.

A flash of movement caught her attention, but she turned
only her eyes to study it. It was several long seconds before
she saw it again, a bit of tanned skin and a green shape that
was not plant or animal, but a cap. The man was moving
slowly, cautiously, making little noise. He carried a rifle,
and he was headed in the general direction of the village.

Jane's heart thudded in her breast. Grant could well
meet him face to face, but Grant might be surprised, while
this man, this guerrilla, was expecting to find him. Jane
didn't doubt that normally Grant would be the victor, but

if he were overtaken from behind he could be shot before he had a chance to act.

The distinctive beating of helicopter blades assaulted the air, still distant, but signaling the intensified search. Jane waited while the noise of the helicopter faded, hoping that its presence had alerted Grant. Surely it had; he was far too wary not to be on guard. For that, if nothing else, she was grateful for the presence of the helicopters.

She had to find Grant before he came face to face with one of the guerrillas and before they found her. This lone man wouldn't be the only one searching for her.

She had learned a lot from Grant these past few days, absorbing the silent manner in which he walked, his instinctive use of the best shelter available. She slid into the jungle, moving slowly, keeping low, and always staying behind and to the side of the silent stalker. Terror fluttered in her chest, almost choking her, but she reminded herself that she had no choice.

A thorny vine caught her hair, jerking it painfully, and tears sprang to her eyes as she bit her lip to stifle a reflexive cry of pain. Trembling, she freed her hair from the vine. Oh, God, where was Grant? Had he been caught already?

Her knees trembled so badly that she could no longer walk at a crouch. She sank to her hands and knees and began crawling, as Grant had taught her, keeping the thickest foliage between herself and the man, awkwardly clutching the pistol in her hand as she moved.

Thunder rumbled in the distance, signaling the approach of the daily rains. She both dreaded and prayed for the rain. It would drown out all sound and reduce visibility to a few feet, increasing her chances for escape—but it would also make it almost impossible for Grant to find her.

A faint crackle in the brush behind her alerted her, bu

she whirled a split second too late. Before she could bring the pistol around, the man was upon her, knocking the gun from her grip and twisting her arm up behind her, then pushing her face into the ground. She gasped, her breath almost cut off by the pressure of his knee on her back. The moist, decaying vegetation that littered the forest floor was ground into her mouth. Twisting her head to one side, Jane spat out the dirt. She tried to wrench her arm free; he cursed and twisted her arm higher behind her back, wringing an involuntary cry of pain from her.

Someone shouted in the distance, and the man answered, but Jane's ears were roaring and she couldn't understand what they said. Then he roughly searched her, slapping his free hand over her body and making her face turn red with fury. When he was satisfied that she carried no other weapons, he released her arm and flipped her onto her back.

She started to surge to her feet, but he swung his rifle around so close that the long, glinting barrel was only a few inches from her face. She glanced at it, then lifted her eyes to glare at her captor. Perhaps she could catch him off guard. "Who are you?" she demanded in a good imitation of a furious, insulted woman, and swatted the barrel away as if it were an insect. His flat, dark eyes briefly registered surprise, then wariness. Jane scrambled to her feet and thrust her face up close to his, letting him see her narrowed, angry eyes. Using all the Spanish she knew, she proceeded to tell him what she thought of him. For good measure she added all the ethnic invective she'd learned in college, silently wondering at the meaning of everything she was calling the soldier, who looked more stunned by the moment.

She poked him repeatedly in the chest with her finger, advancing toward him, and he actually fell back a few paces. Then the other soldier, the one she'd spotted before, joined them, and the man pulled himself together.

"Be quiet!" he shouted.

"I won't be quiet!" Jane shouted in return, but the other soldier grabbed her arms and tied her wrists. Incensed, Jane kicked out behind her, catching him on the shin with her boot. He gave a startled cry of pain, then whirled her around and drew his fist back, but at the last moment stayed his blow. Turego probably had given orders that she wasn't to be hurt, at least until he'd gotten the information he wanted from her.

Shaking her tangled hair away from her eyes, Jane glared at her captors. "What do you want? Who are you?"

They ignored her, and pushed her roughly ahead of them. With her arms tied behind her, her balance was off, and she stumbled over a tangled vine. She couldn't catch herself, and pitched forward with a small cry. Instinctively one of the soldiers grabbed for her. Trying to make it look accidental, she flung out one of her legs and tangled it through his, sending him crashing into a bush. She landed with a jolt on a knotted root, which momentarily stunned her and made her ears ring.

He came out of nowhere. One moment he wasn't there; the next he was in the midst of them. Three quick blows with the side of his hand to the first soldier's face and neck had the man crumpling like a broken doll. The soldier who Jane had tripped yelled and tried to swing his rifle around, but Grant lashed out with his boot, catching the man on the chin. There was a sickening thud; the man's head jerked back, and he went limp.

Grant wasn't even breathing hard, but his face was set and coldly furious as he hauled Jane to her feet and roughly turned her around. His knife sliced easily through the bonds around her wrists. "Why didn't you stay where I left you?" he grated. "If I hadn't heard you yelling—"

She didn't want to think about that. "I did stay," she protested. "Until those two almost walked over me. I was trying to hide, and to find you before you ran straight into them!"

He gave her an impatient glance. "I would've handled them." He grabbed her wrist and began dragging her after him. Jane started to defend herself, then sighed. Since he so obviously *had* handled them, what could she say? She concentrated instead on keeping her feet under her and dodging the limbs and thorny vines that swung at her.

"Where are we going?"

"Be quiet."

There was a loud crack, and Grant knocked her to the ground, covering her with his body. Winded, at first Jane thought that the thunder of the approaching storm had startled him; then her heart convulsed in her chest as she realized what the noise had been. Someone was shooting at them! The two soldiers hadn't been the only ones nearby. Her eyes widened to dark pools; they were shooting at Grant, not at her! They would have orders to take her alive. Panic tightened her throat, and she clutched at him.

"Grant! Are you all right?"

"Yeah," he grunted, slipping his right arm around her and crawling with her behind the shelter of a large mahogany tree, dragging her like a predator carrying off its prey. "What happened to the Bren?"

"He knocked it out of my hand…over there." She waved her hand to indicate the general area where she'd lost the gun. Grant glanced around, measuring the shelter available to him and swearing as he decided it was too much of a risk.

"I'm sorry," Jane said, her dark eyes full of guilt.

"Forget it." He unslung the rifle from his shoulder, his motions sure and swift as he handled the weapon. Jane hugged the ground, watching as he darted a quick look around the huge tree trunk. There was a glitter in his amber eyes that made her feel a little in awe of him; at this moment he was the quintessential warrior, superbly trained and toned, coolly assessing the situation and determining what steps to take.

Another shot zinged through the trees, sending bark flying only inches from Grant's face. He jerked back, then swiped at a thin line of blood that trickled down from his cheekbone, where a splinter had caught him.

"Stay low," he ordered, his tone flat and hard. "Crawl on your belly through those bushes right behind us, and keep going no matter what. We've got to get out of here."

She'd gone white at the sight of the blood ribboning down his face, but she didn't say anything. Controlling the shaking of her legs and arms, she got down on her stomach and obeyed, snaking her way into the emergent shrubs. She could feel him right behind her, directing her with his hand on her leg. He was deliberately keeping himself between her and the direction from which the shots had come, and the realization made her heart squeeze painfully.

Thunder rumbled, so close now that the earth shuddered from the shock waves. Grant glanced up. "Come on, rain," he muttered. "Come on."

It began a few minutes later, filtering through the leaves with a dripping sound, then rapidly intensifying to the thunderous deluge that she'd come to expect. They were soaked to the skin immediately, as if they'd been tossed into a waterfall. Grant shoved her ahead of him, heedless now of any noise they made, because the roar of the rain obliterated everything else. They covered about a hundred yards on their hands and knees, then he pulled her upright and brought his mouth close to her ear. "Run!" he yelled, barely making himself heard over the din of the pummeling rain.

Jane didn't know how she could run but she did. Her legs were trembling, she was dizzy and disoriented, but somehow her feet moved as Grant pulled her through the forest at breakneck speed. Her vision was blurred; she could see only a confused jumble of green, and the rain, always the rain. She had no idea where they were going, but trusted Grant's instincts to guide them.

Suddenly they broke free of the jungle's edge, where man had cut back the foliage in an attempt to bring civilization to a small part of the tropical rain forest. Staggering across fields turned into a quagmire by the rain, Jane was held upright only by Grant's unbreakable grip on her wrist. She fell to her knees once and he dragged her for a few feet before he noticed. Without a word he scooped her up and tossed her over his shoulder, carrying her as effortlessly as ever, showing no trace of the exhaustion she felt.

She closed her eyes and hung on, already dizzy and now becoming nauseated as her stomach was jolted by his hard shoulder. Their surroundings had become a nightmare of endless gray water slapping at them, wrapping them in a curtain that obliterated sight and sound. Terror lay in her stomach in a cold, soggy lump, triggered by the sight of the blood on Grant's face. She couldn't bear it if anything happened to him, she simply couldn't....

He lifted her from his shoulder, propping her against something hard and cold. Jane's fingers spread against the support, and dimly she recognized the texture of metal. Then he wrenched open the door of the ancient pickup truck and picked her up to thrust her into the shelter of the cab. With a lithe twist of his body he slid under the wheel, then slammed the door.

"Jane," he bit out, grabbing her shoulder in a tight grip and shaking her. "Are you all right? Are you hit?"

She was sobbing, but her eyes were dry. She stretched out a trembling hand to touch the red streak that ran down his rain-wet face. "You're hurt," she whispered; he couldn't hear her over the thunder of the rain pounding on the metal top of the old truck, but he read her lips and gathered her in his arms, pressing hard, swift kisses to her dripping hair.

"It's just a scratch, honey," he reassured her. "What about you? Are you okay?"

She managed a nod, clinging to him, feeling the incredible warmth of his body despite the soggy condition of his clothes. He held her for a moment, then pulled her arms from around his neck and put her on the other side of the truck. "Sit tight while I get this thing going. We've got to get out of here before the rain stops and everyone comes out."

He bent down and reached under the dash of the truck, pulling some wires loose.

"What are you doing?" Jane asked numbly.

"Hot-wiring this old crate," he replied, and gave her a quick grin. "Pay close attention, since you've been so insistent that I do this. You may want to steal a truck someday."

"You can't see to drive in this," she said, still in that helpless, numb tone of voice, so unlike her usual cheerful matter-of-fact manner. A frown drew his brows together, but he couldn't stop to cradle her in his arms and reassure her that everything was going to be all right. He wasn't too sure of that himself; all hell had broken loose, reminding him how much he disliked being shot at—and now Jane was a target as well. He hated this whole set-up so much that a certain deadly look had come into his eyes, the look

hat had become legend in the jungles and rice paddies of
outheast Asia.

"I can see well enough to get us out of here."

He put two wires together, and the engine coughed and
urned over, but didn't start. Swearing under his breath, he
ried it again, and the second time the engine caught. He put
he old truck in gear and let up on the clutch. They lurched
nto motion with the old vehicle groaning and protesting.
The rain on the windshield was so heavy that the feeble
ipers were almost useless, but Grant seemed to know
where he was going.

Looking around, Jane saw a surprisingly large number
f buildings through the rain, and several streets seemed to
ranch away from the one they were on. The village was a
rosperous one, with most of the trappings of civilization,
nd it looked somehow incongruous existing so close to
he jungle.

"Where are we going?" she asked.

"South, honey. To Limon, or at least as far as this crate
ill carry us down the road."

CHAPTER NINE

LIMON. THE NAME SOUNDED like heaven, and as she clung to the tattered seat of the old truck, the city seemed just as far away. Her dark eyes were wide and vulnerable as she stared at the streaming windshield, trying to see the road. Grant gave her a quick look, all he could safely spare when driving took so much of his attention. Keeping his voice calm, he said, "Jane, scoot as far into the corner as you can. Get your head away from the back window. Do you understand?"

"Yes." She obeyed, shrinking into the corner. The old truck had a small window in back and smaller windows on each side, leaving deep pockets of protection in the corners. A broken spring dug into the back of her leg, making her shift her weight. The upholstery on this side of the seat was almost nonexistent, consisting mostly of miscellaneous pieces of cloth covering some of the springs. Grant was sitting on a grimy patch of burlap. Looking down, she saw a large hole in the floorboard beside the door.

"This thing has character," she commented, regaining a small portion of her composure.

"Yeah, all of it bad." The truck skewed sideways on a sea of mud, and Grant gave all his attention to steering the thing in a straight line again.

"How can you tell where we're going?"

"I can't. I'm guessing." A devilish grin twisted his lips, a sign of the adrenaline that was racing through his system.

It was a physical high, an acute sensitivity brought on by pitting his wits and his skills against the enemy. If it hadn't been for the danger to Jane, he might even have enjoyed this game of cat and mouse. He risked another quick glance at her, relaxing a little as he saw that she was calmer now, gathering herself together and mastering her fear. The fear was still there, but she was in control.

"You'd better be a good guesser," she gasped as the truck lurched sickeningly to the side. "If you drive us off a cliff, I swear I'll never forgive you!"

He grinned again and shifted his weight uncomfortably. He leaned forward over the wheel. "Can you get these packs off? They're in the way. And keep down!"

She slithered across the seat and unbuckled the backpacks, pulling them away from him so he could lean back. How could she have forgotten her pack? Stricken that she'd been so utterly reckless with it, she drew the buckles through the belt loops of her pants and fastened the straps.

He wasn't paying any attention to her now, but was frowning at the dash. He rapped at a gauge with his knuckle. "Damn it!"

Jane groaned. "Don't tell me. We're almost out of gas!"

"I don't know. The damned gauge doesn't work. We could have a full tank, or it could quit on us at any time."

She looked around. The rain wasn't as torrential as it had been, though it was still heavy. The forest pressed closely on both sides of the road, and the village was out of sight behind them. The road wasn't paved, and the truck kept bouncing over the uneven surface, forcing her to cling to the seat to stay in it—but it was a road and the truck was still running along it. Even if it quit that minute, they were still better off than they had been only a short while before. At least they weren't being shot at now. With any luck Turego would think they were still afoot and continue searching close by, at least for a while. Every moment was precious now, putting distance between them and their pursuers.

Half an hour later the rain stopped, and the temperature immediately began to climb. Jane rolled down the window on her side of the truck, searching for any coolness she could find. "Does this thing have a radio?" she asked.

He snorted. "What do you want to listen to, the top forty? No, it doesn't have a radio."

"There's no need to get snippy," she sniffed.

Grant wondered if he'd ever been accused of being "snippy" before. He'd been called a lot of things, but never that; Jane had a unique way of looking at things. If they *had* met up with a jaguar, she probably would have called it a "nice kitty"! The familiar urge rose in him, making him want to either throttle her or make love to her. His somber expression lightened as he considered which would give him the most pleasure.

The truck brushed against a bush that was encroaching on the narrow road. Jane ducked barely in time to avoid being slapped in the face by the branches that sprang through the open window, showering them with the raindrops that had been clinging to the leaves.

"Roll that window up," he ordered, concern making his voice sharp. Jane obeyed and sat back in the corner again. Already she could feel perspiration beading on her face, and she wiped her sleeve across her forehead. Her hand touched her hair, and she pushed the heavy mass away from her face, appalled at the tangled ringlets she found. What she wouldn't give for a bath! A real bath, with hot water and soap and shampoo, not a rinsing in a rocky stream. And clean clothes! She thought of the hairbrush in her pack, but she didn't have the energy to reach for it right now.

Well, there was no sense in wasting her time wishing for something she couldn't have. There were more important issues at hand. "Did you get any food?"

"In my pack."

She grabbed the pack and opened it, pulling out a towel-wrapped bundle of bread and cheese. That was all there was, but she wasn't in the mood to quibble about the limited menu. Food was food. Right now, even field rations would have been good.

Leaning over, she took his knife from his belt and swiftly sliced the bread and cheese. In less than a minute, she'd made two thick cheese sandwiches and returned the knife to its sheath. "Can you hold the sandwich and drive, or do you want me to feed you?"

"I can manage." It was awkward, wrestling with the steering wheel and holding the sandwich at the same time, but she would have to slide closer to him to feed him, and that would expose her head in the back window. The road behind them was still empty, but he wasn't going to take any chances with her welfare.

"I could lie down with my head in your lap and feed you," she suggested softly, and her dark eyes were sleepy and tender.

He jerked slightly, his entire body tensing. "Honey, if you put your head in my lap, I might drive this crate up a tree. You'd better stay where you are."

Was it only yesterday that he'd taken her so completely in that cave? He'd made her his, possessed her and changed her, until she found it difficult to remember what it had been like before she'd known him. The focus of her entire life had shifted, redirected itself onto him.

What she was feeling was plainly revealed in her eyes, in her expressive face. A quick glance at her had him swallowing to relieve an abruptly dry throat, and his hands clenched on the wheel. He wanted her, immediately; he wanted to stop the truck and pull her astride him, then bury himself in her inner heat. The taste and scent of her lingered in his mind, and his body still felt the silk of her skin beneath his. Perhaps he wouldn't be able to get enough of her to satisfy him in the short time they had remaining, but he was going to try, and the trying would probably drive him crazy with pleasure.

They wolfed down the sandwiches, then Jane passed him the canteen. The Perrier was flat, but it was still wet, and he gulped it thirstily. When he gave the canteen back to her, she found herself gulping, too, in an effort to replenish the moisture her body was losing in perspiration. It was so hot in the truck! Somehow, even trekking through the jungle hadn't seemed this hot, though there hadn't been even a hint of breeze beneath the canopy. The metal shell of the truck made her feel canned, like a boiled shrimp. She forced herself to stop drinking before she emptied the canteen, and capped it again.

Ten minutes later the truck began sputtering and coughing; then the engine stopped altogether, and Grant coasted to a stop, as far to one side of the narrow road as he could get. "It lasted almost two hours," he said, opening the door and getting out.

Jane scrambled across the truck and got out on his side, since he'd parked so close to the edge that her door was blocked by a tree. "How far do you think we got?"

"Thirty miles or so." He wound a lock of her hair around his forefinger and smiled down at her. "Feel up to a walk?"

"A nice afternoon stroll? Sure, why not?"

He lowered his head and took a hard kiss from her mouth. Before she could respond he'd drawn away and pushed her off the road and into the shelter of the forest again. He returned to the truck, and she looked back to see him obliterating their footprints; then he leaped easily up the low bank and came to her side. "There's another village down the road a few more miles; I hoped we'd make it so we could buy more gas, but—" He broke off and shrugged at the change of plans. "We'll follow the road and try to get to the village by nightfall, unless they get too close to us. If they do, we'll have to go back into the interior."

"We're not going to the swamp?"

"We can't," he explained gently. "There's too much open ground to cover, now that they know we're in the area."

A bleak expression came and went in her eyes so fast that he wasn't certain he'd seen it. "It's my fault. If I'd just hidden from them, instead of trying to find you…"

"It's done. Don't worry about it. We just have to adjust our plans, and the plan now is to get to Limon as fast as we can, any way we can."

"You're going to steal another truck?"

"I'll do whatever has to be done."

Yes, he would. That knowledge was what made her feel so safe with him; he was infinitely capable, in many different areas. Even wearily following him through the overgrown tangle of greenery made her happy, because she was with him. She didn't let herself think of the fact that they would soon part, that he'd casually kiss her goodbye and walk away, as if she were nothing more than another job finished. She'd deal with that when it happened; she wasn't going to borrow trouble. She had to devote her energies now to getting out of Costa Rica, or at least to some trustworthy authorities, where Grant wouldn't be in danger of being shot while trying to protect her. When she'd seen the blood on his face, some vital part inside of her had frozen knowing that she couldn't survive if anything happened to him. Even though she'd been able to see that he wasn't badly hurt, the realization of his vulnerability had frightened her. As strong as he was, as vital and dangerous, he was a man, and therefore mortal.

They heard only one vehicle on the road, and it was moving toward the village where they'd stolen the truck. The sun edged downward, and the dim light in the forest began to fade. Right before the darkness became total, they came to the edge of a field, and down the road about half a mile they could see the other village spread out. It was really more of a small town than a village; there were bright electric lights, and cars and trucks were parked on the streets. After days spent in the jungle, it looked like a booming metropolis, a cornerstone of civilization.

"We'll stay here until it's completely dark, then go into town," Grant decided, dropping to the ground and stretching out flat on his back. Jane stared at the twinkling lights of the town, torn between a vague uneasiness and an eagerness to take advantage of the comforts a town offered. She wanted a bath, and to sleep in a bed, but after so much time spent alone with Grant, the thought of once more being surrounded by other people made her wary. She couldn't relax the way Grant did, so she remained on her feet, her face tense and her hands clenched.

"You might as well rest, instead of twitching like a nervous cat."

"I am nervous. Are we going on to Limon tonight?"

"Depends on what we find when we get into town."

She glared down at him in sudden irritation. He was a master at avoiding straight answers. It was so dark that she couldn't make out his features; he was only a black form on the ground, but she was certain that he was aware of her anger, and that the corner of his mouth was turning up in that almost-smile of his. She was too tired to find much humor in it, though, so she walked away from him a few paces and sat down, leaning her head on her drawn-up knees and closing her eyes.

There wasn't even a whisper of sound to warn her, but suddenly he was behind her, his strong hands massaging the tight muscles of her shoulders and neck. "Would you like to sleep in a real bed tonight?" he murmured in her ear.

"And take a real bath. And eat real food. Yes, I'd like that," she said, unaware of how wistful her tone was.

"A town this size probably has a hotel of some sort, but we can't risk going there, not looking the way we do. I'll try to find someone who takes in boarders and won't ask many questions."

Taking her hand, he pulled her to her feet and draped his arm over her shoulder. "Let's go, then. A bed sounds good to me, too."

Walking across the field, ever closer to the beckoning lights, Jane became more conscious of how she looked, and she pushed her fingers through her tangled hair. She knew that her clothes were filthy, and that her face was probably dirty. "No one is going to let us in," she predicted.

"Money has a way of making people look past the dirt."

She glanced up at him in surprise. "You have money?"

"A good Boy Scout is always prepared."

In the distance, the peculiarly mournful wail of a train whistle floated into the air, reinforcing the fact that they'd left the isolation of the rain forest behind. Oddly, Jane felt almost nakedly vulnerable, and she moved closer to Grant. "This is stupid, but I'm scared," she whispered.

"It's just a mild form of culture shock. You'll feel better when you're in a tub of hot water."

They kept to the fringes of the town, in the shadows. It appeared to be a bustling little community. Some of the streets were paved, and the main thoroughfare was lined with prosperous-looking stores. People walked and laughed and chatted, and from somewhere came the unmistakable sound of a jukebox, another element of civilization that jarred her nerves. The universally known red and white sign of a soft drink swung over a sidewalk, making her feel as if she had emerged from a time warp. This was definitely culture shock.

Keeping her pushed behind him, Grant stopped and carried on a quiet conversation with a rheumy-eyed old man who seemed reluctant to be bothered. Finally Grant thanked him and walked away, still keeping a firm grip on Jane's arm. "His sister-in-law's first cousin's daughter takes in boarders," he told her, and Jane swallowed a gasp of laughter.

"Do you know where his sister-in-law's first cousin's daughter lives?"

"Sure. Down this street, turn left, then right, follow the alley until it dead ends in a courtyard."

"If you say so."

Of course he found the boarding house easily, and Jane leaned against the white adobe wall that surrounded the courtyard while he rang the bell and talked with the small, plump woman who answered the door. She seemed reluctant to admit such exceedingly grimy guests. Grant passed her a wad of bills and explained that he and his wife had been doing field research for an American pharmaceutical company, but their vehicle had broken down, forcing them to walk in from their camp. Whether it was the money or the tale of woe that swayed Señora Trejos, her face softened and she opened the grill, letting them in.

Seeing the tautness of Jane's face, Señora Trejos softened even more. "Poor lamb," she cooed, ignoring Jane's dirty state and putting her plump arm around the young woman's sagging shoulders. "You are exhausted, no? I have a nice cool bedroom with a soft bed for you and the *señor*, and I will bring you something good to eat. You will feel better then?"

Jane couldn't help smiling into the woman's kind dark eyes. "That sounds wonderful, all of it," she managed in her less-than-fluent Spanish. "But most of all, I need a bath. Would that be possible?"

"But of course!" Señora Trejos beamed with pride. "Santos and I, we have the water heated by the tank. He brings the fuel for the heating from San Jose."

Chatting away, she led them inside her comfortable house, with cool tiles on the floors and soothing white walls. "The upstairs rooms are taken," she said apologetically. "I have only the one room below the stairs, but it is nice and cool, and closer to the conveniences."

"Thank you, Señora Trejos," Grant said. "The downstairs room will more than make us happy."

It did. It was small, with bare floors and plain white walls, and there was no furniture except for the wood-framed double bed, a cane chair by the lone, gracefully arched window, and a small wooden washstand that held a pitcher and bowl. Jane gazed at the bed with undisguised longing. It looked so cool and comfortable, with fat fluffy pillows.

Grant thanked Señora Trejos again; then she went off to prepare them something to eat, and they were alone. Jane glanced at him and found that he was watching her steadily. Somehow, being alone with him in a bedroom felt different from being alone with him in a jungle. There, their seclusion had been accepted. Here there was the sensation of closing out the world, of coming together in greater intimacy.

"You take the first turn at the bath," he finally said. "Just don't go to sleep in the tub."

Jane didn't waste time protesting. She searched the lower floor, following her nose, until she found Señora Trejos happily puttering about the kitchen. "Pardon, *señora*," she said haltingly. She didn't know all the words needed to explain her shortage of a robe or anything to wear after taking a bath, but Señora Trejos caught on immediately. A few minutes later Jane had a plain white nightgown thrust into her hands and was shown to the *señora's* prized bathroom.

The bathroom had cracked tile and a deep, old-fashioned tub with curved claw feet, but when she turned on the water it gushed out in a hot flood. Sighing in satisfaction, Jane quickly unbuckled the backpack from her belt and set it out of the way, then stripped off her clothes and got into the tub, unwilling to wait until it was full. The heat seeped into her sore muscles and a moan of pleasure escaped her. She would have liked to soak in the tub for hours, but Grant was waiting for his own bath, so she didn't allow herself to lean against the high back and relax. Quickly she washed away the layers of grime, unable to believe how good it felt to be clean again. Then she washed her hair, sighing in relief as the strands came unmatted and once again slipped through her fingers like wet silk.

Hurrying, she wrapped her hair in a towel and got her safety razor out of the backpack. Sitting on the edge of the tub, she shaved her legs and under her arms, then smoothed moisturizer into her skin. A smile kept tugging at her mouth as she thought of spending the night in Grant's arms again. She was going to be clean and sweet-smelling, her skin silky. After all, it wasn't going to be easy to win a warrior's love, and she was going to use all the weapons at her disposal.

She brushed her teeth, then combed out her wet hair and pulled the white nightgown over her head, hoping that she wouldn't meet any of Señora Trejos's other boarders on the short trip back to her room. The *señora* had told her to leave her clothes on the bathroom floor, that she would see that they were washed, so Jane got the backpack and hurried down the hall to the room where Grant waited.

He had closed the shutters over the arched window and was leaning with one shoulder propped against the wall, declining to sit in the single chair. He looked up at her entrance, and the inky pupils at the center of his golden irises expanded until there was only a thin ring of amber circling the black. Jane paused, dropping the pack beside the bed, feeling abruptly shy, despite the tempestuous lovemaking she'd shared with this man. He looked at her as if he were about to pounce on her, and she found herself crossing her arms over her breasts, aware that her nakedness was fully apparent beneath the thin nightgown. She cleared her throat, her mouth suddenly dry. "The bathroom is all yours."

He straightened slowly, not taking his eyes from her. "Why don't you go on to bed?"

"I'd rather wait for you," she whispered.

"I'll wake you up when I come to bed." The intensity of his gaze promised her that she wasn't going to sleep alone that night.

"My hair...I have to dry my hair."

He nodded and left the room, and Jane sat down on the chair weakly, shaking inside from the way he'd looked at her. Bending over, she rubbed her hair briskly, then began to brush it dry. It was so thick and long that it was still damp when Grant came back into the room and stood silently, watching her as she sat bent over, her slender arms curving as she drew the brush through the dark mass. She sat up, tossing her head to fling her hair back over her shoulders, and for a moment they simply stared at each other.

They had made love before, but now sensual awareness was zinging between them like an electric current. Without even touching each other, they were both becoming aroused, their heartbeats quickening, their skin growing hot.

He had shaved, probably using the razor she'd left in the bathroom. It was the first time she'd seen him without several days' growth of beard, and the clean, hard lines of his scarred face made her breath catch. He was naked except for a towel knotted around his lean waist, and as she watched he pulled the towel free and dropped it to the floor. Reaching behind him, he locked the door. "Are you ready for bed?"

"My hair...isn't quite dry."

"Leave it," he said, coming toward her.

The brush dropped to the floor as he caught her hand and pulled her up. Instantly she was in his arms, lifted off her feet by his fierce embrace. Their mouths met hungrily, and her fingers tangled in his water-darkened hair, holding him to her. His mouth was fresh and hot, his tongue thrusting deep into her mouth in a kiss that made her whimper as currents of desire sizzled her nerves.

He was hard against her, his manhood pushing against her softness, his hands kneading her hips and rubbing her over him. Jane pulled her mouth free, gasping, and dropped her head to his broad shoulder. She couldn't contain the wild pleasure he was evoking, as if her body were out of control, already reaching for the peak that his arousal promised. She'd been quite content to live celibately for years, the passion in her unawakened until she met Grant. He was as wild and beautiful and free as the majestic jaguars that melted silently through the tangled green jungle. The wildness in him demanded a response, and she was helpless to restrain it. He didn't have to patiently build her passion; one kiss and she trembled against him, empty and aching and ready for him, her breasts swollen and painful, her body growing wet and soft.

"Let's get this thing off you," he whispered, pulling at the nightgown and easing it up. Reluctantly she released him, and he pulled the gown over her head, dropping it over the chair; then she was back in his arms, and he carried her to the bed.

Their naked bodies moved together, and there was no more waiting. He surged into her, and she cried out a little from the delicious shock of it. Catching the small cry with his mouth, he lifted her legs and placed them around his waist, then began to move more deeply into her.

It was like the night before. She gave no thought to anything but the man with shoulders so broad that they blocked out the light. The bed was soft beneath them, the sheets cool and smooth, and the rhythmic creak of the springs in time with his movements was accompanied by the singing of insects outside the window. Time meant nothing. There was only his mouth on hers, his hands on her body, the slow thrusts that went deep inside her and touched off a wildfire of sensation, until they strained together in frenzied pleasure and the sheets were no longer cool, but warm from their damp, heated flesh.

Then it was quiet again, and he lay heavily on her, drawing in deep breaths while her hands moved over his powerful back. Her lips trembled with the words of love that she wanted to give him, but she held them back. All her instincts told her that he wouldn't want to know, and she didn't want to do anything to spoil their time together.

Perhaps he had given her something anyway, if not his

love, something at least as infinitely precious. As her sensitive fingertips explored the deep valley of his spine, she wondered if he had given her his baby. A tremor of pleasure rippled down her body, and she held him closer, hoping that her body would be receptive to his seed.

He stirred, reaching out to turn off the lamp, and in the darkness he moved to lie beside her. She curled against his side, her head on his shoulder, and after a moment he gave a low chuckle.

"Why don't you just save time and get on top of me now?" he suggested, scooping her up and settling her on his chest.

Jane gave a sigh of deep satisfaction, stretching out on him and looping her arm around his neck. With her face pressed against his throat she was comfortable and safe, as if she'd found a sheltering harbor. "I love you," she said silently, moving her lips without sound against his throat.

THEY WOKE WITH THE bright early morning sun coming through the slats of the shutters. Leaving Jane stretching and grousing on the bed, Grant got up and opened the shutters, letting the rosy light pour into the room. When he turned, he saw the way the light glowed on her warm-toned skin, turning her nipples to apricot, catching the glossy lights in her dark hair. Her face was flushed, her eyes still heavy with sleep.

Suddenly his body throbbed, and he couldn't bear to be separated from her by even the width of the small room. He went back to the bed and pulled her under him, then watched the way her face changed as he slowly eased into her, watched the radiance that lit her. Something swelled in his chest, making it difficult for him to breathe, and as he lost himself in the soft depths of her body he had one last, glaringly clear thought: she'd gotten too close to him, and letting her go was going to be the hardest thing he'd ever done.

HE DRESSED, PULLING ON the freshly washed clothes that one of Señora Trejos's daughters had brought, along with a tray of fruit, bread and cheese. Jane flushed wildly when she realized that Señora Trejos must have brought a tray to them the night before, then discreetly left when she heard the sounds they had been making. A quick glance at Grant told her that he'd had the same thought, because the corner of his mouth was twitching in amusement.

The *señora* had also sent along a soft white off-the-shoulder blouse, and Jane donned it with pleasure, more than glad to discard her tattered black shirt. After selecting a piece of orange from the tray, she bit into the juicy fruit as she watched him pull his dark green undershirt over his head.

"You're going to be pretty noticeable in those camouflage fatigues," she said, poking a bit of the orange into his mouth.

"I know." He quickly kissed her orange-sticky lips. "Put the shirt in your pack and be ready to go when I get back."

"Get back? Where are you going?"

"I'm going to try to get some sort of transport. It won't be as easy this time."

"We could take the train," she pointed out.

"The rifle would be a mite conspicuous, honey."

"Why can't I go with you?"

"Because you're safer here."

"The last time you left me, I got into trouble," she felt obliged to remind him.

He didn't appreciate the reminder. He scowled down at her as he reached for a spear of melon. "If you'll just keep your little butt where I tell you to, you'll be fine."

"I'm fine when I'm with you."

"Damn it, stop arguing with me!"

"I'm not arguing. *I'm* pointing out some obvious facts! *You're* the one who's arguing!"

His eyes were yellow fire. He bent down until they were almost nose to nose, his control under severe stress. His teeth were clenched together as he said, evenly spacing the words out, "If you make it home without having the worst spanking of your life, it'll be a miracle."

"I've never had a spanking in my life," she protested.

"It shows!"

She flounced into the chair and pouted. Grant's hands clenched; then he reached for her and pulled her out of the chair, hauling her up to him for a deep, hard kiss. "Be good, for a change," he said, aware that he was almost pleading with her. "I'll be back in an hour—"

"Or so!" she finished in unison with him. "All right, I'll wait! But I don't like it!"

He left before he completely lost his temper with her, and Jane munched on more of the fruit, terribly grateful for something fresh to eat. Deciding that he'd meant only for her to stay in the house, not in the room, she first got everything ready for them to leave, as he'd instructed, then sought out the *señora* and had a pleasant chat with her. The woman was bustling around the kitchen preparing food for her boarders, while two of her daughters diligently cleaned the house and did a mountain of laundry. Jane had her arms deep in a bowl of dough when Grant returned.

He'd gone first to their room, and when he found her in the kitchen there was a flicker of intense relief in his eyes before he masked it. Jane sensed his presence and looked up, smiling. "Is everything arranged?"

"Yes. Are you ready?"

"Just as soon as I wash my hands."

She hugged the *señora* and thanked her, while Grant leaned in the doorway and watched her. Did she charm everyone so effortlessly? The *señora* was beaming at her, wishing her a safe journey and inviting her back. There would always be a room for the lovely young *señora* and her husband in the Trejos house!

They collected their packs, and Grant slung the rifle over his shoulder. They risked attracting attention because of it, but he didn't dare leave it behind. With any luck they would be on a plane out of Costa Rica by nightfall, but until they were actually on their way he couldn't let his guard down. The close call the day before had been proof of that. Turego wasn't giving up; he stood to lose too much.

Out in the alley, Jane glanced up at him. "What exactly did you arrange?"

"A farmer is going into Limon, and he's giving us a ride."

After the adventure of the last several days that seemed almost boringly tame, but Jane was happy to be bored. A nice, quiet ride, that was the ticket. How good it would be not to feel hunted!

As they neared the end of the alley, a man stepped suddenly in front of them. Grant reacted immediately, shoving Jane aside, but before he could swing the rifle around there was a pistol in his face, and several more men stepped into the alley, all of them armed, all of them with their weapons pointed at Grant. Jane stopped breathing, her eyes wide with horror. Then she recognized the man in the middle, and her heart stopped. Was Grant going to die now, because of her?

She couldn't bear it. She had to do something, anything.

"Manuel!" she cried, filling her voice with joy. She ran to him and flung her arms around him. "I'm so glad you found me!"

CHAPTER TEN

IT WAS A NIGHTMARE. Grant hadn't taken his narrowed gaze off her, and the hatred that glittered in his eyes made her stomach knot, but there was no way she could reassure him. She was acting for all she was worth, clinging to Turego and babbling her head off, telling him how frightened she'd been and how this madman had knocked her out and stolen her away from the plantation, all the while clinging to Turego's shirt as if she couldn't bear to release him. She had no clear idea of what she was going to do, only that somehow she had to stay unfettered so she could help Grant, and to do that she had to win Turego's trust and soothe his wounded vanity.

The entire situation was balanced on a knife edge; things could go in either direction. Wariness was in Turego's dark eyes, as well as a certain amount of cruel satisfaction in having cornered his prey. He wanted to make her suffer for having eluded him, she knew, yet for the moment she was safe from any real harm, because he still wanted the microfilm. It was Grant whose life was threatened, and it would take only a word from Turego for those men to kill him where he stood. Grant had to know it, yet there wasn't even a flicker of fear in his expression, only the cold, consuming hatred of his glare as he stared at Jane. Perhaps it was that, in the end, that eased Turego's suspicions somewhat. He would never relax his guard around her again, but Jane could only worry about one thing at a time. Right now, she had to protect Grant in any way she could.

Turego's arm stole around her waist, pulling her tightly against him. He bent his head and kissed her, a deeply intimate kiss that Jane had to steel herself not to resist in any way, even though she shuddered at having to endure the touch and taste of him. She knew what he was doing; he was illustrating his power, his control, and using her as a weapon against Grant. When he lifted his head, a cruel little smile was on his handsome mouth.

"I have you now, *chiquita*," he reassured her in a smooth tone. "You are quite safe. This...madman, as you called him, will not bother you again, I promise. I am impressed," he continued mockingly, inclining his head toward Grant. "I have heard of you, *señor*. Surely there can be only one with the yellow eyes and scarred face, who melts through jungles like a silent cat. You are a legend, but it was thought that you were dead. It has been a long time since anything was heard of you."

Grant was silent, his attention now on Turego, ignoring Jane as if she no longer existed. Not a muscle moved; it was as if he'd turned to stone. He wasn't even breathing. His utter stillness was unnerving, yet there was also the impression of great strength under control, a wild animal waiting for the perfect moment to pounce. Even though he was only one against many, the others were like jackals surrounding a mighty tiger; the men who held their weapons trained on him were visibly nervous.

"Perhaps it would be interesting to know who now pays you for your services. And there are others who would like very much to have an opportunity to question you, yes? Tie him, and put him in the truck," Turego ordered, still keeping his arm around Jane. She forced herself not to watch as Grant was roughly bound and dragged over to a two-ton military-type truck, with a canvas top stretched over the back. Instead she gave Turego her most dazzling smile and leaned her head on his shoulder.

"I've been so frightened," she whispered.

"Of course you have, *chiquita*. Is that why you resisted my men when they found you in the forest yesterday?"

She might have known he was too sharp to simply believe her! She let her eyes widen incredulously. "Those were *your* men? Well, why didn't they say so? They were shoving me around, and I was afraid they wanted to…to attack me. I had managed to slip away from that crazy man; I'd have made it, too, if it hadn't been for all the noise your men made! They led him right to me!" Her voice quivered with indignation.

"It is over; I will take care of you now." He led her to the truck and assisted her into the cab, then climbed in beside her and gave terse instructions to the driver.

That was exactly what she was afraid of, being taken care of by Turego, but for the moment she had to play up to him and somehow convince him that she was totally innocent of her escape from under the noses of his guards. He hadn't gotten where he was by being a gullible idiot; though she'd successfully fooled him the first time, the second time would be much more difficult.

"Where are we going?" she asked innocently, leaning against him. "Back to the plantation? Did you bring any of my clothes with you? *He* brought me this blouse this morning," she said, plucking at the soft white fabric, "but I'd really like to have my own clothes."

"I have been so worried about you that I did not think of your clothes, I confess," Turego lied smoothly. His hard arm was around her shoulders, and Jane smiled up at him. He was unnaturally handsome, with perfect features that would have done better on a statue than a man, though perhaps Turego wasn't quite human. He didn't show his age; he looked to be in his twenties, though Jane knew that he was in his early forties. Emotion hadn't changed his face; he had no wrinkles, no attractive crinkles at the corners of his eyes, no signs that time or life had touched him. His only weakness was his vanity; he knew he could force himself on Jane at any time, but he wanted to seduce her into giving herself willingly to him. She would be another feather in his cap; then, once he had the microfilm, he could dispose of her without regret.

She had only the microfilm to protect her, and only herself to protect Grant. Her mind raced, trying to think of some way she could free him from his bonds, get some sort of weapon to him. All he needed was a small advantage.

"Who *is* he? You seem to know him."

"He hasn't introduced himself? But you have spent several days alone with him, my heart. Surely you know his name."

Again she had to make a split-second decision. Was Grant's real name commonly known? Was Grant his real name, anyway? She couldn't take the chance. "He told me that his name is Joe Tyson. Isn't that his real name?" she asked in an incredulous voice, sitting up to turn the full force of her brown eyes on him, blinking as if in astonishment.

Oddly, Turego hesitated. "That may be what he calls himself now. If he is who I think he is, he was once known as the Tiger."

He was uneasy! Grant was tied, and there were ten guns on him, but still Turego was made uneasy by his presence! Did that slight hesitation mean that Turego wasn't certain of Grant's real name and didn't want to reveal his lack of knowledge—or was the uncertainty of a greater scope? Was he not entirely certain that Grant was the Tiger? Turego wouldn't want to make himself look foolish by claiming to have captured the Tiger, only to have his prisoner turn out to be someone much less interesting.

Tiger. She could see how he had gained the name, and the reputation. With his amber eyes and deadly grace, the comparison had been inevitable. But he was a man, too, and she'd slept in his arms. He'd held her during the long hours of darkness, keeping the night demons away from her, and he'd shown her a part of herself that she hadn't known existed. Because of Grant, she felt like a whole person, capable of love and passion, a warm, giving woman. Though she could see what he had been, the way she saw him now was colored by love. He was a man, not a supernatural creature who melted through the dark, tangled jungles of the world. He could bleed, and hurt. He could laugh, that deep, rusty laugh that caught at her heart. After Grant, she felt contaminated just by sitting next to Turego.

She gave a tinkling laugh. "That sounds so cloak-and-daggerish! Do you mean he's a spy?"

"No, of course not. Nothing so romantic. He is really just a mercenary, hiring himself out to anyone for any sort of dirty job."

"Like kidnapping me? Why would he do that? I mean, no one is going to pay any ransom for me! My father doesn't even speak to me, and I certainly don't have any money of my own!"

"Perhaps something else was wanted from you," he suggested.

"But I don't have anything!" She managed to fill her face and voice with bewilderment, and Turego smiled down at her.

"Perhaps you have it and are not aware of it."

"What? Do you know?"

"In time, love, we shall find out."

"No one tells me anything!" she wailed, and lapsed into a pout. She allowed herself to hold the pout for about thirty seconds, then roused to demand of him again, like an impatient child, "Where are we going?"

"Just down this street, love."

They were on the very fringes of the town, and a dilapidated tin warehouse sat at the end of the street. It was in sad shape, its walls sagging, the tin roof curled up in several places, sections of it missing altogether in others. A scarred blue door hung crookedly on its hinges. The warehouse was their destination, and when the truck stopped beside the blue door and Turego helped Jane from the cab, she saw why. There were few people about, and those who were in the vicinity quickly turned their eyes away and scurried off.

Grant was hauled out of the back of the truck and shoved toward the door; he stumbled and barely caught his balance before he would have crashed headlong against the building. Someone chuckled, and when Grant straightened to turn his unnerving stare on his captors, Jane saw that a thin trickle of blood had dried at the corner of his mouth. His lip was split and puffy. Her heart lurched, and her breath caught. Someone had hit him while he had his hands tied behind his back! Right behind her first sick reaction came fury, raw and powerful, surging through her like a tidal wave. She shook with the effort it took to disguise it before she turned to Turego again.

"What are we going to do here?"

"I just want to ask a few questions of our friend. Nothing important."

She was firmly escorted into the building, and she gasped as the heat hit her in the face like a blow. The tin building was a furnace, heating the air until it was almost impossible to breathe. Perspiration immediately beaded on her skin, and she felt dizzy, unable to drag in enough oxygen to satisfy her need.

Evidently Turego had been using the warehouse as a sort of base, because there was equipment scattered around. Leaving Grant under guard, Turego led Jane to the back of the building, where several small rooms connected with each other, probably the former offices. It was just as hot there, but a small window was opened and let in a measure of fresh air. The room he took her to was filthy, piled with musty-smelling papers and netted with cobwebs. An old wooden desk, missing a leg, listed drunkenly to one side, and there was the unmistakable stench of rodents. Jane wrinkled her nose fastidiously. "Ugh!" she said in completely honest disgust.

"I apologize for the room," Turego said smoothly, bestowing one of his toothpaste-ad smiles on her. "Hopefully, we won't be here long. Alfonso will stay with you while I question our friend about his activities, and who hired him to abduct you."

What he meant was that she was also under guard. Jane didn't protest, not wanting to arouse his suspicions even more, but her skin crawled. She was very much afraid of the form his "questioning" would take. She had to think of something fast! But nothing came to mind, and Turego tilted her chin up to kiss her again. "I won't be long," he murmured. "Alfonso, watch her carefully. I would be very upset if someone stole her from me again."

Jane thought she recognized Alfonso as one of the guards who had been at the plantation. When Turego had gone, closing the door behind him, Jane gave Alfonso a slow glance from under lowered lashes and essayed a tentative smile. He was fairly young and good-looking. He had probably been warned against her, but still he couldn't help responding to her smile.

"You were a guard at the plantation?" she asked in Spanish.

He gave a reluctant nod.

"I thought I recognized you. I never forget a good-looking man," she said with more enthusiasm than precision, her pronunciation mangled just enough to bring a hint of amusement to Alfonso's face. She wondered if he knew what Turego was up to, or if he had been told some fabrication about protecting her.

Whatever he had been told, he wasn't inclined toward conversation. Jane poked around the room, looking for anything to use as a weapon, but trying not to be obvious about it. She kept straining her ears for any sound from the warehouse, her nerves jumping. What was Turego doing? If he harmed Grant...

How long had it been? Five minutes? Ten? Or less than that? She had no idea, but suddenly she couldn't stand it any longer, and she went to the door. Alfonso stretched his arm in front of her, barring her way.

"I want to see Turego," she said impatiently. "It's too hot to wait in here."

"You must stay here."

"Well, I won't! Don't be such a stuffed shirt, Alfonso; he won't mind. You can come with me, if you can't let me out of your sight."

She ducked under his arm and had the door open before he could stop her. With a muffled oath he came after her, but Jane darted through the door and the connecting offices. Just as she entered the main warehouse she heard the sickening thud of a fist against flesh, and the blood drained from her face.

Two men held Grant between them, holding him up by his bound arms, while another stood before him, rubbing his fist. Turego stood to the side, a small, inhuman smile on his lips. Grant's head sagged forward on his chest, and drops of blood spotted the floor at his feet.

"This silence will gain you nothing but more pain, my friend," Turego said softly. "Tell me who hired you. That is all I want to know, for now."

Grant said nothing, and one of the men holding him grabbed a fistful of hair, jerking his head up. Just before Alfonso took her arm, Jane saw Grant's face, and she jerked free, driven by a wild strength.

"Turego!" she cried shrilly, drawing everyone's attention to her. Turego's brows snapped together over his nose.

"What are you doing here? Alfonso, take her back!"

"No!" she yelled, pushing Alfonso away. "It's too hot back there, and I won't stay! Really, this is too much! I've had a miserable time in that jungle, and I thought when you rescued me that I'd be comfortable again, but no, you drag me to this miserable dump and leave me in that grungy little room. I insist that you take me to a hotel!"

"Jane, Jane, you don't understand these things," Turego said, coming up to her and taking her arm. "Just a few moments more and he will tell me what I want to know. Aren't you interested in knowing who hired him?" He turned her away, leading her back to the offices again. "Please be patient, love."

Jane subsided, letting herself be led docilely away. She risked a quick glance back at Grant and his captors, and saw that they were waiting for Turego's return before resuming the beating. He was sagging limply in their grasp, unable even to stand erect.

"You are to stay here," Turego said sternly when they reached the office again. "Promise me, yes?"

"I promise," Jane said, turning toward him with a smile on her face; he never saw the blow coming. She caught him under the nose with the bridge of her hand, snapping his head back and making blood spurt. Before he could yell with pain or surprise, she slammed her elbow into his solar plexus and he doubled over with an agonized grunt. As if in a well-choreographed ballet, she brought her knee up under his unprotected chin, and Turego collapsed like a stuffed doll. Jane cast a quick thought of thanks to her father for insisting that she take all of those self-defense classes, then bent down and quickly jerked the pistol from Turego's holster.

Just as she started through the doorway again, a shot reverberated through the tin building, and she froze in horror. "No," she moaned, then launched herself toward the sound.

WHEN JANE HAD HURLED herself into Turego's arms, Grant had been seized by a fury so consuming that a mist of red had fallen over his vision, but he'd been trained to control himself, and that control had held, even though he had been on the edge of madness. Then the mist had cleared, and cold contempt had taken its place. Hell, what had he expected? Jane was a survivor, adept at keeping her feet. First she had charmed Turego, then Grant had stolen her from Turego and she'd charmed him as effortlessly as she had put Turego under her spell. Now Turego was back, and since he had the upper hand, it was a case of So long, Sullivan. He even felt a sort of bitter admiration for the way she had so quickly and accurately summed up the situation, then known exactly the tone to set to begin bringing Turego back to heel.

Still, the sense of betrayal was staggering, and nothing would have pleased him at that moment as much as to get his hands on her. Damn her for being a lying, treacherous little bitch! He should have known, should have suspected at her patented look of wide-eyed innocence was nothing but a well-rehearsed act.

The old instincts, only partially shelved, suddenly returned in full force. Forget about the bitch. He had to look out for himself first, then see to her. She was curling in Turego's arms like a cat, while Grant knew that his own future was nonexistent unless he did some fast thinking.

Part of the thinking was done for him when Turego put two and two together and came up with an accurate guess about Grant's identity. A year had been far too short a time for people in the business to even begin forgetting him. After he'd disappeared, his absence had probably made his reputation grow to legendary proportions. Well, let Turego think that he was after the missing microfilm, too; Grant felt no compunction about using Jane in any way he could. She'd not only used him, she'd had him dancing to her tune like a puppet on a fancy little string. If he hadn't agreed to bring her out of Costa Rica, he would have wished the joy of her on Turego, and gotten himself out any way he could. But he'd taken the job, so he had to finish it—if he came out of this alive. When he got his hands on her again she'd find that there would be no more kid-glove treatment.

Turego was curious. With his hands tied behind his back, supported between two of the hired goons, Grant found out just how curious.

"Who hired you? Or are you an independent now?"

"Naw, I'm still a Protestant," Grant said, smiling smoothly. At a nod from Turego, a fist crashed into his face, splitting his lip and filling his mouth with blood. The next blow was into his midsection, and he'd have jacknifed if it hadn't been for the cruel support of his twisted arms.

"Really, I don't have the time for this," Turego murmured. "You are the one known as the Tiger; you aren't a man who works for nothing."

"Sure I am; I'm a walking charity."

The fist landed on his cheekbone, snapping his head back. This guy was a real boxer; he placed his blows with precision. The face a couple of times, then the ribs and kidneys. Pain sliced through Grant until his stomach heaved. He gasped, his vision blurred even though his mind was still clear, and he deliberately let all his weight fall on his two supporters, his knees buckling.

Then he heard Jane's voice, petulant and demanding, as he'd never heard it before, followed by Turego's smooth reassurances. The men's attention wasn't on him; he sensed its absence, like a wild animal acutely sensitive to every nuance. He sagged even more, deliberately putting stress on the bonds around his wrists, and fierce satisfaction welled in him as he felt them slip on his right hand.

He had powerful hands, hands that could destroy. He used that power against the cord that bound him, extending his hand to the fullest and stretching the cord, then relaxing and letting the cord slip even lower. Twice he did that, and the cord dropped around his fingers in loose coils.

Looking about through slitted eyes, he saw that no one was paying much attention to him, not even the boxer, who was absently rubbing his knuckles and waiting for Turego to return from wherever he'd gone. Jane was nowhere in sight, either. Now was the time.

The two men holding him were off guard; he threw them away from him like discarded toys. For a split second everyone was disconcerted, and that split second was all he needed. He grabbed a rifle and kicked its butt up under the chin of the soldier he'd taken it from, sending him staggering backward. He whirled, lashing out with his feet and the stock of the rifle. The soldiers really didn't have much of a chance; they didn't have a fraction of the training he'd had, or the years of experience. They didn't know how to react to an attacker who struck and whirled away before anyone could move. Only one managed to get his rifle up, and he fired wildly, the bullet zinging far over Grant's head. That soldier was the last one standing; Grant took him out with almost contemptuous ease. Then he hesitated only the barest moment as he waited for movement from any of them, but there was none. His gaze moved to the door at the far end of the warehouse, and a cold, twisted smile touched his bruised and bloody lips. He went after Jane.

SHE'D NEVER KNOWN such terror; even her fear of the dark was nothing compared to the way she felt now. She couldn't move fast enough; her feet felt as if they were slogging through syrup. Oh, God, what if they'd killed him? The thought was too horrible to be borne, yet it swelled in her chest until she couldn't breathe. No, she thought, no, no, *no*!

She burst through the door, the pistol in her hand, half-crazed with fear and ready to fight for her man, for her very life. She saw a confused scene of sprawled men and her mind reeled, unable to comprehend why so many were lying there. Hadn't there been only one shot?

Then an arm snaked around her neck, jerking her back and locking under her chin. Another arm reached out, and long fingers clamped around the hand that held the pistol, removing it from her grip.

"Funny thing, sweetheart, but I feel safer when you're unarmed," a low voice hissed in her ear.

At the sound of that voice, Jane's eyes closed, and two tears squeezed out from under the lids. "Grant," she whispered.

"Afraid so. You can tell me how glad you are to see me later; right now we're moving."

He released his arm lock about her neck, but when she

tried to turn to face him, he caught her right arm and pulled it up behind her back, not so high that she was in pain, but high enough that she would be if he moved it even a fraction of an inch higher. "Move!" he barked, thrusting her forward, and Jane stumbled under the force of the motion, wrenching her arm and emitting an involuntary cry.

"You're hurting me," she whimpered, still dazed and trying to understand. "Grant, wait!"

"Cut the crap," he advised, kicking open the door and shoving her out into the searing white sunlight. The transport truck was sitting there, and he didn't hesitate. "Get in. We're going for a ride."

He opened the door and half-lifted, half-threw Jane into the truck, sending her sprawling on the seat. She cried out, her soft cry knifing through him, but he told himself not to be a fool; she didn't need anyone to look after her. Like a cat, she always landed on her feet.

Jane scrambled to a sitting position, her dark eyes full of tears as she stared at his battered, bloody face in both pain and horror. She wanted to reassure him, tell him that it had all been an act, a desperate gamble to save both their lives, but he didn't seem inclined to listen. Surely he wouldn't so easily forget everything they'd shared, everything they'd been to each other! Still, she couldn't give up. She'd lifted her hand to reach out for him when a movement in the door beyond them caught her eye, and she screamed a warning.

"Grant!"

He whirled, and as he did Turego lifted the rifle he held and fired. The explosive crack of sound split the air, but still Jane heard, felt, sensed the grunt of pain that Grant gave as he dropped to one knee and lifted the pistol. Turego lunged to one side, looking for cover, but the pistol spat fire, and a small red flower bloomed high on Turego's right shoulder, sending him tumbling back through the door.

Jane heard someone screaming, but the sound was high and far away. She lunged through the open door of the truck, falling to her hands and knees on the hot, rocky ground. Grant was on his knees, leaning against the running board of the truck, his right hand clamped over his upper left arm, and bright red blood was dripping through his fingers. He looked up at her, his golden eyes bright and burning with the fire of battle, fierce even in his swollen and discolored face.

She went a little mad then. She grabbed him by his undershirt and hauled him to his feet, using a strength she'd had no idea she possessed. "Get in the truck!" she screamed, pushing him in the door. "Damn it, get in the truck! Are you trying to get yourself killed?"

He winced as the side of the seat smashed into his bruised ribs; Jane was shoving at him and screaming like a banshee, tears streaming down her face. "Would you shut up!" he yelled, painfully pulling himself inside.

"Don't you tell me to shut up!" she screamed, pushing him until he moved over. She slapped the tears from her cheeks and climbed into the truck herself. "Get out of the way so I can get this thing started! Are there any keys? Where are the keys? Oh, damn!" She dove headfirst under the steering wheel, feeling under the dash and pulling wires out frantically.

"What're you doing?" Grant groaned, his mind reeling with pain.

"I'm hot-wiring the truck!" she sobbed.

"You're tearing the damned wiring out!" If she was trying to disable their only transportation, she was doing a good job of it. He started to yank her out from under the steering wheel when suddenly she bounced out on her own, jamming the clutch in and touching two wires together. The motor roared into life, and Jane slammed the door on her side, shoved the truck into gear and let out on the clutch. The truck lurched forward violently, throwing Grant against the door.

"Put it in low gear!" he yelled, pulling himself into a sitting position and getting a tighter grip on the seat.

"I don't know where the low gear is! I just took what I could find!"

Swearing, he reached for the gear shift, the pain in his wounded arm like a hot knife as he closed his hand over the knob. There was nothing he could do about the pain, so he ignored it. "Put the clutch in," he ordered. "I'll change gears. Jane, put the damned clutch in!"

"Stop yelling at me!" she screamed, jamming in the clutch. Grant put the truck in the proper gear and she let out on the clutch; this time the truck moved more smoothly. She put her foot on the gas pedal, shoving it to the floor, and slung the heavy truck around a corner, sending its rear wheels sliding on the gravel.

"Turn right," Grant directed, and she took the next right.

The truck was lunging under her heavy urging, its transmission groaning as she kept her foot down on the gas pedal.

"Change gears!"

"Change them yourself!"

"Put in the clutch!"

She put in the clutch, and he geared up. "When I tell you, put in the clutch, and I'll change the gears, understand?"

She was still crying, swiping at her face at irregular intervals. Grant said, "Turn left," and she swung the truck in a turn that sent a pickup dodging to the side of the road to avoid them.

The road took them out of town, but they were only a couple of miles out when Grant said tersely, "Pull over." Jane didn't question him; she pulled over to the side of the road and stopped the truck.

"Okay, get out." Again she obeyed without question, jumping out and standing there awkwardly as he eased himself to the ground. His left arm was streaked with blood, but from the look on his face Jane knew that he wasn't about to stop. He shoved the pistol into his belt and slung the rifle over his shoulder. "Let's go."

"Where are we going?"

"Back into town. Your boyfriend won't expect us to double back on him. You can stop crying," he added cruelly. "I didn't kill him."

"He's not my boyfriend!" Jane spat, whirling on him.

"Sure looked like it from where I was."

"I was trying to catch him off guard! One of us had to stay free!"

"Save it," he advised, his tone bored. "I bought your act once, but it won't sell again. Now, are you going to walk?"

She decided that there was no use trying to reason with him now. When he'd calmed down enough to listen, when she'd calmed down enough to make a coherent explanation, then they'd get this settled. As she turned away from him, she looked in the open door of the truck and caught a glimpse of something shoved in the far corner of the floor. Her backpack! She crawled up in the truck and leaned far over to drag the pack out from under the seat; in the excitement, it had been totally overlooked and forgotten.

"Leave the damned thing!" Grant snapped.

"I need it," she snapped in return. She buckled it to her belt-loop again.

He drew the pistol out of his belt and Jane swallowed,

her eyes growing enormous. Calmly he shot out one of the front tires of the truck, then stuck the pistol back into his belt.

"Why did you do that?" she whispered, swallowing again.

"So it'll look as if we were forced to abandon the truck."

He caught her upper arm in a tight grip and pulled her off the road. Whenever he heard an engine he forced her to the ground and they lay still until the sound had faded. Her blouse, so white and pretty only an hour or so before, became streaked with mud and torn in places where the thorns caught it. She gave it a brief glance, then forgot about it.

"When will Turego be after us again?" she panted.

"Soon. Impatient already?"

Grinding her teeth together, she ignored him. In twenty more minutes they approached the edge of the town again, and he circled it widely. She wanted to ask him what he was looking for, but after the way he'd just bitten her head off, she kept silent. She wanted to sit down to wash his bruised face, and bandage the wound in his arm, but she could do none of those things. He didn't want anything from her now.

Still, what else could she have done? There was no way she could have known he was going to be able to escape. She'd had to use the best plan she had at the time.

Finally they slipped into a ramshackle shed behind an equally ramshackle house and collapsed on the ground in the relatively cool interior. Grant winced as he inadvertently strained his left arm, but when Jane started toward him, he gave her a cold glare that stopped her in her tracks. She sank back to the ground and rested her forehead on her drawn up knees. "What are we going to do now?"

"We're getting out of the country, any way we can," he said flatly. "Your daddy hired me to bring you home, and that's what I'm going to do. The sooner I turn you over to him, the better."

CHAPTER ELEVEN

AFTER THAT JANE SAT quietly, keeping her forehead down on her knees and closing her eyes. A cold desolation was growing inside her, filling her, thrusting aside anxiety and fear. What if she could never convince him that she hadn't betrayed him? With the life he'd led, it was probably something that he'd had to guard against constantly, so he wasn't even surprised by betrayal. She would try again to reason with him, of course; until he actually left her, she wouldn't stop trying. But…what if he wouldn't listen? What would she do then? Somehow she just couldn't imagine her future without Grant. The emotional distance between them now was agonizing, but she could still lift her head and see him, take comfort in his physical proximity. What would she do if he weren't there at all?

The heat and humidity began building, negating the coolness of the shade offered by the old, open-sided shed, and in the distance thunder rumbled as it announced the approach of the daily rain. A door creaked loudly, and soon a stooped old woman, moving slowly, came around the side of the house to a small pen where pigs had been grunting occasionally as they lay in the mud and tried to escape the heat. Grant watched her, his eyes alert, not a muscle moving. There wasn't any real danger that she would see them; weeds and bushes grew out of control, over waist-high, between the house and the shed, with only a faint little-used path leading to the shed. The pigs squealed in loud enthusiasm when the old woman fed them, and after chatting fondly to them for a moment she laboriously made her way back into the shack.

Jane hadn't moved a muscle, not opening her eyes even when the pigs had begun celebrating the arrival of food. Grant looked at her, a faint puzzlement creeping into the coldness of his eyes. It was unlike her to sit so quietly and not investigate the noise. She knew it was the pigs, of course, but she hadn't looked up to see what was making them squeal so loudly, or even when the old woman had begun talking to them. She was normally as curious as a cat, poking her nose into everything whether it concerned her or not. It was difficult to tell, the way she had her head down, but he thought that she was pale; the few freckles he could see stood out plainly.

An image flashed into his mind of Turego bending his head to press his mouth to Jane's, and the way Jane had stood so quiescently to accept that kiss. Rage curled inside him again, and his fists knotted. Damn her! How could she have let that slime touch her?

The thunder moved closer, cracking loudly, and the air carried the scent of rain. Wind began to swirl, darting through the shed and bringing with it welcome coolness. The air was alive, almost shining with the electrical energy it carried. The small creatures began to take shelter, birds winging back and forth in an effort to find the most secure perch to wait out the storm.

During the rain would be a good time to leave, as everyone else would take shelter until it was over, but his body ached from the beating he'd received, and his left arm was still sullenly oozing blood. They were in no immediate danger here, so he was content to rest. Night would be an even better time to move.

The rain started, going from a sprinkle to a deluge in

less than a minute. The ground wasn't able to soak up that enormous amount of water, and a small stream began to trickle through the shed. Grant got up, stifling a groan as his stiff body protested, and found a seat on top of a half-rotten vegetable crate. It gave a little, but held his weight.

Jane still hadn't moved. She didn't look up until the moisture began to dampen the seat of her pants; then her head lifted and she realized that a river was beginning to flow around her. She didn't look at Grant, though she moved away from the water, shifting to the side. She sat with her back to him and resumed her earlier posture, with her knees drawn up, her arms locked around her legs, and her head bent down to rest on her knees.

Grant knew how to wait; patience was second nature to him. He could hold a position all day long, if necessary, ignoring physical discomfort as if it didn't exist. But the silence and lack of motion in the shed began to grate on his nerves, because it wasn't what he'd learned to expect from Jane. Was she planning something?

Eventually the rain stopped, and the steamy heat began to build again. "Are we going to sit here all day?" Jane finally asked fretfully, breaking her long silence.

"Might as well. I don't have anything better to do. Do you?"

She didn't answer that, or ask any more questions, realizing that he wasn't in the mood to tell her anything. She was so hungry that she was sick, but there wasn't any food in her pack, and she wasn't about to complain to him. She dropped her head back to her knees and tried to seek refuge in a nap; at least then she could forget how miserable she was.

She actually managed to sleep, and he woke her at twilight, shaking her shoulder. "Let's go," he said, pulling her to her feet. Jane's heart stopped because just for that moment his touch was strong but gentle, and she had the crazy hope that he'd cooled down and come to his senses while she was napping. But then he dropped her arm and stepped away from her, his face hard, and the hope died.

She followed him like a toy on a string, right in his footsteps, stopping when he stopped, always the same distance behind him. He went boldly into the center of town, walking down the streets as if no one at all was looking for him, let alone a small army. Several people looked at them oddly, but no one stopped them. Jane supposed they did look strange: a tall blond man with a bruised, swollen face and a rifle carried easily in one hand, followed by a woman with wild tangled hair, dirty clothes and a backpack buckled to her belt and swinging against her legs as she walked. Well, everything seemed strange to her, too. She felt as if they'd gotten lost in a video game, with crazy neon images flashing at her. After a moment she realized that the images were real; a street sign advertising a cantina flashed its message in neon pink and blue.

What was he doing? They were attracting so much notice that Turego would have to hear of it if he asked any questions at all. For all Grant knew, Turego could have the local law enforcement looking for them under trumped-up charges; Turego certainly had enough authority to mobilize any number of people in the search. It was as if Grant *wanted* Turego to find them.

He turned down a side street and paused outside a small, dimly lit cantina. "Stay close to me, and keep your mouth shut," he ordered tersely, and entered.

It was hot and smoky in the small bar, and the strong odor of alcohol mixed with sweat permeated the air. Except for the waitress, a harried-looking girl, and two sultry prostitutes, there were no other women there. Several men eyed Jane, speculation in their dark eyes, but then they looked at

Grant and turned back to their drinks, evidently deciding that she wasn't worth the trouble.

Grant found them space at a small table at the back, deep in the shadows. After a while the waitress made it over to them, and without asking Jane her preference, Grant ordered two tequilas.

Jane stopped the waitress. "Wait—do you have lime juice?" At the young woman's nod, she heaved a sigh of relief. "A glass of lime juice, instead of the tequila, please."

Grant lit a cigarette, cupping his hands around the flame. "Are you on the wagon or something?"

"I don't drink on an empty stomach."

"We'll get something to eat later. This place doesn't run to food."

She waited until their drinks were in front of them before saying anything else to him. "Isn't it dangerous for us to be here? Any of Turego's men could have seen us walking down the street."

His eyes were narrow slits as he stared at her through the blue smoke of his cigarette. "Why should that worry you? Don't you think he'd welcome you back with open arms?"

Jane leaned forward, her own eyes narrowed. "Listen to me. I had to buy time, and I did it the only way I could think of. I'm sorry I didn't have time to explain it to you beforehand, but I don't think Turego would have let me call 'time out' and huddle with you! If he'd tied me up, too, there would have been no way I could help you!"

"Thanks, honey, but I can do without your sort of help," he drawled, touching his left eye, which was puffy and red.

Anger seared her; she was innocent, and she was tired of being treated like Benedict Arnold. She thought of pouring the lime juice in his lap, but her stomach growled and revenge took a distant second place to putting something in her empty stomach, even if it was just fruit juice. She sat back in her chair and sipped, wanting to make the juice last as long as possible.

The minutes crawled by, and Jane began to feel a twitch between her shoulder blades. Every second they sat there increased the danger, gave Turego a better chance of finding them. The abandoned truck wouldn't fool him for long.

A man slipped into the chair beside her and Jane jumped, her heart flying into her throat. He gave her only a cursory glance before turning his attention to Grant. He was a nondescript character, his clothing worn, his face covered by a couple of days' growth of beard, and his smell of stale alcohol made Jane wrinkle her nose. But then he said a few words to Grant, so quietly that she couldn't understand them, and it all clicked into place.

Grant had advertised their presence not because he wanted Turego to find them, but because he wanted someone else to find them. It had been a gamble, but it had paid off. He was no longer in the business, but he was known, and he'd trusted his reputation to pull in a contact. This man was probably just a peripheral character, but he would have his uses.

"I need transport," Grant said. "Within the hour. Can you manage it?"

"*Sì,*" the man said, slowly nodding his head for emphasis.

"Good. Have it sitting behind the Blue Pelican exactly one hour from now. Put the keys under the right seat, get out, and walk away."

The man nodded again. "Good luck, amigo."

That hard, lopsided smile curved Grant's lips. "Thanks. I could use some about now."

The man blended in with the crowd, then was gone. Jane slowly twirled the glass of juice between her palms, keeping her eyes on the table. "Now that you've made your contact, shouldn't we get out of here?"

Grant lifted the tequila to his mouth, his strong throat working as he swallowed the sharp-tasting liquid. "We'll wait a while longer."

No, it wouldn't do to follow the other man too closely. George had always told her how important it was to make contact without seeming to. The man had taken a chance by walking up to them so openly, but then, Grant had taken a chance by making himself so available. It had probably been clear that the situation was desperate, though Grant looked as if he was thinking about nothing more important than going to sleep. He was sprawled in his chair, his eyes half-closed, and if Jane hadn't noticed that he kept his left hand on the rifle she would have thought that he was totally relaxed.

"Do you suppose we could find a bathroom?" she asked, keeping her tone light.

"In here? I doubt it."

"Anywhere."

"Okay. Are you finished with that?" He downed the rest of his tequila, and Jane did the same with her lime juice. Her skin was crawling again; she felt that tingling on the back of her neck, and it intensified as she stood up.

They threaded their way through the tangle of feet and tables and chairs to the door, and as soon as they stepped outside Jane said, "I think we were being watched."

"I know we were. That's why we're going in the opposite direction of the Blue Pelican."

"What on earth is the Blue Pelican? How do you know so much about this town? Have you been here before?"

"No, but I keep my eyes open. The Blue Pelican is the first cantina we passed."

Now she remembered. It was the cantina with the flashing neon sign, the one that had given her such an intense feeling of unreality.

They were walking down the small side street into a yawning cave of darkness. The street wasn't paved, and there were no sidewalks, no street lights, not even one of the incongruous neon signs to lend its garish light. The ground was uneven beneath her boots, and the sour smell of old garbage surrounded her. Jane didn't think; her hand shot out, and she grabbed Grant's belt.

He hesitated, then resumed walking without saying anything. Jane swallowed, belatedly realizing that she could have found herself sailing over his shoulder again, as she had the first time she'd grabbed him from behind. What would she do if she no longer had him to cling to in the dark? Stand around wringing her hands? She'd already come a long way from the child who had sat in a terrified stupor for days, and perhaps it was time for one step more. Slowly, deliberately, Jane released her grip on his belt and let her arm drop to her side.

He stopped and looked around at her, darkness shrouding his features. "I don't mind you holding on to my belt."

She remained silent, feeling his reluctant curiosity, but unable to give him any explanation. All her milestones had been inner ones, attained only by wrenching effort, and this wasn't something she could easily talk about. Not even the frighteningly expensive child psychologist to whom her parents had taken her had been able to draw her out about the kidnapping. Everyone knew about the nightmares she'd had, and her abrupt, unreasonable fear of the dark, but she'd never told anyone the details of her experience. Not her parents, not even Chris, and he'd been her best friend long before he'd been her husband. In all the years since the kidnapping, she'd told only one person, trusted only one person enough. Now there was a distance between them that she'd tried to bridge, but he kept pushing her away. No matter how she wanted to throw herself into his arms, she had to stand alone, because soon she might have no choice in the matter.

The fear of being alone in the dark was nothing compared to the fear that she might be alone for the rest of her life.

He wove a crazy path through the town, crisscrossing, backtracking, changing their route so many times that Jane completely lost her sense of direction. She chugged along doggedly, staying right on his heels. He stopped once, and stood guard while Jane sneaked in the back of the local version of a greasy spoon. The plumbing was pre-World War II, the lighting was a single dim bulb hanging from the ceiling, and the carcass of an enormous cockroach lay on its back in the corner, but she wasn't in the mood to quibble. At least the plumbing worked, and when she turned on the water in the cracked basin a thin, lukewarm stream came out. She washed her hands and, bending over, splashed water on her face. There was no towel, so she wiped her hands on her pants and left her face to dry naturally.

When she tiptoed out of the building, Grant stepped from the shadows where he had concealed himself and took her arm. They weren't far from the Blue Pelican, as it turned out; when they turned the corner, she could see the blue and pink sign flashing. But Grant didn't walk straight to it; he circled the entire area, sometimes standing motionless for long minutes while he waited, and watched.

At last they approached the old Ford station wagon that

was parked behind the cantina, but even then he was cautious. He raised the hood and used his cigarette lighter to examine the motor. Jane didn't ask what he was looking for, because she had the chilling idea that she knew. He closed the hood as quietly as possible, evidently reassured.

"Get in, and get the keys out from under the seat."

She opened the door. The dome light didn't come on, but that was to be expected. Doing a little checking on her own, she peered over the back of the seat, holding her breath in case there was actually someone there. But the floorboard was empty, and her breath hissed out of her lungs in relief.

Leaning over, she swept her hand under the seat, searching for the keys. The other door opened, and the car swayed under Grant's weight. "Hurry," he snapped.

"I can't find the keys!" Her scrabbling fingers found a lot of dirt, a few screws, a scrap of paper, but no keys. "Maybe this isn't the right car!"

"It'll have to do. Check again."

She got down on the floor and reached as far under the seat as she could, sweeping her hands back and forth. "Nothing. Try under yours."

He leaned down, extending his arm to search under his seat. Swearing softly, he pulled out a single key wired to a small length of wood. Muttering under his breath about damned people not being able to follow simple instructions, he put the key in the ignition and started the car.

Despite its age, the engine was quiet and smooth. Grant shifted into gear and backed out of the alley. He didn't turn on the headlights until they were well away from the Blue Pelican and the well-lit main street.

Jane leaned back in the musty-smelling seat, unable to believe that at last they seemed to be well on their way. So much had happened since that morning that she'd lost her sense of time. It couldn't be late; it was probably about ten o'clock, if that. She watched the road for a while, hypnotized by the way it unwound just ahead of the reach of their headlights, tired but unable to sleep. "Are we still going to Limon?"

"Why? Is that what you told your lover?"

Jane sat very still, clenching her teeth against the anger that shook her. All right, she'd try one more time. "He isn't my lover, and I didn't tell him anything. All I was trying to do was to stay untied until I could catch one of them off guard and get his gun." She spat the words out evenly, but her chest was heaving as she tried to control her anger. "Just how do you think I got the pistol that you took away from me?"

She felt that was a point that he couldn't ignore, but he did, shrugging it away. "Look, you don't have to keep making explanations," he said in a bored tone. "I'm not interested—"

"Stop the car!" she shouted, enraged.

"Don't start pitching one of your fits," he warned, slanting her a hard look.

Jane dived for the steering wheel, too angry to care if she caused them to crash. He pushed her off with one hand, cursing, but Jane ducked under his arm and caught the wheel, wrenching it violently toward her. Grant hit the brake, fighting to keep the car under control with one hand while he held Jane off with the other. She caught the wheel again and pulled it, and the car jolted violently as it hit the shoulder of the road.

Grant let go of her and wrestled with the car as it slewed back and forth on the narrow road. He braked sharply, finally bringing the car to a complete halt so he could give his full attention to Jane, but even before the car had completely stopped she threw the door open and jumped out. "I'll get myself out of Costa Rica!" she yelled, slamming the door.

He got out of the car. "Jane, come back here," he warned as she started walking off.

"I'm not going another mile with you, not another *inch*!"

"You're going if I have to hog-tie you," he said, coming after her, his stride measured.

She didn't stop. "That's your remedy for everything, isn't it?" she sneered.

Without warning, he sprinted. He moved so fast that Jane didn't have time to run. She gave a startled cry, twisting away as he reached her; his outstretched hand caught her blouse and Jane jerked as he stopped her. It was doubly infuriating to find herself so easily caught, and with a fresh burst of rage she threw herself away from him, twisting and doubling her lithe body, trying to break his grip.

He caught her wildly flailing arm and pinned it to her side. "Damn, woman, why do you have to do everything the hard way?" he panted.

"Let...*go!*" she shouted, but he wrapped his arms around her, holding her arms pinned down. She kicked and shrieked, but he was too strong; there was nothing she could do as he carried her back to the car.

But he had to release her with one arm so he could open the car door, and when he did she twisted violently, at the same time lifting her feet. The combination of the twist and the sudden addition of weight broke his grip, and she slid under his arm. He grabbed for her again, his fingers hooking in the low neckline of the blouse. The fabric parted under the strain, tearing away from her shoulders.

Tears spurted from Jane's eyes as she scrambled to cover her breasts, holding the ruined cloth over them. "Now look what you've done!" Turning away from him, she burst into sobs, her shoulders shaking.

The raw, hard sobs that tore from her throat were so violent that he dropped his outstretched arms. Wearily he rubbed his face. Why couldn't she cry with sedate little sniffles, instead of these sobs that sounded as if she had been beaten? Despite everything that had happened, he wanted to take her in his arms and hold her head to his chest, stroke her dark hair and whisper that everything was going to be all right.

She whirled on him, wiping her face with one hand and clutching the ruined blouse to her breasts with the other. "Think about a few things!" she said hoarsely. "Think about how I got that pistol. And think about Turego. Remember when he came up behind you with the rifle, and I warned you? Did you notice, before you shot him, that his face was bloody? Do you remember the way his nose was bleeding? Do you think it was the altitude that made his nose bleed? You big, stupid, boneheaded *jackass*!" she bellowed, so beside herself with fury that she was shaking her fist under his nose. "Damn it, can't you tell that I love you?"

Grant was as still as stone, not a muscle moving in his face, but he felt winded, as if he'd just taken a huge blow in the chest. Everything hit him at once, and he staggered under the weight of it. She was right. Turego's face had been bloody, but he hadn't thought anything about it at the time. He'd been so damned angry and jealous that he hadn't been thinking at all, only reacting to what had looked like betrayal. Not only had she done some quick thinking to avoid being tied up, she'd charged to his rescue as soon as she could, and when he remembered the way she'd looked when she came through that door, so white and wild— Turego's goons were probably lucky that he'd gotten free first. *She loved him!* He stared down at her, at the small fist that was waving dangerously close to his nose. She was utterly magnificent, her hair a wild tangle around her shoulders, her face filled with a temper that burned out of control, yelling at him like some banshee. She clutched that ridiculous scrap of cloth to her breasts with the hand that wasn't threatening his profile. Indomitable. Courageous. Maddening. And so damned desirable that he was suddenly shaking with need.

He caught her fist and jerked her to him, holding her to him so tightly that she gasped, his face buried against her hair.

She was still struggling against him, beating at his back with her fists and crying again. "Let me go! Please, just let me go."

"I can't," he whispered, and caught her chin, turning her face up to him. Fiercely he ground his mouth down on hers and, like a cornered cat, she tried to bite him. He jerked his head back, laughing, a wild joy running through him. The torn blouse had fallen away, and her naked breasts were flattened against him, their soft fullness reminding him of how good it felt when she wasn't fighting him. He kissed her again, roughly, and cupped her breast in his palm, rubbing his thumb over the velvet nipple and making it tighten.

Jane whimpered under the onslaught of his mouth, but her temper had worn itself out, and she softened against him, suddenly aware that she'd gotten through to him. She wanted to hold on to her anger, but she couldn't hold a grudge. All she could do was kiss him back, her arms sliding up to lock around his neck. His hand burned her breast, his thumb exciting her acutely sensitive skin and beginning to tighten the coil of desire deep in her loins. He had no need to hold her still for his kisses now, so he put his other hand on her bottom and urged her against him, demonstrating graphically that she wasn't the only one affected.

He lifted his mouth from hers, pressing his lips to her forehead. "I swear, that temper of yours is something," he whispered. "Do you forgive me?"

That was a silly question; what was she supposed to say, considering that she was hanging around his neck like a Christmas ornament? "No," she said, rubbing her face into the hollow of his throat, seeking his warm, heady male scent. "I'm going to save this to throw up at you the next time we have a fight." She wanted to say "for the rest of our lives," but though his arms were hard around her, he hadn't yet said that he loved her. She wasn't going to dig for the words, knowing that he might not be able to say them and mean it.

"You will, too," he said, and laughed. Reluctantly his arms loosened, and he reached up, removing her arms from his neck. "I'd like to stay like this, but we need to get to Limon." He looked down at her breasts, and a taut look came over his battered face. "When this is over with, I'm going to take you to a hotel and keep you in bed until neither of us can walk."

They got back in the car, and Jane removed the remnants of the blouse, stuffing it in the backpack and pulling on Grant's camouflage shirt that she'd put in the pack that morning. It would have wrapped around her twice, and the shoulder seams hung almost to her elbows. She rolled the sleeves up as far as they would go, then gathered the long tails and tied them at her waist. Definitely not high fashion, she thought, but she was covered.

The Ford rolled into Limon in the early hours of the morning, and though the streets were nearly deserted, it was obvious that the port was a well-populated city of medium size. Jane's hands clenched on the car seat. Were they safe, then? Had Turego been fooled by the abandoned truck?

"What now?"

"Now I try to get in touch with someone who can get us out tonight. I don't want to wait until morning."

So he thought Turego's men were too close for safety. Was it never going to end? She wished they had remained in the jungle, hidden so deeply in the rain forest that no one would ever have found them.

Evidently Grant had been in Limon before; he negotiated the streets with ease. He drove to the train station, and Jane gave him a puzzled look. "Are we going to take the train?"

"No, but there's a telephone here. Come on."

Limon wasn't an isolated jungle village, or even a tiny town at the edge of the forest; it was a city, with all of the rules of a city. He had to leave the rifle in the back of the station wagon, but he stuck the pistol into his boot. Even without his being obviously armed, Jane thought there was no chance at all of them going anywhere without being noticed. They both looked as if they'd come fresh from a battle, which, in effect, they had. The ticket agent eyed them with sharp curiosity, but Grant ignored him, heading straight for a telephone. He called someone named Angel, and his voice was sharp as he demanded a number. Hanging up, he fed more coins into the slot, then dialed another number.

"Who are you calling?" Jane whispered.

"An old friend."

The old friend's name was Vincente, and intense satisfaction was on Grant's face when he hung up. "They're pulling us out of here. In another hour we'll be home free."

"Who's 'they'?" Jane asked.

"Don't ask too many questions."

She scowled at him, then something else took her attention. "While we're here, could we clean up a little? You look awful."

There was a public bathroom—empty, she was thankful to see—and Grant washed his face while Jane brushed her hair out and quickly pulled it back into a loose braid. Then she wet a towel and painstakingly cleaned the wound on Grant's arm; the bullet hadn't penetrated, but the graze was deep and ugly. After washing it with a strong-smelling soap, she produced a small first-aid kit from her backpack.

"One of these days I'm going to see what all's in that thing," Grant growled.

Jane uncapped a small bottle of alcohol and poured it on the graze. He caught a sharp breath, and said something extremely explicit. "Don't be such a baby," Jane scolded. "You didn't make this much fuss when you were shot."

She smeared an antibiotic cream on the wound, then wrapped gauze snugly around his arm and tied the ends together. After replacing the kit, she made certain the pack was still securely buckled to her belt-loop.

Grant opened the door, then abruptly stepped back and closed it again. Jane had been right behind him, and the impact of their bodies made her stagger. He caught her arm, keeping her from falling. "Turego and a few of his men just came into the station." He looked around, his eyes narrowed and alert. "We'll go out a window."

Her heart pounding, Jane stared in dismay at the row of small, high windows that lined the restroom. They were well over her head. "I can't get up there."

"Sure you can." Grant bent down and grasped her around the knees, lifting her until she could reach the windows.

"Open one, and go through it. Quick! We only have a minute."

"But how will you get up—"

"I'll make it! Jane, get through that window!"

She twisted the handle and shoved the window open. Without giving herself time to think about how high above the ground on the other side it might be, she grasped the bottom edge of the frame and hauled herself through, jumping into the darkness and hoping she didn't kill herself on a railroad tie or something. She landed on her hands and knees in loose gravel, and she had to bite back a cry of pain as the gravel cut her palms. Quickly she scrambled out of the way, and a moment later Grant landed beside her.

"Are you all right?" he asked, hauling her to her feet.

"I think so. No broken bones," she reported breathlessly.

He started running along the side of the building, dragging her behind him. They heard a shot behind them, but didn't slow down or look back. Jane stumbled and was saved from falling only by his grip on her hand. "Can't we go back for the Ford?" she wailed.

"No. We'll have to get there on foot."

"Get where?"

"To the pick-up point."

"How far is that?"

"Not too far."

"Give it to me in yards and miles!" she demanded

He dodged down a street and pulled her into the deep shadows of an alley. He was laughing. "Maybe a mile," he said, and kissed her, his mouth hard and hungry, his tongue finding hers. He hugged her fiercely.

"Whatever you did to Turego, honey, he looks like hell."

"I think I broke his nose," she admitted.

He laughed again. "I think you did, too. It's swollen all over his face. He won't forget you for a long time!"

"Never, if I have anything to do with it. We're going to tell the government about that man," she vowed.

"Later, honey. Right now, we're getting out of here."

CHAPTER TWELVE

A HELICOPTER CAME IN low and fast, and settled lightly on its runners, looking like a giant mosquito. Grant and Jane ran across the small field, bent low against the wind whipped up by the rotors, which the pilot hadn't cut. Behind them people were pouring out of their houses to see what the uproar was about. Jane began to giggle, lightheaded with the triumph of the moment; by the time Grant boosted her into the helicopter, she was laughing so hard she was crying. They'd done it! Turego couldn't catch them now. They would be out of the country before he could mobilize his own helicopters to search for them, and he wouldn't dare pursue them across the border.

Grant flashed her a grin, telling her that he understood her idiotic laughter. He shouted, "Buckle up!" at her, then levered himself into the seat beside the pilot and gave him the thumbs-up sign. The pilot nodded, grinned, and the helicopter rose into the night. Grant put on the headset that would allow him to talk to the pilot, but there wasn't one in the back. Jane gave up trying to hear what they were saying and gripped the sides of her seat, staring out through the open sides of the helicopter. The night air swirled around her, and the world stretched out beyond the small craft. It was the first time she'd ever been in a helicopter, and it was a totally different sensation from being in a jet. She felt adrift in the velvet darkness, and she wished that it wasn't night, so she could see the land below.

The flight didn't take long, but when they set down, Jane recognized the airport and reached up to grab Grant's shoulder. "We're in San Jose!" she yelled, anxiety filling her voice. This was where it had all begun. Turego had plenty of men in the capitol!

Grant took off the headset. The pilot cut the rotors, and the noise began to decrease. They shook hands, and the pilot said, "Nice to see you again! Word filtered down that you were in the area, and that we should give you any assistance you asked for. Good luck. You'd better run. You have just enough time to get on that flight."

They jumped to the asphalt and began running toward the terminal. "What flight is that?" Jane panted.

"The flight to Mexico City that's leaving in about five minutes."

Mexico City! That sounded more like it! The thought lent her strength.

The terminal was almost deserted at that time of night, because the flight for Mexico City had already boarded. The ticket clerk stared at them as they approached, reminding Jane once again of how they looked. "Grant Sullivan and Jane Greer," Grant said tersely. "You're holding our tickets."

The clerk had regained his composure. "Yes, sir, and the plane," he returned in perfect English, handing over two ticket folders. "Ernesto will take you directly aboard."

Ernesto was an airport guard, and he led the way, running. Grant held Jane's hand to make certain she kept up with them. She had a fleeting thought about the pistol stuck in his boot, but they bypassed all checkpoints. Grant certainly had connections, she thought admiringly.

The jet was indeed waiting, and the smiling stewardess welcomed them aboard as calmly as if there was nothing unusual about them. Jane wanted to giggle again; maybe they didn't look as outlandish as she felt they did. After all, camouflage clothing was all the rage in the States. So what if Grant was sporting an almost black eye, a puffy lip and a bandage on his arm? Maybe they looked like journalists who had had a rough time in the field.

As soon as they were seated, the plane began rolling. As they buckled their seat belts, Grant and Jane exchanged glances. It was well and truly over now, but they still had some time together. The next stop was Mexico City, an enormous international city with shops, restaurants…and hotels. Her body longed for a bed, but even deeper than her weariness ran the tingling awareness that Grant would be in that bed with her. He lifted the armrest between their seats and pulled her over so her head nestled into the hollow of his shoulder. "Soon," he murmured against her temple. "In a couple of hours we'll be in Mexico. Home free."

"I'm going to call Dad as soon as we get there, so he and Mom will stop worrying." Jane sighed. "Do you have anyone to call? Does your family know where you were?"

His eyes took on that remote look. "No, they don't know anything about what I do. I'm not close to my family, not anymore."

That was sad, but Jane supposed that when someone was in the business Grant had been in, it was safer for his family not to be close to him. She turned her face into his neck and closed her eyes, holding tightly to him in an effort to let him know that he wasn't alone anymore. Had his nights been spent like hers, lying awake in bed, so achingly alone that every nerve in her body cried out against it?

She slept, and Grant did, too, exhaustion finally sweeping over him as he allowed his bruised body to relax. With her in his arms, it was easy to find the necessary relaxation. She nestled against him as trustingly as a child, but he could never forget that she was a woman, as fierce and elemental as wind or fire. She could have been the spoiled debutante he'd expected. It was what she *should* have been, and no one would have thought the less of her for being the product of her environment—no one expected her to be any more than that. But she'd risen above that, and above the crippling trauma of her childhood, to become a woman of strength and humor and passion.

She was a woman in whose arms a wary, battered, burnt-out warrior could sleep.

The sky was turning pearl pink with dawn when they landed in Mexico City. The terminal was teeming with people scurrying to catch early flights, a multitude of languages and accents assailing the air. Grant hailed a cab, which took them on a hair-raising ride through traffic that made every moment an exercise in survival—or it would have been hair-raising if Jane had had the energy to care. After what she'd been through, the Mexico City traffic looked mundane.

The city was beautiful at dawn, with its wide avenues and fragrant trees; and the white of the buildings glowed rosily in the early morning sun. The sky was already a deep blue bowl overhead, and the air carried that velvet feel that only the warmer climes achieved. Despite the odor of exhaust fumes she could smell the sweetness of orange blossoms, and Grant was warm beside her, his strong leg pressed against hers.

The desk clerk in the pristine white, high-rise hotel was reluctant to give them a room without a reservation. His black eyes kept wandering to Grant's bruised face as he rattled off excuses in rapid-fire Spanish. Grant shrugged, reached into his pocket and peeled off a couple of bills from a roll. The clerk suddenly smiled; that changed everything. Grant signed them in, and the clerk slid a key across the desk. After taking a few steps, Grant turned back. "By the way," he said easily, "I don't want any interruptions. If anyone calls or asks, we aren't here. *¿Comprende?* I'm dead tired, and I get irritable if I'm jerked out of a sound sleep."

His voice was full of silky, lazy menace, and the clerk nodded rapidly.

With Grant's arm draped across her shoulders, they walked over to the bank of elevators. He punched the button for the nineteenth floor, and the doors slid silently shut. Jane said dazedly, "We're safe."

"Having trouble believing it?"

"I'm going to get that man. He's not going to get off scot-free!"

"He won't," Grant drawled. "He'll be taken care of, through channels."

"I don't want 'channels' to take care of him! I want to do it myself!"

He smiled down at her. "You're a bloodthirsty little wench, aren't you? I almost think you enjoyed this."

"Only parts of it," she replied, giving him a slow smile.

Their room was spacious, with a terrace for sunning, a separate sitting area with a dining table and a stunningly modern bath. Jane poked her head into it and withdrew with a beatific smile on her face. "All the modern conveniences," she crowed.

Grant was studying the in-house registry for room service. Picking up the phone, he ordered two enormous breakfasts, and Jane's mouth watered at the thought. It had been almost twenty-four hours since they'd eaten. While they were waiting for their food, she began the process of making a phone call to Connecticut. It took about five minutes for the call to go through, and Jane sat with the receiver gripped tightly in her hand, taut with the need to hear her parents' voices.

"Mom? Mom, it's Jane! I'm all right—don't cry, I can't talk to you if you're crying," Jane said, and wiped away a few tears herself. "Put Dad on the line so I can tell him what's going on. We'll blubber together just as soon as I get home, I promise." She waited a few moments, smiling mistily at Grant, her dark eyes liquid.

"Jane? Is it really you?" Her father's voice boomed across the line.

"Yes, it really is. I'm in Mexico City. Grant got me out; we just flew in a few minutes ago."

Her father made a choked sound, and Jane realized that he was crying, too, but he controlled himself. "Well, what now?" he demanded. "When are you going to be here? Where are you going from there?"

"I don't know," she said, lifting her brows at Grant and taking the receiver from her ear. "Where are we going next?"

He took the phone from her. "This is Sullivan. We'll probably be here for a couple of days, getting some paperwork straightened out. We came in here without being checked for passports, but I'll have to make some calls before we can get into the States. Yes, we're okay. I'll let you know as soon as I find out something."

When he hung up, he turned to find Jane surveying him with pursed lips. "How *did* we get here without being checked for passports?"

"A few people turned their heads, that's all. They knew we were coming through. I'll report our passports as being lost, and get duplicates from the American Embassy. No big deal."

"How did you manage to set all that up so quickly? I know this wasn't the original plan."

"No, but we had some inside help." Sabin had been as good as his word, Grant reflected. All the old contacts had been there, and they had all been notified to give him whatever he needed.

"Your...former business associates?" Jane hazarded a guess.

"The less you know, the better. You pick up on this too damned quickly. Like hot-wiring that truck. Had you ever done it before?"

"No, but I watched you do it the first time," she explained, her eyes full of innocence.

He grunted. "Don't waste your time giving me that wide-eyed look."

A tap on the door and a singsong voice announced that room service had arrived in record time. Grant checked through the fish-eye viewer, then unbolted the door and let the young boy in. The aroma of hot coffee filled the room, and Jane's mouth started watering. She hovered over the boy as he set the food out on the table.

"Look at this," she crooned. "Fresh oranges and melon. Toast. Apricot Danish. Eggs. Butter. Real coffee!"

"You're drooling," Grant teased, giving the boy a generous tip, but he was just as ravenous, and between them they destroyed the array of food. Every crumb was gone and the pot of coffee was empty before they looked at each other and smiled.

"I feel almost human again," Jane sighed. "Now for a hot shower!"

She began unlacing her boots, pulling them off and sighing in relief as she wiggled her toes. Glancing at him, she saw that he was watching her with that lopsided smile that she loved so much. Her heart kicked into time-and-a-half rhythm. "Aren't you going to shower with me?" she asked innocently, sauntering into the bathroom.

She was already under the deliciously warm spray of water, her head tilted up so it hit her directly in the face, when the shower door slid open and he joined her. She turned, wiping the moisture from her eyes, a smile ready on her lips, but the smile faded when she saw the mottled bruises on his ribcage and abdomen. "Oh, Grant," she whispered, reaching out to run her fingers lightly over the dark, ugly splotches. "I'm so sorry."

He gave her a quizzical look. He was sore and stiff, but nothing was broken and the bruises would fade. He'd suffered much worse than this, many times. Of course, if Turego had been able to carry the beating as far as he'd wanted, Grant knew that he probably would have died of internal injuries. But it hadn't happened, so he didn't worry about it. He caught her chin, turning her face up to him. "We're both covered with bruises, honey, in case you haven't noticed. I'm okay." He covered her mouth with his, tasting her sweetness with his tongue, easing her against him.

Their wet, naked bodies created a marvelous friction against each other, heating them, tightening the coil of desire. The rather boring process of soaping and rinsing became a lingering series of strokes, her hands slipping over the muscles and intriguing hardness of his body, his finding the soft curves and slopes of hers, the enticing depths. He lifted her off her feet and bent her back over his arm, kissing her breasts and sucking at her nipples until they were hard and reddened, tasting the freshness of newly soaped skin and the sweetness of her flesh that no soap could ever disguise. Jane writhed against him, her legs twining with his, and heat fogged his mind as he thrust himself against the juncture of her thighs.

She wanted him, wanted him, wanted him. Her body ached and burned. The bed was suddenly too far away.

Her legs parted, lifting to wrap around his waist, and with a hoarse cry he pinned her to the wall. She shuddered as he drove into her, going as deep as he could with a single, powerful thrust, as if any distance at all between them was far too much. Digging his fingers into her hair, he pulled her head back and kissed her, his mouth wild and rough, the kiss deep, his tongue twining with hers, the water beating down on them. The power of his thrusts made her consciousness dim, but she clung to him, whimpering, begging him not to stop. He couldn't have stopped, couldn't even have slowed, his body demanding release inside her. The red mists that clouded his mind blocked out everything but the hot ecstasy of the way her body sheathed him, so softly, so tightly.

She cried out again and again as the almost unbearable waves of pleasure crashed over her. She clung tightly to his shoulders, trembling and shivering, the velvet clasp of her body driving him to the edge. He poured himself into her, heaving against her, feeling that he was dying a little, and yet so intensely alive that he almost screamed from the conflict.

They barely made it to the bed. Drying off had taken all their energy, and Jane was so weak she could barely walk. Grant was shaking in every muscle of his big body. They tumbled onto the bed, not caring that their wet hair soaked the pillows.

Grant reached out for her. "Crawl up here," he rumbled, hauling her on top of him. Blissfully, her eyes closing, she made herself comfortable on the hard expanse of his chest. He adjusted her legs, parting them, and her lashes fluttered open as he eased into her. A purr of pleasure escaped her lips, but she was so sleepy, so tired… "Now we can sleep," he said, his lips moving on her hair.

THE ROOM WAS HOT when they awoke, the Mexican sun broiling through the closed curtains. Their skin was stuck together with perspiration and made a wet, sucking noise as Grant lifted her off him. He got up and turned the air-conditioning on full blast, and stood for a moment with the cold air hitting his naked body. Then he came back to the bed and turned her onto her back.

They scarcely left the bed that day. They made love, napped and woke to make love again. She couldn't get enough of him, nor he, it seemed, of her. There was no sense of urgency now to their lovemaking, only a deep reluctance to be parted from each other. He taught her the unlimited reaches of her own sensuality, tasting her all over, making love to her with his mouth until she was shivering and shuddering with pleasure, mindless, helpless. She told him that she loved him. She couldn't keep the words unsaid, not now, when she'd already told him anyway and soon the world would intrude on them again.

Night came, and finally they left the room. Walking hand in hand in the warm Mexican night, they sought out some shops that were open late. Jane bought a pink sundress that made her tanned skin look like honey, a pair of sandals and new underwear. Grant wasn't much on shopping, so she blithely picked out jeans, loafers and a white polo shirt for him. "You might as well change," she instructed, pushing him toward the dressing room. "We're going out to eat tonight."

There wasn't any talking her out of it, either. It wasn't until he was seated across from her in a dimly lit restaurant with a bottle of wine between them that he realized this was the first time in years that he'd been with a woman in a strictly social setting. They had nothing to do but eat and talk, sip the wine, and think about what they were going to do when they got back to the hotel. Even after he'd

etired, he'd kept to himself on the farm, sometimes going
for weeks without seeing another human being. When the
need for supplies had forced him to go into town, he'd gone
straight there and back, a lot of times without speaking to
anyone. He hadn't been able to stand anyone else around
him. But now he was relaxed, not even thinking about the
strangers surrounding him, accepting their presence but
not noticing them, because his mind and his senses were
on Jane.

She was radiant, incandescent with energy. Her dark
eyes shone; her tanned skin glowed; her laughter sparkled.
Her breasts thrust against the bodice of the sundress, her
nipples puckered by the coolness of the restaurant, and
desire began to stir inside him again. They didn't have
much more time together; soon they would be back in the
States, and his job would be finished. It was too soon, far
too soon. He hadn't had his fill yet of the taste of her, the
wild sweetness of her body beneath him, or the way her
laughter somehow eased all the knots of tension inside
him.

They went back to the hotel, and back to bed. He made
love to her furiously, trying to sate himself, trying to hoard
enough memories to hold him during the long, empty years
ahead. Being alone was a habit deeply ingrained in him;
he wanted her, but couldn't see taking her back to the farm
with him, and there was no way he could fit into her world.
She liked having people around her, while he was more
comfortable with a wall at his back. She was outgoing,
while he was controlled, secretive.

She knew, too, that it was almost over. Lying on his
chest, with the darkness wrapped around them like a blanket, she talked. It was a gift that she gave him, the tales of
her childhood, where she'd gone to school, her food and
music preferences, what she liked to read. Because she

talked, he found it easier to return the favor, his voice low and rusty as he told her about the white-haired young boy he'd been, his skin burned dark by the hot, south Georgia summers, running wild in the swamp. He'd learned to hunt and fish almost as soon as he'd learned how to walk. He told her about playing football during high school, chasing after the cheerleaders, getting drunk and raising hell, then trying to sneak into the house so his mother wouldn't catch him.

Her fingers played in the hair on his chest, aware that silence had fallen because he'd reached the point in his story where his life had changed. There were no more easy tales of growing up.

"Then what happened?" she whispered.

His chest rose and fell. "Vietnam happened. I was drafted when I was eighteen. I was too damned good at sneaking through jungles, so that's where they put me. I went home, once, for R & R, but the folks were just the same as always, while I was nothing like what I had been. We couldn't even talk to each other. So I went back."

"And stayed?"

"Yeah. I stayed." His voice was flat.

"How did you get into the secret-agent business, or whatever you call it?"

"Covert activities. High-risk missions. The war ended, and I came home, but there was nothing for me to do. What was I going to do, work in a grocery store, when I'd been trained to such an edge that people would be taking their lives in their hands to walk up to me and ask the price of eggs? I guess I'd have settled down eventually, but I didn't want to hang around to find out. I was embarrassing the folks, and I was a stranger to them anyway. When an old colleague contacted me, I took him up on his offer."

"But you're retired now. Did you go back to Georgia?"

"Just for a few days, to let them know where I'd be. I couldn't settle there; too many people knew me, and I wanted to be left alone. So I bought a farm close to the mountains in Tennessee, and I've been hibernating there ever since. Until your dad hired me to fetch you home."

"Have you ever married? Been engaged?"

"No," he said, and kissed her. "That's enough questions. Go to sleep."

"Grant?"

"Hmmm?"

"Do you think he's really given up?"

"Who?"

"Turego."

Amusement laced his voice. "Honey, I promise you, he'll be taken care of. Don't worry about it. Now that you're safe and sound, steps can be taken to neutralize him."

"You're using some ominous-sounding phrases. What do 'taken care of' and 'neutralize' mean?"

"That he's going to be spending some time in those gracious Central American jails that everyone hears so much about. Go to sleep."

She obeyed, her lips curved in a contented smile, his arms securely around her.

SOMEONE HAD PULLED strings again. It could have been her father, or the mysterious "friend" of Grant's who kept arranging things, or possibly Grant had intimidated someone at the embassy. However it happened, the next afternoon they had passports. They could have taken the next flight to Dallas, but instead they spent another night together, making love in that king-size bed, the door securely bolted. She didn't want to leave. As long as they were still in Mexico City, she could pretend that it wasn't over, that the job wasn't finished. But her parents were waiting for her, and Grant had his own life to go back to. She had to find another job, as well as take care of the little chore that had gotten her into so much trouble to begin with. There was no way they could stay in Mexico.

Still, tears burned the back of her eyes when they boarded the jet that would take them to Dallas. She knew that Grant had booked separate flights for them from Dallas; she was going on to New York, and he was flying to Knoxville. Their goodbyes would be said in the vast, busy Dallas/Ft. Worth airport, and she couldn't stand it. If she didn't get a tight hold on herself she'd be squalling like a baby, and he wouldn't want that. If he wanted more of her than what he'd already had, he'd have asked her, because she'd made it more than obvious that she was willing to give him whatever he wanted. But he hadn't asked, so he didn't want her. She'd known that this time would come, and she'd accepted it, taken the risk, grabbed for what happiness she could get. Pay-up time had come.

She controlled her tears. She read the airline magazine; and was even able to comprehend what she was reading. For a while she held his hand, but she released it when the in-flight meal was served. She ordered a gin and tonic, gulped it down, then ordered another.

Grant eyed her narrowly, but she gave him a bright, glittering smile, determined not to let him see that she was shattering on the inside.

Too soon, far too soon, they landed at Dallas and filed out of the plane through the portable tunnel. Jane clutched the dirty, battered backpack, for the first time realizing that his boots and fatigues were in it along with her clothing. "I need your address," she chattered brightly, nervously. "To mail your clothes to you. Unless you want to buy a bag in the airport shop, that is. We have plenty of time before our flights."

He checked his watch. "You have twenty-eight minutes, so we'd better find your gate. Do you have your ticket?"

"Yes, it's right here. What about your clothes?"

"I'll be in touch with your father. Don't worry about it."

Yes, of course; there was the matter of payment for dragging her out of Costa Rica. His face was hard and expressionless, his amber eyes cool. She held out her hand, not noticing how it was shaking. "Well, goodbye, then. It's—" She broke off. What could she say? *It's been nice meeting you?* She swallowed. "It's been fun."

He looked down at her extended hand, then back up at her, disbelief edging into the coolness of his eyes. He said slowly, "The hell you say," caught her hand, and jerked her into his arms. His mouth was hot, covering hers, his tongue curling slowly into her mouth as if they weren't surrounded by curiously gawking people. She clung to him, shaking.

He set her away from him. His jaw was clenched. "Go on. Your folks are waiting for you. I'll be in touch in a few days." The last slipped out; he'd intended this to be the final break, but her dark eyes were so lost and full of pain, and she'd kissed him so hungrily, that he couldn't stop the words. One more time, then. He'd give himself one more time with her.

She nodded, drawing herself up. She wasn't going to break down and cry all over him. He almost wished she would cry, because then he'd have an excuse to hold her again. But she was stronger than that. "Goodbye," she said, then turned and walked away from him.

She barely saw where she was going; people blurred in her vision, and she stubbornly blinked her eyes to keep the tears back. Well, she was alone again. He'd said he'd be in touch, but she knew he wouldn't. It was over. She had to accept that and be grateful for the time she'd had. It had been obvious from the first that Grant Sullivan wasn't a man to be tied down.

Someone touched her arm, the touch warm and strong, a man's touch. She stopped, wild hope springing into her breast, but when she turned she found that it wasn't Grant who had stopped her. The man had dark hair and eyes, and his skin was dark, his features strongly Latin. "Jane Greer?" he asked politely.

She nodded, wondering how he'd known her name and recognized her. His grip tightened on her arm. "Would you please come with me," he said, and though his voice remained polite, it was an order, not a question.

Alarm skittered through her, jerking her out of her misery. She smiled at the man and swung the backpack by its straps, catching him on the side of the head with it and sending him staggering. From the solid 'thunk' it made, she knew Grant's boots had hit him.

"Grant!" she screamed, her voice slicing through the bustle of thousands of people. *"Grant!"*

The man caught himself and lunged for her. Jane began running back in the direction she'd come from, dodging around people. Up ahead she saw Grant coming through the crowd like a running back, shoving people out of his path. The man caught up with her, catching her arm; then Grant was there. People were screaming and scattering, and the airport guards were running toward them. Grant sent the man sprawling, then grabbed Jane's arm and ran for the nearest exit, ducking past the milling crowds and ignoring the shouts to stop.

"What the hell's going on?" he roared, jerking her out into the bright Texas sunlight. The humid heat settled over them.

"I don't know! That man just came up to me and asked if my name was Jane Greer; then he caught my arm and told me to come with him, so I hit him in the head with the backpack and started screaming."

"Makes perfect sense to me," he muttered, flagging a cab and putting her in it, then crawling in beside her.

"Where to, folks?" the cab driver asked.

"Downtown."

"Any particular place downtown?"

"I'll tell you where to stop."

The driver shrugged. As they pulled away from the curb there seemed to be a lot of people spilling out of the terminal, but Jane didn't look back. She was still shaking. "It can't be Turego again, can it?"

Grant shrugged. "It's possible, if he has enough money. I'm going to make a phone call."

She'd thought she was safe, that they were both safe. After the two peaceful days spent in Mexico, the sudden fear seemed that much sharper and more acrid. She couldn't stop trembling.

They didn't go all the way into Dallas. Grant instructed the driver to drop them at a shopping mall. "Why a shopping mall?" Jane asked, looking around.

"There are telephones here, and it's safer than standing in a phone booth on the side of a street." He put his arm around her and hugged her briefly to him. "Don't look so worried, honey."

They went inside and found a bank of pay telephones, but it was a busy day and all the lines were in use. They waited while a teenager argued extensively with her mother about how late she could stay out that night, but at last she hung up and stormed away, evidently having lost the argument. Grant stepped in and commandeered the telephone before anyone else could reach it. Standing close by him, Jane watched as he dropped in the coins, punched in a number, then dropped in more coins. He leaned casually against the fieldstone nook that housed the telephone, listening to the rings on the other end.

"Sullivan," he finally drawled when the phone was answered. "She was nearly grabbed in DFW." He listened a moment; then his eyes flicked to Jane. "Okay, I got it. We'll be there. By the way, that was a dumb move. She could've killed the guy." He hung up, and his lips twitched.

"Well?" Jane demanded.

"You just belted an agent."

"An agent? You mean, one of your friend's men?"

"Yeah. We're taking a little detour. You're going to be debriefed. It was left up to some other people to pick you up, and they decided to pick you up after we'd parted company, since I'm no longer in the business and this doesn't officially concern me. Sabin will pin their ears back."

"Sabin? Is he your friend?"

He was smiling down at her. "He's the one." He stroked her cheekbone very gently with the backs of his fingers. "And that's a name you're going to forget, honey. Why don't you call your parents and let them know that you won't be in tonight? It'll be tomorrow; you can call them again when we know something definite."

"Are you going, too?"

"I wouldn't miss it." He grinned a little wolfishly, already anticipating Kell's reaction to Jane.

"But where are we going?"

"Virginia, but don't tell your parents that. Just tell them that you missed your flight."

She reached for the phone, then stopped. "Your friend must be pretty important."

"He's got some power," Grant understated.

So, they must know about the microfilm. Jane punched in her credit card number. She'd be glad to get the whole thing over with, and at least Grant was going to be with her one more day. Just one more day! It was a reprieve, but she didn't know if she'd have the strength for another good-bye.

CHAPTER THIRTEEN

THE VIRGINIA COUNTRYSIDE around the place was quiet and serene, the trees green, the flowering shrubs well-tended. It looked rather like her father's Connecticut estate. Everyone was polite, and several people greeted Grant, but Jane noticed that even the ones who spoke to him did so hesitantly, as if they were a little wary of him.

Kell's office was right where it had always been, and the door still had no name on it. The agent who had escorted them knocked quietly. "Sullivan is here, sir."

"Send them in."

The first thing Jane noticed was the old-fashioned charm of the room. The ceilings were high; the mantel was surely the original one that had been built with the house over a hundred years before. Tall glass doors behind the big desk let in the late afternoon sun. They also placed the man behind the desk in silhouette, while anyone who came in the door was spotlighted by the blazing sun, something George had told her about. He rose to his feet as they entered, a tall man, maybe not quite as tall as Grant, but lean and hard with a whipcord toughness that wasn't maintained by sitting behind a desk.

He stepped forward to greet them. "You look like hell, Sullivan," he said, and the two men shook hands; then he turned his eyes on her, and for the first time Jane felt his power. His eyes were so black that there was no light in them at all; they absorbed light, drawing it into the depths of the irises. His hair was thick and black, his complexion dark, and there was an intense energy about him that seared her.

"Ms. Greer," he said, holding out his hand.

"Mr. Sabin," she returned, calmly shaking his hand.

"I have a very embarrassed agent in Dallas."

"He shouldn't be," Grant drawled behind her. "She let him off easy."

"Grant's boots were in the pack," Jane explained. "That's what stunned him so badly when I hit him in the head."

There was the first hint in Sabin's eyes that Jane wasn't quite what he'd expected. Grant stood behind her, his arms calmly folded, and waited.

Sabin examined her open expression, the catlike slant of her dark eyes, the light dusting of freckles across her cheekbones. Then he quickly glanced at Grant, who was planted like the Rock of Gibraltar behind her. He could question her, but he had the feeling that Grant wouldn't let her be harrassed in any way. It wasn't like Sullivan to get involved, but he was out of the business now, so the old rules didn't apply. She wasn't a great beauty, but there was a lively charm about her that almost made Sabin want to smile. Maybe she'd gotten close to Sullivan. Sabin didn't trust that openness, however, because he knew more about her now than he had in the beginning.

"Ms. Greer," he began slowly, "did you know that George Persall was—"

"Yes, I did," Jane interrupted cheerfully. "I helped him sometimes, but not often, because he liked to use different methods every time. I believe this is what you want." She opened the backpack and began digging in it. "I know it's in here. There!" She produced the small roll of film, placing it on his desk.

Both men looked thunderstruck. "You've just been carrying it around?" Sabin asked in disbelief.

"Well, I didn't have a chance to hide it. Sometimes I put

it in my pocket. That way Turego could search my room all he wanted and he'd never find anything. All of you spy types try to make everything too complicated. George always told me to keep it simple."

Grant began to chuckle. He couldn't help it; it was funny. "Jane, why didn't you tell me you had the microfilm?"

"I thought it would be safer for you if you didn't know about it."

Again Sabin looked thunderstruck, as if he couldn't believe anyone would actually feel the need to protect Grant Sullivan. As Kell was normally the most impassive of men, Grant knew that Jane had tilted him off balance, just as she did everyone she met. Sabin coughed to cover his reaction.

"Ms. Greer," he asked cautiously, "do you know what's on the film?"

"No. Neither did George."

Grant was laughing again. "Go ahead," he told Sabin. "Tell her about the film. Or, better yet, show her. She'll enjoy it."

Sabin shook his head, then picked up the film and pulled it out, unwinding it. Grant produced his cigarette lighter, leaned forward, and set the end of the film on fire. The three watched as the flames slowly ate up the length of celluloid until it burned close to Sabin's fingers and he dropped it into a large ashtray. "The film," Sabin explained, "was a copy of something we don't want anyone else to know. All we wanted was for it to be destroyed before anyone saw it."

With the stench of burning plastic in her nostrils, Jane silently watched the last of the film curl and crumble. All they'd wanted was for it to be destroyed, and she'd hauled it through a jungle and across half a continent—just to hand it over and watch it burn. Her lips twitched; she was afraid of making a scene, so she tried to control the urge. But it was irresistible; it rolled upward, and a giggle escaped. She turned, looking at Grant, and between them flashed the memory of everything they'd been through. She giggled again, then they were both laughing, Jane hanging on to his shirt because she was laughing so hard her knees had gone limp.

"I fell down a cliff," she gasped. "We stole a truck...shot another truck...I broke Turego's nose...all to watch it *burn*!"

Grant went into another spasm of laughter, holding his sore ribs and bending double. Sabin watched them clinging to each other and laughing uproariously. Curiosity seized him. "Why did you shoot a truck?" he asked; then suddenly he was laughing, too.

An agent paused outside the door, his head tilted, listening. No, it was impossible. Sabin never laughed.

THEY LAY IN BED in a hotel in the middle of Washington, D.C., pleasantly tired. They had made love as soon as the door was locked behind them, falling on the bed and removing only the necessary clothing. But that had been hours before, and now they were completely nude, slipping gradually into sleep.

Grant's hand moved up and down her back in a lazy pattern. "Just how involved were you in Persall's activities?"

"Not very," she murmured. "Oh, I knew about them. I had to know, so I could cover for him if I had to. And he sometimes used me as a courier, but not very often. Still, he talked to me a lot, telling me things. He was a strange, lonely man."

"Was he your lover?"

She lifted her head from his chest, surprised. "George? Of course not!"

"Why 'of course not'? He was a man, wasn't he? And he was in your bedroom when he died."

She paused. "George had a problem, a medical one. He wasn't capable of being anyone's lover."

"So that part of the report was wrong, too."

"Deliberately. He used me as a sort of shield."

He put his hand in her hair and held her for his kiss. "I'm glad. He was too old for you."

Jane watched him with wise, dark eyes. "Even if he hadn't been, I wasn't interested. You might as well know, you're the only lover I've ever had. Until I met you, I'd never...wanted anyone."

"And when you met me...?" he murmured.

"I wanted." She lowered her head and kissed him, wrapping her arms around him, slithering her body over his until she felt his hardening response.

"I wanted, too," he said, his words a mere breath over her skin.

"I love you." The words were a cry of pain, launched by desperation, because she knew this was definitely the last time unless she took the chance. "Will you marry me?"

"Jane, don't."

"Don't what? Tell you that I love you? Or ask you to marry me?" She sat up, moving her legs astride him, and shook her dark hair back behind her shoulders.

"We can't live together," he explained, his eyes turning dark gold. "I can't give you what you need, and you'd be miserable."

"I'll be miserable anyway," she said reasonably, striving for a light tone. "I'd rather be miserable with you than miserable without you."

"I'm a loner. Marriage is a partnership, and I'd rather go it alone. Face it, honey. We're good together in bed, but that's all there is."

"Maybe for you. I love you." Despite herself, she couldn't keep the echo of pain out of her voice.

"Do you? We were under a lot of stress. It's human

nature to turn to each other. I'd have been surprised if we hadn't made love."

"Please, spare me your combat psychology! I'm not a child, or stupid! I know when I love someone, and damn it, I love you! You don't have to like it, but don't try to talk me out of it!"

"All right." He lay on his back, looking up into her angry eyes. "Do you want me to get another room?"

"No. This is our last night together, and we're going to spend it *together*."

"Even if we're fighting?"

"Why not?" she dared.

"I don't want to fight," he said, lunging up and twisting. Jane found herself on her back, blinking up at him in astonishment. Slowly he entered her, pushing her legs high. She closed her eyes, excitement spiraling through her. He was right; the time was far better spent making love.

She didn't try again to convince him that they had a future together. She knew from experience just how hardheaded he was; he'd have to figure it out for himself. So she spent her time loving him, trying to make certain that he never forgot her, that no other woman could begin to give him the pleasure that she did. This would be her goodbye.

Late in the night she leaned over him. "You're afraid," she accused softly. "You've seen so much that you're afraid to let yourself love anyone, because you know how easily a world can be wrecked."

His voice was tired. "Jane, let it be."

"All right. That's my last word, except for this: if you decide to take a chance, come get me."

She crept out of bed early the next morning and left him sleeping. She knew that he was too light a sleeper not to have awakened sometime during the shower she took, or while she was dressing, but he didn't roll over or in any way indicate that he was awake, so she preserved the pretence between them. Without even kissing him, she slipped out the door. After all, they'd already said their goodbyes.

At the sound of the door closing Grant rolled over in the bed, his eyes bleak as he stared at the empty room.

JANE AND HER PARENTS fell into each other's arms, laughing and crying and hugging each other exuberantly. Her return called for a family celebration that lasted hours, so it was late that night before she and her father had any time alone. Jane had few secrets from her father; he was too shrewd, too realistic. By silent, instinctive agreement, they kept from her mother the things that would upset her, but Jane was like her father in that she had an inner toughness.

She told him how the entire situation in Costa Rica had come about, and even told him about the trek through the rain forest. Because he was shrewd, he picked up on the nuances in her voice when she mentioned Grant.

"You're in love with Sullivan, aren't you?"

She nodded, sipping her glass of wine. "You met him. What did you think about him?" The answer was important to her, because she trusted her father's judgment of character.

"I thought him unusual. There's something in his eyes that's almost scary. But I trusted him with my daughter's life, if that tells you what you want to know, and I'd do so again."

"Would you mind having him in the family?"

"I'd welcome him with open arms. I think he could keep you in one place," James said grumpily.

"Well, I asked him to marry me, but he turned me down. I'm going to give him a while to stew over it; then I'm going to fight dirty."

Her father grinned, the quick, cheerful grin that his daughter had inherited. "What are you planning?"

"I'm going to chase that man like he's never been chased before. I think I'll stay here for a week or two; then I'm going to Europe."

"But he's not in Europe!"

"I know. I'll chase him from a distance. The idea is for him to know how much he misses me, and he'll miss me a lot more when he finds out how far away I am."

"But how is he going to find out?"

"I'll arrange that somehow. And even if it doesn't work, a trip to Europe is never a waste!"

IT WAS ODD HOW MUCH he missed her. She'd never been to the farm, but sometimes it seemed haunted by her. He'd think he heard her say something and turn to find no one there. At night…God, the nights were awful! He couldn't sleep, missing her soft weight sprawled on top of him.

He tried to lose himself in hard physical work. Chores piled up fast on a farm, and he'd been gone for two weeks. With the money he'd been paid for finding Jane, he was able to free the farm from debt and still have plenty left over, so he could have hired someone to do the work for him. But the work had been therapy for him when he'd first come here, still weak from his wounds, and so tightly drawn that a pine cone dropping from a tree in the night had been enough to send him diving from the bed, reaching for his knife.

So he labored in the sun, doing the backbreaking work of digging new holes for the fence posts, putting up new sections of fencing, patching and painting the barn. He reroofed the house, worked on the old tractor that had come with the farm, and thought about doing more planting the next spring. All he'd planted so far was a few vegetables for himself, but if he was going to own a farm, he might as well farm it. A man wouldn't get rich at it, not on this scale, but he knew how to do it. Working the earth gave him a measure of peace, as if it put him in contact with the boy he'd once been, before war had changed his life.

In the distance loomed the mountains, the great, misty mountains where the ghosts of the Cherokee still walked. The vast slopes were uninhabited now, but then, only a few hardy souls other than the Cherokee had ever called the mountains home. Jane would like the mountains. They were older, wreathed in silvery veils, once the mightiest mountain range on earth, but worn down by more years than people could imagine. There were places in those mountains where time stood still.

The mountains, and the earth, had healed him, and the process had been so gradual that he hadn't realized he was healed until now. Perhaps the final healing had come when Jane had shown him how to laugh again.

He had told her to let it be, and she had. She had left in the quiet morning, without a word, because he'd told her to go. She loved him; he knew that. He'd pretended that it was something else, the pressure of stress that had brought them together, but even then he'd known better, and so had she.

Well, hell! He missed her so badly that he hurt, and if this wasn't love, then he hoped he never loved anyone, because he didn't think he could stand it. He couldn't get her out of his mind, and her absence was an empty ache that he couldn't fill, couldn't ease.

She'd been right; he was afraid to take the chance, afraid to leave himself open to more hurt. But he was hurting anyway. He'd be a fool if he let her get away.

But first there were old rifts to try to heal.

He loved his parents, and he knew they loved him, but

they were simple people, living close to the earth, and he'd turned into someone they didn't recognize. His sister was a pretty, blond woman, content with her job at the local library, her quiet husband, and her three children. It had been a couple of years since he'd even seen his nephew and two nieces. When he'd stopped by the year before to tell his parents that he'd retired and had bought a farm in Tennessee, they'd all been so uncomfortable that he'd stayed for only a few hours, and had left without seeing Rae, or the kids.

So he drove down to Georgia, and stood on the weathered old porch, knocking on the door of the house where he'd grown up. His mother came to the door, wiping her hands on her apron. It was close to noon; as always, as it had been from the time he could remember, she was cooking lunch for his father. But they didn't call it lunch in this part of the country; the noon meal was dinner, and the evening meal was supper.

Surprise lit her honey-brown eyes, the eyes that were so like his, only darker. "Why, son, this is a surprise. What on earth are you knocking for? Why didn't you just come in?"

"I didn't want to get shot," he said honestly.

"Now, you know I don't let your daddy keep a gun in the house. The only gun is that old shotgun, out in the barn. What makes you say a thing like that?" Turning, she went back to the kitchen, and he followed. Everything in the old frame house was familiar, as familiar to him as his own face.

He settled his weight in one of the straight chairs that were grouped around the kitchen table. This was the table he'd eaten at as a boy. "Mama," he said slowly, "I've been shot at so much that I guess I think that's the normal way of things."

She was still for a moment, her head bent; then she resumed making her biscuits. "I know, son. We've always known. But we didn't know how to reach you, how to bring you back to us again. You was still a boy when you left, but you came back a man, and we didn't know how to talk to you."

"There wasn't any talking to me. I was still too raw, too wild. But the farm that I bought, up in Tennessee…it's helped."

He didn't have to elaborate, and he knew it. Grace Sullivan had the simple wisdom of people who lived close to the land. She was a farm girl, had never pretended to be anything else, and he loved her because of it.

"Will you stay for dinner?"

"I'd like to stay for a couple of days, if I won't be messing up any plans."

"Grant Sullivan, you know your daddy and I don't have any *plans* to go off gallivanting anywhere."

She sounded just like she had when he had been five years old and had managed to get his clothes dirty as fast as she could put them on him. He remembered how she'd looked then, her hair dark, her face smooth and young, her honey-gold eyes sparkling at him.

He laughed, because everything was getting better, and his mother glanced at him in surprise. It had been twenty years since she'd heard her son laugh. "That's good," he said cheerfully. "Because it'll take me at least that long to tell you about the woman I'm going to marry."

"What!" She whirled on him, laughing, too. "You're pulling my leg! Are you really going to get married? Tell me about her!"

"Mama, you'll love her," he said. "She's nuts."

HE'D NEVER THOUGHT that finding her would be so hard. Somehow he'd thought that it would be as simple as calling her father and getting her address from him, but he should have known. With Jane, nothing was ever as it should be.

To begin with, it took him three days to get in touch with her father. Evidently her parents had been out of town, and the housekeeper either hadn't known where Jane was, or she'd been instructed not to give out any information. Considering Jane's circumstances, he thought it was probably the latter. So he cooled his heels for three days until he was finally able to speak to her father, but that wasn't much better.

"She's in Europe," James explained easily enough. "She stayed here for about a week, then took off again."

Grant felt like cursing. "Where in Europe?"

"I don't really know. She was vague about it. You know Jane."

He was afraid that he did. "Has she called?"

"Yes, a couple of times."

"Mr. Hamilton, I need to talk to her. When she calls again, would you find out where she is and tell her to stay put until I get in touch?"

"That could be a couple of weeks. Jane doesn't call regularly. But if it's urgent, you may know someone who knows exactly where she is. She did mention that she's talked to a friend of yours…let's see, what was his name?"

"Sabin," Grant supplied, grinding his teeth in rage.

"Yes, that's it. Sabin. Why don't you give him a call? It may save you a lot of time."

Grant didn't want to call Kell; he wanted to see him face to face and strangle him. Damn him! If he'd recruited Jane into that gray network…!

He was wasting time and money chasing over the country after her, and his temper was short when he reached Virginia. He didn't have the clearance to go in, so he called Kell directly. "Sullivan. Clear me through. I'll be there in five minutes."

"Grant—"

Grant hung up, not wanting to hear it over the phone.

Ten minutes later he was leaning over Kell's desk. "Where is she?"

"Monte Carlo."

"Damn it!" he yelled, pounding his fist on the desk. "How could you drag her into this?"

"I didn't drag her," Kell said coolly, his dark eyes watchful. "*She* called *me*. She said she'd noticed something funny and thought I might like to know. She was right; I was highly interested."

"How could she call you? Your number isn't exactly listed."

"I asked her the same thing. It seems she was standing beside you when you called me from Dallas."

Grant swore, rubbing his eyes. "I should have known. I should have been expecting it after she hot-wired that truck. She watched me do it, just once, then did it herself the next time."

"If it's any consolation, she didn't get it exactly right. She remembered the numbers, but not the right order. She told me I was the fifth call she'd placed."

"Oh, hell. What kind of situation is she in?"

"A pretty explosive one. She's stumbled across a high-rolling counterfeiter. He has some high-quality plates of the pound, the franc and several denominations of our currency. He's setting up the deal now. Some of our comrades are very interested."

"I can imagine. Just what does she think she can do?"

"She's going to try to steal the plates."

Grant went white. "And you were going to let her?"

"Damn it, Grant!" Kell exploded. "It's not a matter of letting her and you know it! The problem is stopping her without tipping the guy off and sending him so deep underground we can't find him. I've got agents tiptoeing all around her, but the guy thinks he's in love with her, and his buyer has watchdogs sniffing around, and we simply can't snatch her without blowing the whole thing sky high!"

"All right, all right. I'll get her out of it."

"How?" Kell demanded.

"I'll get the plates myself, then jerk her out of there and make damned certain she never calls you again!"

"I would deeply appreciate it," Kell said. "What are you going to do with her?"

"Marry her."

Something lightened in Kell's dark face, and he leaned back in his chair, looping his hands behind his head. "Well, I'll be damned. Do you know what you're getting into? That woman doesn't think like most people."

That was a polite way of saying it, but Kell wasn't telling him anything he didn't already know. Within moments of meeting her, Grant had realized that Jane was just a little unorthodox. But he loved her, and she couldn't get into too much trouble on the farm.

"Yeah, I know. By the way, you're invited to the wedding."

JANE SMILED AT FELIX, her eyes twinkling at him. He was such a funny little guy; she really liked him, despite the fact that he was a counterfeiter and was planning to do something that could really damage her country. He was slightly built, with shy eyes and a faint stutter. He loved to gamble, but had atrocious luck; that is, he'd had atrocious luck until Jane had started sitting beside him. Since then he'd been winning regularly, and he was now devoted to her.

Despite everything she was having fun in Monte Carlo. Grant was being slow coming around, but she hadn't been bored. If she had trouble sleeping, if she sometimes woke to find her cheeks wet, that was something she had to accept. She missed him. It was as if part of herself were gone. Without him there was no one she could trust, no one in whose arms she could rest.

It was a dangerous tightrope she was walking, and the excitement of it helped keep her from settling into depression. The only thing was, how much longer was it going to last? If she saw that Felix was finally going to make up his mind who to sell to, she would be forced to do something— fast—before the plates got into the wrong hands.

Felix was winning again, as he had every night since he'd met Jane. The elegant casino was buzzing, and the chandeliers rivaled in brilliance the diamonds that were roped about necks and dripping from ears. The men in their formal evening wear, the women in their gowns and jewels, casually wagering fortunes on the roll of the dice or the turn of a card, all created an atmosphere that was unequaled anywhere in the world. Jane fit into it easily, slim and graceful in her black silk gown, her shoulders and back bare. Jet earrings dangled to her shoulders, and her hair was piled on top of her head in a careless, becoming twist. She wore no necklace, no bracelets, only the earrings that touched the glowing gold of her skin.

Across the table Bruno was watching them closely. He was becoming impatient with Felix's dithering, and his impatience was likely to force her hand.

Well, why not? She'd really waited as long as she could. If Grant had been interested, he'd have shown up before now.

She stood and bent down to kiss Felix on the forehead. "I'm going back to the hotel," she said, smiling at him. "I have a headache."

He looked up, dismayed. "Are you really ill?"

"It's just a headache. I was on the beach too long today. You don't have to leave; stay and enjoy your game."

He began to look panicky, and she winked at him. "Why don't you see if you can win now without me? Who knows, it may not be me at all."

He brightened, the poor little man, and turned back to his game with renewed fervor. Jane left the casino and hurried back to the hotel, going straight to her room. She always allowed for being followed, because she sensed that she always was. Bruno was a very suspicious man. Swiftly she stripped off her gown, and she was reaching into the closet for a dark pair of pants and a shirt when a hand closed over her mouth and a muscular arm clamped around her waist.

"Don't scream," a low, faintly raspy voice said in her ear, and her heart jumped. The hand left her mouth, and Jane turned in his arms, burying her face against his neck, breathing in the delicious, familiar male scent of him.

"What are you doing here?" she breathed.

"What do you think I'm doing here?" he asked irritably, but his hands were sliding over her nearly-naked body, reacquainting himself with her flesh. "When I get you home, I just may give you that spanking I've threatened you with a couple of times. I get you away from Turego, and as soon as my back is turned you plunge right back into trouble."

"I'm not in trouble," she snapped.

"You couldn't prove it by me. Get dressed. We're getting out of here."

"I can't! There are some counterfeit plates that I've got to get. My room is being watched, so I was going to climb out the window and work my way around to Felix's room. I have a pretty good idea where he's hidden them."

"And you say you're not in trouble."

"I'm not! But really, Grant, we've got to get those plates."

"I've already got them."

She blinked, her brown eyes owlish. "You do? But...how?

I mean, how did you know—never mind. Kell told you, didn't he? Well, where did Felix have them hidden?"

She was enjoying this. He sighed. "Where do you think he had them?"

"In the ceiling. I think he pushed up a square of the ceiling and hid the plates in there. It's really the only good hiding place in the room, and he isn't the type to put them in a safety deposit box in a bank, which is where I'd have put them."

"No, you wouldn't," he said, annoyed. "You'd have put them in the ceiling, just like he did."

She grinned. "I was right!"

"Yes, you were right." And he probably never should have told her. Turning her around, he gave her a pat on the bottom. "Start packing. Your little friend is probably the nervous sort who checks his hidey-hole every night before he goes to bed, and we want to be long gone before he does."

She dragged down her suitcases and started throwing clothes into them. He watched her, sweat popping out on his brow. She looked even better than he remembered, her breasts ripe and round, her legs long and shapely. He hadn't even kissed her. He caught her arm, swinging her around and catching her close to him. "I've missed you," he said, and lowered his mouth to hers.

Her response was instantaneous. She rose on tiptoe, moving against him, her arms coiled around his neck and her fingers deep in his hair. He'd had a haircut, and the dark blond strands slipped through her fingers to fall back in place, shaped perfectly to his head. "I've missed you, too," she whispered when he released her mouth.

His breathing was ragged as he reluctantly let her go. "We'll finish this when we have more time. Jane, would you please put on some clothes?"

She obeyed without question, pulling on green silk trou-
ers and a matching green tunic. "Where are we going?"

"Right now? We're driving to the beach and turning the
ates over to an agent. Then we're going to catch a flight
Paris, London and New York."

"Unless, of course, Bruno is waiting just outside the door,
d instead we end up sailing across the Mediterranean."

"Bruno isn't waiting outside the door. Would you
urry?"

"I'm finished."

He picked up the suitcases and they went downstairs,
here he checked her out. It all went like clockwork.
here was no sign of Bruno, or any of the men she had
bbed "Bruno's goons." They turned the plates over to
e promised agent and drove to the airport. Jane's heart
as thudding with a slow, strong, powerful beat as Grant
ipped into the seat beside her and buckled himself in.
You know, you never did actually tell me what you're
ing here. You're retired, remember? You're not supposed
be doing things like this."

"Don't play innocent," he advised, giving her a look
om molten gold eyes. "I saw your fine hand in this from
e beginning. It worked. I came after you. I love you; I'm
king you to Tennessee; and we're going to be married.
ut you'd better remember that I'm on to your tricks now,
d I know you're too slick for your own good. Did I leave
ything out?"

"No," Jane said, settling back in her seat. "I think you
ave everything covered."

* * * * *

YOUR PARTICIPATION IS REQUESTED!

Dear Reader,

Since you are a lover of romance fiction – we would like to get to know you!

Inside you will find a short Reader's Survey. Sharing your answers with us will help our editorial staff understand who you are and what activities you enjoy.

To thank you for your participation, we would like to send you 2 books and 2 gifts – **ABSOLUTELY FREE!**

Enjoy your gifts with our appreciation,

Pam Powers

SEE INSIDE FOR READER'S SURVEY

YOUR READER'S SURVEY
"THANK YOU" FREE GIFTS INCLUDE:
- ▶ 2 Romance books
- ▶ 2 lovely surprise gifts

PLEASE FILL IN THE CIRCLES COMPLETELY TO RESPOND

1) What type of fiction books do you enjoy reading? (Check all that apply)
- ○ Suspense/Thrillers
- ○ Action/Adventure
- ○ Modern-day Romances
- ○ Historical Romance
- ○ Humour
- ○ Paranormal Romance

2) What attracted you most to the last fiction book you purchased on impulse?
- ○ The Title
- ○ The Cover
- ○ The Author
- ○ The Story

3) What is usually the greatest influencer when you <u>plan</u> to buy a book?
- ○ Advertising
- ○ Referral
- ○ Book Review

4) How often do you access the internet?
- ○ Daily ○ Weekly ○ Monthly ○ Rarely or never.

5) How many NEW paperback fiction novels have you purchased in the past 3 months?
- ○ 0 - 2
- ○ 3 - 6
- ○ 7 or more

FDH2   FDJE   FDJQ

YES! I have completed the Reader's Survey. Please send me the 2 FREE books and 2 FREE gifts (gifts are worth about $10) for which I qualify. I understand that I am under no obligation to purchase any books, as explained on the back of this card.

194/394 MDL

FIRST NAME   LAST NAME

ADDRESS

APT.#   CITY

STATE/PROV.   ZIP/POSTAL CODE

The Reader Service — Here's How It Works:

BUSINESS REPLY MAIL

FIRST-CLASS MAIL   PERMIT NO. 717   BUFFALO, NY

POSTAGE WILL BE PAID BY ADDRESSEE

THE READER SERVICE
PO BOX 1341
BUFFALO NY 14240-8571

NO POSTAGE
NECESSARY
IF MAILED
IN THE
UNITED STATES

DIAMOND BAY

CHAPTER ONE

THE CLEAN GOLDEN SUN still burned its heat into his flesh, all along his bare chest and long legs, even though it was near sundown. The lengthening rays threw dancing sparkles onto the tips of the waves, mesmerizing him as he stared at them. No, it wasn't the glittering water that mesmerized him, it was the fact that he had nothing more important to do than simply stare at it. He'd forgotten how peace sounded, how it *felt*. For a long, wonderful month of pure solitude he could relax and be only a man. He would fish when he felt like it, or cruise the warm, hypnotic waters of the Gulf if he felt restless. The water drew him on endlessly. Here it was midnight blue; there it was brilliant turquoise; over there it was a pale, shimmering green. He had money for fuel and provisions, and only two people in the world knew where he was or how to reach him. At the end of the month's vacation he would return to the gray world he'd chosen and lose himself in the shadows, but for now he could lie in the sun, and that was all he wanted. Kell Sabin was tired, tired of the endless struggle, the secrecy and maneuvering, the danger and deception of his job. It was a vitally important job, but for this month he would let someone else do it. This month was his; he could almost understand what had lured Grant Sullivan, his old friend and the best agent he'd ever had, to the quiet mystery of the Tennessee mountains.

Sabin had been a top agent himself, a legend prowling

the Golden Triangle and, later, the Middle East and South America, all the hot spots of the world. Now he was a department chief, the shadowy figure behind a group of crack agents who followed his directions and his training. Little was known about him; the security surrounding him was almost absolute. Sabin preferred it that way; he was a loner, a dark man who faced the hard realities of life with both cynicism and acceptance. He knew the drawbacks and dangers of his chosen career, he knew it could be dirty and vicious, but he was a realist and he had accepted all that when he took the job.

Still, it got to him sometimes, and he had to get away from it, live for a little while like a normal citizen. His private escape valve was his custom-made cabin cruiser. His vacations, like everything else about him, were highly guarded secrets, but the days and nights at sea were what kept him human, the only times when he could relax and think, when he could lie naked in the sun and reestablish his link with his own humanity, or watch the stars at night and regain his perspective.

A white gull soared overhead, giving its plaintive cry. Idly he watched it, free and graceful, framed against the cloudless blue bowl of the sky. The sea breeze brushed lightly over his naked skin, and pleasure brought a rare smile to his dark eyes. There was a streak of untamed savage in him that he had to keep under tight control, but out here, with only the sun and the wind and the water, he could let that part of himself surface. The restrictions of clothing seemed almost sacrilegious out here, and he resented having to dress whenever he went into a port for fuel, or whenever another boat pulled up beside him for a chat, as people were wont to do down here.

The sun had moved lower, dipping its golden edge into the water, when he heard the sound of another motor. He turned his head to watch the cabin cruiser, a little larger than his own, cut leisurely through the waves. That was the only way to get around out here: leisurely. The warmer the clime, the slower the time. Sabin kept his gaze on the boat, admiring the graceful lines and the smooth, powerful sound of the motor. He liked boats, and he liked the sea. His own boat was a prized possession, and a closely guarded secret. No one knew it belonged to him; it was registered to an insurance salesman in New Orleans who had no knowledge at all of Kell Sabin. Even the name of the boat, *Wanda*, had no meaning. Sabin knew no one named Wanda; it was simply a name that he'd chosen. But *Wanda* was completely his, with secrets and surprises of her own. Anyone who really knew him wouldn't have expected anything else, but only one man in the world had ever known the man behind the mask, and Grant Sullivan gave away no secrets.

The sound of the other boat's motor changed as it slowed and turned in his direction. Sabin swore irritably, looking around for the faded denim cutoffs he usually kept on deck for such situations. A voice drifted to him over the water, and he looked at the other boat again. A woman was standing at the forward rail, waving her arm back and forth over her head in a manner that held no urgency, so he guessed they were just looking for a chat and weren't having any sort of trouble. The afternoon sunlight glinted on her red hair, turning it into fire, and for a moment Sabin stared at it, his attention caught by that unusual, glowing shade of red.

A frown put furrows in his brow as he quickly stepped into his cutoffs and zipped them. The boat was still too far away for him to see her face, but that red hair had aggravated some hidden little memory that was trying to surface. He stared at her as the other boat idled toward him, his black eyes glittering with intensity. There was something about that hair....

Suddenly every instinct in Sabin shrilled an alarm and he hit the deck, not questioning that spine-tingling uneasiness; it had saved his life too many times for him to hesitate. He spread his fingers on the warm wood of the deck, acknowledging that he could be making a fool of himself, but he'd rather be a live fool than a dead wise man. The sound of the other motor dropped off, as if it had slowed even more, and Sabin made another decision. Still on his stomach, with the scent of polish in his nostrils and the scrape of wood on his bare flesh, he snaked his way over to a storage compartment.

He never went anywhere without some means of self-defense. The rifle that he pulled out of the storage compartment was powerful and accurate, though he knew it would be a temporary deterrent at best. If his instincts were wrong, then he would have no use for it at all; if his instincts were right, they would have far more firepower than this rifle, because they would have prepared for this.

Swearing under his breath, Sabin checked that the rifle was on full automatic fire and crawled back over to the rail. Coolly choosing his cover, he let the barrel of the rifle be seen, and he eased his head around just enough to let him see the other boat. It was still closing on him, less than a hundred yards away.

"That's close enough!" he yelled, not knowing if his voice would carry clearly enough to be understood over the noise of the motor. But that didn't matter, as long as they could tell he was yelling something.

The boat slowed, barely moving through the water now, seventy-five yards away. Suddenly it seemed to be swarming with people, and none of them looked like the ordinary Gulf fishermen or leisure boaters, because every one of them was armed, even the red-haired woman. Sabin scanned them quickly, his extraordinary eyesight picking up details of shape and size. He was able to identify the types of weapons without having to think about it, he was so familiar with them. It was the people he watched, and his eyes darted back to one man. Even at that distance, and even though he stood a little behind everyone else, there was something familiar about him, just as there was something familiar about the woman.

There was no doubt now, and icy, deadly calm settled over him, just as it always did in combat situations. He didn't waste time worrying about how badly outnumbered he was; instead he began weighing and discarding options, each decision made in the flash of a second.

A flat CRACK! split the twilight—the sound of rifle fire over open water. He caught the faint, warm percussion of the bullet as it split the air over his head and splintered the wood of the cabin behind him. With a motion as smooth as oiled silk Sabin took aim and fired, then pulled his head down, all in one continuous flow. He didn't need the involuntary sharp cry that pierced the air to tell him that he hadn't missed; Sabin would have been both surprised and furious if he *had*.

"Sabin!" The amplified voice echoed tinnily across the water. "You know you don't have a chance! Make it easy on yourself."

The accent was very good, but it wasn't quite American. The offer was only what he'd expected. His best chance was to outrun them; *Wanda*'s speed was just one of her unusual features. But to outrun them, he had to get to the controls up top, which meant exposing himself to their fire during the climb up the ladder.

Sabin weighed the situation and accepted that he had perhaps a fifty-fifty chance of reaching the top, maybe less, depending on how surprised they were by his move. On the other hand, he had no chance at all if he simply sat there and tried to hold them off with one rifle. He had a lot of ammunition, but they would have more. Moving was a risk he had to take, so he didn't waste time worrying about his diminishing chances. He took a deep breath, held it, then exhaled slowly, coiling his steely body in preparation. He needed to get as high up the ladder with the first jump as he could. Gripping the rifle firmly, he took another breath and leaped. His finger pressed the trigger as he moved, the automatic fire making the weapon buck in his hand and forcing everyone on the other boat to take cover. His outstretched right hand caught the top rung of the ladder, and his bare feet barely touched before launching him higher. Out of the corner of his eye he saw the white bursts even as he swung himself over the top and two red-hot sledgehammers slammed into his body. Only sheer momentum and determination carried him onto the deck, and kept him from falling to the lower one. Black mist almost obscured his vision, and the sound of his own breathing was loud in his ears.

He'd dropped the rifle. *"Goddammit." He'd dropped the rifle!* he thought furiously. He took a deep breath, forcing the black mist away, and summoned the strength to turn his head. The rifle still lay there, clutched in his left hand, but he couldn't feel it. The left side of his body was washed with his own blood, almost black in the dwindling light. His chest heaving with his rapid breathing, Sabin reached across with his right hand and got the rifle. The feel of it in his hand made things a little better, but not much. Sweat broke out and ran off him in rivers, mixing with his blood. He had to do something, or they'd be on him.

His left arm and leg wouldn't obey the commands of his brain, so he ignored them, dragging himself over to the side using only his right arm and leg. Bracing the rifle against his right shoulder, he fired at the other boat again, letting them know he was still alive and dangerous so they wouldn't come rushing in.

Glancing down, he took stock of his injuries. A bullet had gone through the outside muscle of his left thigh, another through his left shoulder; each was serious enough on its own. After the first burning impact his shoulder and arm had gone numb, useless, and his leg wouldn't support his weight, but he knew from experience that the numbness would soon begin to fade, and with the pain he would regain some use of his wounded muscles, if he could afford to wait that long.

He risked another look and saw that the other boat was circling behind him. The upper deck was open at the rear, and they would have a clear shot at him.

"Sabin! We know you're hurt! Don't make us kill you!"

No, they would much rather have him alive, for "questioning," but he knew they wouldn't take any chances. They would kill him if they had to, rather than let him escape.

Grinding his teeth, Sabin dragged himself over to the controls and reached up to turn the key in the ignition. The powerful engine coughed into life. He couldn't see where he was going, but that didn't matter, even if he rammed the other cruiser. Panting, he slumped back to the deck, trying to gather his strength; he had to reach the throttle, and he had only a few moments left. Hot pain was spreading over his entire left side, but his arm and leg were beginning to respond now, so he figured that was a fair trade. He ignored the growing pain and levered himself up on his right arm, forcing his left arm to move, to reach, until his bloody fingers touched the throttle and shoved it into forward gear. The cruiser began sliding through the water with slowly increasing speed, and he heard the shouts from the other boat.

"That's it, girl," he panted, encouraging the boat. "Let's go, let's go." He stretched again, every muscle in his body shaking from the effort, and managed to reach far enough to push the throttle wide open. The boat leaped beneath him, responding to the surge of power with a deep-throated roar.

At full speed he had to see where he was going. He was taking another chance, but those chances were getting better with every foot of distance he put between himself and the other boat. A grunt of pain exploded from his throat as he hauled himself to his feet, and salty sweat stung his eyes; he had to keep most of his weight on his right leg, but the left one didn't buckle beneath him, which was all he asked. He glanced over his shoulder at the other cruiser. He was rapidly pulling away from them, even though they were giving chase.

There was a figure on the top deck of the other boat, and he was settling a bulky pipe onto his shoulder.

Sabin didn't even have to think to know what it was; he'd seen rocket launchers too many times not to recognize them on sight. Only a second before the flash, and barely two seconds before the rocket exploded his boat, Sabin went over the right side, into the turquoise water of the Gulf.

He went deep, as deep as he could, but he had very little time, and the percussion rolled him through the water like a child's toy. Pain seared his wounded muscles and everything went black again; it was for only a second or two, but it was enough to completely disorient him. He was choking, and he didn't know where the surface was. The water wasn't turquoise now, it was black, and it was pressing down on him.

The years of training saved him. Sabin had never

panicked, and now wasn't the time to start. He stopped fighting the water and forced himself to relax, and his natural buoyancy began carrying him to the surface. Once he could tell which direction was up, he began swimming as well as he could, though he could barely move his left arm and leg. His lungs were burning when he finally bobbed to the surface and gulped the warm, salt-scented air.

Wanda was burning, sending black smoke billowing into a pearlescent sky that held only the last few moments of light. Darkness had already spread over the earth and sea, and he seized it as his only available cover. The other boat was circling the *Wanda*, playing its spotlight over the burning wreckage and the surrounding ocean; he could feel the water vibrating with the power of the engines. Unless they found his body—or as much of it as they could realistically expect to remain—they would search for him; they'd have to. They couldn't afford to do anything else. His priority remained the same: he had to put as much distance as he could between himself and them.

Clumsily he rolled to his back and began a one-sided backstroke, not stopping until he was well away from the glare of the burning boat. His chances weren't good; he was at least two miles from shore, probably closer to three. He was weak from loss of blood, and he could barely move his left arm and leg. Added to that were the chances that the predators of the sea would be drawn to him by his wounds before he got anywhere close to land. He gave a low, cynical laugh, and choked as a wave hit him in the face. He was caught between the human sharks and the sharks of the sea, and damned if it really made any difference which one got him, but they would both have to work for it. He didn't intend to make it easy for them.

He took a deep breath and floated while he struggled out of his shorts, but his twisting efforts made him sink, and he had to fight his way back to the surface. He held the garment in his teeth while he considered the best tactics to use. The denim was old, thin, almost threadbare; he should be able to tear it. The problem was in staying afloat while he did it. He would have to use his left arm and leg, or he'd never be able to manage it.

He had no choice; he had to do what was necessary, despite the pain.

He thought he might pass out again when he began treading water, but the moment passed, though the pain didn't lessen. Grimly he chewed on the edge of the shorts, trying to get a tear started in the fabric. He forced the pain out of his mind as his teeth shredded the threads, and he hastily tore the garment up to the waistband, where the reinforced fabric and double-stitching stopped his progress. He began tearing again, until he had four loose strips of cloth attached to the waistband; then he began chewing along the waistband. The first strip came loose, and he held it in his fist while he freed the second strip.

He rolled to his back and floated, groaning as his wounded leg relaxed. Quickly he knotted the two strips together to get enough length to wrap around his leg. Then he tied the makeshift tourniquet around his thigh, making certain that the cloth covered both the entrance and exit wounds. He pulled it as tightly as he could without cutting off circulation, but he had to put pressure on the wounds to stop them from bleeding.

His shoulder was going to be more difficult. He bit and pulled until he tore the other two strips from the waistband, then knotted them together. How was he going to position this makeshift bandage? He didn't even know if he had an exit wound in his back, or if the bullet was still in his shoulder. Slowly, awkwardly, he moved his right hand and felt his back, but his water-puckered fingers could find only smooth skin, which meant that the bullet was still in him. The wound was high on his shoulder, and bandaging it would be almost impossible with the materials he had.

Even tied together, the two strips weren't enough. He began chewing again, tore off two more strips, then tied them to the other two. The best he could manage was to sling the strip over his back, bring it around under his armpit and tie it in a tight loop over his shoulder. Then he folded the remnant of his cutoffs into a pad and slipped it under the loop, positioning it over the wound. It was a clumsy bandage at best, but his head was swimming, and deadly lethargy was creeping into his limbs. Grimly Sabin pushed both sensations away, staring fixedly at the stars in an effort to orient himself. He wasn't going to give up; he could float, and he could manage to swim for short periods of time. It might take a while, but unless a shark got him, he was damned well going to make it to shore. He rolled onto his back and rested for a few minutes before he began the slow, agonizing process of swimming to shore.

IT WAS A HOT NIGHT, even for mid-July in central Florida. Rachel Jones had automatically adjusted her habits to the weather, taking it easy, either doing her chores early in the morning or putting them off until late afternoon. She had been up at sunrise, hoeing the weeds out of her small vegetable garden, feeding the geese, washing her car. When the temperature soared into the nineties she moved inside and put a load of clothes in the washer, then settled down for a few hours of research and planning for the journalism course she had agreed to teach at night in Gainesville when the fall quarter began. With the ceiling fan whirring serenely overhead, her dark hair pinned on top of her head, and wearing only a tank top and an old pair of shorts, Rachel was comfortable despite the heat. A glass of iced tea sat constantly beside her elbow, and she sipped at it as she read.

The geese honked peacefully as they waddled from one section of grass to the other, herded by Ebenezer Duck, the cantankerous old leader. Once there was an uproar when Ebenezer and Joe, the dog, got into a dispute over which one had the right to the patch of cool green grass beneath the oleander shrub. Rachel went to the screen door and shouted at her rambunctious pets to be quiet, and that was the most exciting event of the day. That was the way most of her days went during the summer. Things picked up during the fall, when the tourist season began and her two souvenir shops in Treasure Island and Tarpon Springs began doing a lively trade. With the journalism course her days would be even busier than usual, but the summers were a time for relaxing. She worked intermittently on her third book, feeling no great pressure to finish it, since her deadline wasn't until Christmas and she was well ahead of schedule. Rachel's energy was deceptive, because she managed to accomplish so much without ever seeming to hurry.

She was at home here, her roots deep in the sandy soil. The house she lived in had been her grandfather's, and the land had been in the family for a hundred and fifty years. The house had been remodeled in the fifties and no longer resembled the original frame structure. When Rachel had moved in she had renovated the inside, but the place still gave her a sense of permanency. She knew the house and the land surrounding it as well as she knew her own face in the mirror. Probably better, because Rachel wasn't given to staring at herself. She knew the tall pine thicket in front of her and the rolling grassland at her back, every hill and tree and bush. A path wound through the pines and down to the beach where the Gulf waters rolled in. The beach

was undeveloped here, partly because of the unusual roughness of the shore, partly because the beachfront property
was owned by people who had had it for generations and
weren't inclined to see condominiums and motels rise in
their faces. This was prime cattle country; Rachel's property was almost surrounded by a huge ranch, owned by
John Rafferty, and Rafferty was as reluctant as she to sell
any land for development.

The beach was Rachel's special haven, a place for walking and thinking and finding peace in the relentless, eternal
surge of the water. It was called Diamond Bay because of
the way the light splintered on the waves as they crashed
over the underwater boulders that lined the mouth of the
little bay. The water shimmied and glittered like thousands of diamonds as it rolled to shore. Her grandfather had
taught her to swim in Diamond Bay; sometimes it seemed
as if her life had begun in the turquoise water.

Certainly the bay had been the center of the golden days
of her childhood, when a visit to Gramps's had been the
most fun a young Rachel could imagine. Then her mother
died when Rachel was twelve, and the bay became her
permanent home. There was something about the ocean
that had eased the sharpness of her grief and taught her acceptance. She'd had Gramps, too, and even now the thought
of him brought a smile to her face. What a wonderful old
man he'd been! He had never been too busy or too embarrassed to answer the sometimes awkward questions an
adolescent girl could ask, and had given her the freedom to
test her wings while still keeping her solidly grounded in
common sense. He had died the year she'd finished college,
but even death had met him on his own terms. He had been
tired and ill and ready to die, and he'd done it with such
humor and acceptance that Rachel had even felt a sort of
peace at his going. She had grieved, yes, but the grief had

been tempered by the knowledge that it was what he had wanted.

The old house had stood empty then, while Rachel pursued her career as an investigative reporter in Miami. She had met and married B. B. Jones, and life had been good. B.B. had been more than a husband, he had been a friend, and they had thought they had the world on a string. Then B.B.'s violent death had ended that dream and left Rachel a widow at the age of twenty-five. She quit her job and returned here to the bay, once again finding solace in the unending sea. She had been crippled emotionally, but time and the peaceful life had healed her. Still, she felt no urge to return to the fast-paced life she'd led before. This was home, and she was happy with what she was doing now. The two souvenir stores provided an adequate living, and she supplemented her income by writing an occasional article as well as the adventure books that had done so surprisingly well.

This summer was almost exactly like all the other summers she had ever spent at Diamond Bay, except it was hotter. The heat and humidity were almost stifling, and some days she felt like doing nothing more strenuous than lying in the hammock and fanning herself. Sundown brought some relief, but even that was relative. The night brought a light breeze from the Gulf to cool her heated skin, but it was still too hot to sleep. She had already taken a cool shower, and now she sat on the front porch swing in the dark, lazily keeping the swing moving with occasional movements of her foot. The chains squeaked in time with the chirping of crickets and the croaking of frogs; Joe lay on the porch in front of the screen door, dozing and dreaming his doggy dreams. Rachel closed her eyes, enjoying the breeze on her face and thinking of what she would do the next day: pretty much what she had done today, and the day before, but she didn't mind the repetition. She had enjoyed the old days of excitement, filled with the peculiar seductive power of danger, yet now she also enjoyed the peace of her present life.

Even though she wore only panties and a man's oversize white shirt, with the sleeves rolled up and first three buttons open, she could still feel small beads of sweat forming between her breasts. The heat made her restless, and finally she got to her feet. "I'm going for a walk," she told the dog, who flicked an ear at her but didn't open his eyes.

Rachel hadn't really expected him to join her; Joe wasn't a friendly dog, not even with her. He was independent and antisocial, backing away from an outstretched hand with his hackles raised and teeth showing. She thought he must have been mistreated before he'd shown up in her yard a few years before, but they had formed a truce. She fed him, and he filled the role of guard dog. He still wouldn't allow her to pet him, but he would come instantly to her side if a stranger drove up, and stand there glaring at the intruder until he either decided there was no danger, or the stranger left. If Rachel worked in her garden, Joe was usually close by. It was a partnership based on mutual respect, and both were satisfied with it.

He really had it easy, Rachel thought as she cut across the yard and took the path that wound down through the tall pines to the beach. He wasn't often called on as a guard; few people came to her house, except for the postman. She was at the dead end of an unpaved road that cut through Rafferty's property and hers was the only house. John Rafferty was her only neighbor, and he wasn't the type to drop in for a chat. Honey Mayfield, the local veterinarian, sometimes came by after a call at the Rafferty ranch, and they had developed a rather close friendship, but other than that Rachel was pretty much left alone, which was one reason she felt comfortable roaming around at night wearing only her underwear and a shirt.

The path sloped down a very gradual incline through the pine thicket. The stars were bright and heavy in the sky, and Rachel had walked the path since childhood, so she didn't bother with a flashlight. Even in the pines she could still see well enough to find her way. It was a quarter of a mile from the house to the beach, an easy walk. She liked walking the beach at night; it was her favorite time to listen to the ocean's power, when the waves were black except for their pearly foam tops. It was also low tide, and Rachel preferred the beach at low tide. It was at low tide that the ocean pulled back to reveal the treasures it had brought in to leave on the sand, like a love offering. She had collected a lot of sea treasures at low tide, and never ceased marveling at the wonders the turquoise Gulf brought to her feet.

It was a beautiful night, moonless and cloudless, and the stars were brighter than she had seen them in years, their light refracted on the waves like countless diamonds. Diamond Bay. It had been well named. The beach was narrow and uneven, with clumps of weeds growing along the edge, and the mouth of the bay was lined with jagged rocks that were especially dangerous at low tide, but for all its imperfections the bay created magic with its combination of light and water. She could stand and watch the glittering water for hours, spellbound by the power and beauty of the ocean.

The gritty sand cooled her bare feet, and she dug her toes deeper. The breeze gusted momentarily, lifting her hair away from her face, and Rachel inhaled the clean salt air. There was only herself and the ocean.

The breeze changed directions, flirting with her, blowing strands of hair across her face. She put up her hand to push her hair out of her eyes and paused in mid-motion, her eyebrows drawing together fractionally as she stared at the water. She could have sworn she'd seen something. Just for a moment there had been a flash of movement, but now her straining eyes picked up nothing but the rhythmic surge of the waves. Perhaps it had been only a fish, or a large piece of driftwood. She wanted to find a really good piece for a flower arrangement, so she walked to the edge of the waves, pushing her hair back so it wouldn't obscure her vision.

There it was again, bobbing in the water! She took an eager step forward, wetting her feet in the foamy surf. Then the dark object moved again and took on a funny shape. The sheen of the silvery starlight made it look just like an arm, flailing weakly forward, like a tired swimmer struggling for coordination. A muscled arm, at that, and the dark bulk beside it could be a head.

Realization burst, and Rachel's entire body tingled with electricity. She was in the water before she realized it, surging through the waves toward the struggling man. The water impeded her progress, the waves pushing her back with increasing strength; the tide was just beginning to come back in. The man sank from view, and a hoarse cry burst from her throat. Wildly she splashed toward him, the water up to her breasts now, the waves crashing into her face. Where was he? The black water gave no hint of his location. She reached the spot where she had last seen him, but her frantically searching hands came up empty.

The waves would wash him toward the beach. She turned and staggered back toward shore and saw him again for a moment before his head disappeared beneath the water once more. She struck out, swimming strongly, and two seconds later her hand closed on thick hair. Fiercely she jerked his head above the water, but he was limp, his eyes closed. "Don't you die on me!" she ordered between clenched teeth, catching him under the shoulders and towing him in. Twice the incoming tide knocked her feet out from under her, and each time she thought she would drown before she could struggle free of the man's confining weight.

Then she was in water to her knees, and he sagged limply. She tugged until he was mostly out of the water, then fell on her hands and knees in the sand, coughing and gasping. Every muscle trembling with reaction, she crawled over to him.

CHAPTER TWO

HE WAS NAKED. Her mind barely registered that fact before it was pushed aside by more urgent matters. She was still gasping for air herself, but she forced herself to hold her breath while she put her hand on his chest to detect a heartbeat, or the up and down movement of breathing. He was still, too still. She could find no hint of life in him, and his skin was so cool....

Of course it was cool! She brought herself up sharply, shaking her head to clear it of the cobwebs of fatigue. He'd been in the water for God only knew how long, but he'd been swimming, however weakly, the first time she'd seen him, and she was letting precious seconds tick past when she should be acting.

It took every ounce of strength she had to roll him onto his stomach, because he wasn't a small man, and the bright starlight revealed that he was solid muscle. Panting, she straddled him and began the rhythmic push-pull action that would stimulate his lungs. That was another thing her grandfather had taught her, and taught her well. Her arms and hands were strong from the gardening and swimming she did, and she worked on the man until she was rewarded by a choking cough and a stream of water gushing out of his mouth.

"There you go," she breathed, not ceasing her efforts. He went into a paroxysm of coughing, his body heaving beneath her; then he groaned hoarsely and shuddered before going limp.

Rachel quickly rolled him onto his back again, bending anxiously over him. His breathing was audible now. It was too rapid and too ragged, but he was definitely breathing. His eyes were closed, and his head rolled to the side when she shook him. He was unconscious.

She sank back on her heels, shivering as the ocean breeze went right through the wet shirt she wore, and stared at the dark head that rested on the sand. Only then did she notice the clumsy binding around his shoulder. She reached to pull it away, thinking that perhaps it was the remnants of the shirt he'd been wearing when he suffered whatever accident had cast him into the ocean. But the wet fabric beneath her fingers was denim, too heavy for a shirt in this weather, and it had been tied into a knot. She pulled at it again, and part of the fabric came away. It had been folded into a pad and shoved under the knot, and high on his shoulder was a wound, a round, obscene mouth where there shouldn't have been one, showing black in the colorless light.

Rachel stared at the wound, her mind jolting with realization. He'd been shot! She'd seen too many gunshot wounds not to recognize one, even in the pale light of the stars that reduced everything to silvery gleam and black shadows. Her head whipped around and she stared out to sea, straining her eyes to see the telltale pinpoint of light that would warn of a boat, but there was nothing. All her senses were alert, her nerves tingling, and she was instantly wary. People didn't get shot without reason, and it was logical to assume that whoever had shot him the first time would be willing to do so again.

He had to have help, but there was no way she could throw him over her shoulder and carry him up to the house. She stood, scanning the dark sea again to make certain she hadn't missed anything, but the expanse of water was empty. She would have to leave him here, at least for as long as it would take her to run up to the house and back.

Once the decision was made Rachel didn't vacillate. Bending, she grasped the man under his shoulders and dug her heels into the sand, grunting with the effort as she pulled him far enough out of the water that the incoming tide wouldn't lap around him before she could get back. Even in the depths of unconsciousness he felt the pain she caused him by tugging on his wounded shoulder and gave a low, hoarse moan. Rachel winced and felt her eyes burn momentarily, but it was something she had to do. When she judged that he was far enough up the beach she let his shoulders down on the sand as easily as she could, muttering a breathless apology to him even though she knew he couldn't hear her. "I'll be right back," she assured him, touching his wet face briefly. Then she ran.

Normally the path up the beach and through the stand of pines seemed like a fairly short one, but tonight it stretched endlessly ahead of her. She ran, not caring about stubbing her bare toes on exposed roots, heedless of the small branches that caught at her shirt. One such limb was strong enough to catch her shirt, halting her flight in mid-step. Rachel threw her entire weight against the fabric, too frantic to pause to untangle it. With a sodden ripping sound the shirt tore, and she was free to resume her wild plunge up the slope.

The welcoming lights of her small house were a beacon in the night, the house an oasis of safety and familiarity, but something had gone very wrong, and she couldn't shut herself inside its refuge. The life of the man on the beach depended on her.

Joe had heard her coming. He stood on the edge of the porch with his hackles raised and a low, rumbling growl issuing from his throat. She could see him silhouetted by the porch light as she sprinted across the yard, but she didn't have time to calm him down. If he bit her, he bit her. She would worry about that later. But Joe didn't even glance at her as she bounded up the steps and slammed the screen door back on its hinges. He remained on guard, facing the pines and the beach, every muscle quivering as he placed himself between Rachel and whatever had sent her flying through the night.

Rachel grabbed the phone, trying to control her breathing so she would be able to talk coherently. Her hands were shaking as she fumbled through the telephone book, looking for an ambulance listing, or a rescue squad—maybe the sheriff's department. Anyone! She dropped the book and swore violently, leaning down to grab it again. Rescue squad—they would have paramedics, and the man needed medical attention more than he needed a police report made out on him.

She found the number and was punching it out, when suddenly her hand froze, and she stared at the phone. A police report. She didn't know why, couldn't logically explain it to herself right then, but abruptly she knew she had to keep this quiet, at least for now. The instincts she had developed during her years as an investigative reporter were sending off steady warning signals, and she obeyed them now as she had obeyed them then. She slammed the receiver back onto its hook, shaking as she stood there and tried to force her thoughts into order.

No police. Not now. The man on the beach was helpless, no threat to her or anyone else. He would have no chance at all if this was more than a simple shooting, an argument that had gotten out of hand. He might be a drug-runner. A terrorist. Anything. But, dear God, he might not be any of those, and she was the only chance he had.

Even as she dragged a quilt from the top of her bedroom closet and bolted from the house again, with Joe right on her heels, jumbled scenes from her past kept skittering through her mind. Scenes of things that weren't quite right, where the glossy surface was accepted and neatly filed away, the real story forever hidden from view. There were other worlds beyond the normal, everyday life that most people lived, layers of danger and deceit and treachery that were never even suspected. Rachel knew about those layers. They had taken B.B.'s life. The man on the beach might be victim or villain, but if he was a villain she would have time to turn him in to the authorities long before he could recover from his wound; on the other hand, if he was a victim, the only time he had was what she could give him.

He was lying just as she'd left him, the tide swirling just inches from his feet. Gasping, Rachel fell to her knees in the sand beside him and put her hand on his chest, shuddering with relief when she felt the steady up and down movement that told her he was still alive. Joe stood beside her, his head lowered and his ears laid back as a low, continuous growl came from his throat, his eyes never leaving the man.

"It's all right, Joe," she said, automatically giving the dog a reassuring pat, and for once he didn't shy away from her touch. She spread the quilt on the sand, then knelt once again to brace her hands against the man's limp body. She rolled him onto the quilt. This time he didn't make a sound, and she was grateful he couldn't feel the pain she had to cause him.

It took her a few minutes to get him positioned; then she had to rest. She stared uneasily at the sea again, but it was still empty. There was no one out there, though it wasn't unusual to see the night lights of passing boats. Joe brushed against her legs, growling again, and she gathered her strength. Then she leaned down, gathered the two corners of the quilt nearest the man's head and dug her heels into the sand. She grunted with the strain; even with her entire weight thrown into the effort, it was all she could do to drag him a few feet. God, he was heavy!

Maybe when she got him off the beach and onto the slippery pine needles it would be easier. If it got much harder she wouldn't be able to budge him at all. She'd known it would be difficult, but she hadn't realized it would be almost beyond her physical capabilities. She was strong and healthy, and his life depended on her. Surely she could drag him up to her house, even if she had to do it an inch at a time!

That was almost what it amounted to. Even when she managed to get him off the beach, although the pine needles were slippery and the quilt slid over them more easily, her path was uphill. The incline wasn't steep, and she normally walked it easily, but it might as well have been vertical for the effort it took her to drag a two-hundred-pound man up it. She couldn't sustain her forward progress for any length of time at all. She lunged and lurched, falling to her knees several times. Her lungs were pumping and wheezing like bellows, and her entire body was one big ache before she had him halfway up the slope. She stopped for a moment and leaned against a pine, fighting the inevitable nausea of overexertion. If it hadn't been for the tree supporting her, she might not have been able to stand at all, because her legs and arms were trembling wildly.

An owl hooted somewhere close by, and the crickets chirped on undisturbed; the events of the night meant nothing to them. Joe hadn't left her side, and every time she stopped to rest he crowded against her legs, which was totally unlike him. But he wasn't pressing against her for protection; rather, he was protecting her, putting himself between her and the man. Rachel took a deep breath and steeled herself for another effort, patting Joe on the side and saying, "Good boy, good boy."

She reached down to take hold of the quilt again, and Joe did something extraordinary; he caught the edge of the quilt between his teeth and growled. Rachel stared at him, wondering if he'd taken it in his head to prevent her from dragging it any farther. Cautiously she braced her shaky legs, then leaned back and pulled with every ounce of strength left in her. Still growling, Joe braced his legs and pulled, too, and with his strength added to hers the quilt slid forward several feet.

Rachel stopped in amazement, staring at the dog. "Good boy," she said again. "Good boy!" Had it been a fluke, or would he do it again? He was a big, strong dog; Honey Mayfield had estimated that he weighed almost eighty pounds. If he could be coaxed into pulling with her, she could have the man up the slope in no time.

"Okay," she whispered, taking a better grip on the quilt. "Let's see if you'll do it one more time." She pulled, and Joe pulled, that low growl still rumbling in his throat, as if he disapproved of what she was doing, but would help her if she was determined to do it.

It was much easier with the dog's help, and soon they were out of the pine thicket, with only the dirt road and the small yard to cross before they reached the house. Rachel straightened and stared at the house, wondering how she would ever get him up the two steps to the porch. Well, she'd gotten him this far; she'd get him in the house, one way or another. Bending, she began tugging again.

He hadn't made a sound since that one groan on the beach, not even when they pulled him across exposed roots or the loose rocks on the dirt road. Rachel let the quilt drop and bent over him again, crouching on the cool, damp grass beside him. He was still breathing; after what she'd put him through, she didn't suppose she could ask for anything more. She stared at the two steps again, a frown puckering her forehead. She needed a conveyor belt to get him up those steps. A growing sense of urgency gnawed at her. Not only did he need attention, but the sooner she got him hidden inside, the better. She was isolated out here at Diamond Bay, so chance visitors weren't likely, but anyone who came looking for the man wouldn't be a chance visitor. Until he was conscious, until she knew more about what was going on, she had to hide him.

The only way she had of getting him up the steps was to catch him under the arms and pull him up them, just as she'd pulled him out of the sea. Joe couldn't help now. She would have to lift the man's head, shoulders and chest—the heaviest part of his body.

She'd gotten her wind back, and sitting there in the grass wasn't going to get anything accomplished. But she was so tired, as if her legs and arms were weighted down with lead; they were sluggish, and she staggered a little when she climbed to her feet. Gently she wrapped the quilt around the man, then positioned herself behind him and slid her hands under his shoulders. Straining, fighting for every bit of leverage, she raised him to a half-sitting position, then quickly propped him up on her legs. He started to fall over, and with a cry Rachel caught him around the chest, looping her arms tightly and locking her hands together. His head fell forward, as limply as a newborn's. Joe worried at her side, growling when he couldn't find a place to catch hold of the quilt.

"It's all right," she panted. "I've got to do it this way now." She wondered if she was talking to the dog or the man. Either was ridiculous, but both seemed important.

The steps were at her back. Keeping her legs under her and her hands tightly locked around the man's chest, Rachel thrust herself backward; her bottom landed on the first step with a jarring thud, and the edge of the top step scraped a raw strip down her back, but she'd managed to lift the man a little. Hot pain seared her back and legs from the strain she was putting on her muscles. "Oh, God," she whispered, "I can't collapse now. In a little while I'll rest, but not now."

Grinding her teeth, she got her feet under her again, using the stronger muscles of her thighs rather than her more vulnerable back muscles. Once more she lunged up and back, pushing with her legs, hauling the man up with her. She was sitting on the top step now, and tears of pain and effort were stinging her eyes. The man's torso was on the steps, his legs still out in the yard, but if she could get his upper body on the porch the rest would be easy. She had to do the agonizing maneuver one more time.

She didn't know how she did it, where she found the strength. She gathered, lunged, pushed. Suddenly her feet went out from under her and she fell heavily on her back on the wooden porch, the man lying on her legs. Stunned, she lay there for a moment, staring up at the yellow porch light with the tiny bugs swarming around it. She could feel her heart pounding wildly inside her rib cage, hear the wheezing sobs as she tried to suck enough oxygen into her lungs to meet the demand being made by overworked muscles. His weight was crushing her legs. But she was lying full-length on the porch, so if he was lying on her legs, that meant she'd done it. She'd gotten him up the steps!

Groaning, crying, she pushed herself into a sitting position, though she thought the planks beneath her made a wonderful bed. It took her a moment to struggle from beneath his confining weight, and then it was more than she could do to stand. She crawled to the screen door and propped it open, then scrambled back to the man. Just a few more feet. Inside the front door, angle to the right, then into her bedroom. Twenty, thirty feet. That was it, all she would ask of herself.

The original method of catching the edge of the quilt and pulling it seemed like a good idea, and Joe was willing to lend his strength again, but Rachel had precious little strength herself, and the dog had to do most of the work. Slowly, laboriously, they inched the man across the porch. She and Joe couldn't get through the door at the same time, so she went first and knelt to reach for a new grip on the quilt. Growling, his husky body braced, Joe pulled back with all his strength, and man and quilt came through the door.

It seemed like a good idea to keep on going while they had him moving; she angled him toward her bedroom, and a scant minute later he was lying on the floor beside her bed. Joe released the quilt as soon as she did and immediately backed away from her, his hackles raised as he reacted to the unfamiliar confines of a house.

Rachel didn't try to pet him now; she'd already asked so much of him, trespassed so far past the set boundaries, that any further overtures would simply be too much. "This way," she said, struggling to her feet and leading him back to the front door. He darted past her, anxious for his freedom again, and disappeared into the darkness beyond the porchlight. Slowly she released the screen door and closed it, slapping at a gnat that had entered the house.

Methodically, her steps slow and faltering, she locked the front and back doors and pulled the curtains over the windows. Her bedroom had old-fashioned venetian blinds, and she closed them. That done, the house as secure as she could make it, she stared down at the naked man sprawled on her bedroom floor. He needed medical attention, skilled medical attention, but she didn't dare call a doctor. They were required to report all gunshot wounds to the police.

There was really only one person who could help her now, one person she trusted to keep a secret. Going to the kitchen, Rachel dialed Honey Mayfield, keeping her fingers crossed that some emergency hadn't already called Honey out. The telephone was picked up on the third ring, and a distinctly drowsy voice said, "This is Mayfield."

"Honey, this is Rachel. Can you come out?"

"Now?" Honey yawned. "Has something happened to Joe?"

"No, the animals are fine. But…can you bring your bag? And put it in a grocery sack or something, so no one can see it."

All traces of drowsiness had left Honey's voice. "Is this a joke?"

"No. Hurry."

"I'll be there as soon as I can."

Two receivers were hung up simultaneously, and Rachel went back to the bedroom, where she crouched beside the man. He was still unconscious, and the handling he had received should have been enough to wake the dead, unless he had lost so much blood that he was in deep shock and near death himself. Sharp, piercing anxiety seized her, and she touched his face with trembling hands, as if she could pass the essence of life to him with her touch. He was warmer now than he had been, and he was breathing with slow, heavy movements of his chest. The wound on his shoulder was sullenly oozing blood, and sand clung to him, even matting his hair, which was still dripping seawater. She tried to brush some of the sand out of his hair and felt something sticky beneath her fingers. Frowning, she looked at the watery redness that stained her hand; then awareness dawned. He had a head injury, as well! And she had dragged him up that slope, then literally manhandled him up the steps and onto the porch! The wonder was that she hadn't killed him!

Her heart pounding, she ran to the kitchen and filled her biggest plastic mixing bowl with warm water, then returned to the bedroom to sit on the floor beside him. As gently as possible, she washed as much blood and sand out of his hair as she could, feeling the thick strands come unmatted between her fingers. Her fingertips found a swelling lump on the right side of his head, just past the hairline at his temple, and she pushed the hair aside to reveal a jagged tear in the skin. Not a gunshot wound, though. It was as if he'd hit his head, or been hit with something. But why was he unconscious now? He had been swimming when she'd first seen him, so he'd been conscious then, coming in on the surge of the tide. He hadn't lost consciousness until he was already inside the mouth of Diamond Bay.

She pressed the cloth to the lump, trying to clean sand out of the cut. Had he hit his head on one of the huge, jagged rocks that lined the mouth of the bay? At low tide they were just under the surface of the water and difficult to avoid unless you knew exactly where they were placed. Knowing what she did about the bay, Rachel decided that that was exactly what had happened, and she bit her lip at the thought of dragging the man around the way she had when he was probably suffering from a concussion. What if her imagination was running wild with her, and she caused the man's death with her fears and hesitation? A concussion was serious, and so was a gunshot wound. Oh, God, was she doing the right thing? Had he been shot by accident and fallen overboard at night, then lost his bearings from pain and confusion? Was someone frantically searching for him right now?

She stared blindly down at him, her hand moving to touch his shoulder as if in apology, her fingers stroking lightly over his warm, darkly tanned skin. What a fool she was! The best thing she could do for this man would be to call the rescue squad immediately and hope that she hadn't done any additional damage to him with her rough handling. She started to get to her feet, to forget her crazy fancies and do the sensible thing, when she realized that she had been staring at his legs, and that the left one had a knotted strip of denim tied around it. Denim. He'd had denim tied around his shoulder, too. Her spine tingled warily, and she left her position by his head to crawl down to his leg, already afraid of what she would find. She couldn't untie the knot; it was pulled too tightly, and the water had only tightened it.

She got a pair of scissors out of her sewing basket and neatly sliced the fabric. The scissors slipped from her suddenly nerveless fingers as she stared down at his thigh, at the ugly wound in the outer muscle. He'd been shot in the leg, too. She examined his leg almost clinically; there were both entry and exit wounds, so at least the bullet wasn't still inside him. He hadn't been so lucky with his shoulder.

No one was shot *twice* by accident. Someone had deliberately tried to kill him.

"I won't let it happen!" she said fiercely, the sound of her own voice startling her. She didn't know the man who lay on the floor, unmoving and unresponsive, but she crouched over him with all the protectiveness of a lioness for a helpless cub. Until she knew what was going on, no one was going to get a chance to hurt this man.

Her hands gentle, she began washing him as best she could. His nudity didn't embarrass her; under the circumstances she felt it would be silly to flinch from his bare flesh. He was wounded, helpless; had she walked up on him sunbathing in the nude, that would have been a different kettle of fish entirely, but he needed her now, and she wasn't about to let modesty prevent her from helping him.

She heard the sound of a car coming down her road and got hastily to her feet. That should be Honey, and though Joe normally wasn't as hostile to women as he was to men, after the unusual events of the night he might be on edge and take it out on the vet. Rachel unlocked the front door and opened it, stepping out on the front porch. She couldn't see Joe, but a low growl issued from beneath the oleander shrub, and she spoke quietly to him as Honey's car turned into the driveway.

Honey got out and reached into the back seat for two grocery sacks, which she clutched to her as she started across the yard. "Thanks for waiting up," she said clearly. "Aunt Audrey wants you to look at these quilting squares for your shops."

"Come on in," Rachel invited, holding open the screen door. Joe growled again as Honey walked up the steps, but remained beneath the oleander.

Honey set the two grocery sacks on the floor and watched as Rachel carefully locked the front door again. "What's going *on*?" she demanded, planting her strong, freckled fists on her hips. "Why am I disguising my bag as quilting squares?"

"In here," Rachel said, leading the way to her bedroom. He still wasn't moving, except for the regular motion of his chest as he breathed. "He's been shot," she said, going down on her knees beside him.

The healthy color washed out of Honey's face, leaving her freckles as bright spots on her nose and cheekbones. "My God, what's going on here? Who is he? Have you called the sheriff? Who shot him?"

"I don't know, to answer three of those questions," Rachel said tensely, not looking at Honey. She kept her eyes trained on the man's face, willing him to open his eyes, wishing he could give her the answers to the questions Honey had asked. "And I'm not going to call the sheriff."

"What do you mean, you're not going to call?" Honey fairly shouted, shaken out of her usual calm capability by the sight of a naked man on Rachel's bedroom floor. "Did *you* shoot him?"

"Of course not! He washed up on the beach!"

"All the more reason to call the sheriff!"

"I *can't*!" Rachel lifted her head, her eyes fierce and strangely calm. "I can't risk his life that way."

"Have you lost your sense of reason? He needs a doctor, and the sheriff needs to investigate why he was shot! He could be an escaped felon, or a drug runner. Anything!"

"I know that." Rachel drew a deep breath. "But the shape he's in, I don't think I'm taking that much of a risk. He's helpless. And if things aren't that…cut and dried… he wouldn't stand a chance in a hospital where someone could get to him."

Honey put her hand to her head. "I don't understand what you're talking about," she said wearily. "What do you mean, 'cut and dried'? And why do you think someone would try to get to him? To finish the job they started?"

"Yes."

"Then it's a job for the sheriff!"

"Listen," Rachel said insistently. "When I was a reporter, I saw some things that were…strange. I was on the scene one night when a body was found. The man had been shot in the back of the head. The sheriff of that county did his report, the body was taken in for identification, but when the one-paragraph report appeared in the newspaper two days later it said that he had died of *natural causes*! In a way, I suppose it is natural to die of a bullet in the brain, but it made me curious, and I poked around a little, looking for the file. The file had disappeared. The coroner's office had no record of a man who had been shot in the head. Finally the word filtered down to me to stop snooping, that certain people in government had taken care of the matter and wanted it dropped."

"This doesn't make any sense," Honey muttered.

"The man was an agent!"

"What sort of agent? DEA? FBI? What?"

"You're on the right track, but go deeper."

"A spy? You're saying he was a spy?"

"He was an agent. I don't know for which side, but the entire thing was hushed up and doctored out of existence. After that I started noticing other things that weren't quite what they seemed. I've seen too much to simply assume that this man will be safe if I turn him over to the authorities!"

"You think *he's* an agent?" Honey stared down at him, her brown eyes wide.

Rachel willed herself to answer calmly. "I think there's a chance of it, and I think we'd be risking his life to turn him over to the sheriff. It would be a matter of public record then, and anyone hunting for him would be able to find him."

"He could still be a drug runner. You could be risking your life by protecting him."

"That's a possibility," Rachel admitted. "But he's wounded, and I'm not. He doesn't have any chance at all, except what I can give him. If the DEA has busted up a drug ring there'll be something about it on the scanner, or in the newspaper. If he's an escaped felon it'll be on the news. He's not in any condition to hurt anyone, so I'm safe."

"And if a drug deal has gone sour, and some other unsavory characters are after him? You wouldn't be safe then, from either him or the others."

"That's a chance I'll have to take," Rachel said quietly, her gray eyes level as she met Honey's worried gaze. "I know all the possibilities, and I know the risks. I may be seeing shadows where there aren't any, but think how terrible it would be for him if I'm right."

Honey drew a deep breath and tried again. "It just isn't likely that a wounded spy would wash up on your beach. Things like that don't happen to normal people, and you're still within the bounds of normalcy, even if you are a little eccentric."

Rachel couldn't believe what she was hearing, from Honey of all people, who was usually the most logical person in the state. The night's events were rattling everyone. "It isn't likely that a wounded man would wash up on my beach period, regardless of his occupation! But he did! He's here, and he needs help. I've done what I can, but he needs medical attention. He still has a bullet in his shoulder. Honey, please!"

If possible, Honey went even whiter. "You want *me* to take care of him? He needs a doctor! I'm a veterinarian!"

"I can't call a doctor! Doctors are required to report all gunshot wounds to the police. You can do it. No vital organs are involved. It's his shoulder and his leg, and I think he has a concussion. Please."

Honey glanced down at the naked man and bit her lip. "How did you get him up here?"

"Joe and I pulled him, on this quilt."

"If he has a severe concussion he may need surgery."

"I know. I'll handle that if it's necessary. I'll think of something."

They were both silent for a few minutes, looking down

at the man who lay so still and helpless at their feet. "All right," Honey finally said, her voice soft. "I'll do what I can. Let's get him up on the bed."

That was as difficult as getting him up from the beach had been. Because Honey was larger and stronger, she got him under the shoulders, while Rachel slid one arm under his hips and the other under his thighs. As Rachel had noted before, he was a big man, and roped with muscles, which meant that he weighed more for his size than a less muscular man would have. He was also deadweight, and they had to be careful of his injuries. "Good God," Honey panted. "How did you manage to get him up that slope and into the house, even with Joe's help?"

"I had to do it," Rachel said, because that was the only explanation she had.

Finally they got him on the bed, and Rachel slumped to the floor, totally exhausted by the night's efforts. Honey bent over the man, her freckled face intent as she examined him.

CHAPTER THREE

IT WAS THREE O'CLOCK in the morning. Honey had left half an hour before, and Rachel had held her weariness at bay long enough to take another much needed shower and wash the salt out of her hair. The heat of the day had finally abated enough that the air was comfortable, but soon it would be sunrise, and the heat would begin to build once more. She needed to sleep now, while she could, but her hair was wet. Sighing, she propped herself against the vanity and turned on the blow-dryer.

The man was still asleep, or unconscious. He was definitely concussed, but Honey hadn't thought it was severe, or that he was in a coma; rather, she'd decided that his continued unconsciousness was due to a combination of fatigue, loss of blood, shock and the blow to his head. She had taken the bullet out of his shoulder, stitched and bandaged his wounds and given him a tetanus injection and an antibiotic; then she and Rachel had cleaned him up, changed the bedding and made him as comfortable as they could. Once she had decided to help, Honey had become her usual capable, unflustered self, for which Rachel would be eternally grateful. Rachel felt that she'd strained herself to the limits physically, yet from somewhere she'd found the strength to help Honey during the nerve-racking operation to remove the bullet from the man's shoulder, then repair the damage done to his body.

Her hair dry, she put on the clean shirt she had brought

into the bathroom with her. The face in the mirror didn't
look like her own, and she stared at it curiously, noting
the colorless skin and the mauve shadows under eyes dark
with fatigue. She was punch-drunk from weariness, and
she knew it. It was time to go to bed. The only problem
was: where?

The man was in her bed, the only bed in the house. She
didn't have a regular-sized couch, only two matching love
seats. There was always the possibility of making a pallet
on the floor, but she was so tired that even the thought of
the effort involved was almost beyond her. Leaving the
bathroom, she stared at her neat bed with its snowy white
sheets, and at the man who lay so quietly between those
sheets.

She needed to sleep, and she needed to be close to him
so she could hear him if he awoke. She was a thirty-year-
old widow, not a trembling ingenue; the most sensible thing
to do would be to crawl into bed beside him so she could
rest. After staring at him for just a moment longer she made
her decision and turned out the lights, then went around to
the other side of the bed and slipped carefully between the
sheets, trying not to jostle him. She couldn't prevent a low
moan as her tired muscles finally relaxed, and she turned
on her side to put her hand on his arm, so she would wake
up if he became restless. Then she slept.

It was hot when she awoke, and she was drenched in
sweat. Alarm flared briefly when she opened her eyes and
saw the dark masculine face on the pillow next to hers;
then she remembered and rose on her elbow to look at
him. Despite the heat he wasn't sweating, and his breathing
seemed a little too fast. Quick concern rose in her; she sat
up and put her hand on his face, feeling the heat there. He
moved his head restlessly, away from her touch. He was
feverish, which wasn't unexpected.

Quickly Rachel got out of bed, noticing that it was past noon. No wonder the house was so hot! She opened windows and turned on the ceiling fans to get some of the hot air out of the house before she turned on the air conditioner to cool things even more. She didn't use it that much, but her patient needed to be cooled down.

She had to take care of him before anything could be done. She dissolved two aspirin in a teaspoon of water, then gently lifted his head, trying not to jar him. "Open your mouth," she crooned, as if he were a baby. "Swallow this for me. Then I'll let you rest." His head lay heavily against her shoulder, his black eyelashes still resting on his cheeks. His hair was thick and silky beneath her fingers, and warm, reminding her of his fever. She put the spoon against his mouth, noting the clear-cut line of his lips; the spoon pressed down on his bottom lip, opening it just a little. "Come on," she whispered. "Open your mouth."

How many levels of consciousness were there? Did he hear her voice? Make sense of the words? Or was it just the low, tender tone that got through to him? Was it her touch? The warm, sleepy scent of her flesh? Something reached him. He tried to turn toward her, his head nuzzling against her shoulder, and his mouth opened a little. Her heart pounded in her chest as she coaxed him to swallow, hoping that he wouldn't choke. It worked so well that she managed to get three more teaspoons of water down him before he lapsed back into deeper unconsciousness.

She wet a washcloth in cold water, folded it and placed it across his brow, then turned the sheet back until it was low across his hips and began sponging him down with the cold water. Slowly, almost mechanically, she drew the wet cloth over his chest and shoulders and down his powerful arms, then to his lean, hard belly, where the hair on his chest narrowed to a thin, silky line. Rachel drew a deep breath, aware of the slight trembling in her body. He was beautiful. She had never seen a more beautiful man.

She hadn't let herself think about it the night before, when it had been important to get help for him and tend to his wounds, but she had realized even then how attractive he was. His features were even and well formed, his nose thin and straight above the mouth she had just touched. That mouth was firm and strong, with a finely chiseled upper lip that hinted of determination and perhaps even ruthlessness, while his lower lip curved with disturbing sensuality. His chin was square, his jaw firm and darkened with a stubble of black beard. His hair was like thick black silk, the color of coal and without any blue shininess to it. His skin was darkened with an allover tan, a deep, olive-bronze hue.

He was very muscular, without having the off-putting bulk of a body-builder. His were the muscles of hard work and physical exercise, the muscles of a man trained for both strength and speed. Rachel picked up one of his hands, cradling it between both of hers. His hands were long fingered and lean, the strength in them apparent even though he was completely limp. His nails were short and well tended. Lightly she felt the calluses on his palm and fingertips; and she felt something else, as well: the hardness of his flesh on the outside edge of his hand. Her breath became shorter, and wariness prickled along her spine again. Cradling his hand against her cheek, she reached out tentatively and touched the scar on his flat belly, a curving, silvery line that almost glowed against the darkness of his tan. It went across his stomach and around his right side, curving down out of view. That wasn't a surgical scar. She went cold, visualizing the terrible ferocity and viciousness of a knife fight. He must have whirled away from the blade, leaving it to slice his side and back.

A man with a scar like that, and with those tell-tale calluses on his hands, wasn't an ordinary man working an ordinary job. No ordinary man could have swum to shore wounded the way he was; that had required incredible strength and determination. How far had he swum? She hadn't been able to see any lights at sea, she remembered. She looked at his hard, lean face and shivered at the thought of the mental toughness hidden behind his closed eyelids. Yet for all his toughness, he was helpless now; his survival depended on her. She had made the decision to hide him, so it was up to her to nurse and protect him as best she could. Her instincts told her that she had made the right decision, but the uneasiness wouldn't leave her until she had some hard facts to back up her intuition.

The aspirin and sponging had lowered his fever, and he seemed to be sleeping deeply, though she wondered how to tell the difference between sleep and unconsciousness. Honey had promised to come by again that day and check him, to make certain the concussion wasn't worse than she had first thought. There was nothing else Rachel could do, except go about her normal business.

She brushed her teeth and combed her hair, then changed into khaki shorts and a sleeveless white cotton shirt. She started to change in her bedroom, as she normally did, then cast a quick glance at the sleeping man in her bed. Feeling foolish, she went into the bathroom and closed the door. B.B. had been dead for five years, and she wasn't used to having a man around, especially a stranger.

She closed the windows and turned on the air conditioning, then stepped outside. Ebenezer Duck and his band of waddling followers rushed up to her, with Ebenezer squawking his displeasure at having to wait so long for the grain she usually scattered first thing in the morning. Ebenezer was the grouchiest goose living, she was sure, but there was a certain majesty about him, so big and fat and white, and she liked his eccentricities. Joe came around the back corner of the house and stood watching as she fed the geese, keeping his distance from them as he always did. Rachel poured Joe's food in his bowl and filled his water dish with fresh water, then stepped away. He never approached while she was still near his food.

She gathered the ripe tomatoes from her small garden and checked the bean vines; the green beans would need gathering in another day or so. By that time her stomach was rumbling emptily, and she realized that it was hours past her normal breakfast time. Her entire schedule was shot, and there didn't seem to be much point in trying to regain it. How could she concentrate on writing when all her senses were attuned to the man in the bedroom?

She went inside and checked on him, but he hadn't moved. She freshened the wet cloth and replaced it on his brow, then turned her attention to her growling stomach. It was so hot that anything cooked seemed too heavy, so she settled for a sandwich of cold cuts and slices from one of the fresh tomatoes she had just picked. With a glass of iced tea in one hand and her sandwich in the other, she turned on the radio and sat down next to it to listen to the news. There was nothing unusual: the standard political maneuverings, both local and national; a house fire; a trial of local interest, followed by the weather, which promised more of the same. None of that offered even a glimmer of an explanation for the presence and condition of the man in her bedroom.

Switching to the scanner, she listened for almost an hour, but again there was nothing. It was a quiet day, the heat inducing most people to stay inside. There was nothing about any searches or drug busts. When she heard a car coming to a stop in front of her house she turned off the scanner and got up to look out the window. Honey was just getting out of her car, carrying still another grocery sack.

"How's he doing?" she asked as soon as they were inside.

"He still hasn't moved. He was feverish when I woke up, so I managed to get two aspirin and a little bit of water down him. Then I sponged him off."

Honey went into the bedroom and carefully checked his pupil responses, then examined her handiwork on his shoulder and thigh and rebandaged the wounds. "I bought a new thermometer for this," she muttered, shaking it down and putting it in his mouth. "I didn't have one for humans."

Rachel had been hovering worriedly. "How does he look?"

"His pupil responses are better, and the wounds look clean, but he's a long way from being out of the woods. He's going to be a sick man for several days. Actually, the longer he stays quiet like this, the better it is for him. He's resting his head and not putting any stress on his shoulder or leg."

"What about his fever?"

Honey counted his pulse, then took the thermometer out of his mouth and read it. "A hundred and two. Not critical, but like I said, he's going to be very sick for a while. Give him aspirin every four hours and get as much water down him as you can. Keep sponging him off with cool water to keep him comfortable. I'll be back tomorrow, but I can't come too often or it'll look suspicious."

Rachel managed a tight smile. "Are you sure your imagination isn't running away with you, too?"

Honey shrugged. "I listened to the radio and read the newspaper. There wasn't anything to account for this guy. Maybe you're rubbing off on me, but all I can think is that only two scenarios are left. One is that he's an agent, and the other is that he's a drug runner hiding from his own people."

Looking down at him, at his tousled black hair, Rachel shook her head. "I don't think he's a drug runner."

"Why not? Do they have identifying tattoos, or something?"

She didn't tell Honey about his hands. "I'm probably just trying to reassure myself that I've done the right thing."

"For what it's worth, I think you have. Last night I didn't, but today I've thought about it, and I struck up a chat with a deputy this morning. He didn't mention anything unusual. If your guy is involved with drugs you'll have time to find out before he's in any shape to be dangerous. So, I guess you were right."

There was still another possibility, one that Rachel had thought of but had no intention of mentioning to Honey. What if he was an agent…for someone else? A drug runner, an agent—neither of those was very savory, considering what she had learned about both occupations while she'd been a reporter. Rachel had been a very good reporter, an ace, digging for the facts even in the face of danger. She knew, far more than Honey did, just how dangerous it was to hide this man, but there was something in her that was incapable of simply washing her hands of responsibility and turning him over to the sheriff, then letting events take their course. She had become responsible for him the second she had seen him feebly swimming in the Gulf, and turning him over to someone else wouldn't change that fact. As long as there was a possibility, however remote, that he was deserving of her protection, she had to offer it. It was a risk she had to take.

"How much longer will it be before he wakes up?" she murmured.

Honey hesitated. "I don't know. I'm a veterinarian, remember? With the fever, the loss of blood, the knock on his head…I just don't know. He should be hooked up to an IV, getting fluids. His pulse is weak and fast, he probably needs some blood and he's shocky, but he's coming out of it. He may wake up at any time, or it may be tomorrow. When he does wake up he may be disoriented, which isn't surprising. Don't let him get excited, and whatever you do, don't let him get up."

Rachel looked at him, at his powerfully muscled torso, and wondered if there was any way on earth she could prevent him from doing anything he set his mind on doing.

Honey was taking gauze and tape out of her bag. "Change his bandages tomorrow morning. I won't be back until tomorrow night, unless you think he's getting worse and call me, and in that case you'd be better off calling a doctor."

Rachel managed a taut smile. "Thanks. I know this hasn't been easy for you to handle."

"At least you brought some excitement into the summer. I've got to go now, or Rafferty will tear a strip off me for keeping him waiting."

"Tell John I said hello," Rachel said as they stepped onto the porch.

"Depends on his mood." Honey grinned, her eyes lighting with the pleasurable prospect of battle. She and John Rafferty had been warring ever since Honey had set up practice in the area; Rafferty had made plain his opinion that a woman wasn't strong enough to handle the job, and Honey had set out to prove him wrong. Their relationship had long since evolved into mutual respect and a continuous wrangle that they both enjoyed. Since Honey had a long-standing engagement to an overseas engineer, with plans to marry during the winter when he returned to the States, she was also safe from Rafferty's legendary tomcatting, because one thing Rafferty didn't do was poach.

Joe stood just at the corner of the house, muscles tight as he warily watched Honey get in her car and drive off. Ordinarily Rachel would have spoken soothingly to him, but today she, too, was tense and wary. "Guard," she said softly, not knowing if he would understand the command. "That's a good boy. Guard the house."

She managed to work for a couple of hours on her manuscript, but she couldn't really concentrate on what she was doing when she kept listening for any sound from the bedroom. Every few minutes she went in to check on him, but each time he was lying just as he had been the time before. She tried several times to get him to drink something, but his head would loll against her shoulder whenever she lifted him, and he didn't respond at all. Late in the afternoon his fever began to rise again, and Rachel abandoned all attempts to write. Somehow she had to rouse him enough to give him more aspirin.

The fever seemed worse this time. His skin burned to the touch, and his face was flushed with hectic color. Rachel talked to him as she lifted his head, crooning and cajoling. With her free hand she stroked his chest and arms, trying to rouse him, and her efforts were rewarded when he suddenly groaned sharply and turned his face against her neck.

The sound and motion, from someone who had been still and silent, startled her. Her heart jumped wildly, and she was unable to move for a moment, simply holding him and feeling the scrape of his growing beard against her neck. It was an oddly erotic sensation, and her body quickened in remembrance. A hot flush colored her cheeks; what was she doing, reacting like that to the unconscious touch of a sick man? Granted, it had been a long time for her, but she'd never considered herself love starved, so hungry for the touch of a man that the most inadvertent contact could turn her on.

She reached for the teaspoon with the dissolved aspirin in it and held it to his mouth, touching his lips with the spoon as she had before. Restlessly he turned his head away, and Rachel followed the movement with the spoon. "No you don't," she crooned. "You aren't getting away. Open your mouth and take this. It'll make you feel better."

A frown puckered his straight black brows and he fretted, evading the spoon once more. Persistently Rachel tried again, and this time she got the bitter aspirin into his mouth. He swallowed, and while he was cooperating she spoon-fed him several ounces of iced tea before he began to sink back into a stupor. Following the routine she had begun that morning, she patiently sponged him down with cool water until the aspirin began to work and the fever subsided again, allowing him to rest.

His response, fretful as it had been, gave her hope that he would soon be waking up, but that hope died during the long night. His fever soared at intervals until she could give him more aspirin and bring it under control again. What rest she got that night came in brief snatches, because she spent most of the time bending over him, patiently wiping him with a cold wet cloth to keep him as cool as she could, and doing all of the other things that were necessary for a bedridden patient.

Toward dawn he groaned again and tried to turn onto his side. Guessing that his muscles were aching from lying in one position for so long, Rachel helped him to roll onto his right side, then took advantage of the new position and sponged his back with cold water. He quieted almost immediately, his breathing becoming deep and even. Her eyes burning and her muscles sore, Rachel continued to rub his back until she was convinced that he was at last resting,

then crept into bed herself. She was so tired.... She stared
at his muscled back, wondering if she dared go to sleep and
how she could possibly stay awake a moment longer. Her
eyelids drooped heavily, and she immediately fell asleep,
instinct moving her closer to his warm back.

It was still early when she awoke; the clock told her that
she had slept a little over two hours. He was lying on his
back again, and had kicked the cover into a twisted heap
around his left leg. Disturbed that his movements hadn't
awakened her, Rachel got out of bed and went around to
straighten the sheet and pull it back over him, trying not
to jar his left leg. Her gaze drifted over his naked body
and hastily she jerked her eyes away, flushing again. What
on earth was wrong with her? She knew what naked men
looked like, and it wasn't even as if this were the first time
she'd seen him. She had been nursing him for almost two
days now; she'd bathed him and helped sew him up. Still,
she couldn't stop the warm feeling that swelled inside every
time she looked at him. It's just lust, she told herself firmly.
Plain, old-fashioned lust. I'm a normal woman, and he's a
good-looking man. It's normal to admire his body, so I've
got to stop acting like a giggly teenager!

She pulled the sheet up to his chest, then coaxed him
into taking more aspirin. Why hadn't he awoken by now?
Was the concussion more severe than Honey had thought?
Yet his condition didn't seem to be getting worse, and in
fact he was a little more responsive than he had been; it
was easier to get him to take the aspirin and liquids now,
but she wanted him to open his eyes, to talk to her. Until
then she couldn't be assured that she hadn't harmed him
by making the decision to keep him hidden.

Hidden from whom? her subconscious jeered. No one
had been looking for him. The jitters she had been suffering
from seemed foolish on this bright, cloudless morning.

While he was quiet she fed the animals and worked in the garden, gathering the green beans and the few tomatoes that had ripened overnight. There were a few yellow squash ready to be picked, and she decided to make a squash casserole for dinner. She weeded the garden and around the shrubs, and by that time the heat had become stifling. Even the usual breeze from the Gulf was missing, and the air lay hot and heavy. She thought longingly of a swim, but didn't dare leave her patient unattended for that long.

When she checked on him again she found the sheet once again kicked down, and he was moving a little, his head turning fretfully. It wasn't time for more aspirin, but he was hot; she got a bowl of cold water and sat on the bed beside him, slowly sponging him with the cold water until he was cool and resting again. When she eased off the bed she glanced down at him and wondered if she would be wasting her time to cover him up. It was simply too hot for him, as feverish as he was, even though she'd left the air conditioning on and the house felt cool to her. Carefully she untangled the sheet from around his feet, her touch light and fleeting; then she paused and her hands returned to his feet. He had nice feet, lean and tanned, masculine and well tended, like his hands. He also had the same tough calluses on the outside ridges of his feet that he had on his hands.

He was a trained warrior.

Tears burned her eyes as she pulled the sheet up to his waist and left it there, deciding to compromise. She had no reason to cry; he'd chosen his life and wouldn't appreciate her sympathy. The people who lived on the edge of danger did so because that was what they wanted; she had lived there herself, and she knew that she had freely chosen to accept the perils that came her way. B.B. had accepted the danger of his job, counting it as the price to be paid for something he thought was worth doing. What neither of them had counted on was that it would be *her* job that would cost him his life.

By the time Honey came that night Rachel had long since controlled herself, and a fragrant squash casserole greeted Honey's nose when she came in the door. "Umm, that smells good," she breathed. "How's our patient?"

Rachel shook her head. "Not much change. He's moving around a little, fretting, when the fever gets high, but he hasn't woken up yet."

She had just twitched the sheet up over him again a few moments before, so he was covered when Honey went in to check on him. "He's doing good," Honey murmured after looking at his wounds and checking his eyes. "Let him sleep. It's just what he needs."

"It's been so long," Rachel murmured.

"He went through a lot. The body has a way of taking over and getting what it needs."

It didn't take much to get Honey to stay for dinner. The casserole, fresh peas and sliced tomatoes did a lot of convincing by themselves. "This is a lot better than the hamburger I'd planned on," Honey said, waving her fork for emphasis. "I think our boy is out of danger, so I wasn't going to come by tomorrow, but if you're cooking again I can always change my mind."

It felt good to laugh, after the tension of the past two days. Rachel's eyes sparkled. "This is the first meal I've cooked since it got so hot. I've been living on fruit and cereal and salad, anything to keep from turning on the stove. But since I've been running the air conditioning to keep him comfortable, tonight cooking didn't seem so bad."

After they'd cleaned the kitchen Honey checked her watch. "It's not too late. I think I'll stop by Rafferty's and check on one of his mares that's due to foal. It may save a trip back out as soon as I get home. Thanks for feeding me."

"Anytime. I don't know what I'd have done without you."

Honey regarded her for a moment, her freckled face serious. "You'd have managed, wouldn't you? You're one of those people who do what has to be done, without fussing about it. That guy in there owes you a lot."

Rachel didn't know if he would see it that way or not. When she came out of the bathroom after showering she watched him intently, willing him to open his eyes and speak to her, to give her some hint of the man behind those closed lids. Every hour that passed increased the mystery that surrounded him. Who was he? Who had shot him, and why? Why was there nothing being mentioned in the news media that could apply to him? An abandoned boat found floating in the Gulf or washed up on shore would have made the news. A missing person's report would have been in the newspaper. A drug bust, a prison escape, anything, but there had been nothing that would explain why he had washed in with the tide.

She got into bed beside him, hoping for at least a few hours of sleep. He was resting better, she thought, the fever not climbing quite as high as it had at first. Her fingers closed over his arm, and she slept.

The shaking of the bed awoke her, startling her out of a sound sleep. She sat straight up in bed, her heart pounding. He was moving restlessly, trying to kick the cover away from him with only his right leg, and finally he succeeded in getting most of it off him. His skin was hot, and he was breathing too heavily. A glance at the clock told her that it was well past the time he should have had more aspirin.

She turned on the lamp beside the bed and went into the bathroom to get the aspirin and fresh water. He swallowed without fuss this time, and Rachel got him to drink almost a full glass of water. She eased his head down onto the pillow again, her fingers slow to move from his hair.

Daydreaming again! She jerked herself sharply away from the dangerous direction those daydreams were taking. He needed to be cooled down, and she was standing there fantasizing about him. Disgusted with herself, she wet a washcloth and bent over him, slowly wiping his torso with the cool cloth.

A hand touched her breast. She froze, her eyes widening. Her nightgown was loose and sleeveless, with a scooped neckline that had fallen well away from her body when she bent over him. His right hand moved slowly inside the neckline, and he brushed the backs of his lean, strong fingers insistently over her nipple, back and forth, until the small bud of flesh tightened and Rachel had to close her eyes at the sharp, unexpected pleasure. Then his hand moved lower, so slowly that her breath halted in her chest, stroking over the velvet underside of her breast. "Pretty," he murmured, his voice deep, the single word slurred.

The word echoed sharply in Rachel's mind, and her head jerked around, her eyes opening. He was awake! For a moment she stared into half-opened eyes that were so black it was as if light drowned in them; then his lashes slowly dropped and he was asleep again, his hand falling away from her breast.

She was so shaken that she could barely move. Her flesh still burned from his touch, and that instant when she had stared into his eyes was a moment that was frozen in time, so imprinted on her memory that she felt branded by his glance. Black eyes, blacker than night, without any hint of brown. They had been hazy with fever and pain, but he had seen something he liked and reached out for it. Looking down, she saw that the gaping neckline of the loose, comfortable cotton shift left her breasts completely exposed to his view, and his touch; she had unwittingly invited both.

Her hands trembled as she automatically continued wiping him down with the cool cloth. Her senses were reeling, her mind scrambling to adjust to the fact that he had been awake, that he had spoken, even if it had been only one word. Somehow during the long two days when he had lain motionless, even though she had longed for him to wake, she had stopped expecting him to. She had taken care of him as totally as one would an infant, and now she was as startled as if an infant had suddenly spoken. But he was no infant; he was a man. All man, if the frank appreciation in that single slurred word was any measurement. "Pretty," he'd said, and her cheeks heated.

Then the implications of that single word hit her, and she jerked upright. He was American! If he'd been anything else the first word he spoke, when he was only half-conscious and burning with fever, would have been in his native language. But that one word had been in English, and the accent, though slurred, had definitely been American. Part of the slur could have come from a natural accent, a southern or western drawl.

American. She wondered at the heritage that had given him his dark coloring, Italian or Arabic, Hungarian or American Indian, maybe even Black Irish? Spanish? Tartar? The high, chiseled cheekbones and thin, hawk-bridged nose could have come from any of those bloodlines, but he was definitely from the huge American melting pot.

Her heart was still hammering in her chest with excitement. Even after she had emptied the bowl of water, turned out the lamp and crawled into bed beside him, she was quivering and unable to sleep. He had opened his eyes and spoken to her, had moved voluntarily. He was recovering! A burden lifted from her shoulders with the knowledge.

She turned on her side and looked at him, barely able to see the outline of his profile in the darkness of the room, but every pore in her skin sensed his nearness. He was warm and alive, and an odd mixture of pain and ecstasy swelled inside her, because somehow he had become important to her, so important that the tenor of her existence had been irrevocably altered. Even when he left, as practicality told her he must, she would never be the same again. Diamond Bay had given him to her, a strange gift from the turquoise waters. She reached out and trailed her fingers lightly down his muscled arm, then withdrew her touch, because the feel of his skin made her heart lurch again. He had come from the sea, but it was she who had suffered the sea change.

CHAPTER FOUR

"HE'S DEAD, I'm telling you."

A slim man, with graying brown hair and a narrow, intense face that belied the self-imposed calmness and control of his manner, gave the speaker a look of contemptuous amusement. "Do you think we can afford to assume that, Ellis? We have found nothing—I repeat, nothing—to assure us of his death."

Tod Ellis narrowed his eyes. "There's no way he could've survived. That boat went up like a fuel tank."

An elegant red-haired woman had been silently listening to the two, and now she leaned forward to put out a cigarette. "And the report from one of the men that he saw something, or someone, go over the side?"

Ellis flushed angrily. These two had deferred to him when it came to setting up the ambush, but now they were treating him like a rank amateur. He didn't like it; he was far from an amateur, and they had damned well needed him when they were after Sabin. The plan hadn't worked out exactly as they'd wanted, but Sabin hadn't escaped, and that was the most important thing. If they had thought it would be easy to capture him, then they were fools, at best. "Even if he got into the water," he said patiently, "he was wounded. We saw him get hit. We were miles out. There's no way he could have gotten to shore. He either drowned, or a shark got him. Why take the chance on drawing attention to ourselves by searching for him?"

The other man's pale blue eyes looked beyond Ellis, into the past. "Ah, but this is Sabin we're talking about, not some ordinary man. How many times has he slipped away from us? Too many for me to trust that it was so easy to kill him. We found no remains on the boat, and if, as you say, he either drowned or was attacked by sharks, there still would have been *some* evidence. We've patrolled these waters for two days without finding anything. The logical thing to do is to move our search to shore."

"We'll be exposing ourselves if we do."

The woman smiled. "Not if we do it right. We must simply be discreet. Our biggest danger is the possibility that he was picked up by another boat and taken to a hospital. If he's had the opportunity to talk to someone, to make some calls, we won't be able to get near him. First we must find him, though. I agree with Charles. Too much is at stake for us to simply assume that he's dead."

Ellis's face was grim. "Do you have any idea how large an area we'll have to cover?"

Charles drew a map of Florida closer. "Our position was here," he said, marking the spot with an X. "Given the distance and the tides, which I've already checked, I think we should concentrate our efforts in this area." He drew a long oval on the map and tapped it with his pen. "Noelle, check all the hospitals in the area, and also the police blotters, to find if anyone has been treated for a gunshot wound. While you're doing that we'll be searching every inch of the coastline." He leaned back in his chair and surveyed Ellis with his arctic gaze. "Can you contact your people and find out without arousing suspicions if he's called anyone?"

Ellis shrugged. "I have a reliable contact."

"Then make it. We may have waited too long as it is."

He would make the call, Ellis thought, but he was sure it would be a waste of time. Sabin was dead; these people persisted in acting as if he were some sort of superman who could disappear into thin air, then miraculously reappear. Okay, so he'd had a reputation when he was in the field; that had been years ago. He would have lost his edge since then, sitting around at a dull desk job the way he'd been doing. No, Sabin was dead; Ellis was certain of it.

RACHEL SAT ON THE FRONT porch swing, a newspaper spread across her lap and heaped with green beans. A dishpan sat on the swing beside her, and she systematically broke the tips off the beans and peeled the string off them, then broke the pods into inch-long sections, which she dropped into the dishpan. She didn't like stringing green beans, but she liked to eat them, so it was a necessary evil. She kept the swing gently swaying and listened to a portable radio set on the windowsill. She was listening to an FM country station, but the volume was turned low because she didn't want to disturb her patient, who was sleeping peacefully.

She had spent the morning expecting him to finally wake up for good, but instead he was still alternating between periods of deep sleep, when the aspirin and sponging got his fever down, and restlessness, when his temperature soared. He hadn't opened his eyes or spoken again, though once he had groaned and held his shoulder with his right hand until Rachel loosened his grip and held his hand, soothing him with soft murmurs of reassurance.

Joe eased up from his position under the oleander bush, a rumble forming in his throat. Rachel glanced at him, then swept her gaze around the yard and toward the road, to the left, but could see nothing. It wasn't like Joe to pay any attention to squirrels or rabbits. "What is it?" she asked, unable to keep the tightness of apprehension out of her voice, and Joe responded to her tone by moving to stand directly in front of the steps. The rumble was a full-fledged growl now, and he was staring toward the pine thicket, toward the slope that led down to Diamond Bay.

Two men were coming out of the thicket.

Rachel continued to string and snap the beans as if she were totally unconcerned, but she felt every muscle in her body tense. She stared at them, openly, deciding that that would be the normal thing to do. They were dressed casually, in lightweight cotton canvas pants and pullover shirts, with loose cotton jackets. Rachel eyed the jackets. The temperature was ninety-nine degrees and it wasn't quite noon yet, so it promised to get hotter. Jackets were anything but practical—unless they were needed to hide shoulder holsters.

As the men crossed the road and approached the house Joe's growls became snarls, and he crouched, the hair along his neck lifted. The men halted, and Rachel caught the movement one man made beneath his jacket before he halted himself. "Sorry about that," she called, leisurely putting aside the beans and getting to her feet. "Joe doesn't like strangers in general, and men in particular. He won't even let the neighbor in the yard. Guess some man abused him once. Are you lost, or has your boat quit on you?" As she talked she came down the steps and laid a calming hand on Joe's back, feeling the way he shifted a little away from her.

"Neither. We're looking for someone." The man who answered her was tall and good-looking, with sandy brown hair and an open, college-boy smile that flashed whitely in his tanned face. He glanced down at Joe. "Uh, do you want to get a better hold on the dog?"

"He'll be all right, as long as you don't come any nearer to the house." Rachel hoped that was true. Giving Joe another pat, she walked past him and approached the men. "I don't think it's me he's protecting as much as his territory. Now what was it you said?"

The other man was shorter, slimmer and darker than Mr. All-American College Boy. "FBI," he said briskly, flashing a badge in front of her nose. "I'm Agent Lowell. This is Agent Ellis. We're looking for a man we think might be in this area."

Rachel wrinkled her forehead, praying she wasn't overdoing it. "An escaped convict?"

Agent Ellis's gaze had been appreciatively measuring Rachel's long, bare legs, but now his eyes lifted to her face. "No, but prison is where we're trying to put him. We think he may have come ashore somewhere in this area."

"Haven't seen any strangers around here, but I'll keep a sharp watch. What does he look like?"

"Six feet tall, maybe a little taller. Black hair, black eyes."

"Seminole?"

Both men looked startled. "No, he's not an Indian," Agent Lowell finally said. "But he's dark, sort of Indian-looking."

"Do you have a picture of him?"

A quick look passed between the two men. "No."

"Is he dangerous? I mean, a murderer, or anything like that?" A lump had formed in her chest and was rising toward her throat. What would she do if they told her he was a murderer? How could she bear it?

Again that look, as if they weren't sure what to tell her. "He should be considered armed and dangerous. If you see anything at all suspicious give us a call at this number." Agent Lowell scribbled a telephone number on a piece of paper and gave it to Rachel, who glanced at it before folding it and putting it in her pocket.

"I'll do that," she said. "Thank you for coming by."

They started to leave; then Agent Lowell paused and turned back to her, his eyes narrowed. "There are some strange marks on the beach down there, as if something has been dragged. Do you know anything about them?"

Rachel's blood froze in her veins. Fool! she told herself numbly. She should have gone down to the beach and obliterated all those marks. At least the tide would have washed away any blood and other signs that had been left where he had fallen. Deliberately she wrinkled her forehead, giving herself time to think, then let her face clear. "Oh, you must mean where I collect shells and driftwood. I pile them all on a tarp and haul it up here. That way I can get it all up the slope with just one trip."

"What do you do with them? The shells and driftwood."

She didn't like the way Agent Lowell was looking at her, as if he didn't believe a word she said. "I sell them," she said, and it was the truth. "I own two souvenir shops."

"I see." He smiled at her. "Well, good luck in your shell hunting." They turned to leave again.

"Do you need a lift?" she asked, raising her voice. "You look hot now, and it's going to get hotter."

Both of them looked up at the blistering sun in the cloudless blue bowl of the sky; their faces were shiny with perspiration. "We came by boat," Agent Ellis said. "We're going to check along the beach some more. Thanks, anyway."

"Anytime. Oh, watch out if you go north. It gets swampy."

"Thanks again."

She watched them disappear into the pines and down the slope, and chills prickled her skin despite the heat. Slowly she returned to the porch and sat down on the swing, automatically returning to the task of breaking the beans. Everything they had said swirled in her mind, and she tried to sort it all out, to get her thoughts in order again. FBI? It was possible, but they had flashed their badges so swiftly she hadn't been able to examine them. They knew what he looked like, but they didn't have any photographs of him; she thought it would be reasonable that the FBI would have some likeness, even if it was just a drawing of someone they were trying to find. And they had side-stepped the question when she asked what he had done, as if they hadn't anticipated that and didn't know how to answer. They had said he should be considered armed and dangerous, but instead he was naked and helpless. Didn't they know he'd been shot? Why hadn't they said something about that?

But what if she were harboring a criminal? That had always been one of the possibilities, though she had discounted it. Now it swarmed back into her mind, and she felt sick.

The beans were finished. She took the pan into the house and set it in the sink, then returned to gather up the paper with the strings and broken ends on it. As she carried it to the kitchen to stuff it in the trash can she cast an apprehensive look at her open bedroom door. She could just see the head of the bed and his black hair on the pillow... her pillow. When he woke up again, and she looked into those night-black eyes, would she be looking into the eyes of a criminal? A killer?

Swiftly she washed her hands and flipped through the telephone book, then punched the number. It rang only once before a harried male voice said, "Sheriff's Department."

"Andy Phelps, please."

"Just a minute."

There was another ring, but this time the answer was absentminded, as if the person had other things on his mind. "Phelps."

"Andy, this is Rachel."

Immediately his voice warmed. "Hi, honey. Everything okay?"

"Fine. Hot, but fine. How are Trish and the kids?"

"The kids are doing okay, but Trish is praying for school to start."

She laughed, sympathizing with Andy's wife. Their boys carried rowdiness to new heights. "Listen, two guys just stopped by the house. They walked up from the beach."

His voice sharpened. "They give you any trouble?"

"No, nothing like that. They said they were FBI, but I didn't get a good look at their badges. They're looking for some man. Are they legitimate? Has your department been notified of anything? I may be paranoid, but I'm out here at the end of the road, and Rafferty's miles away. After B.B...." Her voice trailed away with the sudden pain of the memory. It had been five years, but there were still times when the loss and regret seared her, when the emptiness got to her.

Like no one else on earth, Andy understood. He had worked with B.B. in the DEA. The memory roughened his tone. "I know. You can't be too careful, honey. Look, we've had orders come down to cooperate with some guys who are looking for a man. It's all hush-hush. They're not the local FBI people. I doubt that they're FBI at all, but orders are orders."

Rachel's hand tightened on the receiver. "And an agency is an agency?"

"Yeah, something like that. Keep quiet about it, but keep your eyes open. I'm not real comfortable with the feel of this."

He wasn't the only one. "I will. Thanks."

"Sure thing. Listen, why don't you come to dinner some night soon? It's been a while since we've seen you."

"Thanks, I'd love to. Have Trish call me."

They hung up, and Rachel drew a deep breath. If Andy didn't think the men were FBI, that was good enough for her. Going into the bedroom, she stood beside the bed and watched the man sleep, his deep chest slowly rising and falling. She had kept the blinds closed since the night she had brought him into the house, so the room was dim and cool, but a thin ray of sunlight crept between two of the slats and slanted across his stomach, making that long, thin scar glow. Whoever he was, whatever he was involved in, he wasn't a common criminal.

They played lethal games, the men and women who peopled the shadowy world of intelligence and counterintelligence. They lived their lives balanced on the razor's edge of death; they were hard and cold, intense but casual. They weren't like other people, the people who worked at the same job every day and went home to their houses, to their families. Was he one of those for whom a normal life was impossible? She was almost certain of it now. But what was going on, and who could she trust? Someone had shot him. Either he had escaped, or he had been dumped in the ocean to drown. Were those two men hunting for him to protect him, or to finish off the job? Did he possess some highly sensitive information, something critical to defense?

She trailed her fingers over his hand, which was lying limply on top of the sheet. His skin was hot and dry; fever still burned inside him as his body tried to mend itself. She had been able to spoon enough sweetened tea and water into him to keep him from becoming dehydrated, but he had to begin eating soon, or she would be forced to take him to a hospital. This was the third day; he had to have nourishment.

Her brow furrowed. If he could swallow tea, he could swallow soup. She should have thought of that before! Briskly she went into the kitchen and opened a can of chicken noodle soup, ran it through the blender until it was liquified, then put it on the stove to simmer. "Sorry it isn't homemade," she muttered to the man in the bedroom. "But I don't have any chicken in the freezer. Besides, this is easier."

She watched him closely, checking on him every few minutes; when he began to stir restlessly, moving his head back and forth on the pillow and kicking at the sheet, she prepared a tray for his first "meal," such as it was. It didn't take her long, less than five minutes. She carried the tray into the bedroom and almost dropped it when he suddenly heaved himself up on his right elbow, staring at her with those piercing, fever-bright black eyes.

Rachel's entire body tensed as desperation flooded her. If he fell off the bed she wouldn't be able to get him back on it without help. He was weaving back and forth on his precarious prop, still staring at her with burning intensity. She plunked the tray down on the floor where she stood, sloshing some of the soup over the side of the bowl, then darted to the side of the bed to catch him. Gently, supporting his head and trying not to jostle his shoulder, she put her arm around his back and eased his head onto her shoulder, bracing herself against his weight. "Lie down," she said in the calm, soothing tone she always used for him. "You can't get up yet."

A frown laced his black eyebrows together, and he resisted her efforts. "It's time for the party," he muttered, his words still drunkenly slurred.

He was awake, but certainly not lucid, drifting in a fever-induced dream world. "No, the party hasn't started yet," she reassured him, catching his right elbow and pulling it forward so he wouldn't be able to prop himself up on it. His weight fell heavily on her supporting arm as she lowered him back onto the pillow. "You have time for a nap."

He lay there, breathing heavily, his brow still furrowed

as he stared at her. His gaze didn't flicker as she retrieved the tray from the floor and placed it on the bedside table; his attention was locked on her, as if he were trying to make sense of things, to fight his way out of the mists that clouded his mind. She talked quietly to him as she propped him up on her extra pillows; she didn't know if he understood what she was saying, but her voice and touch seemed to calm him. Sitting on the side of the bed, she began to feed him, talking to him all the while. He was docile, opening his mouth whenever she put the spoon to his lips, but soon his eyelids began to droop as he tired. Quickly she gave him aspirin, elated at how easy it had been to feed him.

As she supported his head and pulled the extra pillows from behind him so he could lie flat again, she had an idea. It was worth a try. "What's your name?"

He frowned, his head jerking restlessly. "Whose?" he asked, his deep voice full of confusion.

Rachel remained bent over him, her hand under his head. Her heart was beating faster. Maybe she could begin getting some answers! "Yours. What's your name?"

"Mine?" The questions were making him fretful, agitated. He stared hard at her as he tried to concentrate, his gaze slipping over her face, then moving lower.

She tried again. "Yes, yours. What's your name?"

"Mine?" He drew a deep breath, then said it again. "Mine." The second time it was a statement, not a question. Slowly he moved, lifting both hands, wincing at the pain in his shoulder. He molded his hands over her breasts, cupping them warmly in his palms and rubbing her nipples with his thumbs. "Mine," he said again, stating what he plainly considered to be his ownership.

For a moment, just for a moment, Rachel was helpless against the unexpected pleasure burning her flesh at his touch. She was frozen in place, her nerve endings going wild, her body flooding with warmth as his thumbs turned her nipples into hardened nubs. Then reality returned with a thud, and she jerked away from him, bolting off the bed. Exasperation at him—and anger at herself—filled her. "That's what you think," she snapped at him. "These are mine, not yours!"

His eyelids drooped sleepily. She stood there glaring down at him. Evidently the only things on his mind were partying and sex! "Damn it, you have a one-track mind!" she angrily accused, half under her breath.

His eyelashes fluttered open, and he looked at her again. "Yes," he said clearly, then closed his eyes and went to sleep.

Rachel stood beside the bed with clenched fists, torn between laughing and swatting him. It was doubtful that he had understood anything she'd said; that last provocative word could have been in answer to her accusation, or to some question that existed only in his own foggy consciousness. Now he was sleeping heavily again, totally relaxed and oblivious to the upheaval he had left behind.

Shaking her head, she picked up the tray and quietly left the room. Her insides were still quivering with mingled indignation and desire. It was an uncomfortable combination, uncomfortable because she wasn't one to delude herself, and she couldn't deny that she was attracted to him more powerfully than she could ever have imagined. Touching him was a compulsion; her hands wanted to linger on his warm skin. His voice made her shiver deep inside, and one look from those black eyes made her feel electrified. And his touch...his touch! Twice now he had put his hands on her, and each time she had turned molten with uncontrollable pleasure.

It was insane to feel so intensely about a man she didn't

know, but no amount of self-lecturing could change her response. Their lives had become linked from the moment she had dragged him out of the surf; in assuming responsibility for his safety, she had committed herself to him on a level that went so deep she was only now beginning to realize its reaches. And he had become hers, as if that act of mercy had created a marriage of their lives, binding them together regardless of their wishes or wants.

Though he was a stranger she already knew a lot about him. She knew that he was hard and fast and well trained; he would have to be, to survive in the world he had chosen. He also possessed a tough-mindedness that was awesome in its intensity, a steely determination that had kept him swimming in the night-dark ocean with two bullet wounds in his body, when a lesser man would have drowned almost immediately. She knew that he was important to the people who were hunting him, though she didn't know if they wanted to protect him or kill him. She knew that he didn't snore and that he had an extremely healthy libido, despite his physical incapacitation. He was still when he slept, except when his bones and muscles ached from his flaring fever; that stillness had bothered her at first, until she realized that it was natural to him.

He also answered no questions, even in his delirium, not even one as elemental as his name. It could be the fever-induced confusion, but it was also more than possible that his training was so deeply ingrained in his subconscious that even illness or drugs couldn't override it.

Soon, tomorrow or the next day, or perhaps even during the coming night, he would wake up and be in full possession of his senses. He would require clothing, and answers to his questions. She wondered what those questions would be, and thought of her own questions, though she was beginning to wonder if he would provide any answers.

She couldn't prepare for what he might or might not say, because she felt it would be useless to try to predict his actions. Clothing, however, was a problem she could do something about. She had nothing there that would fit him; though she often wore men's shirts she had bought them specifically for herself, and they would be far too small for him. She hadn't kept any of B.B.'s clothing, though that would have been useless in any case, as B.B. had weighed a good thirty pounds less than this man.

Mentally she made a list of the things he would need. She didn't like leaving him alone for the length of time it would take her to drive to the nearest discount store, but it was either that or ask Honey to do the shopping and bring the things out. She considered that. It was tempting, but the arrival of the two men that morning made her reluctant to involve Honey any deeper in the situation. It should be safe to leave him alone for an hour. She would do her shopping early the next morning, which would give those men time to move out of the immediate area.

SHE CAREFULLY LOCKED the house when she left, and told Joe to stand guard. Her patient was sleeping quietly; she had just gotten him settled, so he should sleep for several hours. Her gun-metal Regal ate up the miles as she pushed her speed as fast as she could, anxiety gnawing at her. It should be all right to leave him alone, but she wouldn't breathe easy until she was back home and could see that for herself.

Though it had just opened for the morning, the local K mart was already swarming with customers who had all decided to do their shopping before the worst heat of the day was upon them. Rachel got a shopping cart and maneuvered it through the crowded aisles, dodging the darting preschoolers who had managed to escape their mothers and were headed, one and all, for the toy department. She steered around browsers, idled behind a frail white-haired woman who walked with a cane, then spotted a clear aisle and broke to the right.

A package of underwear, a few pairs of socks and a pair of jogging shoes, size ten, went into the cart. She had measured his feet that morning, so she was fairly certain the shoes would fit. Two button-up shirts and a cotton terry pullover shirt were piled on top of the shoes. She was uncertain of what size pants to get, but finally selected a pair of jeans, a pair of black denim cutoffs in case the jeans were too uncomfortable on his leg and a pair of khaki chinos. She was ready to head for the checkout counter when a tingle ran up her spine, and her head lifted. Glancing around, she saw a man casually examining some sale items, and the tingle became a full-fledged chill. It was Agent Lowell.

Without breaking stride, she diverted her path to the women's section. The men's clothes, though androgynous enough that they couldn't be recognized as men's unless the sizes were examined, would be a dead giveaway under close scrutiny. Unfortunately Agent Lowell was exactly the type to subject everything to just such an examination. The undershorts, socks and shoes, beneath the pants and shirts, could have no logical explanation.

Ruthlessly she went through the underwear section. Several pairs of panties, all lace and satin, were thrown on top of the pile. A frothy confection of a bra and a matching half-slip were added; she hoped she could trust in the normal male's aversion to handling female lingerie in a public place to keep Agent Lowell from examining the contents of her shopping cart. Out of the corner of her eye she saw him casually moving closer, pausing every so often to examine certain items with absent interest. He was good;

he slid through the crowds without attracting notice. He tracked, while giving no appearance of being a hunter.

A grim look entered Rachel's eyes. He would have to be determined indeed to get to the bottom of her cart. Wheeling around, she headed for the drug-and-health section. Intimate female items, some of which she never used but chose now for their conspicuous packaging, were thrown into the cart. If he dared reach for anything she would accuse him of being a pervert in a voice loud enough to bring every store security guard at a run.

He was closing in again. Rachel chose her moment, then turned her cart and all but rammed it into his knee.

"Oh, my goodness, I'm sorry!" she gasped in apology. "I didn't see you—oh," she said again, startled recognition in her voice. "Ag—" She stopped, looked around, then lowered her voice to little more than a whisper. "Agent Lowell."

It was an Academy Award–winning performance, but it might have been wasted on Agent Lowell, who was preoccupied with rubbing his knee. He straightened, a look of pain still in his eyes. "Hello again, Ms....I don't believe I got your name yesterday."

"Jones," she said, holding out her hand. "Rachel Jones."

His hand was hard, but his palm was a little moist. Agent Lowell wasn't quite as relaxed as he appeared.

"You're out early," he commented.

"With the heat the way it is, it's best to either get out early or wait until after sundown. You really should wear a hat if you're going to be walking around today the way you were yesterday." His face was already sunburned, so her advice was too late.

His expressionless eyes drifted down to the contents of the cart, then jerked back up abruptly. Rachel felt a moment's grim satisfaction at her choices. His presence could be pure coincidence, or it could be deliberate, but he was automatically curious; it was part of his job. She sensed that he had been less disarmed by her studied nonchalance and innocence than the other agent had been.

"You, uh, may have to float a loan to pay for all that," he said after a slight pause.

She ruefully examined the cart. "You may be right. Every time I go off on a trip it seems as if I never have what I need."

His eyes sharpened with interest. "You're going on a trip?"

"In a couple of weeks. I'm doing some research on the Keys, and it always helps to see an area firsthand."

"Research?"

She shrugged. "I dabble in several things. I have my souvenir shops. I do a little writing, teach a few night courses. It keeps me from getting bored with myself." Looking at the checkout counters, where the lines were growing, she said blithely, "I'd better get in line before everyone in the store gets ahead of me. Oh—did you find anything yesterday?"

His face was a blank mask, though his eyes were once again peering at her cart. "No, nothing. It may have been a false lead."

"Well, good luck. Remember to get a cap or something while you're here."

"Sure. Thanks."

She joined one of the lines at the row of checkout counters and selected a magazine to flip through while she waited, gradually nudging the cart forward. He had moved to the side and was looking at paperback books. Damn, would he never leave? When it came her time, she unloaded the cart and tried to keep her body between Lowell and the counter. The clerk picked up the package of undershorts and held them in front of her while she punched in the code number on the computerized cash register. Rachel shifted to that side, and when the clerk set the package down she pushed a shirt over it. Lowell was moving closer.

"One-forty-six eighteen," the clerk said, reaching for a large bag.

Rachel checked her wallet, inwardly grimacing. She seldom carried that much cash, and this was no exception. Disgruntled, she plunked down a plastic credit card and the clerk ran it through the imprinting machine, then called to get an okay on the amount. Lowell had walked around to the front of the store and was coming down in front of the checkout counters. Rachel grabbed the bag the clerk had laid on the counter and began shoving her purchases into it.

"Sign here," the clerk said, pushing the credit slip toward her. Rachel scribbled her name and a moment later the bag was stapled shut. She loaded it in the cart and began wheeling it out of the store.

"Need any help?" Lowell asked, falling into step beside her.

"No, rolling it in the cart is easier than carrying it. Thanks, anyway."

The humid heat settled on them like a suffocating blanket as soon as they left the cool confines of the store, and Rachel squinted her eyes against the almost painful brightness. After opening the trunk of the car she dumped the bag in and slammed the lid shut, agonizingly aware of Lowell's acute interest.

She pushed the cart to a buggy-return stand, then walked back to the car. "Goodbye," she said casually.

He was still watching as she drove out of the lot. Rachel wiped the perspiration off her face, aware that her heart was thudding in a panicky rhythm. She was out of practice for this! She only hoped he hadn't been too suspicious.

CHAPTER FIVE

THE DREAMS WERE STILL SO vivid that it was several minutes before he realized he was awake, but awareness did
not necessarily bring understanding. He lay quietly, looking
around the cool, dim, unfamiliar room and groping for any
details in his mind that would give him a hint of what was
going on and where he was. There seemed to be no connection between his only memories and this silent room.
But were they memories, or dreams? He had dreamed of
a woman, a warm and pliant woman, with eyes as clear
and gray as a highland lake under cloudy skies, her hands
tender as she caressed him, her velvety breasts swelling
against his palms. His fingers twitched on the sheets; the
dream was so real he almost ached to feel her under his
hands.

Still, that had been only a dream, and he had to deal with
reality. He lay there until certain things began to return,
and he knew that *they* weren't dreams. The attack on his
boat; the endless, agonizing swim in the dark, driven on
by his own sheer inability to give up. Then, after that...
nothing. Not even a glimmer of what had happened.

Where was he? Had he been captured? They would give
almost anything, risk almost anything, to take him alive.

He moved cautiously, his mouth setting grimly at the
amount of effort it took. There was pain in his left shoulder and lacing through his left thigh, and he had a dull
headache, but both his leg and arm obeyed his mental

command to move. Awkwardly using his right hand, he threw the sheet back and struggled to a sitting position. Dizziness assailed him, but he gripped the side of the bed until the feeling subsided, then he took stock once again. A pristine bandage was wrapped around his thigh, thickly padded over the wounds. The same treatment had been given to his shoulder; gauze had been wrapped around it, then anchored around his chest. He was totally naked, but that didn't bother him. His first priority was to establish his mobility; his second was to find out where the hell he was.

He stood, the wounded muscle in his thigh quivering in outrage at being forced into motion. He wavered, but didn't fall, merely stood there until the room stopped swaying and his leg was steady under him. Despite the coolness of the room a fine sheen of sweat began to form on his body.

There was no sound except for the gentle whir of a ceiling fan that hung over the bed and the distant mechanized sound of an air conditioner. He listened intently, but could detect nothing else. Keeping his right hand braced against the bed, he took a step toward the window, grinding his teeth together at the searing pain in his leg. The closed slats of the old-fashioned blinds drew him. Reaching the window, he used one finger to lift a slat and peer through the crack. A yard, a vegetable garden. Nothing unusual, but nothing in sight, either, human or animal.

An open door was in front of him, revealing a bathroom. Slowly he moved to the doorway, his black eyes taking note of the items on the vanity. Hair spray, lotions, cosmetics. A woman's bathroom, then. Perhaps the red-haired woman who had been on the boat? Everything was neat, impeccably clean, and there was a certain spare luxury to both the bath and bedroom, as if everything had been chosen for maximum comfort while still leaving a lot of what was

simply bare space. The next door over was a closet. He
pushed racks aside and checked sizes. Again, everything
was for a woman, or a small, very slender man of undecided
sexuality. The clothes ranged from remarkably ragged to
sleekly sophisticated. A disguise?

Cautiously he opened the next door slightly, putting his
eye to the small crack to make certain there was no one
out there. The small hallway was empty, as was the room
he could see beyond it. He eased the door open, balancing
himself with a hand on the frame. Nothing. No one. He
was alone, and that made no sense at all.

Damn, he was weak, and so thirsty that the fires of
hell seemed to be in his throat. Limping badly, occasionally staggering, he made his way through the empty living
room. A small, sunlit alcove was next, and the glaring sun
streaming through the windows made him blink as his eyes
adjusted to the sudden excess of light. Next was a kitchen,
small and sunny and extremely modern. A colorful array
of fresh vegetables lay on a counter, and there was a bowl
of fresh fruit sitting on the center work island.

Cotton lined his mouth and throat. He groped toward the
sink, then opened cabinet doors until he found the glasses.
Turning on the cool tap water, he filled a glass and turned
it up, pouring the water into his mouth so thirstily that
some of it spilled down his chest. With that first terrible
urgency satisfied, he drank another glass of water and this
time managed to get it all in his mouth.

How long had he been here? The blanks in his memory
made him furious. He was vulnerable, uncertain of where
he was or what had happened, and vulnerability was one
thing he couldn't afford. But he was starving, too. The bowl
of fresh fruit beckoned, and he wolfed down a banana, then
half an apple. Abruptly he was too full to eat another bite,

so he tossed both the banana skin and the half-eaten apple into the trash.

Okay, he could get around. Slowly, but he wasn't helpless. His next priority was to find some means of self-defense. The most available weapon was a knife, and he examined the kitchen knives before choosing the one with the sharpest, strongest blade. With that in his hand he began a slow, methodical search of the house, but there were no other weapons of any sort to be found.

The outside doors all had extremely strong dead-bolt locks on them. They weren't fancy, but they would damned sure slow down anyone trying to get in. He looked at them, trying to remember if he had ever seen any locks exactly like them, and decided that he hadn't. They were locked, but what sense did it make to put the locks on the inside, where he could get to them? He turned the lock, and it opened with a smooth, almost silent movement. Warily he reached for the knob and opened the door a little, again checking through the crack to see if anyone was in view. The door was heavy, too heavy to be an ordinary door. He opened it a little more, running his fingers along the edge. Steel reinforced, he guessed.

It was a snug little prison, but the locks were on the wrong side of the doors, and there were no wardens.

He opened the door completely, looking out through a screen door at a neat little yard, a tall pine thicket and a flock of fat white and gray geese searching for insects in the grass. The heat coming through the screen door was thick and heavy, hitting him like a blow. A dog appeared as if by magic from beneath a bush, leaping up onto the porch and staring at him with unblinking eyes as its ears went back and snarls twisted the canine muzzle.

Dispassionately he examined the dog, weighing his chances. A trained attack dog, German shepherd, weighing eighty or ninety pounds. In his weakened condition he didn't have a chance against a dog like that, even with a knife in his hand. He was effectively caged, after all.

His leg would barely support his weight. He was naked, weak, and didn't know where he was. The odds weren't in his favor, but he was alive and filled with a cold, controlled rage. Now he also had the advantage of surprise, because whoever had brought him here wouldn't be expecting him to be up and armed. He closed the door and locked it again, then watched the dog through the window until it left the porch and resumed its position beneath the bush.

He had to wait.

An enormous, purplish-black thunderhead was looming in the sky when Rachel turned into the driveway. She eyed it, wondering if it would dump its load of rain out at sea or hold it until it was over land. The rain would be torrential, and the temperature would drop sharply, but as soon as the cloud had passed the heat would rise again, and the rain would evaporate in a suffocating cloud of steam. Ebenezer Duck and his flock scattered, honking irritably, as she pulled the car under the shade of the oak tree where they had been lazily pecking at the grass. Joe lifted his head to look at her, then returned to his snooze. Everything was calm, just as it had been when she'd left. Only then did she feel an easing of the tight constriction in her chest.

She got the bag out of the trunk, unaware of the sharp black eyes that followed her every move. Holding the bag in one arm and the keys in the other hand, she climbed the steps to the porch, paused to shove her sunglasses on top of her head, then held the screen door open with her hip while she unlocked the door and pushed it open. The air-conditioned coolness was such a shocking contrast to the searing heat outside that goose bumps rose on her flesh, and she shivered. Taking deep breaths, she dropped the bag and her purse on one of the love seats and went to check on her patient.

Just as her hand touched the doorknob a hard arm circled her throat and she was jerked backward, her neck arched unnaturally. A brightly gleaming knife was held in front of her face. She had been too stunned to react, but now sheer terror flooded her as her gaze locked on the knife. How had they gotten in? Had they already killed him? The anguish that rose in her was wild and ferocious, consuming her.

"Don't fight and I won't hurt you," a deep voice murmured in her ear. "I want some answers, but I won't take any chances. If you make a wrong move—" He didn't finish the sentence, but he didn't have to. How calm the voice was, as cool and unemotional as stone. It made her blood congeal.

The arm under her chin was choking her, and she automatically raised both hands, clutching at him. The knife moved menacingly closer. "No, none of that," he whispered, his mouth close to her ear. Rachel shrank from the knife, her head digging into his shoulder, her body crowding frantically against his in an attempt to put distance between herself and that shining blade. Every detail of his body was imprinted against her, and suddenly her dazed senses realized what she was feeling. He was naked! And if he were naked, then it had to be…

Sharp, piercing relief, as painful in its own way as the fear and anguish had been, made her muscles suddenly tremble as the tension left them. Her hands relaxed on his forearm.

"That's better," the low voice growled. "Who are you?"

"Rachel Jones," she said, her voice breathless because of the pressure he was putting on her throat.

"Where am I?"

"In my house. I pulled you out of the surf and brought you here." She could feel him hesitate, though perhaps it was simply that he was growing weaker. His strength was astonishing under the circumstances, but he had been very ill, and his stamina must be wavering. "Please," she whispered. "You shouldn't be out of bed."

That was the truth, Sabin thought grimly. He was exhausted, as if he'd run a marathon; his legs felt as if they would give out on him at any moment. He didn't know her, and he couldn't trust her; he had only this one chance, and a wrong guess could cost him his life, but he didn't have much choice. Damn, he was weak! Slowly he relaxed his right arm from around her throat and let his left hand, the one holding the knife, drop to his side. His shoulder throbbed, and he doubted that he would be able to lift his arm again.

Rather than jerking away from him, she turned cautiously, as if afraid of startling him into an attack, and wedged her shoulder under his right arm, while her arms went around him and supported him. "Lean on me before you fall," she said, her voice still a little breathless. "It would be a mess if you tore all those stitches out."

He didn't have much choice except to drape his arm over her slender shoulders and lean heavily on her. If he didn't either sit down or lie down—soon—he was going to fall, and he knew it. Slowly she helped him into the bedroom, supporting him as he virtually collapsed onto the edge of the bed, then holding his head in the crook of her left arm as she lowered him into a supine position while she reached around him with her other hand to arrange the pillow. Sabin drew a deep breath, his senses automatically reacting to her warm female scent and the softness of her breast against his cheek. He had only to turn his head to press his mouth against her nipple, and the image teased at him with a curious urgency.

He lay with his eyes closed, breathing rapidly in exhaustion, while she lifted his legs onto the bed and pulled the sheet up to his waist. "There," she said softly. "You can rest now." She stroked her hand over his chest, as she had done so many times in the past few days, an action that had become automatic because it seemed to calm his restlessness. He was much cooler; the fever had finally lost its grip on him. The knife was still clutched in his left hand, and she reached to take it, but his fingers tightened at her touch, and his eyes flew open, his gaze black and fierce.

Rachel kept her hand on the knife, levelly meeting his eyes. "Why do you need it?" she asked. "If I meant you any harm I've had a lot of opportunities to do something about it before now."

Her eyes were gray, completely so, without any hint of blue. They were almost charcoal in color, but warm, and with an utter clarity that made them seem fathomless. He felt a shock of recognition. The eyes, and the woman, had filled his recent dreams with a tender eroticism that made his loins tighten. But...were they dreams? The woman wasn't a dream. She was real, warm and firm of flesh, and her hands had moved over him with the ease of familiarity. She didn't act like a guard, but he couldn't afford to take the chance. If he relinquished the knife he might not be able to get it back. "I'll keep it," he said.

Rachel hesitated, wondering if she should press the issue, but there was something in his quiet, flat tone that made her decide to let it go. Even though he was weak and barely able to get around on his own, there was something about him that told her he couldn't be pushed. He was a dangerous man, this stranger sleeping in her bed. She moved her hand from his.

"All right. Are you hungry?"

"No. I ate a banana and an apple."

"How long have you been awake?"

He hadn't checked a clock, but he didn't need a clock to give him a sense of time. "Almost an hour." His gaze hadn't wavered from her. Rachel felt as if he could see through her, as if he were probing her mind.

"You woke up a couple of times before, but you were still feverish and talking nonsense."

"What kind of nonsense?" he asked sharply.

Rachel regarded him calmly. "No state secrets or anything like that. You thought you were going to a party."

Was there a double meaning to that crack about state secrets? Did she know anything, or had that just been a coincidence? Sabin wanted to question her, but he hardly had the upper hand at the moment, and his exhaustion was changing into acute sleepiness. As if she knew, she touched his face, her fingers cool and light. "Go to sleep," she said. "I'll still be here when you wake up."

It was, ridiculously, the reassurance he needed to let him relax into sleep.

Quietly Rachel left the room and went to the kitchen, where she leaned weakly against the work island. Her legs were shaking, her insides quivering like gelatin, in reaction to all that had happened to her already…and it wasn't even noon yet! Nor did she have any of the answers she had promised herself she would get as soon as he woke up; rather than asking questions, she had been answering his. She hadn't been prepared for the intensity of his gaze, so piercing that it was difficult to meet his eyes for any length of time. Warlock's eyes… She certainly hadn't been prepared for having a knife held to her throat! And she had been helpless, unable to do anything against a strength that was far superior to hers, even though he was undoubtedly weak from his wounds and illness.

The terror that had held her in its icy grip for those few moments had been worse than she had ever imagined. She had been frightened before, but not to that degree. She was still shaking in reaction, and her eyes burned with tears that she refused to let fall. Now wasn't the time for tears; she had to get herself under control. He might sleep for half a day, or he might wake up in an hour, but she was going to be in complete command of herself whenever he woke. He would also need feeding, she thought, seizing gratefully on something practical to do. Banana and apple notwithstanding, his system would probably demand frequent feedings until he had recovered.

Her movements jerky, she set beef tips simmering for beef stew and began dicing potatoes, carrots and celery. Maybe the meal would be ready by the time he awoke; if not, he could settle for soup and a sandwich. When everything was in the pot she darted out to the vegetable garden and gathered the ripe tomatoes, then ignored the heat and began pulling up weeds. It wasn't until she finally fell to her knees on a wave of dizziness that she realized how erratically she had been behaving, spurred on by the overdose of adrenaline her system had absorbed that morning. It was insanity to work out in the broiling sun, especially without a hat!

She went inside and washed her face with cold water; she felt calmer now, though her hands were still trembling slightly. There was nothing to do but wait: wait until the stew was ready; wait until he woke up; wait until she got some answers...wait.

It was a tribute to her self-possession and concentration that she was actually able to do some research for the course she would be teaching in the fall. Like a manuscript, the course would require pacing and plotting to hold the students' interest, to make them stretch. Yet even though she was deeply involved in her reading and notes, she was so attuned to him that she heard the slight rustle made by the bedcovers when he moved, and she knew he was awake. Checking her watch, she saw that he had slept for a little over three hours; the stew would be ready, if he was hungry.

He was sitting up, yawning and rubbing his bearded face, when she entered the bedroom. Instantly she felt his attention settle on her like a beam of pure energy, tingling on her skin.

"Are you hungry now? You've slept for three hours."

He considered that, then gave a brief nod. "Yes. I need a bathroom, a shower and a shave first, though."

"Sorry, the shower is out while you still have stitches," she said, hurrying to his side as he threw back the sheet and eased his feet to the floor, wincing in pain and holding his left thigh. Rachel put a supporting arm around him until he was steady on his feet. "I'll put a new blade in my razor for you, though." Sensing that he preferred to get across the room on his own power, she let her arm drop and watched anxiously as he took each painful step. He was a loner; he wasn't accustomed to aid and didn't welcome it, though he had to know that he simply wasn't capable of some things right now. He would let her help him only when it was necessary. Still, she felt compelled to ask, "Shall I shave you, or do you think you're steady enough to do it yourself?"

He paused at the door to the bathroom and glanced over his shoulder at her. "I'll do it."

She nodded and started toward him. "I'll just put the new blade—"

"I'll find them," he said quietly, stopping her before she

could reach him. Rachel accepted her dismissal, turning instead toward the other door.

It hurt to have him reject her help after the days he had been totally helpless and dependent on her for everything, after the nights she had spent leaning over him, sponging him down to keep him cool, and especially after the mental strain she had endured. As she set the table she tried to deal with that hurt, to push it away. After all, she was even more of a stranger to him than he was to her, and it was only natural that he would try to regain control of himself as soon as possible. To a man like him, control would be vital. She had to stop hovering over him like a mother hen.

It was easy to tell herself that, but when at last she heard the water cut off in the bathroom she hesitated for only a moment before giving in to the compulsion to check on him. He was standing in the middle of the bedroom floor, looking around as if considering his options. A towel was knotted low on his lean hips, and contrary to logic it made him seem even more naked than when he had been completely unclothed. Rachel's pulse leaped. Even with the stark contrast of the white bandages on his leg and shoulder, he still seemed immensely powerful, and so male that she felt her mouth go dry.

He had shaved, and the clean line of his jaw made her fingers twitch with the urge to stroke it—another gesture he wouldn't appreciate.

"Is there anything I could wear, or do I just go around naked?" he finally asked, when Rachel made no move either to approach him or to speak.

She groaned as she remembered and hit the heel of her palm against her forehead. "I have something for you to wear. That's where I was this morning, picking up some things you would need." The shopping bag still lay where she had dropped it in the living room; she grabbed it and carried it into the bedroom, where she deposited it on the bed.

He opened the bag and a curious expression crossed his face; then he pulled out a lacy pair of panties and held them up to examine them before Rachel could explain. "Size five," he commented, and looked at her as though measuring her for the fit. The scrap of lace and nylon dangled from one finger. "Nice, but I don't think they'll fit me."

"They weren't meant to," Rachel said calmly, still tingling from the once-over he'd given her. "They were camouflage, that's all. Anything you find in there that you don't ordinarily use, put back in the bag." She refused to be embarrassed, since she had only done what had seemed necessary. The "camouflage" had been darned expensive, too! Leaving him to dress in whatever he chose, she returned to the kitchen and popped buttered fresh bread into the oven, then ladled up the stew and poured tea into tall glasses full of ice.

"I need help with the shirt."

She hadn't heard him approach, and she whirled, startled by both his nearness and what he'd said. He was standing right behind her, clad in the black denim cutoffs and holding the terry-cloth pullover in his hand. His chest filled her vision, tautly powerful muscles covered with black, curling hair and the white bulk of the bandage wrapped around his left shoulder. How long had he struggled with the shirt before admitting that he couldn't manage it by himself? She was astonished that he hadn't simply exchanged it for one that buttoned, so he wouldn't have to ask for her help.

"Sit down so I can reach you better," she said, taking the shirt from his hand. He held the corner of the cabinets for support as he slowly limped to the table in the dining alcove and eased himself down onto one of the chairs.

Rachel carefully worked the shirt up his arm, a look of intent concentration on her face as she tried not to jostle his shoulder. When she had it in place she said, "Put your other arm in the sleeve while I keep it from pulling on your shoulder."

Without a word he did as she directed, and together they pulled the shirt over his head. Rachel tugged it into place, much as a mother would dress a toddler, but the man sitting motionless under her ministrations was no child in any sense she could imagine. She didn't linger over the chore, well aware of his dislike for having to rely on her aid. Briskly she got the bread out of the oven and put it in the napkin-lined breadbasket, then placed the basket on the table and took her own chair. "Are you left-handed or right-handed?" she asked, not looking at him, even though she could feel the burning energy of his gaze on her face.

"Ambidextrous. Why?"

"The spoon could be difficult for you to handle if you were left-handed," she replied, nodding at the stew. "Would you like bread?"

"Please."

He was very good at one-word sentences, she thought as she put the bread on his plate. Actually, she should have thought of asking him if he could handle the razor, too, but his clean-shaven face said that he evidently could. They ate in silence for a few moments, and he really did justice to the stew. She hadn't expected his appetite to be so good so early in his recovery.

The bowl was nearly empty when he put his spoon down and pinned her with the ebony fire of his eyes. "Tell me what's going on."

It was a demand that Rachel didn't feel like meeting. Carefully she put her own spoon down. "I think it's my turn to ask a few questions. Who are you? What's your name?"

He didn't like the counterdemand. She sensed his displeasure, though his expression didn't flicker. The hesitation lasted for barely a second, but she noticed it and had the immediate impression that he wasn't going to answer. Then he drawled, "Call me 'Joe'."

"I can't do that," she replied. "'Joe' is what I call the dog, because he wouldn't tell me his name, either. Make up another one." Driven by the electric surge of tension in the air she began clearing off the table, moving swiftly and automatically.

He watched her for a moment, then said quietly, "Sit down."

Rachel didn't pause. "Why? Do I have to be sitting down to listen to more lies?"

"Rachel, sit down." He didn't raise his voice, didn't change the calm, dead-level inflection of his tone, but suddenly it was a command. She stared at him for a moment, then lifted her chin and returned to her chair. When she merely waited in silence, looking at him, he gave a little sigh.

"I appreciate your help, but the less you know, the better it is for you."

Rachel had always hated it when anyone presumed to know what was best for her and what wasn't. "I see. Was I not supposed to notice that you had two bullet holes in you when I pulled you out of the surf? Was I supposed to turn my head when two men pretending to be FBI agents came looking for you, and just turn you over to them? Was it supposed to pass my notice that you held a knife to my throat this morning? I'm a little curious, I admit! I've nursed you for four days, and I really would like to know your name, if that isn't too much to ask!"

One level black brow lifted at her sarcasm. "It could be."

"All right, forget it. Play your little games. You don't answer my questions and I won't answer yours. Deal?"

He watched her for a little longer, and Rachel kept her gaze level, not backing down an inch. "My name is Sabin," he finally said, the words slowly drawn out of him, as if he begrudged every syllable.

She absorbed the name's sound, her mind lingering over the feel and form of it. "And the rest of it?"

"Is it important?"

"No. But I'd like to know, anyway."

He paused only a fraction of a second. "Kell Sabin."

She held out her hand. "Glad to meet you, Kell Sabin."

Slowly he took her hand, his callused palm sliding against her softer one and his hard, warm fingers wrapping around hers. "Thank you for taking care of me. I've been here four days?"

"This is the fourth day."

"Fill me in on what's happened."

He had the manner of a man accustomed to command; rather than requesting, he ordered, and it was clear that he expected his orders to be obeyed. Rachel pulled her hand from his, disturbed by his warm touch and the shivery way it affected her. Clasping her fingers together to dispel the tingling in them, she rested her hands on the table. "I pulled you out of the water and brought you here. I think you hit your head on one of the rocks that line the mouth of the bay. You had a concussion and were in shock. The bullet was still in your shoulder."

He frowned. "I know. Did you take it out?"

"Not me. I called the vet."

At least something could startle him, though the expression was quickly gone. "A veterinarian?"

"I had to do something, and a doctor has to report all gunshot wounds."

He eyed her thoughtfully. "You didn't want it reported?"

"I thought *you* might not want it reported."

"You thought right. What happened then?"

"I took care of you. You were out of it for two days. Then you started waking up, but the fever had you out of your head. You didn't know what was going on."

"And the FBI agents?"

"They weren't FBI. I checked."

"What did they look like?"

Rachel began to feel as if she were being interrogated. "The one who calls himself Lowell is thin, dark, about five foot ten, early forties. The other one, Ellis, is tall, good-looking in a toothpaste-ad sort of way, sandy-brown hair, blue eyes."

"Ellis," he said, as if to himself.

"I played dumb. It seemed the safest thing to do until you woke up. Are they friends of yours?"

"No."

Silence fell between them. Rachel studied her hands, waiting for another question. When none came she tried one of her own. "Should I have called the police?"

"It would have been safer for you if you had."

"I took a calculated risk. I figured the odds were more in my favor than yours." She took a deep breath. "I'm a civilian, but I used to be an investigative reporter. I saw some things in those days that didn't add up, and I did a little digging, found out some things before I was warned not to go any deeper. You could have been a drug runner or an escaped convict, but there wasn't any hint of anything like that on the scanner. You could also have been an agent. You had been shot twice. You were unconscious and couldn't protect yourself or tell me anything. If... people...

were hunting you, you wouldn't have had a chance in a hospital."

His lashes had dropped, shielding his expression. "You've got quite an imagination."

"Haven't I," she agreed mildly.

He leaned back in his chair, wincing a little as he tried to get his shoulder comfortable. "Who else knows I'm here, other than the vet?"

"No one."

"Then how did you get me up here? Or did the vet help you? You're not Superwoman."

"I put you on a quilt and dragged you up here, with help from the dog. Maybe he thought it was a game." Her gray eyes darkened as she thought of the Herculean effort she had made to get him inside the house. "When Honey got here, we lifted you onto the bed."

"Honey?"

"The vet. Honey Mayfield."

Sabin watched her quiet face, wondering at what she wasn't saying. How far had she dragged him? How had she gotten him up the steps to the porch? He had carried wounded men out of battle, so he knew how difficult it was, even with his strength and training. He outweighed her by at least eighty pounds; there was no way she could have lifted him. She could be lying about not having anyone else help her, but there wasn't any reason for her to do so; all he could do was read between the lines. Almost anyone would have called the police immediately on finding a man unconscious on their beach, but she hadn't. Few people would ever have considered the options and circumstances that had occurred to her. People just didn't think about such things. It wasn't a part of their normal lives; it only happened in movies and books and therefore wasn't real. What life had she led that would make her so cautious, so aware of something that should have been beyond her experience?

They both heard the approaching car at the same time. Instantly she was out of her chair, her hand on his shoulder. "Go to the bedroom and close the door," she said evenly, not noticing the way his eyebrows lifted at her order. She went to the window and looked out; then the tension visibly left her body.

"It's Honey. Everything's okay. I guess she stayed away as long as her curiosity would let her."

CHAPTER SIX

"How's the headache?" the veterinarian asked, peering into his eyes. She was a big, strong-boned woman with a friendly, freckled face and a light touch. Sabin decided that he liked her; she had a good bedside manner.

"Hanging in there," he grunted.

"Help me get his shirt off," she said to Rachel, and the two women gently and efficiently stripped him. He was glad that he'd chosen to wear the cutoffs, or they would have had his pants off, too. He didn't have any modesty to worry about, but it still disconcerted him to be handled like a Barbie doll. He dispassionately observed the purpled, puckered skin around the stitches in his leg, wondering about the extent of the muscle damage. It was essential that he be able to do more than hobble, and soon. The damage to his shoulder, with its complex system of muscle and tendons, was likely to be more permanent, but mobility was his greatest concern at the moment. Once he had decided what course of action to take he would need to move fast.

Fresh bandages were applied, and he was put back inside his shirt. "I'll be back in a couple of days to take out the stitches," Honey said, repacking her bag. It struck Sabin that not once had she asked his name or any other question that didn't deal with his physical well-being. Either she was remarkably incurious or she had decided that the less she knew, the better. It was a view that he wished Rachel

shared. Sabin had always made it a rule not to involve innocent citizens; his work was too dangerous, and though
he knew the risks of his job and accepted them, there was
really no way Rachel could comprehend the extent of the
risk she was taking in helping him.

Rachel went out with Honey, and Sabin hobbled to the
door to watch as they stood by Honey's car, talking in
low voices. The dog, Joe, took up a position at the foot of
the steps, a low growl working in his throat as he turned
first to watch Sabin at the door, then back to Rachel, as if
he couldn't decide where to place his attention. His fore-
most instinct was to guard Rachel, but those same instincts
couldn't allow him to ignore Sabin's alien presence at the
door.

Honey got in the car and drove off, and after a final
wave Rachel walked back to the porch. "Calm down," she
admonished the dog softly, daring to give him a swift touch
on the neck. His growl intensified, and she looked up to
see Sabin coming out on the porch.

"Don't come too close to him," she warned. "He doesn't
like men."

Sabin regarded the dog with remote curiosity. "Where
did you get him? He's a trained attack dog."

Astonished, Rachel looked down at Joe, standing so
close by her leg. "He just wandered up one day, all skinny
and beat-up. We reached an understanding. I feed him, and
he stays around. He's not an attack dog."

"Joe," Sabin said sharply. "Heel."

She felt the animal quiver as if he'd been struck, and
blood-chilling snarls worked up from his throat as he stared
at the man, every muscle in his big body quivering as if he
longed to launch himself at his enemy but was chained to
Rachel's side. Before she thought of the danger she went
down on one knee and put her arm around his neck, talking

softly to him in reassurance. "It's all right," she crooned. "He won't hurt you, I promise. Everything's all right."

When Joe was calmer Rachel went up on the porch and deliberately stroked Sabin's arm, letting the dog see her. Sabin watched Joe, unafraid of the dog, but not pushing him, either. He needed to have Joe accept him, at least enough to let him leave the house without attacking.

"He was probably abused by his owner," he said. "You're lucky he didn't have you for breakfast the first time you walked out of the house."

"I think you're wrong. It's a possibility that he was a guard dog, but I don't think he was trained to attack. You owe him a lot. If it hadn't been for him, I couldn't have gotten you up from the beach." Suddenly she realized that her hand was still on his arm, slowly moving up and down, and she let her arm fall to her side. "Are you ready to go back inside? You must be tired by now."

"In a minute." He slowly surveyed the pine thicket to the right and the road that curved away to the left, committing distances and details to memory for future use. "How far are we from a main road?"

"About five or six miles, I guess. This is a private road. It joins the road from Rafferty's ranch before it runs into U.S. 19."

"Which way is the beach?"

She pointed to the pine thicket. "Down through the pines."

"Do you have a boat?"

Rachel looked at him, her gray eyes very clear. "No. The only means of escape are on foot or driving."

The faintest smile lifted one corner of his mouth. "I wasn't going to steal your car."

"Weren't you? I still don't know what's going on, why you were shot, or even if you're a good guy."

"With those doubts, why haven't you called the police?" he returned, his voice cool. "I obviously wasn't wearing a white hat when you found me."

He was going to stonewall it to the end, the ultimate professional, alone and unemotional. Rachel accepted that she wasn't entitled to full knowledge of his situation, even though she had saved his life, but she would very much like to know that she had done the right thing. Though she had acted on her instincts, the uncertainty was gnawing at her. Had she saved a rogue agent? An enemy of her country? What would she do if it turned out to be that way? The worst part of it was the undeniable and growing attraction she felt for him, even against her own better judgment.

He didn't say anything else, and she didn't respond to his provoking mention of his lack of clothing when she'd found him. She glanced at Joe and turned to open the screen door. "I'm getting out of this heat. You can take your chances with Joe if you want to stay out here."

Sabin followed her inside, measuring the unyielding straightness of her back. She was angry, but she was also disturbed. He would have liked to reassure her, but the hard truth was that the less she knew, the safer she was. He had no way of protecting her in his present condition and circumstances. The fact that she was protecting him, willingly endangering herself even though her guesses ranged uncomfortably close to the truth, did something unwanted to his insides. Hell, he thought in disgust at himself, everything about her did something to his insides. He was already familiar with the scent of her flesh and the tender, startlingly intimate touch of her hands. His body still felt the press of hers against him, making him want to reach out and pull her back. He had never needed another human being's closeness, except for the physical closeness required for sex. He eyed her bare, slender legs and softly rounded buttocks; the sexual urge was there, all right, and damned strong, considering his general physical condition. The dangerous part of it was that the thought of lying in the darkness with her and simply holding her was at least as attractive as the thought of taking her.

He leaned in the doorway and watched as she efficiently finished cleaning the dishes. There was a brisk, economical grace to her movements, even while she was doing such a mundane task. Everything was organized and logical. She wasn't a fussy woman. Even her clothing was plain and unadorned, though her beige shorts and simple blue cotton shirt didn't need any adornment other than the soft feminine curves beneath them. Again he was aware of the tantalizing image of those curves, just as if he knew how she looked naked, had already had his hands on her.

"Why are you staring?" she asked without looking at him. She had been as aware of his gaze as she would have been of his touch.

"Sorry." He didn't explain, but, then, he doubted that she would really want to know. "I'm going back to bed. Will you help me with the shirt?"

"Of course." She wiped her hands on a towel and went ahead of him to the bedroom. "Let me change the sheets first."

Fatigue pulled at him as he leaned against the dresser to ease the strain of his weight on his left leg. His shoulder and leg throbbed, but the pain was to be expected, so he ignored it. The real problem was his lack of strength; he wouldn't be able to protect Rachel or himself if anything happened. Did he dare remain here while he healed? His brooding gaze remained fixed on her as she put fresh linens on the bed, his available options running through his mind. Those options were severely limited. He had no money, no identification, and he didn't dare call to be picked up, because he had no idea of the extent to which the agency had been compromised, or who he could trust. He wasn't in any shape to do anything anyway; he had to recuperate, so it might as well be here. The small house had its advantages: the dog outside was a damned good defense; the locks were strong; he had food and medical care.

There was also Rachel.

Looking at her was easy; it could become an uncontrollable habit. She was slim and healthy-looking, with a honeyed tan that made her skin look luscious. Her hair was thick and straight and shiny, a dark ash-brown so completely lacking in any warm highlights that it almost had a silvery sheen. It went well with her wide, clear, lake-gray eyes. She wasn't tall, less than medium height, but she carried herself so straight that she gave the impression of being a tall woman. And she was soft, with rounded breasts that nestled into his palms....

Damn! The image was so real, so strong, that it kept creeping back. If it was only a fever-induced dream, it was the most realistic he had ever known. But if it had really happened, when and how? He had been unconscious most of the time, and out of his head with fever even when he'd been awake. Yet he kept reliving the sensation of her hands on him, stroking gently, with the open intimacy of lovers, and he had either had his hands on her or his imagination had lurched into overdrive.

She plumped the pillows and turned to him. "Do you want to sleep in your shorts?"

For an answer he unsnapped the cutoffs and let them drop, then sat down on the bed so she could work the shirt off his shoulder. The warm, faintly floral scent of her enveloped him as she leaned close, and he instinctively turned his head toward it, his mouth and nose pressing into her shoulder. She hesitated, then quickly freed him from the shirt and moved away from his touch. The moist warmth of his breath had heated her skin through the fabric of her shirt and played havoc with the even rhythm of her heartbeat. Trying not to let him see how his nearness had affected her, she neatly folded the shirt and placed it on a chair, then picked up his cutoffs and placed them on top of the shirt. When she looked at him again he was lying on his back, his right leg bent at the knee and raised, his right arm resting across his stomach. His white briefs contrasted sharply with his bronzed skin, reminding her that he didn't have any tan lines on his body. She groaned inwardly. Why did she have to think about that now?

"Do you want the sheet over you?"

"No, the fan feels good." He lifted his right hand from his stomach and held it out to her. "Sit here for a minute."

Her mind told her that it wasn't a good idea. She sat down, anyway, just as she had done so many times since he'd been in her bed, her body angled to face him and her hip against his side. He draped his arm over her thighs, his hand cradling the curve of her hip as if to keep her nestled against him. His fingers, curving around to her buttock, began to move caressingly, and her heart started pounding again. She looked up to meet his eyes and was unable to look away, caught by the mesmerizing black fire.

"I can't give you all the answers you want," he murmured. "I don't know them myself. Even if I tell you I'm a good guy, you'd still only have my word for it, and why would I cut my own throat by telling you anything else?"

"Don't play devil's advocate," she said sharply, wishing she could find the will to break away from the seductive power of his gaze and touch. "Let's deal in facts. You were shot. Who shot you?"

"I was ambushed, set up by one of my own men—Tod Ellis."

"Bogus-FBI-agent Ellis?"

"The same, from the description you gave."

"Then make a call and turn him in."

"It isn't as simple as that. I'm on a month's vacation from the agency. Only two men knew my location, both of them my superiors."

Rachel sat very still. "One of them betrayed you, but you don't know which one."

"Perhaps both of them."

"Can't you contact someone higher up?"

Something cold and furious flashed in his eyes. "Sweetheart, you can't get much higher. I'm not even certain I can get through. Either one of them has the power to declare me an outlaw, and calling from here would endanger you."

Rachel felt the icy power of his rage and shivered inside, thankful that she wasn't the one who had crossed him. The look in his eyes was in direct contrast to the touch of his fingertips on her hip. How could his touch remain so gentle, while the wrath of hell glittered in his eyes?

"What are you going to do?"

His fingers trailed down her hip to her thigh and rubbed across the hem of her shorts, then gently glided beneath it. "Recuperate. I can't do a damned thing right now, including dress myself. The problem is that I'm putting you in danger just by being here."

She couldn't control her breathing, or her pulse rate. Heat was building inside her, destroying her ability to think and leaving her to operate purely on her senses. She knew she should move his hand, but the rasp of his rough fingertips on her thigh was so pleasurable that all she could do was sit there, quivering slightly like a leaf in a soft spring breeze. Did he normally treat women as if they were his to touch as he wished, or had he picked up on her uncontrollable responses to him? She thought she had disguised them well, kept them to herself, but perhaps his job had made his senses and intuitions more acute. Desperately she made herself move, putting her hand on top of his to prevent it from moving any higher.

"You didn't put me in danger," she said, her voice a little hoarse. "I made the decision without your help."

Despite her controlling hand, his fingers moved higher and found the edge of her panties. "I have a question that's been driving me crazy," he admitted in a low voice. He moved his hand again, delving beneath the elastic leg of her panties and curving his fingers over the cool bareness of her buttock.

A whimper escaped her before she bit her lip, controlling the wild little sound. How could he do this to her with just his touch? "Stop," she whispered. "You have to stop."

"Have we been sleeping together?"

Her breasts had tightened painfully, begging for that touch to be transferred to them, for him to claim them as he had before. His question destroyed what little concentration she had left. "This...there's only this one bed. I don't have a couch, only the love seats—"

"So we've been in the same bed for four days," he interrupted, stopping a flow of words that she had felt edging toward incoherency. His eyes were glittering again, but this time with a different fire, and she couldn't look away. "You've been taking care of me."

She drew a deep, shuddering breath. "Yes."

"All alone?"

"Yes."

"You've been feeding me."

"Yes."

"Bathing me."

"Yes. Your fever—I had to sponge you with cool water to keep it down."

"You did everything that had to be done, took care of me like a baby."

She didn't know what to say, what to do. His hand was still on her, his palm warm and hard against the softness of her flesh.

"You touched me," he said. "All over."

She swallowed. "It was necessary."

"I remember your hands on me. I liked it, but when I woke up this morning I thought it was a dream."

"You did dream," she said.

"Have I seen you naked?"

"No!"

"Then how do I know what your breasts look like? How they feel in my hands? It wasn't all a dream, Rachel. Was it?"

A hot, wild blush colored her face, giving him an answer even before she spoke. Her voice was stifled, and she looked away from him, her embarrassment at last freeing her from his gaze. "Twice, when you woke up, you… uh…grabbed me."

"Helped myself to the goodies?"

"Something like that."

"And I saw you?"

She made a helpless gesture toward her neck. "My night-gown drooped when I bent over you. The neckline was hanging open…."

"Was I rough?"

"No," she whispered.

"Did you like it?"

This had to stop, right now, though she had a feeling that it was already too late, that she should never have sat down on the bed. "Move your hand," she said, trying desperately to put some strength into her voice. "Let me go."

He obeyed without hesitation, triumph stamped on his hard, dark face. She shot up from the bed, her face on fire. What an utter fool she had made of herself! He probably wouldn't be able to sleep for laughing at her. She was at the door before he spoke, his voice momentarily freezing her to the spot.

"Rachel."

She didn't want to turn, didn't want to look at him, but the way he said her name was a command that pulled at her like a magnet. Lying down didn't diminish his power; being wounded didn't diminish it. He was a man born to dominate, and he did it effortlessly, with the sheer strength of his will.

"If I could, I'd come after you. You wouldn't get away."

Her voice was as quiet as his, rising only slightly above the whir of the ceiling fan in the cool, dim room. "I might," she said, and closed the door gently behind her as she left the room.

She wanted to cry, but she didn't, because crying never solved anything. She hurt inside, and she felt restless. Lust. She had identified it almost immediately, had properly labeled the source of her undeniable and, evidently, uncontrollable attraction to him. She could have handled it if it had remained merely lust, for lust was a human appetite, the perfectly normal reaction of one sex to another. She could have acknowledged it, then ignored it. What she couldn't ignore was the growing emotional impact he had on her. She had sat there on the bed and let him fondle her, not because she was physically attracted to him, though God knew that was the truth, but because he had rapidly become far too important to her.

Rachel's refuge was work; it had saved her when B.B. died, and she sought it instinctively now. Her study was small and cluttered with both her work and memorabilia: books, magazines, clipped articles and family photographs crowded together on every available space. It was comfortable for her; it was here that she immersed herself in her interests, and despite the clutter she knew where everything was. It wasn't until her eyes fell on her favorite picture of B.B. that she realized she wasn't going to find the comfort she sought in this room. There couldn't be any hiding from herself; she had to face it, and face it now.

Slowly her fingers traced B.B.'s smiling face. He had been best friend, husband and lover, a man whose cheerful manner had hidden a strong character and firm sense of responsibility. They had had so much fun together! There were still times when she missed him so much that she thought she would never get over the sense of loss, even though she knew that wasn't what B.B. would have wanted. He would have wanted her to enjoy her life, to love again with all the passion she was capable of, to have children, to pursue her career, to have everything. She wanted that, too, but somehow she had never been able to imagine having it without B.B., and he was gone.

They had both known and accepted the risks of their jobs. They had even talked about them, holding hands in the night and discussing the danger they faced, as if by bringing it out in the open they could hold it at bay. Her job as an investigative reporter had made it inevitable that she would step on toes, and Rachel was very good at anything she chose to do. B.B.'s job with the Drug Enforcement Administration was inherently dangerous.

Perhaps B.B. had had a premonition. His hand strong around hers in the darkness, he had once said, "Honey, if anything ever happens to me, remember that I know the possibilities and I'm willing to take the risks. I think it's a job worth doing, and I'm going to do my best at it, the same way you won't back down from a story that's getting too hot for comfort. Accidents happen to people who never take any risks at all. Playing it safe isn't a guarantee. Who knows? With the noses you put out of joint, your job may turn out to be more dangerous than mine."

Prophetic words. Within the year B.B. was dead. An investigation Rachel was making into a politician's background had turned up a connection with illegal drugs. She didn't have any proof, but her questions must have been making the politician itchy. One morning she had been late to catch a flight to Jacksonville and her car had been low on gas. B.B. had tossed her the keys to his. "Drive mine," he'd said. "I have plenty of time to get gas on the way to work. See you tonight, honey."

But he hadn't. Ten minutes after her flight left the ground B.B. started her car and a bomb wired to the ignition killed him instantly.

Haunted by grief, she had finished the investigation, and now the politician was serving a life sentence without parole for both his drug dealings and his part in B.B.'s death. Then she had given up investigative reporting and returned to Diamond Bay to try to find again some sense of life for herself. Peace, hard won but finally hers, had let her find pleasure in work again, and in the quiet tenor of life here on the bay. She had contentment, peace and pleasure, but hadn't come close to loving again; she hadn't even been tempted. She hadn't wanted to date, hadn't wanted a man's kiss, or touch, or company.

Until now. Her forefinger gently touched the glass that covered B.B.'s crooked grin. It was incredibly painful and difficult to fall in love. What an apt phrase it was! "Falling in love." She was definitely falling, unable to stop her whirling, headlong plunge, even though she wasn't certain she was ready for it. She felt like a fool. After all, what did she know about Kell Sabin? Enough for her emotions to go wildly out of control, that was for certain! She had somehow started loving him from the first, her intuition sensing that he would be important to her. Why else had she fought so desperately to hide him, to protect him? Would she have taken the risk of caring for any other stranger? It would be romantic of her to assume that it was predestination; another explanation was an ancient one, that a life belonged to the one who saved it. Was it a primitive predilection, a sort of bonding forged by danger?

At that point in her thoughts Rachel gave a wry laugh at herself. What difference did it make? She could sit there all night thinking of plausible and implausible explanations, but they wouldn't change a thing. She was, regardless of will and logic, already half in love with the man, and it was getting worse.

He was trying to seduce her. Oh, he wasn't in any physical shape for it, but given his superb conditioning and strength he would probably recover much faster than an ordinary person. Part of her shivered in excitement at the thought of making love with him, but another part, more cautious, warned her not to let herself become that involved with him. To do so would be to take an even larger risk than hiding him and nursing him back to health had been. She wasn't afraid of the physical risk, but the emotional price she might have to pay for loving such a man could be crippling.

She took a deep breath. She couldn't limit her emotions and responses to carefully measured dollops, like following a recipe. Her nature wasn't that controlled and unemotional. All she could do was accept the fact that she loved him, or was growing to love him, and deal with it from there.

B.B.'s photographed gaze looked back at her. It wasn't a betrayal to love someone else; he would want her to love again.

It was wrenching to accept the idea; Rachel didn't love lightly. When she gave herself it was with all the passion of her emotions, which wasn't an easy or casual way to love. The man in her bed wouldn't welcome her devotion; it didn't take a crystal ball to tell that he was one of those men who combined icy unemotionalism with fiery sensuality. He lived for the danger of his job, and it was a job that didn't encourage emotional ties. He could take her with raw, hungry passion, then calmly walk away and return to the life he had chosen.

Wryly she looked around the study; she wasn't going to be able to work, after all. Her emotions were too turbulent to allow her to sink into either planning her class or working on her manuscript. She had gotten her hero into a sticky situation, but could it be any stickier than the one she found herself in? Actually, she could use some practical advice. A smile suddenly lit her face. She had an expert in her bedroom; why not use his knowledge while he was there? If nothing else, it would help occupy his time. To occupy her time, she could finish weeding the garden now that it was late afternoon and the sun's ferocious heat had abated somewhat. She might as well do something practical.

The twilight was rapidly fading and she had almost finished her chore, when she heard the simultaneous creak of the screen door at the back steps and Joe's explosive, furious spring from his position at the end of the row where she was working. Rachel screamed Joe's name as she jumped to her feet, knowing that she'd never be able to reach the dog in time to stop him.

Sabin didn't retreat. Joe hesitated when Rachel screamed at him, his attention momentarily split, and Sabin used the interval to ease himself down into a sitting position on the steps. It left him vulnerable, but it also took him out of a threatening position. Joe stopped four feet away, his face contorted, the fur on his neck raised as he crouched.

"Stay back," Sabin said evenly as Rachel approached from the side, trying to put herself between Sabin and the dog. She was far too willing to use herself as a shield; he didn't think the dog would intentionally hurt her, but if the dog attacked and Rachel tried to protect him... He had to reach an understanding with Joe, and it might as well be now.

Rachel stopped as he'd directed, but she spoke softly to the dog, trying to calm him. If he attacked she wasn't strong enough to wrestle him off of Sabin. What was he thinking of, coming out like that, when he knew Joe didn't like men?

"Joe, heel," Sabin said firmly.

Just as it had earlier, the command sent Joe into a paroxysm of rage. She edged closer, ready to leap if Joe made any move to attack. Sabin gave her a warning glance.

"Joe, heel." He repeated the command over and over, always in a quiet, level voice, and Joe made a lunge that brought his sharp teeth within inches of Sabin's bare foot. Rachel gasped and threw herself at the dog, wrapping her arms around his neck. He was quivering in every muscle of his body. He ignored her, his attention locked on the man.

"Turn him loose and back away," Sabin instructed.

"Why don't you just go back in the house while I hold him?"

"Because I'm a prisoner as long as he doesn't accept me. I may need to leave in a hurry, and I don't want to have to worry about the dog."

Rachel crouched by Joe, her fingers buried in his fur and

gently rubbing. Already Sabin was planning to leave, but,
then, she had known how it would be. Slowly she released
the dog and stepped back.

"Joe, heel," Sabin said again.

Rachel held her breath, waiting for another violent reaction. She could see Joe shake, and his ears went back. Sabin
repeated the command. For a moment the dog quivered on
the verge of attack, then, abruptly, he went to Sabin's side
and took up the heeling position.

"Sit," Sabin said, and Joe sat.

"Good boy, good boy." Stiffly he moved his left arm
to pat the dog's head. For a moment Joe's ears went back
and he snarled softly, but he made no move to bite. Rachel
slowly released her pent-up breath, relief making her legs
wobble.

Sabin slanted her a quick glance from his midnight eyes.
"Now you come sit beside me."

"Just like the dog?" she quipped, sinking gratefully onto
the step beside him. At her action Joe sprang up and moved
to stand in front of them, his ears going back again.

Sabin put his right arm around her shoulders and hugged
her against his bare chest, carefully watching the dog. Joe
didn't like it at all; a growl began rumbling in his chest.

"He's jealous," Sabin observed.

"Or he thinks you might hurt me." His arm around her
was interfering with her breathing, and to take her mind off
it she held her hand out to Joe. "It's all right. Come here,
boy. Come on."

Warily Joe came closer. He sniffed at Rachel's outstretched hand, then Sabin's knee. After a moment he
dropped to the ground at their feet and put his head on his
paws.

"It's a shame someone abused him. He's an intelligent,
expensive animal, and he isn't old. He's about five."

"That's what Honey thinks."

"Have you always had a penchant for taking in strays?" he asked, and she knew he wasn't just talking about Joe.

"Only the interesting ones." She could hear the tightness creeping into her voice and wondered if he could hear it, too, if he could guess what caused it. His right hand was lightly rubbing her bare arm, an innocent touch if it hadn't been for the warm pleasure it gave her. A flash of lightning in the darkening sky made her look up, glad for an interruption.

"It looks like there's a chance of rain. A thunderhead passed right over us this morning and didn't leave a drop." Right on cue, thunder rumbled and a few fat drops of rain splashed down on them. "We'd better go in the house."

Sabin let her help him to his feet, but he negotiated the steps on his own. Joe got up and took shelter under the car. Just as Rachel latched the screen door thunder cracked deafeningly directly overhead, and the heavens opened to release a deluge of rain. The temperature plummeted while they stood there, the rain fresh and cool, and the wind blew a fine mist through the screen door. Laughing, Rachel shut the wooden door and locked it, then turned to find herself in Sabin's arms.

He didn't say anything. He simply closed his fist in her hair and held her head back, and his mouth came down on hers. Her world shuddered, then tilted off-balance. She stood there, her hands on his bare chest, and let him have her mouth as he pleased, unable to do anything except give him what he wanted. His mouth was hard, as she had known it would be. Hungry, as she had known it would be. He kissed her with the slow, hot skill of experience, his tongue on hers, the roughness of his faint beard scraping her softer skin.

The exquisite pleasure stunned her, and she jerked her mouth from his, her eyes wide as she stared up at him.

His fist tightened in her hair. "Are you afraid of me?" he asked roughly.

"No," she whispered.

"Then why did you pull away?"

She couldn't do anything but give him the truth, staring up at him in the growing darkness while the storm raged over their heads. "Because it was too much."

There was a storm in his black eyes, glittering and snapping with hot fire. "No," he said. "It wasn't enough."

CHAPTER SEVEN

Tension was coiling tightly inside Rachel; it had been increasing as the night wore on. He hadn't kissed her again, hadn't touched her again, but he had watched her, and in some ways that was worse. The power of his gaze was like a physical touch, stroking and burning. She couldn't make small talk to lessen the tension, because every time she looked up at him, he was watching her. They ate; then she turned on the television for diversion. Unfortunately the programs weren't very diverting, and he watched her, instead, so she turned the set off again. "Do you want something to read?" she finally asked in desperation.

He shook his head. "I'm too tired, and this damned headache is worse. I think I'll go back to bed."

He did look tired, but that wasn't surprising. He had been on his feet a lot, considering that he had just recovered full consciousness that morning. She was tired, too, the events of the day having sapped her energy. "Let me take a shower first. Then I'll help you get settled," she said, and he nodded in agreement.

She hurried through her shower and pulled on her most modest nightgown, then belted a light robe around her. He was waiting in the bedroom when she left the bath, and the rest of the house was dark. "That was fast," he said, smiling faintly. "I didn't know a woman could get out of a bathroom in less than half an hour."

"Chauvinist," she said mildly in reply, wondering if his smiles ever reached his eyes.

He unfastened the cutoffs and let them drop, then stepped out of them and limped into the bathroom. "I'll wash what I can reach, then call you to do the rest, all right?"

"Yes," she said, her throat tightening at the thought of feeling his body under her hands again. It wasn't as if she hadn't washed him before, but he was awake now, and he had kissed her. It was her own response to him that was making her nervous, not worrying over anything he might do. He was still too much of an invalid to make any serious advances.

There was no need for her to sleep with him now; it would be easier on both of them if she didn't make a big deal out of it and simply made a pallet before he came out of the bathroom. Thinking that, she took a couple of quilts from the top of the closet and unfolded them on the floor, then dragged a pillow from the bed and tossed it down. She wouldn't need a cover; her robe would be enough.

After twenty minutes he opened the door. "I'm ready for the reinforcements."

He wore only a towel knotted around his lean waist, and he was literally weaving on his feet. Rachel looked at him closely, concern driving away her nervousness. He was pale, the skin stretched tautly over his high cheekbones, but his lips were very red. "I think you're feverish again," she said, laying her hand against his cheek. He was too warm, but the fever wasn't nearly as high as it had been before. Quickly she lowered the lid on the toilet and helped him to sit down, then gave him two aspirin and a glass of water before she finished washing his torso, working as fast as she could. The sooner he was in bed, the better. She should have been looking for the fever to flare again after the way he'd pushed himself that day.

"Sorry about this," he muttered as she dried him. "I didn't intend to give out on you this way."

"You're not Superman," Rachel told him briskly. "Come on, let's get you in bed."

She helped him to stand, and he said, "Wait." Removing his right arm from around her shoulders, he tugged the towel loose from his waist and draped it over one of the towel racks. Totally and unconcernedly nude, he put his arm back around her shoulders and leaned on her heavily as she helped him walk to the bed. Rachel didn't know if she should laugh or get huffy with him, but in the end she decided to ignore his lack of clothing. It wasn't as if she hadn't seen him before, and if it didn't bother him, it shouldn't bother her.

Even though he was feverish and exhausted, nothing escaped his notice. He saw the pallet at the foot of the bed, and his dark, level brows lowered as his eyes narrowed. "What's that?"

"My bed."

He looked at it, then at her. His voice was quiet. "Get that damned thing up from there and get in bed with me, where you belong."

She gave him a long, cool look. "You're presuming a lot on the basis of one kiss. You're a lot better now. I won't need to get up with you during the night, so I don't need to sleep with you."

"After sleeping with me that many times, why stop now? God knows it can't be modesty at this stage, and sex is out of the question. Any pass I made would be false advertising, and you know it."

She didn't want to laugh, didn't want him to know that his logic seemed very…logical. It wasn't the thought of what he might do that made her wary of sleeping with him now, but rather the knowledge of what it would mean to her to lie beside him in the night, to feel his weight and warmth in the bed next to her. She'd gotten used to sleeping alone, and it was painful to rediscover the subtle but powerful pleasure of sharing the dark hours with a man.

He put his hand on her throat, his callused thumb rubbing the sensitive tendons running down to her shoulder and making her shiver. "There's another reason why I want you to sleep with me."

She didn't know if she wanted to hear it. That cold, lethal expression was in his eyes again, the look of a man for whom there were no illusions, who had seen the worst and not been surprised. "I'll be right there, at the foot of the bed," she whispered.

"No. I want you at hand, so I'll know exactly where you are at all times. If I have to use the knife I want to make certain you don't accidentally get in the way."

She turned her head and looked at the knife, still lying there on the table beside the bed. "No one can break in without waking us."

"I'm not taking that chance. Get in the bed. Or we'll both sleep on the floor."

He meant it, and with a sigh she gave in; there was no use in both of them being uncomfortable. "All right. Let me get my pillow."

His hand dropped to his side, and Rachel retrieved her pillow, tossing it into place on the bed. Gingerly he eased between the sheets, and a low groan escaped him as he lay back, putting strain on his shoulder. She turned out the light and got into bed on the opposite side, pulling the sheet up over both of them and curling up in her usual position, just as if they had done this for years, but the casual pose was completely superficial. She was tightly knotted inside; his caution was catching. She doubted that he really expected the men who were hunting him to break into the house in the middle of the night, but he prepared himself, anyway.

The old house settled around them with comfortable squeaks and groans; in the evening silence she could hear the crickets chirping outside the window, but the familiar noises didn't reassure her. Her thoughts roamed restlessly, trying to piece her snippets of information into a coherent picture. He was on vacation, but he'd been ambushed? Why were they trying to get rid of him? Had he learned something they wanted suppressed? She wanted to ask him, but his quiet, even breathing told her that he had already gone to sleep, worn out from the day.

Without thinking, she reached out and put her hand on his arm. It was a purely automatic gesture, left over from the nights she had needed to be aware of his every movement.

There was no warning, only the lightning-fast strike of his right hand as his hard fingers clamped around her wrist with a force that bruised and twisted. Rachel cried out, in fear as much as pain, every nerve in her jolted by his attack. The hand that held her wrist slackened a little, and he muttered, "Rachel?"

"You're hurting me!" The involuntary protest was wrung from her, and he released her completely, sitting up in the bed and swearing softly under his breath.

Rachel rubbed her bruised wrist, staring up at the faint outline of his body against the darkness. "I think the pallet would be safer," she finally said, trying for lightness. "I'm sorry. I didn't mean to touch you. It just...happened."

His voice was rough. "Are you all right?"

"Yes. My wrist is bruised, that's all."

He tried to turn toward her, but his injured shoulder stopped him, and he swore again, halting the movement.

"Climb over on this side, so I can sleep on my right side and hold you."

"I don't need holding, thank you." She was still feeling a little shaken by the way he'd reacted, as violently and swiftly as a snake striking. "You must have a hard time keeping bed partners."

"You're the only woman I've slept with, in the literal sense, in years," he snapped. "Now do you want to take your chances on startling me again, or are you going to crawl over here?"

She got out of bed and walked around to the other side, and he slid over enough to make room for her. Without a word she lay down, turned her back to him and pulled the sheet up to cover them. In equal silence he positioned himself against her like a spoon, his thighs against the backs of hers, her bottom snuggling his loins, her back against his hard, broad chest. His right arm went under her head, and his left one curved around her waist, anchoring her in place. Rachel closed her eyes, branded by his heat and wondering how much of it was fever. She'd forgotten how it felt to lie like this with a man, to feel his strength wrapped around her like a blanket. "What if I bang against your shoulder or leg?" she whispered.

"It'll hurt like hell," he replied dryly, his breath stirring her hair. "Go to sleep. Don't worry about it."

How could she not worry about hurting him, when she would rather die than cause him pain? She nestled her head into the pillow, feeling the iron hard strength of his arm beneath it; her hand slid beneath the pillow and lightly closed over his wrist, a touch that she had to have now. "Good night," she said, sinking into his warmth and letting drowsiness take over.

Sabin lay there, feeling her softness in his arms, the female sweetness of her scent in his nostrils and the remembered taste of her on his tongue. It felt too good, and that made him wary. It had been years since he'd actually *slept* with anyone; he had trained to such a fine, sharp edge that he hadn't been able to tolerate anyone close to him while he slept, including his ex-wife. Even while he'd been married he had still been essentially alone, both mentally and physically. It was odd that he could feel so comfortable now, with Rachel sleeping in his arms, as if he didn't need to be distant with her. He was innately cautious and solitary, on guard with everyone, including his own men; that trait had saved his life more than once. Maybe it was because he was already subconsciously accustomed to sleeping with her, to touching her and being touched by her, though that light touch on his arm had startled him into a violent reaction before he could catch himself.

For whatever reason, it felt good to hold her, to kiss her. She was a remarkably dangerous woman, because she tempted him in ways he'd never been tempted before. He thought of having sex with her. Every muscle in his body tightened, and he began to harden. Too bad he wasn't able to roll her onto her back and do all the things to her he wanted to do, but that would have to wait. He would have her, but he'd have to be very careful that it didn't become anything more than a good time. He couldn't afford to let it be anything else, for both of them.

RACHEL WOKE SLOWLY, so completely comfortable she was loath to open her eyes and start the day. She was normally an early riser, wide-awake as soon as her feet hit the floor, and she really liked the morning. But on this particular morning she had burrowed deeply into her pillow, her body warm and relaxed, and she was aware of having slept better than she had in years. But where was Kell? She was immediately aware that he wasn't in the bed; her eyes popped open, and she was out of bed before the thought was even completed. The bathroom door was open, so he wasn't in there. "Kell?" she called, hurrying out of the bedroom.

"Out here."

The answering call came from the back, and she almost ran to the rear door, which was standing open. He was sitting on the steps, wearing only the denim shorts, and Joe was lying on the grass at his feet. Ebenezer Duck and his faithful flock were waddling around the backyard, peacefully hunting insects. The rain the night before had left everything so fresh it almost hurt to look at it, and now the sun lit a dark-blue sky that didn't have a cloud in sight. It was a remarkably peaceful morning, warm and sweet.

"How did you get out of bed without waking me?"

Bracing his hand on the step, he pushed himself to a standing position; she noticed that he seemed to be moving more easily than he had the day before. He faced her through the screen. "You were tired after taking care of me for four days."

"You're getting around better."

"I feel stronger, and my head isn't hurting." He opened the screen door and hesitated for a moment, his black eyes swiftly running down her body. It was all she could do to keep from folding her arms across her chest, but she knew that the gown she'd chosen didn't reveal anything, so the gesture would have been futile. She probably looked a mess, with her hair uncombed, but she'd seen him at his worst, so she wasn't going to worry about that, either.

"I'm too used to playing mother hen," she said, laughing a little. "When you weren't in the bed I panicked. But since you're all right, I'll go get dressed and make breakfast."

"Don't get dressed on my account," he drawled, a comment she ignored as she walked away. Kell watched until she was out of sight, then slowly made his way back up the steps and inside. He latched the screen door behind him. She didn't play games by wearing slinky nightgowns and then pretending to be embarrassed by what was revealed, but she didn't have to. With that pink flowered nightgown and her tousled hair, she looked warm and sleepy and so damned soft a man could sink into her. That was exactly what he'd wanted to do when he awoke to find that her nightgown had ridden up during the night and he was pressed against her bare thighs, with only the thin nylon of her panties keeping him from her. He'd become so aroused that he'd had to get out of bed, to remove himself from the temptation of her body. He swore impatiently at his own physical disability, because it kept him from taking her the way he wanted to take her, hard and fast and deep.

In only a few minutes she came back into the kitchen, her hair brushed out and pulled up on each side of her head with a wine-red butterfly clip. She was still barefoot, and she wore denim shorts so old that they were almost white, along with an oversize maroon jersey with the tail knotted at her waist. Her tanned face was completely free of makeup. She was comfortable with herself, he realized. She could probably stop traffic when she did deck herself out in silk and jewels, but she would do so only when she felt like it, not for someone else's benefit. She was self-assured, and Kell liked that; he was so dominant that it took a strong woman not to be completely overpowered by him, not to shrink from him both in bed and out.

Working with an economy of motion, she put on the coffee and started the bacon frying. Until those twin aromas started filling the air he hadn't been aware of how hungry he was, but abruptly his mouth began watering. She put biscuits in the oven, whipped four eggs for scrambling, then peeled and sliced a cantaloupe. Her clear gray eyes turned toward him. "This would be easier if I had my best knife."

Sabin seldom laughed or was even amused, but the dry, chiding tone of her voice made him want to smile. He leaned against the work island to take the weight off his injured leg, unwilling to argue. He needed a means of self-defense, even if it was just a kitchen knife. Both logic and instinct insisted on it. "Do you have any sort of gun around here?"

Rachel deftly turned the bacon. "I have a .22 rifle under the bed, and a .357 loaded with ratshot in the glove compartment of the car."

Swift irritation rose in him; why hadn't she said anything about them the day before? Then she gave him another of those long, level looks, and he knew she was just waiting for him to say something. Why should she give a gun to a man who had held a knife on her? "What if I'd needed them during the night?"

"I don't have any shells for the .357 other than ratshot, so I discounted it," she replied calmly. "The .22 was within reach, and I not only know how to use it, I have two good arms as opposed to your one." She felt safe at Diamond Bay, but common sense dictated that she have some means of protection; she was a woman who lived alone, without close neighbors. Both the weapons she had were for what her grandfather had called "varmints," though anyone looking down the barrel of the .357 wouldn't know that it was loaded with ratshot. She had chosen both for self-protection, not for killing.

He paused, his black eyes narrowed. "Why tell me now?"

"One, because you told me who you are. Two, because you asked. Three, even without the knife, you weren't unarmed. Handicapped, but not helpless."

"What do you mean?"

She looked down at his hard, brown bare feet. "The calluses on the outside edges of your feet, and on your hands. Not many people have them. You work out barefoot, don't you?"

When he spoke his voice was quiet and silky, and it raised a chill along her spine. "You notice a lot, honey."

She nodded in agreement. "Yes."

"Most people wouldn't think anything about calluses."

Just for a moment Rachel hesitated, her gaze turned inward, before she resumed setting the table and checking the food. "My husband took extra training. He had calluses on his hands, too."

Something tightened inside him, twisting, and his fingers slowly curled. He darted a quick glance at her slim, tanned, ringless hands. "You're divorced?"

"No. I'm a widow."

"I'm sorry."

She nodded again and began dishing up the eggs and bacon, then checked the biscuits in the oven. They were just right, golden brown on top, and she quickly turned them out into the breadbasket. "It's been a long time," she finally said. "Five years." Then her voice changed and became brisk again. "Wash up before the biscuits get cold."

She was, he reflected a few minutes later, a damned good cook. The eggs were fluffy, the bacon crisp, the biscuits light, the coffee just strong enough. Homemade pear preserves dripped golden juice over the biscuits, and the yellow cantaloupe was ripe and sweet. There was nothing fancy about it, but it all fit together, and even the colors were harmonious. It was simply another facet of her competent nature. Just as he was savoring his third biscuit she said serenely, "Don't expect this every day. Some mornings I have cereal and fruit for breakfast. I'm just trying to build up your strength." Her manner hid the satisfaction she felt in watching this coldly controlled man eat with such obvious enjoyment.

He leaned back in his chair, taking his time as he examined the twinkle in her eyes and the smile that was barely hidden by the coffee cup she held in her elegant hands. She was teasing him, and he couldn't remember the last time anyone had actually dared to tease him. Probably back in high school, some giddy, giggling teenage girl trying out her newfound powers of seduction and daring to use them on the boy even the teachers considered "dangerous." He'd never actually done anything to make them think that; it had simply been the way he looked at them, with that cold, level gaze as black as a night in hell. Rachel dared to tease him because she was certain of herself, and because of that certainty she met him as an equal. She wasn't afraid of him, despite what she knew, or had guessed.

In time. He'd have her, sooner or later.

"You're going about it the right way," he said, finally responding to her teasing statement. Rachel wondered if he did it deliberately, waiting so long before answering. He could either be thinking about what he wanted to say, or those long pauses could be designed to tilt the other person a little off-balance. Everything he did was so controlled that she didn't think it was a habit; it was a deliberate tactic.

There could be a double meaning to his words, but Rachel chose to take them at face value. "If that's a bribe to keep me cooking like this, it won't work. It's too hot to eat a big meal three times a day. More coffee?"

"Please."

As she poured the coffee she asked, "How long are you planning to stay?"

He waited until she had set the pot back on its warming pad and returned to her seat before he answered. "Until

I get over this, and can walk and use my shoulder again. Unless you want me gone, and then it's up to you when you throw me out."

Well, that was plain enough, Rachel thought. He'd stay while he was recuperating, but that was it. "Do you have any idea what you're going to do?"

He leaned his forearms on the table. "Get well. That's the first item on the list. I have to find out how deeply we've been compromised. There's still one man I can call when I need him, but I'll wait until I've recovered before I do anything. One man alone won't stand much of a chance. I have three weeks left of my vacation. Three weeks that they'll have to keep this quiet, unless my body just 'happens' to wash up somewhere. Without my body they're stalled. They can't make any moves to replace me until I'm officially dead, or missing."

"What happens if you don't turn up at work in three weeks?"

"My file will be erased from all records. Codes will be changed, agents reassigned, and I will officially cease to exist."

"Presumed dead?"

"Dead, captured, or turned."

Three weeks. At the most she would have three weeks with him. The time seemed so pitifully short, but she wasn't going to ruin it by moaning and sulking because things weren't turning out just the way she wanted. She had learned the hard way that "forever" could be heartbreakingly brief. If these three weeks were to be all she had with him, then she would smile and take care of him, even argue with him if she felt like it, help him in any way she could…cherish him… then wave goodbye to this dark warrior and keep her tears for herself, after he had gone.

It didn't give her much comfort to know that women had probably been doing that exact thing for centuries.

He was thinking, his lashes lowered over his eyes while he stared into his coffee cup. "I want you to make another shopping trip."

"Sure," Rachel said easily. "I meant to ask you if the pants were the right size."

"Everything's the right size. You have a good eye. No, I want you to get hollowpoint ammunition for that .357, a good supply of it. The same for the rifle. You'll be reimbursed."

Being reimbursed was the last of Rachel's worries, and she felt a flare of resentment that he'd even mentioned it. "Are you sure you don't want me to buy a couple of deer rifles while I'm at it? Or a .44 Magnum?"

To her surprise he took her sarcasm seriously. "No. I don't want you on record as having purchased any type of weapon since the date I disappeared."

That startled her, and she leaned back. "You mean records of this sort that are likely to be checked?"

"For anyone in this area."

Rachel looked at him for a long, long time, her gray eyes drifting over the hard planes of his face and the closed expression in his eyes, eyes that were older than time. At last she whispered, "Who are you, that anyone would go to such lengths to kill you?"

"They'd rather take me alive," he replied dryly. "It's my job to make certain that never happens."

"Why you?"

One corner of his mouth quirked upward in what passed for a smile, though it was totally humorless. "Because I'm the best at what I do."

It wasn't much of an answer, but then he was good at answering questions without giving any information. The details that he'd told her had been carefully considered, chosen to exact the response from her that he wanted. It wasn't necessary; Rachel knew that she would do whatever she could to help him.

She drained the last of her coffee and stood up. "I have chores to do before it gets too hot; the dishes can wait until later. Do you want to come outside with me, or stay in here and rest?"

"I need to move around," he said, getting up and following her outside. He slowly limped around the yard, taking in every detail, while Rachel fed Joe and the geese, then set to work gathering the ripe vegetables from the garden. When he tired, Kell sat down on the back steps and watched her work, his eyes narrowed against the sun.

Rachel Jones had a comfortable way about her that made him feel relaxed. Her life was peaceful, her small house cozy, and that hot Southern sun burned down on his skin…. Everything here was seductive, in one way or another. The meals she cooked and shared with him brought up stray thoughts of what it would be like to have breakfast with her every day, and those thoughts were more dangerous to him than any weapon.

He'd tried to have a normal private life once, but it hadn't worked out. Marriage hadn't brought the intimacy he'd expected; the sex had been good, and regular, but after the act was finished he'd still been solitary, set apart by nature and circumstance from the rest of the world. He'd been fond of his wife, as far as it went, but that was it. She hadn't been able to scale the barriers to reach the inside man; maybe she'd never even realized he existed. Certainly she either hadn't realized or hadn't wanted to face the true nature of his job. Marilyn Sabin had looked on her husband as merely one of the thousands of men who held civil service desk jobs in Washington, D.C. He went to work in the mornings and he returned—usually—at night. She was busy with her own growing law practice and often had to work late hours, so she understood. She was a fastidious woman, so Kell's cool, distant character had suited her perfectly, and she'd never made any effort to see beyond the surface to the complicated man beneath.

Kell turned his face up to the sun, feeling everything in him loosen up and slow down. Marilyn…it had been years since he'd even thought of her, an illustration of how shallowly she had touched him. The divorce hadn't elicited any response from him other than a shrug; hell, she would have been crazy to have stayed with him after what happened.

The attempt on his life had been clumsy, not well planned or well executed at all. He and Marilyn had been out to dinner, one of the few times in their married life that they had been out together socially, and never to one of the ritzy "in" places that Marilyn loved so dearly. Kell had seen the sniper as soon as they left the restaurant and acted immediately, shoving Marilyn down and rolling for cover himself. His action had saved Marilyn's life, because she had kept walking and ended up between Kell and the sniper, who had fired almost simultaneously with Kell's shove, wounding Marilyn in the right arm.

That night had forever changed the way Marilyn viewed her husband, and she hadn't liked the new view at all. She'd seen the cool way he had tracked and cornered his assailant, seen the short, vicious fight that left the other man unconscious on the ground, heard the biting authority in Kell's voice as he gave orders to the men who arrived shortly and took over. One of those men took her to a hospital, where she was treated and kept overnight, while Kell spent the night piecing together how the sniper had learned where he would be that evening. The answer, obviously, had been Marilyn. She saw no reason to be secretive about her movements or the fact that she would be dining with her husband that night, or where; she'd truly had no idea how dangerous and highly classified her husband's job was, nor had she been interested in learning.

By the time Kell collected her at the hospital the next day their marriage was over in every way except legally. The first words Marilyn had said to him, very calmly, were that she wanted a divorce. She didn't know what it was he did, didn't want to know, but she wasn't going to risk her own life being married to him while he did it. It might have piqued her vanity a bit when Kell agreed so easily, but he'd been doing some thinking during the night, too, and had reached basically the same conclusion, though for different reasons.

Kell didn't blame her for getting a divorce; it had been the wise thing to do. The close call had shaken him, because it had illustrated how easily he could be reached through the very person who was supposed to be closest to him. It had been a mistake for him even to attempt to have a normal private life, considering who he was and what he did. Other men could manage it, but other men weren't Kell Sabin, whose particular talents put him on the leading edge of danger. If there was any one man in intelligence whom other agencies wanted to take out of commission, it was Kell Sabin. Because he was a target, anyone close to him was automatically a target, too.

It had taught him a lesson. He had never again let anyone get close enough to him that they could be used against him, or hurt in an effort to get to him. He had chosen his life, because he was both a realist and a patriot, and he was willing to pay whatever price he had to, but he was determined to never again involve an innocent, a civilian, one of the very people whose lives and freedom he was sworn to protect.

He'd never been tempted to marry again, or even to take a mistress. Sex was casual, never on a regular basis with the same woman, and he always carefully limited the number of times he saw anyone in particular. It had worked out well.

Until Rachel. She tempted him. Damn, how she tempted him! She was nothing like Marilyn; she was comfortable and casual, where Marilyn had been fastidious and chic. She knew—somehow, she *knew*—too much about his way of life in general, while Marilyn hadn't realized even a fraction that much about him in the years they were married.

But it simply wouldn't work. He couldn't allow it to work. He watched Rachel as she worked in her small garden, content with her chores. Sex with her would be hot and long, writhing on that bed with her, and she wouldn't worry if he mussed her hair or smeared her makeup. To protect her, he had to make certain that sex was all it ever was. When he walked out of her life it would be for good, and for her own good. He owed her too much to risk any harm coming to her.

She straightened from her bent position and stretched, reaching her arms high in the air; the movement thrust her breasts upward against the thin fabric of her shirt. Then she picked up her basket and picked her way across the rows of vegetables toward him; Joe left his position at the end of the row and followed her to find shade under the back steps. There was a smile on Rachel's face as she approached Kell, her gray eyes warm and clear, her slim body moving gracefully. He watched her approach, aware of her in every cell of his body. No, there was no way he'd endanger her by staying any longer than was necessary; the real danger was that he was so hungry for her that he might be tempted to see her again, something he couldn't let happen.

CHAPTER EIGHT

THE NEXT FEW DAYS were slow, hot and peaceful. Now that Kell was on the mend and didn't require her constant attention Rachel resumed her normal work schedule; she finished planning her course and began working on her manuscript again, as well as tending the garden and doing all the other small chores that never seemed to end. She got the requested hollowpoint bullets for Kell, and the .357 was never far from his hand. If they were inside he sometimes placed it on the table in the bedroom, but usually he kept it stuck into his waistband at the small of his back, instantly accessible.

Honey came to take the stitches out of his wounds and professed to be amazed at how well he had healed. "Your metabolic rate must be something else," she said admiringly. "Of course, I did a terrific job on you. The muscle in your leg was a mess, but I did some repair work, and I think you're going to come out of this without even a limp."

"You did a helluva job, doc," he drawled, smiling at her.

"I know," Honey returned cheerfully. "You were just plain lucky on your shoulder. You may lose some of your rotation ability, but not much, I don't think. Take it easy on both the leg and shoulder for another week or so, but you can start working the stiffness out if you're careful."

He had already been working the stiffness out; Rachel had seen him exercising his shoulder and arm carefully, as though testing the limits of the stitches. He hadn't put any weight on either his leg or shoulder, but he had been doing exercises to ease his movements, and as a result his limp was much better, no worse than if he'd had a sprained ankle.

Honey hadn't even blinked when he removed the pistol from his waistband and placed it on the table while he took off his khaki pants and blue cotton shirt. Wearing only his briefs, he'd sat at the table and observed expressionlessly while she removed the stitches and Rachel leaned over to watch. Then he put his clothes back on and returned the heavy pistol to its accustomed place at the small of his back.

"Stay for lunch," Rachel invited. "Tuna salad and fresh tomatoes, light and cool."

Honey made it a practice never to refuse one of Rachel's invitations. "Done. I've been craving a fresh tomato."

"Southerners serve tomatoes with almost everything," Kell observed.

"That's because almost everything tastes better with a tomato," Honey defended. She was from Georgia, and passionately fond of tomatoes.

"Love apples," Rachel said absently. "Tomatoes, that is. Though I don't know why they were called that, since most people thought they were poisonous because they're a member of the nightshade family, like belladonna."

Honey chuckled. "Oh, ho! You've been reading up on old poisons, haven't you? Is someone in one of your books going to kick the bucket from an overdose of belladonna?"

"Of course not. I don't write whodunits." Not at all perturbed by Honey's teasing, Rachel glanced at Kell as she set the table. "You're not a Southerner, are you? You have a drawl, but it isn't Southern."

"Most of it comes from spending a lot of time with a

man from Georgia. We were in Vietnam together. I was born in Nevada."

That was probably the limit of the personal information he would give about himself, so Rachel didn't ask any more questions. They ate the simple meal, with Kell sitting between the two women, and though he ate well as always and kept up with the conversation, she noticed that he sat where he could watch both the window and the door. It was habit with him; he did it at every meal, even though he knew no one could approach the house without Joe giving warning.

As Honey was leaving she smiled at Kell and held out her hand. "If I don't see you again, goodbye."

He took her hand. "Thanks, doc. Goodbye." Rachel noticed that he made no pretense about staying.

Honey eyed him consideringly. "I'm literally bursting with questions, but I think I'm going to follow my own good advice and not ask them. I don't want to know. But be careful, you hear?"

He gave his crooked half smile. "Sure thing."

She winked at him. "If anyone asks, I don't know a thing."

"You're a smart woman, doc. After I'm gone Rachel can fill you in on the details."

"Maybe. But maybe I'll just make up my own answers. That way I can get as wild and romantic as I want but still play it safe."

Probably Honey's outlook *was* the best, Rachel thought after she and Kell were alone. Honey allowed herself to be wild and romantic in her fantasies, but in real life she opted for safety. Honey would never do anything as risky as falling in love with a man like Kell Sabin. She would clean the kitchen, just as Rachel was doing, and forget about the rest.

Rachel turned and found him watching her in that steady, unnerving way of his. Her chin lifted. "What is it?"

For answer he walked up to her and cupped her chin in his hand, then bent and covered her mouth with his. Surprise held Rachel motionless for a moment; he hadn't kissed her after that first time, though she sometimes thought there was a touch of possessiveness in the way he held her at night. She hadn't betrayed the pleasure she felt in sleeping in his arms, but there was no way she could hide the heavy surge of desire that made her respond to his mouth, her lips parting at the pressure of his, her hands sliding up the hard, warm wall of his chest. His tongue curled against hers, and she made a sound deep in her throat, her breasts and loins tightening as if he had touched them.

Slowly Kell moved forward, backing her up until she was jammed against the cabinets. Rachel freed her mouth and gasped, "What brought this on?"

His mouth moved down to the curve of her jaw and explored the soft skin below her ear. "Must be all those love apples you've been feeding me," he murmured. "Stop turning your head away. Kiss me. Open your mouth." She did, her hands clenching his shirt, and he took her mouth in a long, deep, mind-drugging way that went on forever and had her standing on tiptoe to press against him. His hands slid down to her buttocks and cupped them, lifting her into even more intimate contact.

The kiss stripped away all pretense and left them clinging together in open passion, hungry for each other, straining to get even closer. Their passion had been building for days, feeding on the memory of intimate touches between them that normally would have come after the first questing kisses, but they had been thrown together in circumstances that had gotten the order mixed. She had seen and touched his hard, beautiful body while caring for him and soothing him. He had felt her in his hands and gotten used to the particular sweet scent of her even before he'd known her name. He had slept with her in his arms for four nights now, and their bodies had grown accustomed to each other. Nature had circumvented all the natural barriers that people threw up to protect their sense of privacy, forcing the two of them together in a hothouse atmosphere forged by circumstance.

The force of what she was feeling frightened her a little, and again she tore her mouth away from his, hiding her face in the warm curve of his throat. She had to slow this down before she went out of control. "You're a fast man," she gulped, trying to steady her voice.

He moved his hands from her buttocks to slide them up her back, holding her tightly. His mouth nuzzled her ear, and his voice was warm and dark. "Not as fast as I wanted to be."

Uncontrollable shivers were vibrating through her entire body, and her nipples were so tight that they ached. He held her even more tightly, crushing her breasts against his hard, muscle-layered body and rubbed his cheek against the top of her head, but the tender caress didn't last long against his hungry need for more. He dug his fingers into her hair and tilted her head back, his mouth once again taking hers, his tongue moving in the rhythm of making love. Rachel's entire body jolted when his other hand covered her breast, sliding inside her blouse to cup her warmly in his palm so he could rasp his callused thumb over her hardened nipple, simultaneously soothing the ache and creating a deeper one.

"I want to be inside you," he murmured, lifting his head to watch the way her nipple rolled under his thumb. "I've been going crazy, wanting you. Will you let me have you for the time we have left together?"

God, he was honest, and she had to swallow hard to keep

from crying out at the pain. Even now, with their bodies fevered with need, he didn't make sweet promises he had no intention of keeping. He would be leaving; the best they could have would be temporary. Still, it would be so simple if she could just forget about the future and go with him now into her bedroom, but his honesty reminded her that she had to think about the future and the day when he would leave her.

Slowly she pushed against him, and he moved back, giving her the space she needed. With a shaking hand she pushed her hair back from her face. "It isn't something that's easy for me," she tried to explain, her voice shaking just like her hand. "I've never had a lover...only my husband."

His eyes were sharp, watchful, and he waited.

She made a helpless gesture. His honesty deserved her own. "I...care about you."

"No," he said sharply, deliberately. "Don't let it happen."

"Is it something I'm supposed to turn off, like a water faucet?" Rachel faced him, her gaze level.

"Yes. This is sex, nothing else. Don't fool yourself into thinking there can be anything more, because even if there were, there'd still be no future in it."

"Oh, I know that." She gave a tight little laugh and turned to look out the window over the sink. "When you walk out of here, that's when it ends."

She wanted him to deny it, but again that brutal honesty destroyed her hopes. "That's it. That's the way it has to be."

It would be useless to argue with him on that point; she had known all along that he was solitary, a lone wolf. "It's that way for you, but I don't have that sort of emotional control. I think I love you—oh, damn, why try to hedge my bets?" Her voice was filled with helpless frustration. "I started loving you the minute I dragged you out of the ocean! It doesn't make sense, does it? But it won't stop just because you leave."

He watched her, accurately reading the tension in her slender back, the tightness of her hands. What had it cost her to confess that? She was the most direct woman he'd ever known, with no use for games or subterfuge. She was the only woman in all these years that he regretted leaving; just the thought of it twisted his guts, but he could handle that a lot easier than the knowledge that keeping her with him would jeopardize her life. She was too fine for him to carelessly endanger her for his own enjoyment.

He put his hands on her shoulders, kneading the tension from them. "I won't pressure you," he murmured. "You have to do what's best for you, but if you decide you want me, I'm here."

Decide she wanted him? She ached with wanting him! But he was giving her the space to decide for herself, rather than seducing her into bed as he knew he easily could; she had no illusions about her self-control where he was concerned. She put her hand on his, and their fingers entwined.

There was a thump as Joe left the shade under the steps and tore around the side of the house, and Kell's hand stiffened under hers, his head snapping around. Rachel went still, then shook herself and moved swiftly to the front door. She didn't have to tell him to stay out of sight; she knew that if she looked around he would already be hidden from view, moving silently through the house.

She opened the door and stepped out onto the front porch, and only then did she remember that Kell had partially unbuttoned her blouse. She rebuttoned it swiftly, looking around for whatever had set Joe off. Then she heard the car approaching down the private road; it wouldn't be

Honey, since she had just left, and on the rare times Rafferty visited he rode his horse over rather than driving.

The car that pulled to a stop in front of the house was a pale-blue Ford, a government car. Joe was crouched facing it, snarling, his ears back. "Steady, steady," Rachel murmured to him, trying to see who was in the car, but the sun was glaring on the window and blocked her vision. Then the car door opened and a tall man got out, but he remained in the open door, looking at her over the top of the vehicle. Agent Ellis, his jacket off and dark sunglasses shading his eyes.

"Oh, hello," Rachel called. "Nice to see you again." The Southern ritual of greeting had its advantages, giving her time to gather her thoughts. Why was he here again? Had Kell been seen when he'd been outside? They had been careful, trusting Joe to warn them if anyone was near, but someone with binoculars might have seen him.

Tod Ellis gave her his bright college smile. "It's nice to see you again, Ms. Jones. I thought I'd check in with you, make sure everything's okay."

It was a pretty weak excuse for driving miles out of his way. Rachel stepped around Joe and walked out to the car in an effort to keep Ellis from looking toward the house. It wasn't likely that Kell would let himself be seen, but she didn't want to take any chances. "Yes, everything's okay," she said cheerfully, going around the car and standing at the door so he had to turn his back to the house in order to face her. "Hot, but okay. Did you ever find that man you were hunting?"

"No, not a trace. You haven't seen anything?"

"Not even at a distance, and Joe always lets me know if anyone's around."

The mention of the dog made Ellis jerk his head around for a quick look as if to check Joe's location; the dog was still standing in the middle of the yard, his eyes locked on the intruder, low growls still rumbling in his chest. Ellis cleared his throat, then turned back to Rachel. "It's a good thing you've got him, living way out here by yourself. You can't be too careful."

She laughed. "Well, actually you can. Look at Howard Hughes. But I feel safe with Joe guarding the place."

She couldn't be certain, because of the dark glasses shading his eyes, but she thought he kept looking at her legs and breasts. Alarm skittered through her, and she had to fight down the urge to check her buttons; had she buttoned the blouse straight? If not, it was too late now, and he had no reason to think she had been in the house, kissing the very man he was hunting.

Then abruptly he laughed, too, and took off his sunglasses, dangling them from his fingers. "I didn't come out here to check on you." He leaned his forearm on top of the open car door, his posture relaxed and confident. With his clean-cut good looks he was accustomed to approval from women. "I came to ask you out to dinner. I know you don't know me, but my credentials are respectable. What do you say?"

Rachel didn't have to fake her confusion; it was real. She had no idea how she should answer him. If she went out with him it would go a long way toward convincing him she knew nothing about Kell, but on the other hand, it might encourage Agent Ellis to come around again, and she didn't want that. Why were they still here, anyway? Why hadn't they moved farther down the coast in their search for Kell?

"Why, I don't know," she replied, stammering a little. "When?"

"Tonight, if you don't have other plans."

God, this was making her paranoid! If they had seen

Kell, then this could be a ploy to get her out of the house so there would be no witnesses. If not, she might make him suspicious if *she* acted too suspicious. All this second-guessing could drive her crazy. Finally she went on her instincts. Agent Ellis hadn't tried to hide his male admiration for her the first time they'd met, so she was going to take his invitation at face value. If nothing else, she might be able to get some information from him.

"I think I'd like that," she finally said. "What did you have in mind? I'm not much of a party person."

He gave her his boyish grin again. "You're safe. I'm not into the punk scene, either. I'm too squeamish to stick safety pins through my cheeks. What I had in mind was a quiet restaurant and a good, thick steak."

And a roll in bed afterward? He'd be disappointed. "You're on," Rachel said. "What time?"

"Say, eight o'clock? It'll be sundown by then and cooling off, I hope."

She laughed. "I would say you get used to it, but all you do is learn to cope with it. The humidity is what gets you. All right, eight o'clock it is. I'll be ready."

He gave her a little salute and folded himself back under the steering wheel. Rachel walked back into the yard so she wouldn't get covered with dust when he drove off, and watched until the blue Ford was out of sight.

Kell was waiting for her inside, his eyes narrow and cold. "What did he want?"

"To ask me out to dinner," she replied slowly. "I didn't know what to say. Going out with him might keep him from being suspicious, or he could be asking me out just to get me out of the house. Maybe they've seen you. Maybe they just want to search."

"They haven't seen me," he said. "Or I wouldn't still be alive. What excuse did you give him?"

"I accepted."

Rachel had known he wouldn't be pleased, but she hadn't expected the reaction she got. His head snapped around, and his eyes burned with black fire, his usual cool remoteness shattered. "Hell, no, you're not. Get that idea out of your head, lady."

"It's too late. It might really make him suspicious if I made some weak excuse now."

He shoved his hands into his pants pockets, and in petrified fascination Rachel watched them ball into fists. "He's a murderer and a traitor. I've been doing a lot of thinking since I recognized him before they blew up my boat, tying together some details about things that went wrong when they shouldn't have, and Tod Ellis is connected in some little way to every one of those plans. You're not going out with him."

Rachel didn't back down. "Yes," she said. "I am. If nothing else, I may be able to pick up some information that will help you—"

She broke off with a gasp; he had jerked his hands out of his pockets and reached for her so rapidly that she hadn't had time to move back. His hard fingers closed on her shoulders in a grip that bruised, and he shook her slightly, his face hard and set with rage.

"Damn you," he whispered, the words barely audible as he pushed them between his clenched teeth. "When will you learn that this isn't something for amateurs to play with? You're in way over your head, and you don't have the sense to realize it! You aren't still in college playing a game of Assassination, sugar. Get that through your skull! Damn it," he swore again, releasing her shoulders and running his hand through his hair. "You've been lucky so far that you haven't blundered around and really screwed things up, but how long do you expect that luck to last? You're dealing with a cold-blooded professional!"

Rachel stepped back from him, putting her hand up to rub her aching shoulder. Something inside her had gone very still at his attack; that stillness was reflected on her face. "Which one?" she finally asked quietly. "Tod Ellis... or you?"

She turned and walked away from him, going into the bathroom and closing the door; it was the one place in the house where he wouldn't follow. She sat down on the rim of the tub, shaking; she had wondered occasionally what it would be like if he slipped the tight rein of his control, but she hadn't wanted to find out like that. She had wanted him to lose control when he kissed her, touched her. Wanted him to shake with need and desire and bury his face against her. She hadn't wanted him to lose control in anger, hadn't wanted to hear what he really thought of her efforts to help. She had been terrified all along of doing something wrong that might jeopardize him; she had agonized over every decision, and he had dismissed her from the start as a bumbling amateur. She knew she didn't have his knowledge or expertise, but she had done the best she could.

It was doubly painful after the way he had kissed her and touched her, but now she remembered that even then he had retained his steely control. It had been she who trembled and yearned, not him. He hadn't even lied to her; he'd told her plainly that it was nothing more to him than casual sex.

Taking a deep breath, Rachel gathered herself together. Since she was in the bathroom she might as well shower now; that would give her straight, heavy hair time to dry naturally and she wouldn't have to do anything to it except give it lift and curve with the curling iron. She might be going out with Tod Ellis with all the enthusiasm of attending an execution, but she wouldn't let him think that she looked on it as anything other than a real date, and that meant taking pains with her appearance.

She stripped off and got in the shower, briskly shampooing her hair and bathing, not allowing herself the luxury of brooding. Self-pity wouldn't accomplish anything except wasting time, time that would be better spent considering how to conduct herself that night, how to be friendly without being encouraging. The last thing she wanted was for Ellis to ask her out again! If he did, she'd have to make up some excuse. She'd told Agent Lowell she was making a trip to the Keys; it had been pure fabrication, but perhaps she could use the lie as an excuse for packing, planning and so on.

She turned off the water and dragged a towel off the top of the shower door, then wrapped it around her head. Just as she started to slide the door open and step out of the tub she caught sight of Kell's blurred image through the frosted door, and she jerked her hand back from the door as if it had burned her.

"Get out of here," she breathed sharply, snatching the towel off her head and wrapping it around her body, instead. The frosted surface of the doors gave her some protection, but if she could see him, he could see just as much of her. Knowing that he had watched her bathe made her feel terribly vulnerable. How long had he been there?

She saw his hand reaching out, and she moved back against the shower wall as he slid the door open on its track. "You didn't answer when I called you," he said curtly. "I wanted to make certain you were okay."

Rachel lifted her chin. "That's not much of an excuse. As soon as you saw I was taking a shower, you should have left."

His eyes raked over her, from her wet, tangled hair to

her glistening shoulders and down to her slim, bare legs, which had rivulets of water running down them. The towel covered her from breast to thigh, but it would take only a tug to bare her completely, and his black, searching eyes had a way of making her feel even more exposed than she was.

"I'm sorry," he said abruptly, finally lifting his gaze to her face. "I didn't intend to imply that you haven't been a help."

"You didn't imply any such thing," Rachel returned, her voice sharp. "You came right out and said it." She felt both insulted and hurt, and she wasn't in the mood to forgive him. After what he had said, he had a lot of nerve to stand there eyeing her the way he was doing!

Suddenly he moved, hooking his right arm around her waist and lifting her out of the tub. Rachel gasped, clutching at him for balance. "Watch out! Your shoulder—"

He stood her on the fuzzy bath mat, his face hard and unreadable as he looked down at her, his right arm still locked around her waist. "I don't want you going out with him," he finally rasped. "Damn it, Rachel, I don't want you taking any risks on my account!"

The towel was slipping, and Rachel grabbed for the ends to anchor it more securely. "Why can't you give me any credit for being an adult, able to accept responsibility for my own actions?" she cried. "You told me Tod Ellis is a traitor, and I believe you. Don't you think I have a moral responsibility to do what I can to stop him and to help you? I think the situation is critical enough to warrant the risk! It's my decision, not yours."

"You never should have been involved."

"Why not? You said yourself that you'll have to have help. You've sent other people into dangerous situations, haven't you?"

"They were trained agents," he snapped, goaded. "And, damn it to hell, I never lay awake at night burning to make love to any of them."

She fell silent, her eyes wide as they searched his. His expression gave away nothing but anger and a faintly startled look, as if he hadn't meant to say that. The arm around her waist had her arched against him, though she had wedged her arm between their bodies in an effort to hold the towel. Only her toes touched the mat. Her thighs were inside his slightly spread legs, his growing hardness nestled against the soft mound at the top of her thighs.

They said nothing, both of them very aware of what was happening. Their chests expanded and fell rapidly as their breathing quickened, and Rachel's knees grew weak as she felt him grow stronger and bolder.

"I'd kill him before I let him touch you," he muttered, the words wrenched from him.

She shuddered at the thought. "*I* wouldn't let him. Never." Staring up at him, she shuddered again, as if she'd been struck between the eyes. Tod Ellis had made her realize anew how much danger stalked Kell's heels. She wasn't guaranteed three weeks with him; she wasn't guaranteed tomorrow, or even tonight. For men such as Kell Sabin there was no tomorrow, only the present; it was the brutal truth that he could be killed, that tragedy and terror could strike without warning. She had already learned that lesson once; how could she have been so stupid as to forget? She had wanted things to be perfect, wanted him to feel as she felt, but life was never perfect. It had to be taken as it was, or it passed by without a second glance. All she had with Kell was right now, the eternal present, because the past is always gone and the future never comes.

His hands were flexing on her flesh, his fingers kneading her as if he were barely able to restrain himself from doing more. His face was rock hard as he stared down at her, his voice raw when he spoke. "I let you back away in the kitchen. By God, I don't think I can do it again. Not now."

Rachel's breath left her lungs at the look in his midnight eyes, the hard, almost cruel look of savage arousal. The skin was pulled tight over his high, prominent cheekbones, and his jaw and mouth were set. Her heart gave a sudden leap as she realized that he meant exactly what he'd said, and fear and excitement rushed through her veins in a dizzying mixture. Control was impossible for him now, and the primitive force of his hunger was burning in his eyes.

Her hands trembled on his chest as her entire body began quivering in reaction to the fiercely male intent that was plain on his face, the look of a predator who had scented female. Heat. Heat was rising in her body, melting her insides, turning them liquid. His hand at her back clenched the towel and pulled it free from the tuck at her bosom. It dropped to the floor in a damp heap. Naked, Rachel stood in his grasp, shaking and yearning and gasping for breath that wouldn't seem to go deep enough.

He looked down at her, and a low rumbling sound started in his chest, working up to the back of his throat. Rachel's thighs turned to water, and she swayed, her throat tight, her heart pounding. Slowly he lifted his hand and touched her breasts, high and round, soft, with small, tight brown nipples, filling his palm with her to discover anew the warm, velvety texture of her flesh. Then, just as slowly, his hand drifted downward, smoothing over the sleek delta of her stomach and the slope of her lower abdomen, his fingers at last sliding into the dark curls of her womanhood. She hung there, shaking wildly and unable to move, paralyzed by the hot river of pleasure that followed his questing touch. One finger made a bolder foray. Her body jerked wildly, and she whimpered as he touched and teased and explored.

His gaze lifted from the gut-wrenching contrast of his hard, sinewy hand cupping the soft, exquisitely female mound and drifted back up to her pretty breasts, then to her face. Her eyes were half closed, glazed with desire; her lips were moist and parted, her breath rushing in and out in gasps. She was a woman on the verge of complete satisfaction, and her look of sweet carnality exploded the slim hold he still had on himself. With a wild, deep sound he bent and hoisted her over his right shoulder, the blood pounding so wildly in his ears that he didn't hear her startled cry.

He made it to the bed in five long steps and dropped her across it, following her down, spreading her thighs and kneeling between them before she had recovered. Rachel reached for him, almost sobbing with need. He tore off his shirt and tossed it to the floor, then jerked at his pants until they were open, and he lowered himself onto her.

Her body arched in shock as he thrust into her, and she cried out at both the moment of pinching discomfort and the jolt to her senses and flesh as he filled her. He was... oh...

"Take it all," he groaned, demanded, pleaded. He hung over her, his face shiny with sweat, his expression at once tortured and ecstatic. "All of me. Please." His voice was hoarse with need. "Let yourself relax—yes. Like that. *More*. Please. Rachel. Rachel! You're mine you're mine you're mine...."

The rawly primitive chant washed over her, and she cried out again as he moved in and out of her, powerfully, their bodies writhing together. It had never been like this for her, so painfully intense that it was unbearable. She had never loved like this, knowing that the breath would still in her lungs and her heart stop beating in her chest if anything ever happened to him. If this was all he wanted of her, then she would give herself to him freely and fervently, branding him with the sweet burning of her own passion.

He rolled his hips against her with a heavy surge, and it was abruptly too much for her to bear, making her senses crest and shatter. She gasped and cried out, writhing beneath him in a shimmer of pure heat that went on and on until it caught him, too. She couldn't see, couldn't breathe, could only feel. She felt the heavy pounding of his thrusts as he drove himself into her, then the convulsive heaving of his body in her arms. His hoarse wild cries filled her ears, then became rough moans. Slowly he stilled, became silent. His body relaxed, and his heavy weight bore down on her, but she cradled him gladly, her hands still clutching his back.

Concern began to nudge her as sanity returned, bringing remembrance of the way he had lifted her onto his shoulder and the unrestrained wildness of his lovemaking. His head lay on her shoulder, and she twined her fingers into his coal-black hair, managing only a husky murmur as she said, "Kell? Your shoulder...are you okay?"

He levered himself onto his right elbow and looked down at her. Her clear gray eyes were dark with concern—for him, after he'd taken her with all the care and finesse of a bull in rut! There were her soft, trembling lips, but he hadn't kissed them, nor had he caressed her pretty breasts and sucked them as he'd done in his dreams. Love was in those eyes, love so pure and shining that it knotted his insides with pain and shattered a wall somewhere deep in his mind and soul, leaving him vulnerable in a way he'd never been before.

Now he knew what hell was. Hell was seeing heaven, bright and tender, but being on the outside of the gates, unable to enter them without risking the destruction of what you most treasured.

CHAPTER NINE

"JUST WHO IS THIS woman Ellis has gone so mad over?" Charles asked calmly, his pale-blue eyes never wavering as he watched Lowell. As always, Charles's manner was detached, but Lowell knew that he missed nothing.

"She lives in a little house close to the beach. Deserted area, nothing around for miles. We questioned her when we first started looking for Sabin."

"And?" The voice was almost gentle.

Lowell shrugged. "And nothing. She hadn't seen anything."

"She must be out of the ordinary to capture Ellis's attention."

After considering it a minute Lowell shook his head. "She's good-looking, but that's all. Nothing fancy. No makeup. Outdoorsy type. But Ellis hasn't stopped talking about her."

"It seems our friend Ellis doesn't have his mind completely on the job at hand." The comment was deceptively casual.

Again Lowell shrugged. "He thinks Sabin died when the boat blew up, so he's not putting a lot of effort into hunting him."

"What do *you* think?"

"It's a possibility. We haven't found any trace of him. He was wounded. Even if by a miracle he'd made it to shore, he'd have needed help."

Charles nodded, his eyes thoughtful as he waved Lowell away. He had worked with Lowell for many years now and knew him as a steady and competent, if uninspired, agent. He had to be competent to have survived. Lowell was no more convinced of Sabin's survival than Ellis was, and Charles wondered if he had allowed Sabin's reputation to override his own common sense. Common sense would certainly seem to indicate that Sabin had died in the explosion or immediately thereafter, drowning in the warm turquoise waters to become food for the denizens of the sea. No one should have survived that, but Sabin... Sabin was one of a kind, except for that blond devil with the golden eyes, who had disappeared and was rumored to be dead, despite the disquieting talk that had floated out of Costa Rica the year before. Sabin was more shadow than substance, instinctively cunning and damnably lucky. No, not lucky, Charles corrected himself. Skilled. To call Sabin "lucky" was to underestimate him, a fatal mistake too many of his colleagues had made.

"Noelle, come here," he called, barely raising his voice, but he didn't need to. Noelle was never far from him. It gave him pleasure to look at her, not because she was extraordinarily beautiful, though she was, but because he enjoyed the incongruity of such lethal skill housed in such a lovely woman. Her job was twofold: to protect Charles and to kill Sabin.

Noelle came into the room, walking with the grace of a model, her eyes sleepy and soft. "Yes?"

He waved his thin, elegant hand to indicate a chair. "Sit, please. I have been discussing Sabin with Lowell."

She sat, crossing her legs to best display them. The gestures that attracted unsuspecting males came naturally to her; she had studied and practiced too long for them to be anything else by now. She smiled. "Ah, Agent Lowell. Sturdy, dependable, if a little shortsighted."

"Like Ellis, he seems to think we're wasting our time in searching for Sabin."

She lit a cigarette and inhaled deeply, then blew smoke through her shapely lips. "It doesn't matter what they think, does it? Only what you think."

"I wonder if I *am* bestowing superhuman powers on Sabin, if I'm so wary of him that I can't accept his death," Charles mused.

Her sleepy eyes blinked. "Until we have proof of his death we can't afford to assume otherwise. It's been eight days. If he somehow survived, he would now be recovered enough to start moving around, which should increase our chances of finding him. The most logical thing would be to intensify our search, rather than slacken it."

Yes, that was indeed logical; on the other hand, if Sabin had survived the explosion and somehow made it to shore, something that seemed impossible, why hadn't he contacted his headquarters for aid? Ellis's contact in Washington was completely certain that Sabin hadn't attempted to get in touch with anyone. That simple fact had convinced almost everyone that Sabin was dead…yet Charles couldn't convince himself. It was sheer instinct that prompted him to keep his men searching, waiting, poised to strike. He could not believe that it had been so easy to kill Sabin, not after all these years when attempt after attempt had failed. It was impossible to have too much respect for his capabilities. Sabin was out there, somewhere. Charles could feel it.

He was abruptly brisk. "You're right, of course," he told Noelle. "We will intensify the search, re-cover every inch of ground. Somehow, somewhere, we have missed him."

SABIN PROWLED THE HOUSE, his savage mood reflected on his face. He'd done some hard things in his life, but none of them had been as difficult as having to watch Rachel get ready to go out with Tod Ellis. It went against every instinct he had, but nothing he'd said could change her mind, and he was helpless, handcuffed by circumstance. He couldn't afford to do anything that would focus attention on her; it would merely increase the danger she was in. If he'd been ready to move he would have gone that night rather than expose her to Ellis, but again he was stymied. He wasn't ready to move, and to move before he was prepared could mean the difference between success and failure, with his country's security at stake. He'd been trained for half his lifetime to put his country first, even at the cost of his own life. Sabin could have sacrificed himself without hesitation or even regret if it had been necessary, but the simple, terrible truth was that he couldn't sacrifice Rachel.

He had to do whatever he could to keep her safe, even if it meant swallowing his pride and possessive instincts. She was safe enough with Ellis as long as he had no reason to suspect her of anything. To jerk her out of the house and take her away before Ellis arrived to pick her up, as Kell had badly wanted to do, *would* arouse the man's suspicions. Kell knew the agent, knew that he was damned good at his job...too good, or he'd never have been able to hide his other activities for so long. He also had a good-sized ego; if Rachel stood him up it would make him furious, and he wouldn't let it pass. He would be back.

Patience, the ability to wait even in the face of great urgency, was one of Sabin's greatest gifts. He knew how to wait, how to pick his moment for optimum success, how to ignore danger and concentrate solely on timing. He could literally disappear into his surroundings, waiting, so much a part of the earth that the wild creatures had ignored him and the Vietcong had at times passed within touching distance of him without ever seeing him. His ability to wait was enhanced by his instinctive knowledge of when patience was useless; then he exploded into action. He explained it to himself as a well-developed sense of timing. Yes, he knew how to wait…but waiting for Rachel to come home was driving him crazy. He wanted her back safe in his arms, in bed. Damn, how he wanted her in bed!

He didn't turn on any lights in the house; he didn't think it likely that the house was being watched, but he couldn't take the chance. Rachel and Ellis might return early, and a lit house could trigger Ellis's suspicions. Instead he moved silently through the darkness, unable to sit still despite the ache in his shoulder and leg. His shoulder had been giving him hell since the afternoon, and he absently massaged it. A humorless smile quirked his lips. He hadn't felt a thing while he'd been making love to Rachel; his senses had been centered completely on her and the unbearable ecstasy of their bodies linked together. But since then the shoulder had been painfully reminding him that he was a long way from being healed; he'd been lucky he hadn't torn it open again.

Abruptly he swore and limped through the kitchen to the back door, so agitated that he couldn't remain inside the confines of the house any longer. As soon as Kell opened the back door he sensed Joe leaving his stakeout under the oleander bush, silently moving through the shadows, and he softly called to the dog in reassurance. Kell no longer feared being attacked; Joe had warily accepted his residency, but Kell didn't trust him enough to refrain from identifying himself before going down the back steps.

Automatically keeping himself in the shadows, Kell circled the house and investigated the pines, assuring himself that the house wasn't under surveillance. Joe padded along about ten feet behind him, stopping when Kell stopped and advancing when Kell moved on.

A new moon was just rising, a thin sickle of light on the horizon. Sabin looked up at the clear sky, so clear, like Rachel's eyes, that infinity seemed within his reach.

His heart twisted again, and his hand clenched into a fist. He whispered a curse into the night. She was too gallant, too strong, for her own good; why couldn't she play it safe and let him take all the risks? Didn't she know what it would do to him if anything happened to her?

No, how could she know? He'd never told her, and he never would, not at the expense of her safety. He'd protect her if it killed him. His mouth twisted wryly; it probably *would* kill him, not physically, but deep inside where he'd never let anyone touch him…until Rachel had slipped past all his defenses and seared herself into his mind and soul.

Of course, there was always the possibility that he wouldn't get out of this alive, anyway, but he didn't dwell on that. He had thought a lot in the past few days, considering and discarding options. His plans were made. Now he was waiting: waiting for his wounds to heal more completely; waiting until he was physically ready; waiting for Ellis and his pals to make some little mistake; waiting until he sensed the time was right…waiting. When the time came he would call Sullivan, and the plan would be put into action. He would rather have Sullivan with him than any ten other men. No one would ever be expecting the two of them to be working together again.

No, his only uncertainty was because of Rachel. He knew what he had to do to protect her, but for the first time in his life he dreaded it. Letting her go was one thing; living without her was another.

He stood there in the night and cursed whatever it was that made him different from other men: the extraordinary skill and cunning, the acute eyesight and athletic body, the extreme coordination between mind and muscle that, all combined, made him a hunter and a warrior. When his emotional aloofness was added to that it had made him a natural for the job he held, the perfect, emotionless soldier in the cold gray shadows. He couldn't remember ever being any different. He hadn't been a noisy, laughing child; he'd been silent and solitary, holding himself aloof even from his parents. He'd always been alone deep inside himself and had never wanted it any other way; perhaps he'd known, even as a child, how much it would hurt to love.

There. He'd let the words form in his thoughts, and even that was so painful that he flinched. He was too intense ever to love casually, lightly, to play the game of romance over and over. His emotional distance had been a defense, but Rachel had shattered it, and it hurt. God, how it hurt.

RACHEL SAT ACROSS FROM Tod Ellis, smiling and chatting and forcing herself to eat her seafood as if she enjoyed it, but it chilled her every time he gave her that toothpaste-ad smile. She knew what that smile concealed. She knew that he had tried to kill Kell; he was a liar, a murderer and a traitor. It took all her strength to continue acting as if she were having a pleasant time, but nothing could keep her thoughts from slipping back to Kell.

She had wanted nothing more than to continue lying in his arms that afternoon, her body limp and throbbing from his rough, fast, but intensely satisfying possession. She had forgotten what it was like…or perhaps it had never been like that before. Being married to B.B. had been warm and fun and loving. Being Sabin's woman would be like burning alive every time he touched her, going soft, hot and moist at his glance, his lightest touch. He wasn't easygoing and cheerful. He was a hard, intense man, the force of his personality radiating from him. He wasn't playful; she'd never heard him laugh, or even seen his rare smiles reach his eyes. But he had reached for her with such desperate, driving need that everything in her had responded immediately, and she had been ready for him, wanting him.

No, Kell wasn't a comfortable man to be around, or an easy man to love, but she didn't waste time railing against fate. She loved him, and accepted him for what he was. She looked at Tod Ellis and her eyes narrowed a little, because Kell was a lion surrounded by jackals, and this man was one of the jackals.

She put down her fork and gave him a bright smile. "How much longer will you be around here, do you think? Or are you permanently assigned to this area?"

"No, I move around a lot," he said, responding to her direct attention by flashing his smile once again. "I never know when I'll be reassigned."

"Is this sort of a special assignment?"

"It's more of a wild-goose chase. We've been wasting our time. Still, if we hadn't been searching the beach I never would have met you."

He'd been throwing out lines like that since he'd picked her up, and Rachel had been determinedly skirting them. He evidently thought he was a modern day Don Juan, and probably a lot of women found him attractive and charming, but, then, they didn't know what Rachel did about him.

"Oh, I'm certain you aren't hurting for casual dates," she said in an offhand manner.

He reached across the table and put his hand on hers. "Maybe I don't consider this a casual date."

Rachel smiled and removed her hand to pick up her wineglass. "I don't see how you could consider it anything else, considering you may be reassigned at any time. Even if you aren't, I'll be leaving on vacation soon and probably won't be back for the rest of the summer."

He didn't like that; it put a small dent in his ego that she wasn't willing to hang around for as long as he was there. "Where are you going?"

"The Keys. I'm going to stay with a friend and do some research in the area. I was planning to stay there until I have to come back to teach a night course in Gainesville when the fall quarter starts."

Anyone else would have asked her about the course she was teaching; Ellis scowled at her and said, "Is your friend male or female?"

Just for a moment she entertained the appealing idea of telling him to take a long walk off a short pier, but it wasn't her plan to antagonize him, not yet. She still wanted to get some information out of him if she could. So instead she gave him a cool look that told him he'd gone too far and said calmly, "A woman, an old college friend."

He wasn't stupid. Arrogant and conceited, but not stupid. He grimaced in a way that was meant to be charming, but left her cold. "Sorry. I overstepped myself, didn't I? It's just that—well, from the moment I saw you, I was really attracted, and I want to get to know you better."

"There doesn't seem to be much point in it," Rachel pointed out. "You would be leaving soon, anyway, even if I hadn't planned my vacation."

He looked as if he'd like to refute that, but he'd told her himself that he moved around a lot. "We may be around for another couple of weeks," he said sulkily.

"Tying up loose ends?"

"Yeah, you know how it is. Paperwork."

"Is it just you and Agent Lowell?"

He hesitated, habit too deeply ingrained in him to make it easy for him to talk in any detail about his work. Rachel held her breath, wondering if his ego would prompt him to try to make up for the ground he had lost by being too personal. After all, it was inherently flattering when someone asked about your work. It was a way of getting better acquainted, of asking innocent questions that still denoted interest. She was interested, all right, but not in Ellis.

"There are nine of us actively investigating," he finally said. "We were all chosen especially for this job."

Because they were unscrupulous? She gave him a wide-eyed, ego-stroking look. "It must be really big to have that many men working on it."

"As I said, we're the active investigators. We can call on about twenty other men for backup if necessary."

She looked suitably impressed. "But you think it's a dead end?"

"We haven't turned up anything, but the top man isn't satisfied yet. You know how it is. People behind a desk think they know more than the men in the field."

She sympathized with him and even made up a few tales to reciprocate, edging the conversation away from his work. If she probed too directly and too often it could rouse his suspicions. Talking to him made her feel unclean and anxious to get away from him, as far away as she could. The knowledge that he would try to kiss her, probably even try to talk her into bed, filled her with sick horror. There was no way she could tolerate his mouth on hers even for a moment. Even if he wasn't a total snake, which he was, she couldn't have kissed him; she was Kell Sabin's woman, a fact that had nothing to do with will or determination. It simply *was*.

She forced herself to chat for another hour, smiling at the appropriate moments and forcing down the increasing urge to gag. He was almost more than she could tolerate. Only the thought that Kell could use any information she got out of Ellis gave her the will to stay. When their dishes had finally been cleared away and they were taking their time over coffee, she put out another feeler. "Where are you staying? This isn't a tourist area, and motel rooms can be hard to find."

"We're actually spread out down the coast," he explained. "Lowell and I are sharing a room at this dinky little motel, Harran's."

"I know where it is," she said, nodding.

"We've been living off fast food since we got here. It's a relief to get a decent meal for a change."

"I imagine so." She pushed her coffee cup back and looked around the restaurant, hoping he'd get the message that she was ready to go. The sketchy details she'd gotten would have to be enough; she simply couldn't sit there with him any longer and pretend that she liked him. She wanted to go home and lock the door behind her, closing Tod Ellis and his cohorts out of her life. Kell was there, waiting for her, and she wanted to be with him, even though she was uneasy about his mood. He had been coldly silent when she left, his rage barely controlled. He had wanted her to play it safe and let all the risk fall on him, but Rachel could quit breathing more easily than she could stand by without doing anything while he was in danger. He wasn't used to his commands being ignored, and he didn't like it one little bit.

For his own reasons Ellis wasn't loath to leave a little early. Rachel imagined that he thought the remainder of the evening would be spent in a more physical manner. He would be disappointed.

She didn't talk much on the way home, both reluctant to have any more to do with Ellis than necessary and because her thoughts were increasingly taken with Kell, though he'd never been far from her mind all evening. Her heartbeat suddenly lurched and her blood skittered through her veins, making her feel flushed and dizzy. The fierce lovemaking they'd shared that afternoon should have clarified their relationship, even if only on that basic level, but it hadn't. Kell had looked at her so oddly afterward, as if she wasn't what he'd expected. Despite his anger with her when she refused to do what he told her, on some deep level he had seemed even more self-contained than ever. He was a difficult, unusual man, but she was so acutely sensitive to him that every faint nuance of his expression, which most people wouldn't notice at all, seemed to shout at her. Why had he looked at her like that, then withdrawn? Why did she feel farther from him now than she had before they had lain locked together in writhing heat?

Ellis turned onto the private road that ended at her house and a few minutes later pulled the car to a stop in front. The house was dark, but she hadn't really expected it to be any other way. Kell wouldn't advertise his presence by turning on lights.

They got out of the car, and as Ellis came around to her side they heard that low snarl. Joe, bless him, didn't miss anything.

Ellis visibly jerked, the sudden alarm starkly etched on his face in the ghastly light from the car's open door. He stopped in his tracks. "Where is he?" he muttered.

Rachel looked around but couldn't see the dog. He was black and tan, with the classic markings of a German shepherd, so his darkness made it difficult to see him. The snarls placed him slightly to her left, close to Ellis, but she still couldn't make him out.

Quickly she seized the opportunity. "Look, you stand still while I walk into the yard. He's behind you, so don't move any closer to him. When I'm out of the way, get in the car on this side and he probably won't bother you."

"That dog's vicious. You should have him chained," Ellis snapped, but he didn't argue with her instructions. He stood absolutely still while Rachel walked up into the yard, then sidled toward the open door on the passenger side of the car.

"I'm sorry," she apologized, hoping he couldn't hear the insincerity in her voice. "I didn't think. Still, he's good protection. He's never yet let a stranger walk into the yard."

Joe moved then, the movement betraying his position. Snarling steadily, he planted himself between Rachel and Ellis.

She wanted to laugh. There was no chance of even a good-night kiss now, and from the look on Ellis's face he wanted nothing more than to be inside the car, with solid steel between him and the dog. Hastily he slid inside and slammed the door, then rolled the window down partway.

"I'll call you, okay?"

She made herself hesitate, rather than shouting out the "No!" she wanted to voice. "I'll be busy getting ready for my vacation. I have some work I have to finish before I leave. I really won't have much free time."

Now that he was safe from the dog his cockiness was returning. "You have to eat, don't you? I'll call you for lunch or something."

She planned on being busy, but she could handle him over the telephone. She didn't want him showing up here unannounced, but that wasn't likely as long as Joe was in residence.

She stood in the yard, watching the taillights as he drove off, then said, "Good boy," to Joe with obvious approval in her voice. Turning toward the house, she wondered why Kell didn't turn on a light for her now that Ellis was out of sight. She started to walk up to the porch but hadn't taken a full step, when a hard arm passed around her waist and jerked her backward.

"Have fun?" a low, angry voice whispered in her ear.

"Kell." She relaxed against him, pleasure flooding warmly through her at even this touch, despite his anger.

"Did he touch you? Kiss you?"

She had expected questioning, but not primarily about that. Kell's voice was rough, almost savage.

"You know he didn't," she replied steadily. "After all, you were out here watching."

"What about before?"

"No. Not at all. I couldn't stand the thought."

A great shudder passed through his body, an extraordinary response in a man as controlled as he normally was, but when he spoke his voice was level again. "Let's go inside."

He locked up while she went into the bedroom to put away her purse and slip out of her shoes; then he joined her in the bedroom. His black eyes were expressionless as he watched her slip the earrings out of her pierced lobes and put the jewelry away in a velvet-lined box. He'd been right; she slipped into stylish sophistication as easily as she puttered barefoot in the garden, and she was gut-wrenchingly sexy in either case.

His silent, unwavering stare was making her uneasy. "I did get some information," she finally offered, taking a nightgown from the dresser and darting a quick look at him. He looked…furious, somehow, though his face was rock hard and his eyes expressionless. His arms were folded across his bare chest; he wore only his jeans and running shoes, and he looked formidable.

He didn't ask, but she condensed it for him, anyway. "There are nine of them actively searching for you, but Ellis let it slip that they have a backup of about twenty more if needed. They're scattered, looking up and down the coast. Ellis and Lowell are staying at Harran's Motel. He thinks you're dead and that they're wasting his time, but the head man on the operation won't give up."

That would be the mysterious "Charles." Sabin had known who had to be behind things from the moment he had recognized the red-haired woman, Noelle, on the boat. He had known it would be only a matter of time until they locked horns again. Charles was the head of an international terrorist organization that had been growing bolder and more challenging, while at the same time Charles himself had kept at a safe distance, protected by a web of technicalities and politics. Now he had come out into the open, to get Sabin. But he'd made one big mistake: his first attempt hadn't succeeded, and now Sabin knew that his own organization had been infiltrated. Charles couldn't afford to stop the search until Sabin was found, dead or alive.

When Kell didn't ask any questions Rachel shrugged and went into the bathroom to take off her makeup and change into her nightgown. His silence was unnerving; he probably used it as a weapon, to shake people off-balance and put them on the defensive. Well, she wasn't one of his minions; she was a woman who loved him.

Five minutes later she left the bathroom, her clothing draped over her arm. Sabin was sitting on the side of the bed, taking off his shoes. He kept his eyes on her while she hung her things in the closet, not looking away even when he stood to unzip his jeans.

"The nightgown is a waste of time," he drawled. "You might as well pull it off and put it back in that drawer."

Startled, Rachel looked around at him. He was standing by the bed, his hands on the fly of his jeans, and he was watching her with the concentrated attention with which a cat watches a mouse. The air around her suddenly sizzled with tension, and her throat went dry, forcing her to swallow. Slowly he slid down the zipper on his jeans, the denim spreading open in a vee to reveal bronzed skin and the vertical line of downy hair that arrowed down his lower abdomen into the thicker growth of hair just visible in his opened pants. The thick bulge beneath the denim clearly demonstrated his intention.

Her body leaped into immediate response, her heart beating faster and her breath racing in and out of her lungs. It had been like that from the beginning, and she had no more control over it now than she'd had then. He wanted her; that was more than obvious. But he didn't *want* to want her, and the knowledge hurt.

She swallowed again, pushing the closet door shut and leaning against it. "It's silly," she said, trying for a wry tone but failing miserably. Her voice was taut and shaking. "After this afternoon you'd think I'd be more comfortable about going to bed with you, but I'm not. I don't know what…what we have, if anything. I thought it would be clearer, but it isn't. What do you want from me?" She made a brief, dismissive gesture. "Other than sex."

Silently Kell swore. He was so good at holding people away from him that now, when he desperately wanted Rachel as close as he could get her for what time they had left, she still thought he was pushing her away. They had so little time together that the thought of not grabbing for every moment with her was unbearable, and he didn't know how to make her see that. Perhaps it was better if she didn't see it; perhaps it would be easier for her if she never knew how tempted he was to forget all his rules and priorities. But he had to have her, had to stockpile memories against the empty days in the future when she wouldn't be there. Even now she wasn't playing games, wasn't trying to hide behind lies to protect her pride. She was so honest that she deserved at least a fraction of the same honesty from him, no matter how it hurt. But the pain wasn't only hers.

He looked at her and said, "Everything. That's what I want. But I can't have it."

She quivered, and tears welled in her eyes. "You know you can have anything you want. All you have to do is reach out and take it."

Slowly he walked up to her and put his hand on her shoulder, sliding his fingers under the strap of her night-gown and stroking his rough fingertips over her warm, satiny skin. "At the risk of your life?" he asked in a low voice. "No. I couldn't live with that."

"You make it sound like a concrete fact that anyone close to you is a target. Other agents—"

"Other agents aren't me," he interrupted quietly, his black eyes level on hers. "There are several renegade governments and terrorist groups that have a bounty on my head. Do you think I'd ask any woman to share that sort of life with me?"

She managed to smile through her tears. "Don't try to tell me you live like a monk. I know there have been women—"

"No one close. No one special. No one who could be used or threatened in an attempt to get at me. I've tried it, honey. I was married, years ago before it got as bad as it is now. She was wounded in an attempt on my life. Being a smart woman, she got the hell away from me as fast as she could."

Not so smart, Rachel thought. She knew that she never would have let that drive her away from him. Her throat was so tight that she was almost choking on her words as she stared up at him, the tears finally overflowing and rolling down her cheeks. "It would be worth it, to be with you," she whispered. "I'd take the chance."

"No," he said, shaking his head. "I won't let you. *I* won't take the chance, not with your life." With one thumb he rubbed away the tears tracking her face.

"Isn't that my decision to make?"

He moved both his hands up to cup her face, sliding his fingers into her thick straight hair and tilting her face closer to his. "Not when you don't have any real idea of the danger involved. You pulled a little stint as an investigative reporter, and you notice more than is good for you, but you're as innocent as a baby when it comes to knowing what my work is really like. There *are* agents who live fairly normal lives, but I'm not one of them. I'm one of a very small minority. My existence isn't even admitted publicly."

She had gone pale, her face very still. "I know more about the risks involved than you think."

"No. You know the movie versions, the cleaned up, romanticized, glamorized crap."

Rachel suddenly jerked her head away from his touch, her hands clenched into fists. "You think so?" she rasped, her voice rough with pain. "My husband was killed by a car bomb meant for me. There was nothing cleaned up, romanticized, or glamorous about that. He died in my place! Ask me what I know about someone else paying the price for a risk I chose to take!" Tears began falling again, and she dashed them away, glaring fiercely at him. "Damn you, Kell Sabin! Do you think I *want* to love you? But at least I'm willing to take the chance, rather than run away from it the way you do!"

CHAPTER TEN

SHE WAS CRYING, and it was like taking a punch in the gut to watch her. Rachel simply wasn't a weepy person, and she was trying hard not to cry, but the tears kept rolling down her face as she faced him, and she kept angrily dashing them away. Slowly Kell reached out and brushed her hair away from her damp face, then eased her into his arms and pressed her head against his uninjured shoulder. "Whatever happens, I can't risk you," he said in a low, tortured voice.

Hearing the finality in his voice, she knew that there was no convincing him otherwise. He would go, and when he did it would be forever. Desperately she clung to him, inhaling deeply to draw the scent of him into her body, her hands trying to memorize the way it felt to touch him. All she had was this.

He tilted her chin up and bent his head then slanted his mouth over hers, the pressure hard and hungry, even a little angry, because they had so little time when forever wouldn't suffice. She sighed and opened her mouth to his probing tongue, her fingers flexing on his muscular back, and as always there was that strong, immediate response to him that tightened her breasts and sent twinges of pleasure through her loins. He sensed it, cupping her bottom in his rough hands and lifting her into grinding contact with his own throbbing flesh while his mouth continued to take hers.

He wanted to wipe out the pain he'd seen in her eyes; he wanted to savor her, take his time with her, as he'd been unable to do that afternoon. Sabin couldn't remember ever before losing control like that, not even when he'd been a young boy on the prowl, driven by a rapacious sexuality. But with Rachel his responses were so extreme that he'd exploded only moments after entering her; she had reached her peak, too, but he knew that he'd rushed her, hurt her with his too-powerful penetration. She was so tight that accommodating him hadn't been easy for her. He wasn't going to let it be that way again; he was going to take his time with her, until she was truly ready for him and trembling on the brink.

She was trembling in his arms, the salty taste of her tears on his tongue. Silently he led her to the bed, leaving the light on because he wanted to see every nuance of her expression while he made love to her. He paused to push his jeans off, and Rachel watched him, her hands automatically lifting to her nightgown.

Quickly he stayed them. "No, leave your gown on for now." Perhaps it would be easier for him if he couldn't see her stretched out naked and waiting for him. He was caught in his own delicious dilemma, wanting to watch her as he made love to her, as he made her ready to receive him, yet knowing that the sight of her naked body would push him closer to the edge than he wanted to be right now. Just thinking about her was torture enough. His loins were heavy and throbbing, his all-too-accurate memory reminding him just how it had felt to be sheathed inside her.

"Why?" Rachel asked huskily when they were lying on the bed and he was leaning over her with an expression on his face that would have frightened her if she hadn't trusted him completely.

He smoothed his hand over her breasts, the motion

deliberately slow as the thin cotton slid across her nipples, bringing them to tingling prominence. "Why the gown?" he clarified.

It was hard to talk when her breath kept catching. "Yes."

"Because I'm inciting myself to riot."

No, it was she who was being incited, tantalized. Everywhere his lightly trailing fingers went they left behind a delicious tingle as her aroused nerve endings pleaded for more. Sometimes he merely brushed her with his fingertips, while at others he stroked her with the flat of his palm, the contact almost hard. And he kissed her: her mouth, her ears, the line of her jaw, the arch of her throat, the exquisitely tender hollow above her collarbones. Finally her breasts knew the warm, moist pressure of his mouth and the probing of his tongue. It was all the more maddening because he didn't remove her gown; even when his mouth closed hotly on her extended nipple and sucked at it with a strength that made her cry out, it was with the thin barrier of cotton between his mouth and her flesh. In frustration she tried to unbutton the two buttons that closed the top of the gown, to give him access to her bareness, but he stopped her and captured her hands, pinning them to the pillow above her head and anchoring them there with his strong right hand.

"Kell!" she protested, writhing to escape, but he was incredibly strong, despite his half-healed wounds, and she couldn't wrest herself free. "You've got a cruel streak in you!"

"No," he murmured against her breast, licking her nipple through the wet fabric. "I only want to make you feel good. Don't you like this?"

There was no way she could deny it; he could easily

read the signs of arousal in her body. "Yes," she admitted, panting. "But I want to touch you, too. Let me—"

"Umm, not yet. You make me feel too much like a teenager, ready to go off like a Fourth of July rocket. I'm going to make it good for you this time."

"It was good before," she said, and moaned as his left hand trailed down to the juncture of her thighs, rubbing delicately. Rachel's breath caught, and her hips lifted blindly to his hand.

"I was too rough, too fast. I hurt you."

She couldn't deny it, but the discomfort hadn't been unexpected, and pleasure had swiftly followed. She started to tell him that, but the words were strangled in her throat. The gown had been pushed between her legs by his exploring hand, stretched tightly across her femininity. With one finger he probed the soft cleft, found and stroked her most sensitive flesh. Rachel's body jolted with pleasure, and a low whimper came from her throat.

His touch was firm but tender, with just the right amount of pressure. Slowly her head rolled back and forth on the pillow between the frame of her arms, and her back arched. If he had tantalized her before, this was torture, the sweetest torture imaginable. Hot coils wound inside her, heat spreading throughout her body until she was flushed and damp. Her breasts were so tight that they ached. Kell knew exactly when she couldn't stand it any longer and bent to suck strongly at her nubbed flesh, wringing another soft, wild sound from her throat.

Then his hand was on her bare thigh, under the nightgown, and the relief of feeling skin on skin was so intense that she jerked again.

"Easy," he breathed, and she held herself as still as she could while his warm, hard hand slowly moved upward, stroking her thigh. Her legs were parted already, in aching need, and she strained toward him.

His palm barely brushed her, then moved to her other thigh and stroked until she thought she would go mad. "You just wait!" she both threatened and promised, hissing the words through her tightly clenched teeth.

He laughed aloud, a low, rough sound of masculine triumph. Dimly she realized that it was the first time she'd heard him laugh. "I'm looking forward to it," he said, his voice strained. He was hot and damp, too, his eyes glittering with barely controlled passion, his face taut, with hectic color on his cheekbones and his lips. "Are you ready, love? Let me see." He touched her, and then the light, teasing touches ceased completely. He parted her soft flesh and slid two long fingers into her. Rachel gave a thin, high cry, her hips heaving as she trembled on the verge of ecstasy.

"Not yet," he breathed. "Not yet. Hold on, honey. I'm not going to let you go just yet. Not until I'm inside you."

His low, rough words washed over her shaking, twisting body. Crying a little, tormented by those long, probing fingers as he brought her to moist readiness, she tried again to free her hands, and this time he let them go.

"Now," he crooned, pulling the nightgown up. Rachel lifted herself up to aid in the removal of the frustrating garment, pulling it over her head herself and throwing it across the room. Kell's face tightened even more as he stared down at her naked body, at her flushed, glowing skin. Briefly his eyes closed, and he ground his teeth together as a heavy surge in his loins threatened his self-control.

Carefully he rolled to his back, favoring his shoulder, and guided her astride him. "Slow and easy," he muttered, his eyes glittering like black fire as he positioned himself for her. "Let's go easy, a little at a time."

"I love you," Rachel whispered achingly, closing her eyes

at the probing of his flesh against her. She braced her hands on his chest, her fingers flexing in the mat of curly hair, and slid onto him. He made a guttural sound and arched beneath her, his hands clenching on the sheet. "I love you," she said again, and another low animal sound came from him as his control shattered and he grabbed for her hips, grinding her in a rotating motion against him.

"Rachel," he groaned, shaking. His body was taut and straining beneath her.

She moved on him, rising, sliding, falling. Now it was her turn, and she did a primeval dance of passion, slowing whenever it seemed that her motions would take either of them past the point of no return. She was no longer so painfully empty; she was filled with him, an intense satisfaction in itself. Time became elastic, expanded, then disappeared altogether. She forgot everything but Kell, and she gave herself to him in a way she'd never known would be possible. He had become irrevocably hers when she pulled him from the surf, and she was irrevocably his, perhaps by the same power. For as long as she lived, she would be his.

She was crying again, but this time she was oblivious to the tears raining down her face. "I love you," she choked, then abruptly she crested, surging against him while her soft inner quivering made the world explode, then fade away and there were only the two of them, straining together, until he cried out hoarsely and heaved beneath her. Later, as she slept in his arms, he lay awake staring into the night, and though his face was as blank as usual, there was a look of desperation in his eyes.

"LET'S DRIVE INTO TOWN," he said the next morning after breakfast.

She drew a deep breath, her hands stilling for a moment

before she resumed washing the last plate. She handed it to him to dry, feeling the dread rising in her chest to choke her. "Why?"

"I need to make a phone call. I'm not going to do it from here."

Her throat was so tight she could scarcely speak. "You're going to call the man you think you can trust?"

"I *know* I can trust him," Kell replied briefly. "I'm staking my life on it." Even more than that, he was staking Rachel's life. Yes, he trusted Sullivan completely.

"I thought you were going to wait until you had recuperated." When she turned to look at him, her eyes were shadowed with a stark pain that twisted the knife inside him once more.

"I was, until Ellis came around again. It'll take Sullivan a few days to check out some things for me and get things organized. I don't want to push it any longer than that."

"Sullivan? That's the man?"

"Yes."

"But you just got your stitches out yesterday," she protested urgently, lacing her fingers together to keep from wringing her hands. "You're still weak, and you can't—" She bit her lip, halting her own desperate flow of words. Arguing wouldn't change his mind. And how could she tell him he was too weak, when he had made love to her twice during the night and woken her that morning when he slid into her again? She was both stiff and sore, and every step she took reminded her of his strength and endurance. He wasn't at his own personal peak of strength, but even so, he was probably stronger than most men.

She closed her eyes, hating her own weakness for trying to hold on to him when she'd known from the first that she couldn't. "I'm sorry," she said quietly. "Of course you can. We'll go now, if you want."

Kell watched her silently; if there was any one moment that revealed the strength of the woman, it was now, and it only made the leaving harder. He didn't want to call Sullivan; he didn't want to hurry the day when this would have to end. He wanted to stretch time to its utmost limits, to spend the hot, lazy days lying on the beach with her, getting to know every minute facet of her personality and making love to her whenever they wanted. And the nights... those long, warm, fragrant nights, spent tangled together on the damp, twisted sheets. Yes, that was what he wanted. Only the sure knowledge that she was in increasing danger could force him to make that call to Sullivan. His instinct told him that time was running out.

He was silent so long that Rachel opened her eyes and found him looking at her with that intent way of his. "What I want," he said deliberately, "is to make love again."

That was all it took, just that look of his and the words, and she felt herself growing warm and moist as her body automatically tightened, but she knew that she wouldn't be able to comfortably accept him. She looked at him with poignant regret. "I don't think I can."

He touched her cheek, his hard, rough fingers stroking the contours of her face with incredible tenderness. "I'm sorry. I should have realized."

She gave him a smile that wasn't as steady as she wished. "Let me change clothes and brush my hair, and we'll leave."

Because she wasn't the type to linger in front of a mirror, they were on their way in five minutes. Sabin was alert, his dark eyes noting every detail of the countryside and examining every car they met. Rachel found herself watching the rearview mirror in case they were being followed.

"I need a phone booth off the main drag. I don't want to be seen by six hundred people on their way to buy groceries." The words were terse, his attention on the traffic.

Obediently she searched out a phone booth next to a service station on the edge of town and parked the car next to it. Kell opened the door, then shut it again without getting out. He turned to her with a smile of real amusement on his lips. "I don't have any money."

His smile relieved the tension inside her, and she chuckled as she reached for her purse. "You could use my credit card number."

"No. If anyone checked it could lead them to Sullivan."

He took the handful of change she gave him and went into the phone booth, closing the door behind him. Rachel watched as he fed coins into the slot, then looked around to see if anyone else was watching him, but the only other person in sight was the man at the service station, and he was sitting in a chair in the front office, leaning back against the wall with the front legs of the chair off the ground while he read a newspaper.

Kell was back in only a few minutes, and Rachel started the car as he slid onto the seat and slammed the door. "That didn't take long," she said.

"Sullivan doesn't waste words."

"He'll come?"

"Yeah." Suddenly he smiled again, that rare, true smile. "His biggest problem is getting out of the house without his wife following him."

The humor, on that particular subject, was unexpected. "She doesn't understand about his job?"

He snorted. "It isn't his job—he's a farmer. And it'll make Jane madder than hell that he didn't take her with him."

"Farmer!"

"He retired from the agency a couple of years ago."

"Was his wife an agent, too?"

"No, thank God," he said with real feeling.

"Don't you like her?"

"It's impossible not to like her. I'm just glad Sullivan has her under control on that farm."

Rachel gave him a dubious glance. "Is he any good? How old is he, anyway?"

"He's about my age. He retired himself. The government would have been glad to keep him another twenty years, but he got out."

"And he's good?"

Kell's dark eyebrows lifted. "He's the best agent I ever had. We trained together in Nam."

That reassured her; even more than her dread at his leaving, she feared the danger he would have to face. Not a hint of it would ever surface in any newspaper, but there would be a small war in the nation's capital. Kell wouldn't rest until his section was clean again, even at the cost of his own life. The knowledge ate at her. If she could, if he would let her, she would go with him and do whatever she could to protect him.

"Stop at a drugstore," he instructed, swiveling in his seat to check behind them.

"What do you want at a drugstore?" She looked at him again and found him watching her with faint amusement.

"Birth control. Or haven't you realized what a chance we've been taking?"

"Yes, I'd realized," she admitted in a low voice.

"You weren't going to say anything or do anything about it?"

Her hands tightened on the steering wheel until the knuckles were white, and she concentrated on the traffic. "No."

Just that one, calmly uttered word had the power to jerk

his head up, and she felt his gaze burning on her. "I don't want to get you pregnant. I can't stay, Rachel. You'd be alone, with a baby to raise."

She braked for a red light and turned her head to meet his gaze. "It would be worth it, to have your baby."

His jaw tightened, and he swore under his breath. Damn, he was hard again just at the thought of getting her pregnant, of her bearing his child and nursing it at her pretty breasts. He wanted to. He wanted to take her with him and go home to her every night, but he couldn't turn his back on his job and his country. Security was critical, now more than ever, and his services were invaluable. It was something he had to do; endangering Rachel was something he couldn't do.

Her gray eyes were dark with mingled love and pain. "I won't make it easy for you to leave me," she whispered. "I won't hide what I feel and wave you off with a smile."

His profile was hard and unreadable as he turned back to watch the road; he didn't answer, and when the light changed to green again she drove carefully to the nearest drugstore. Without speaking, she took a twenty from her purse and handed it to him.

His hand clenched on the crisp bill, and he looked like murder. "It's either this or abstinence."

She drew a deep breath. "Then I suppose you'd better go in, hadn't you?"

No, she wasn't making it any easier; she was making it so difficult that it was tearing him apart. Damn it, he'd give her a baby every year if things were different, he thought savagely as he went into the drugstore and made his purchase. Maybe he was too late; maybe she was already pregnant. Only the naive or the careless could discount the possibility.

He left the cash register and had started for the door,

when Rachel came through it, her face strained, her eyes wide and urgent. Without hesitation he turned and walked several aisles over to intently examine a high stack of insulated beverage coolers. Rachel walked past, to the cosmetic department. Sabin waited, and a moment later the door opened again. He caught a glimpse of sandy hair and ducked his own head down, automatically reaching behind his back for the pistol, but his waistband was empty. The pistol was in the car. His eyes narrowed, and a cold, deadly look settled over his features; moving silently, he began trailing Ellis.

Rachel had seen the blue Ford driving down the street and had known immediately that it was Ellis; her only thought had been to warn Kell before he walked out of the drugstore and let Ellis see him. If Ellis had been following them it was already too late, but she was fairly certain that wasn't the case. This was just an unhappy coincidence; it had to be. She had pretended not to see him, getting out of the car and walking into the drugstore as if she'd just driven up herself. She had heard a car door close behind her just as she went inside, and she knew Ellis would be there in a few seconds. Kell had taken one look at her face and detoured; now all she had to do was get rid of Ellis, even if she had to get back in the car and drive away without Kell. She could circle back to pick him up.

"I thought it was you. Didn't you hear me call?" Ellis asked behind her as she surveyed the array of lipsticks.

She jerked around, pretending that he'd startled her. "Tod! You scared me!" she gasped, holding a hand to her chest.

"Sorry. I thought you knew I was behind you."

He seemed to be thinking a lot this morning; she hoped it didn't strain him too much. She gave him an abstracted smile. "I've got so much on my mind I'm just walking around in a daze. I'm trying to get everything together for my trip, but I left my shopping list at home, and it's driving me crazy trying to remember everything."

He looked at the display, his easy grin flashing. "I guess lipstick is essential."

"No, but lip balm is, and I thought it would be here." Condescending mongrel! She wondered how he'd look if she told him to shove off. The problem with someone with an enormous ego was that any slight sent them around the bend, hell-bent on revenge. Still, she couldn't keep the tartness out of her voice, and he looked at her in surprise.

"Is something wrong?"

"I've got a vicious headache," she muttered. She caught sight of Kell, moving just behind Ellis; his face was set, his eyes narrowed and cold, and he moved like a stalking panther. What was he doing? He was supposed to stay out of sight until she got rid of Ellis, not attack the man! All the color drained from her face as Ellis peered at her.

"You do look sick," he finally admitted.

"I think it was too much wine last night." She turned on her heel and marched down the aisle, away from Kell. Damn the man! If he wanted to jump Ellis, he'd have to chase him down to do it! She didn't stop until she got to the insect repellent section; she grabbed a bottle and scowled as she read the directions on the back.

Ellis was still right behind her. "Do you think you'd feel like going out tonight?"

Rachel ground her teeth in frustration. She couldn't believe he was that thick-skinned. It was an effort to take a deep breath and answer calmly. "I don't think so, Tod, but thanks for asking. I really feel rotten."

"Sure, I understand. I'll call you in a day or so."

From somewhere she dredged up enough control for a

wan smile. "Yes, do that. Maybe I'll feel better then, unless this is some sort of virus."

Like most people, he backed off a little at the mention of anything contagious. "I'll let you get back to your shopping, but you really should go home and take it easy."

"That's good advice. I just might do that." *Would he never leave?*

But still he lingered, chatting, being so obviously charming that she wanted to gag. Then she saw Kell again, silently working his way around behind Ellis, his eyes never wavering from his prey. Desperately she grabbed her stomach and said clearly, "I think I may throw up."

It was really amazing how fast Ellis retreated, looking at her warily. "You'd better go home," he said. "I'll call you later." The last words were said as he went out the door. She waited until he got in the Ford and drove off before she turned to look at Kell as he walked up to her.

"Stay in here," she said curtly. "I'll drive around the block to make certain he's gone."

She walked off before he could say anything. She was seething, and driving around the block would give her time to cool down. It made her furious that he would take that sort of risk right now, when he wasn't a hundred percent physically fit. When she was in the car she leaned her head on the steering wheel for a moment, shaking. What if Ellis had seen Kell go into the drugstore and had just been playing it cool, making sure it was Kell so he could report back to his superiors? She didn't think so, unless Ellis was much more cunning than she'd given him credit for, but even the possibility was horrifying.

Shaking, she started the car and circled the block, looking up and down all the streets for a blue Ford parked anywhere. She didn't just have to look for Ellis; she had to look for Lowell, too, and she had no idea what he might be driving. And how many other men were in this area now?

Returning to the drugstore, she pulled up close to the door and Kell came out, sliding into the car beside her. "See anyone?"

"No, but I don't know what kind of cars the others might have." She pulled into traffic, heading in the opposite direction from the one Ellis had taken. That wasn't where she wanted to go, but she could always cut back.

"He didn't see me," Kell said quietly, hoping to ease some of the tension evident in her face.

"How do you know? He could have decided to report you and wait for backup, catch you out later rather than trying something in the middle of a crowded drugstore."

"Relax, honey. He's not that smart. He'd try to take me himself."

"If he's so stupid, why did you hire him?" Rachel shot back.

He looked thoughtful. "I didn't. Someone else 'acquired' him."

Rachel glanced at him. "One of the two men who knew where you were?"

"That's right," he said grimly.

"That narrows it down for you, doesn't it?"

"I wish it did, but I can't afford to take that for granted. Until I know for certain, both of them are suspects."

It made sense; if he had to err, it would be on the side of caution. He couldn't afford even one mistake.

"Why were you trailing him like that? Why didn't you just stay out of sight until I'd gotten rid of him?" she demanded, her knuckles showing white again.

"If he had seen me, it could have been his plan to grab you for bait, to draw me out. I wasn't going to let that happen." The quiet, calm way he said it made Rachel shiver, as if the air had suddenly turned cold.

"But you aren't up to something like that yet! Your leg could give out on you, and your shoulder is so stiff you can barely move it. What if you'd torn everything open again?"

"It didn't happen. Anyway, I didn't anticipate a fight, just one good crack at him."

His male arrogance made her want to scream; instead she ground her teeth together. "It didn't occur to you that something could have gone wrong?"

"Sure, but if he'd grabbed you, I wouldn't have had any choice, so I wanted to be in position."

And he was willing to do whatever was necessary, despite his stiff shoulder and lame leg. He was one of a rare breed, able to see the cost and still be willing to pay it, though he would do everything he could to tip the scales the other way.

She was still pale, her eyes shadowed, and he reached over to slide his hand down her thigh. "It's all right," he said gently. "Nothing happened."

"But it could have. Your shoulder—"

"Forget my damned shoulder, and my leg. I know how far I can push them, and I don't go into anything unless I think I can win."

She was silent for the remainder of the drive, until she parked the car under the tree. "I think I'll go for a swim," she said tightly. "Want to come along?"

"Yes."

Joe came up to her car door as always, his dark eyes trained on her even though he remained just out of touching distance, and he walked beside her as she went up the steps to the porch. He accepted Kell, but if the two of them were outside he was never far from Rachel. He was one warrior who was content to stay, she thought wistfully, then resolutely pushed away the creeping self-pity. Life would go on, even if it was without Kell. It hurt to think about it, and she didn't want to, but she knew that she would survive somehow, though her life had been irrevocably changed by the time she had spent with him, quiet days punctuated by moments of sheer terror.

She changed into her sleek black bathing suit and Kell put on his denim shorts, and after grabbing a couple of towels, they walked through the pines down to the beach. Joe followed them and lay down in the scant shade of a clump of sea oats. Rachel dropped the towels on the sand and pointed out to the bay, where the water was rising and breaking over the submerged rocks. "See the line where the water breaks? That's where the rocks are. I'm pretty sure you hit your head on one of them that night. The tide was just starting to come in, so the water was low." She pointed again. "I dragged you out here."

Kell looked at the beach, then turned and stared up the slope, where the pines were standing tall and straight, a thicket of wooden sentinels. She had somehow dragged him up that slope and gotten him into the house, a feat that he couldn't imagine when he looked at her slender body. "You damn near killed yourself getting me up there, didn't you?" he asked quietly.

She didn't want to think about that night, or what it had cost her physically. Part of it had already been blocked from her brain; she remembered that she'd been in pain, but the exact nature of the pain escaped her. Perhaps adrenaline was responsible for both her strength that night and the selective amnesia that followed. She looked at him for a long moment, then turned and walked into the sea. He watched until the water reached her knees, then pulled the pistol out of his waistband and carefully laid it on a towel, covering it with the other to keep the blowing sand out of it. Then he dropped his shorts and walked naked into the water after her.

Rachel was a strong swimmer, having spent most of her life living on the Gulf, but Kell stayed even with her despite his stiff shoulder. At first, when she realized he was in the water, she had started to protest that he shouldn't get his wounds wet, but she swallowed the words. After all, he had swum with open wounds, and the exercise would be good therapy. They swam in the bay for half an hour before he decided that he'd had enough, and Rachel returned to the beach with him. It wasn't until the water reached his waist that she realized he was nude, and the familiar quiver shook her insides as she watched him wade out of the water. He was so lean and hard and perfect, darkly tanned and roped with muscle, even his tight buttocks. She watched as he moved the pistol and lay down on one of the towels, his glistening body offered to the sun.

She left the water, too, bending over to wring out her hair. When she straightened again she found him watching her. "Take off the bathing suit," he said softly.

She looked out to sea, but there were no boats in sight. Then she looked at him again, lying there like a bronzed, naked statue, except that she'd never seen a statue in a state of arousal. Slowly she reached up for the straps on her shoulders and drew them down, and immediately she felt the heat of the hot sun kissing her wet breasts. A slight breeze suddenly kicked up, whispering across her nipples and making them pucker. Sabin's breath caught in his chest, and he held his hand out to her. "Come here."

She pushed the bathing suit down and off, then walked to the towels. He sat up and reached for her, drawing her down beside him and stretching her out. Amusement was twinkling in his dark eyes as he looked down at her. "Guess what I forgot to bring."

She began to laugh, the sound pure and deep in this world where only the two of them existed.

"Ah, well, you're too sore for that, anyway," he murmured, sliding his hand over her breasts and bringing her nipples to tingling awareness. "I'll just have to... improvise."

He leaned over her, his shoulders so broad that they blocked out the sun, and his mouth burned on hers, then down on her body.

He was very good with improvisations. He lingered over her as if she were a willing, sun-kissed sacrifice offered up for his delectation, until her body finally arched to his rapacious mouth and she cried out in intolerable pleasure, her cry rising to the white inferno of the sun.

CHAPTER ELEVEN

RACHEL DIDN'T LET HERSELF think about time, though she knew they had only a few more days at the most, however long it took this Sullivan to make his arrangements and travel down to meet Kell. She lived completely in the present, reveling in his company whatever they were doing. He began helping her gather the vegetables from the garden and he worked some with Joe, gaining more of the dog's trust and showing Rachel how highly trained Joe was. After the first swim they also spent a lot of time down at the bay; they swam every morning and again in the afternoon, after the worst of the heat was over. It was marvelous therapy, and every day he got stronger, his shoulder more flexible and his limp improving. He also did other exercises, continually working to bring his body back up to par, and she could only watch in amazement. She was athletic and strong herself, but her endurance was nothing compared to his. He was often in pain; she sensed it, even though he never said anything, but he ignored it as if it weren't there. Ten days after she'd found him he was gingerly jogging around the house, his thigh tightly wrapped to brace the injured muscle. After a moment of anger Rachel joined him and jogged along beside him, ready to catch him if his leg gave out and he fell. It wouldn't have done any good to yell at him, because it was important for him to be able to meet whatever demands might be placed on him when he left.

And whatever they did, they talked. He was reticent

bout himself, both naturally and as a result of his training, but he did have a lot of fascinating inside details about
the political and economic considerations of governments
round the world. He probably also knew more than anyone
would want him to know about military forces and capabilities, but he didn't talk about those. Rachel learned as
much about him from his omissions as she did from the
subjects he would talk about.

No matter what they did, whether weeding the garden,
jogging around the house, cooking a meal or arguing politics, desire ran between them like an invisible current, link-
ing them together in a state of heightened awareness. Her
senses were filled with him; she knew his taste, his smell,
his touch, every nuance of his deep voice. Because he was
normally so expressionless she watched him closely for
each small movement of his brows or twitch of his lips.
Even though he was relaxed with her and smiled more
often, sometimes teasing her, his laughter was rare, and
therefore doubly treasured, the occasions pressed into her
memory. Their desire couldn't be quenched by lovemaking,
because it was more than a physical need. She immersed
herself in him, knowing that she had only the present.

Still, physical desire couldn't be denied. Rachel had
never been so thoroughly enjoyed before, even in the early
days of marriage. Kell had a strong sexual appetite, and
the more he made love to her, the more they both wanted it
again. He was exquisitely careful with her until she became
more accustomed to him, his lovemaking both sophisticated
and earthy. There were times when they lingered, savoring
each sensation like sexual gourmets until the tension was
so strong that they exploded together. There were also the
times when their loving was fast and hard, when there
was no foreplay because their need to be together was too
urgent.

The third day after he'd called Sullivan, Kell made love to her with barely controlled violence, and she knew that he was thinking this might be the last day they had together. She clung to him, her arms tight around his neck when he lay on her in heavy, damp exhaustion. A lump lodged in her throat, and she squeezed her eyes tightly shut in an effort to deny the march of time. She couldn't bear to let him go.

"Take me with you," she said thickly, unable to let it lie, to simply let him walk away from her. Rachel was too much of a fighter to let him go without trying to change his mind.

He stiffened, then withdrew from her to lie on his back beside her, his forearm thrown up to cover his eyes. The ceiling fan whirred overhead, wafting a cool breeze across their overheated skin and making her feel a little chilled without the heat of his body pressed over her. She opened her eyes to stare at him, her gaze burning with desperation.

"No," he finally said, and left it at that, the single word filled with a finality that almost broke her heart.

"Something could be worked out," she pressed. "At worst we could see each other occasionally. I'm mobile. I can work anywhere—"

"Rachel," he interrupted tiredly. "No. Leave it." He took his forearm down from his eyes and looked at her. Though his expression changed very little, she could tell that he was annoyed by her persistence.

She was too desperate to stop. "How can I leave it? I love you! This isn't a game I'm playing, that I can just pick up my marbles and go home when I get tired of it!"

"Damn it, I'm not playing games, either!" he roared, bolting upright in the bed and seizing her arm to shake her, finally goaded past his limits. His eyes were hot and arrowed, his teeth clenched. "You could be killed because of me! Didn't it teach you anything when your husband died?"

She went pale, staring at him. "I could be killed driving into town," she finally said shakily. "Would that make me any less dead? Would you grieve any less?" Suddenly she stopped, wrenching her arm free and rubbing it where his fingers had bitten into her flesh. She was so white that her eyes burned darkly in her colorless face. Finally she said with an attempt at lightness, "Or would you grieve at all? I'm being rather presumptuous, aren't I? Maybe I'm the only one involved here. If so, just forget everything I've said."

Silence stretched between them as they faced each other on the bed; her face was strained, his grim. He wasn't going to say anything. Rachel inhaled sharply at the pain squeezing her insides. Well, she'd asked for it. She'd pushed him, fighting to change his mind, to get a commitment from him, and she had lost…everything. She had thought that he cared for her, loved her, even though he'd never said anything about love. She had put it down to his natural reticence. Now she had to face the unpleasant truth that it was his brutal honesty that had kept him from saying he loved her. He wouldn't spout pretty words that he didn't mean just to soothe her feelings. He liked her. She was a reasonably attractive woman, and she was convenient; he was highly sexed. The reason for his attentions was obvious, and she'd made a complete fool of herself.

The worst of it was that even facing the hard, unpalatable reality didn't stop her from loving him. That was another reality, and she couldn't wish it away.

"Sorry," she mumbled, scrambling off the bed and reaching for her clothes, suddenly embarrassed by her nudity. It was different now.

Sabin watched her, every muscle coiled tightly. Th
look on her face ate at him, the abrupt embarrassmer
the sudden extinguishing of the light in her eyes as s
fumbled with her clothing in an attempt to cover herse
He could let her go. She might get over him more easily
she thought he had just used her sexually, without retur
ing any of her emotion. Emotion made Sabin uneasy; h
wasn't accustomed to it. But damned if he could stand th
look on her face! Maybe he couldn't give her much, but h
couldn't leave with her thinking she'd been nothing mo
than a sexual convenience.

Rachel was out of the room before he could catch he
and then he heard the screen door slam. Going to the doc
he saw her disappearing into the pines with Joe right besic
her, as usual. He cursed steadily as he jerked on his pan
and started after her. She wasn't going to be inclined t
listen to him now, but listen she would even if he had t
hold her down.

When Rachel reached the beach she kept walking, wor
dering how she was going to find the courage to go back t
the house and act as if everything were normal, as if sh
weren't a shriveled knot of pain inside. Still, it was prob
ably only for one more day; she could manage that. Sh
could endure it for twenty-four hours. Part of her was gla
that it could be measured in hours; then she could forge
about a stiff upper lip and cry until the tears were all gone
But the rest of her screamed silently at the thought of no
seeing him again, no matter what he felt—or didn't feel—
for her.

A pastel pink shell was half-hidden by a clump of sea
weed, and she paused to push the seaweed aside with he
foot, hoping to find something beautiful to lighten he
heart. But the shell was broken, most of it gone, and she
kept walking. Joe left her side, trotting up the beach to d

is own exploring; he had been changed by Kell's arrival,
oo, for the first time allowing a man to touch him and
earning to accept someone other than Rachel. She watched
he dog, wondering if he would miss Kell, too.

A warm hand closed on her shoulder, bringing her to a
alt. Even without looking around she knew it was Kell;
he knew his touch, the rasp of his roughened fingertips.
he felt him at her back, tall and warm, so intense that her
kin tingled whenever he was near. All she had to do was
urn around and her head would fit right into the hollow
f his shoulder, her body would fit into his arms, but he
vouldn't allow her to fit into his life. She didn't want to
reat him to tears and hysterics, and she was very much
fraid she would if she turned around, so she kept her back
o him.

"This isn't easy for me, either," he said roughly.

"I'm sorry," she broke in, wanting to make a quick end
o it. "I didn't mean to start a scene, or put you on the spot.
ust forget it, if you can."

His hand tightened on her shoulder, and he turned her
round, sliding his other hand into her hair and tilting
er face up so he could see her eyes. "Don't you see that
 couldn't work between us? I can't leave my job. What I
o...it's hard and it's ugly, but it's necessary."

"I haven't asked you to give up your job," she said, her
ace proud.

"It's not the damn job I'm worried about!" he shouted,
is dark face furious. "It's you! God, it would tear my guts
ut if anything happened to you! I love you." He paused,
ook a deep breath, and continued more quietly. "I've never
aid that to anyone before, and I shouldn't be saying it now,
ecause there's no use in it."

The wind whipped her hair around her face as she
ared up at him, her gray eyes fathomless. Slowly his fist

loosened in her hair and he moved his hand down to he
neck, rubbing his thumb over the fluttering pulse at th
base of her throat. Rachel swallowed. "We could try it fo
a little while," she whispered, but he shook his head.

"I want to know that you're safe. I *have* to know that,
I can't function the way I should. I can't make a mistak
because if I did it could mean that people died, good me
and women. And if you were kidnapped—" He stopped, h
face almost savage. "I'd sell my soul to keep you safe."

Rachel felt herself shattering on the inside. "No, it car
be like that. No negotiation—"

"*I love you,*" he said harshly. "I've never loved anyor
before in my life, not my parents, any of my relatives,
even my wife. I've always been alone, different from e
eryone else. The only friend I've ever had is Sullivan, ar
he's as much of a lobo as I am. Do you really think I cou
sacrifice you? Sweet hell, woman, you're my one chance
a lifetime—" He broke off, a muscle in his jaw twitchir
as he stared at her. "And I don't dare take it," he finishe
quietly.

She understood, and she wished she didn't. Because I
loved her, he didn't trust himself not to betray his countr
if she were kidnapped and used as a weapon against hir
He wasn't like people who had loved before and would lo
again; he was too remote, too chillingly alone. For whatev
reason, whatever particular chemistry and circumstance, I
loved her, and it was the only time in his life he would ev
love a woman. Living with him would make her vulnerab
to attack; merely loving her would make him vulnerab
because for a man such as he, love was something bo
wonderful and terrible.

He took her hand, and they walked silently back to th
house. It was time for lunch; Rachel went into the kitche
with the intention of trying to busy herself cooking so sl

wouldn't be able to think. Kell leaned against the cabinets and watched her, his black eyes burning her flesh. Suddenly he reached out and caught her hand, removing the pot from her grasp and setting it back on the countertop. "Now," he said gutturally, pulling her toward the bedroom.

He stripped down her shorts but didn't take the time to remove her shirt; nor did he take the time to shed his pants, merely opening them and shoving them down. They didn't make it to the bed. He took her on the floor, so desperate to be inside her, to sheathe himself in her and eliminate all distance between them, that he couldn't wait. Rachel clung to him as he pounded into her, every inch of her flesh, every cell, branded by his possession. And even then they both knew it wouldn't be enough.

Late that afternoon she walked out to the garden to gather a few fresh peppers to add to the spaghetti sauce she was cooking. Kell was taking a shower, and Joe, oddly, was nowhere in sight. She started to call him, but decided that he must be asleep under the oleander bush, taking refuge from the heat. The temperature had to be pushing a hundred, and the humidity was high, prime conditions for a thunderstorm. With her hand full of peppers she crossed the small backyard to the house. Later she could never decide where he came from; there had been no one in sight, and no place for him to hide. But as she went up the back steps he was suddenly there behind her, his hand clamping over her mouth and jerking her head back. His other arm went around her in almost exactly the same movement Kell had used when he had jumped her from behind, but instead of a knife this man carried a gun clutched in his fist; it glinted in the sun with a dull blue sheen.

"Don't make a sound and I won't hurt you," the man murmured in her ear, his voice easy on consonants and pure liquid on the vowels. "I'm looking for a man. He's supposed to be in this house."

She clawed at his hand, trying to scream a warning even though Kell might still be in the shower and wouldn't be able to hear her. But what if Kell did hear her? He could be shot trying to help her. The thought paralyzed her, and she sagged against the man, struggling to organize her mind and think of something she could do. "Shhh, that's right," the man said in that low, soft voice that made chills run over her body. "Open the door now, and we'll go in nice and easy."

She didn't have any choice but to open the screen door. If he had wanted to kill her he already would have, but he could still easily knock her unconscious, and the end result would be the same: she would be unable to help Kell if the opportunity arose. The man pushed her up the back steps with his big body, holding her so securely against him that she couldn't struggle. She stared at the gun in his hand. If he tried to shoot Kell, she could hit his arm, throw off his aim. Where was Kell? She tried to listen for the shower, but her thundering heartbeat made a roaring in her ears that blotted out sound. Was he dressing? Had he heard the back door close? Even if he had, would he think anything of it? They relied on Joe to let them know if anyone was close by. Hard on the heels of that thought came another one, and pain welled in her again. Had he killed Joe? Was that why the dog hadn't come around the house when she went out to the garden?

Then Kell walked out of the bedroom, wearing only his jeans and carrying his shirt in his hand. He stopped, his face very still as he looked first at the man holding her, then at her terrified eyes above the hand clamped over her mouth. "You're scaring her to death," he said in a cool, controlled tone.

The hand over her mouth loosened, but the man didn't completely release her. "Is she yours?"

"She's mine."

Then the big man let her go, gently setting her away from him. "You didn't tell me anything about a woman, so I wasn't taking any chances," he said to Kell, and Rachel realized who he was.

She held herself very still, fighting for control and taking slow, deep breaths until she thought she could speak without her voice trembling. "You must be Sullivan," she said with admirable calm as she gradually relaxed her clenched hands.

"Yes, ma'am."

She didn't know what she'd expected, but it wasn't this. He and Kell were so much alike that it staggered her. It wasn't the way he looked, but they both had the same stillness about them, the same aura of power. He had sun-streaked, shaggy hair, and his eyes were as piercing and golden as an eagle's. A scar cut across his left cheekbone, testimony to some past battle. He was a warrior, lean and hard and dangerous…like Kell.

While she had been looking at him, he'd been giving her the same treatment, studying her while she struggled for control. One corner of his mouth kicked up in an almost-smile. "Sorry for scaring you, ma'am. I admire your self-control. Jane would've kicked me in the shins."

"She probably did," Kell commented, his tone still cool, but now with an undercurrent of amusement.

Sullivan's dark brows snapped down over his golden eyes. "No," he said dryly. "That wasn't where she kicked me."

That sounded like a fascinating story, but though Kell still looked amused, he didn't pursue it. "This is Rachel

Jones," he said, holding out his hand to her in a quiet command. "She dragged me out of the ocean."

"Glad to meet you." Sullivan's drawl was soft and raspy as he watched Rachel immediately go to Kell in response to his outstretched hand.

"I'm glad to meet you, Mr. Sullivan...I think."

Kell gave her a brief, comforting touch, then began pulling on his shirt; it was an action that still caused him some difficulty, as his shoulder was stiff and sore. Sullivan looked at the tender, red, newly formed scar tissue where the bullet had torn into Kell's shoulder. "How much damage?"

"I've lost some flexibility, but there's still some swelling. Part of it may return as the swelling goes down."

"Did you get it anywhere else?"

"Left thigh."

"Will it hold up?"

"It'll have to. I've been jogging, loosening it up."

Sullivan grunted. Rachel sensed the man's reluctance to talk freely in front of her, the same ingrained caution that characterized Kell. "Are you hungry, Mr. Sullivan? We're having spaghetti."

That wild-animal gaze turned on her. "Yes, ma'am. Thank you." The soft slurring of his drawl and the grave courtesy of his manners made such a contrast to the fierceness of his eyes that she felt off-balance. Why hadn't Kell warned her?

"I'll finish while you two talk, then. I must have dropped the peppers when you grabbed me," she said. She started toward the door, then turned back, distress in her eyes. "Mr. Sullivan?"

He and Kell were walking into the living room, and Sullivan stopped, looking back at her. "Ma'am?"

"My dog," she said, a faint trembling in her voice. "He's always there when I go outside. Why didn't he—"

Understanding was in those wild golden eyes. "He's all right. I've got him tied up in that pine thicket. Had a helluva time outsmarting him. That's a nice animal."

Relief made her weak. "I'll go untie him, then. You didn't...hurt him in any way?"

"No, ma'am. He's about a hundred yards down, just to the left of that little trail."

She ran down the trail, her heart thudding; Joe was right where Sullivan had said he would be, tied securely to a tall pine, and the dog was furious. He even snarled at Rachel, but she talked softly to him and approached him at a slow, measured pace, calming him before she knelt beside him to untie the rope around his neck. Even then she kept talking, giving him small, quick pats, and the snarls diminished in his throat. Finally he accepted a hug from her, and for the first time gave her a welcoming lick. A lump rose in her throat. "Come on, let's go home," she said, getting to her feet.

She collected the peppers from where she had dropped them on the back steps and left Joe prowling around the house. She washed her hands and began preparing the sauce, listening to the quiet rumble of the men's voices from the living room. Now that she had met Sullivan she understood Kell's confidence in him. He was...incredible. And Kell was even more so. Seeing them together made her realize anew the caliber of the man she loved, and she reeled under the shock of that realization.

It was almost an hour before she called them to the table, and the sun was a fierce red ball low on the horizon, a reminder that now her time with Kell was truly running out. Or was it already gone? Would they be leaving soon?

Deliberately, to get her mind off her fears, she kept

the conversation going. It was remarkably difficult, with both men being the way they were, until finally she hit on the right subject. "Kell told me that you're married, Mr. Sullivan."

He nodded, a curious lightening of his expression making him seem less formidable. "Jane is my wife." He said it as if everyone knew Jane.

"Do you have any children?"

There was no mistaking the look of intense pride that came over the hard, scarred face. "Twin sons. They're six months old."

For some reason Kell was looking amused again. "I didn't know twins ran in your family, Grant."

"They don't," Sullivan growled. "Or in Jane's, either. Even the damn doctor didn't know. She took everybody by surprise."

"That's not unusual," Kell said, and they looked at each other, grinning.

"The hell of it is, she went into labor two weeks early, in the middle of a snowstorm. All the roads were closed, and I couldn't get her to a hospital. I had to deliver them." For a moment there was a look of desperation in his eyes, and a faint sheen of perspiration broke out on his forehead. "Twins," he said faintly. "Damn. I told her not to ever do that to me again, but you know Jane."

Kell laughed out loud, his rare deep laugh making pleasure shimmer through Rachel. "Next time she'll probably have triplets."

Sullivan glared at him. "Don't even think it," he muttered.

Rachel lifted a forkful of spaghetti to her mouth. "I don't think it's Jane's fault that she had twins, or that it snowed."

"Logically, no," Sullivan admitted. "But logic flies out the window when Jane walks in the door."

"How did you meet her?"

"I kidnapped her," he said offhandedly, leaving Rachel gasping, because he offered no other explanation.

"How did you get away from her?" Kell asked, provoking another glare.

"It wasn't easy, but she couldn't leave the kids." Sullivan leaned back in his chair, an unholy light entering his eyes. "You're going to have to go back with me to explain."

Kell looked alarmed, then resigned; finally he grinned. "All right. I want to see you with these babies."

"They're already crawling. You have to watch where you step," the proud father said, grinning in return. "Their names are Dane and Daniel, but beats the hell out of me which one is which. Jane said we can let them decide when they get older."

That was it. The three of them looked at one another, and Rachel gulped helplessly. Kell made a rough choking sound. In a perfectly choreographed move three forks were laid down on the table and three people held their heads and laughed until they hurt.

CHARLES READ THE HASTILY gathered intelligence report on Rachel, frowning as he rubbed his forehead with one thin finger. According to both Agents Lowell and Ellis, Rachel Jones was a good-looking but otherwise ordinary woman, even though Ellis was enamored of her. Ellis was enamored of women in general, so that wasn't unusual. The problem was that the report painted her as anything but ordinary. She was a well educated, well traveled, multitalented woman, but again the problem went even deeper than that. She had been an investigative reporter of extraordinary talent, nerve and perseverance, which meant that she was more knowledgeable than the ordinary person about things that were usually kept from public knowledge. According to her record she had been very successful in her field. Her husband had been murdered by a car bomb meant for her when she began investigating a powerful politician's connection with illegal drugs; rather than backing down as many people would have done, this Rachel Jones had kept after the politician and not only proved that he was involved with drug smuggling and dealing, she had proved that he was behind her husband's death. The politician was now serving a life sentence in prison.

This wasn't the rather unsophisticated woman Lowell and Ellis had described. What particularly troubled Charles was why she had projected such an image; she had to have a reason, but what was it? Why had she wanted to deceive them? For amusement, or had there been a more serious motivation?

Charles wasn't surprised that she had lied; in his experience most people lied. In his profession it was necessary to lie. What he didn't like was not knowing *why*, because the why of something was the heart of it.

Sabin had disappeared, possibly dead, though Charles couldn't convince himself of that. No trace of him had been found, not by Charles's men, a fishing trawler, a pleasure boater, or any law enforcement agency. Even though Sabin's boat had exploded there should have been some identifiably human remains—if Sabin had been on the boat. The only explanation was that he had gone overboard and swum for shore. It almost defied belief to think that he could actually have made it in his wounded condition, but this was Sabin, not some ordinary man. He *had* made it to shore, but where? Why hadn't he surfaced yet? No one had found a wounded man; no unaccounted-for gunshot wounds had been reported to the police; he hadn't been admitted to any of the hospitals in the area. He had simply disappeared into thin air.

So, on the one hand he had Sabin, who had vanished. The only possibility was that someone was hiding him, but there were no clues. On the other hand, there was this Rachel Jones, who, like Sabin, was not ordinary. Her house was in the prime search area, the area where Sabin would have most likely made it to shore. Neither Lowell nor Ellis thought she had anything to hide, but they didn't know everything about her. She had projected a false image; she was more familiar than could have been suspected with undercover agents and tactics. But what reason could she have for acting like less than what she was...unless she had something to hide? More to the point, did she have some*one* to hide?

"Noelle," he said softly. "I want to talk to Lowell and Ellis. Immediately. Find them."

An hour later both men were sitting across from him. Charles folded his hands and smiled absently at them. "Gentlemen, I want to discuss this Rachel Jones. I want to know everything you can remember about her."

Ellis and Lowell exchanged looks; then Ellis shrugged. "She's a good-looking woman—"

"No, I am not interested in her looks. I want to know what she has said and done. When you searched the beach in her area and went up to her house, did you go inside?"

"No," Lowell replied.

"Why not?"

"She's got this damned big guard dog who hates men. He won't let a man in the yard," Ellis explained.

"Even when you took her out to dinner?"

Ellis looked discomfited, as if he disliked admitting that a dog had scared him off. "She came out to the car. When

I took her home the dog was there waiting, ready to take my leg off if I moved in the wrong direction."

"So no one has been inside her house."

"No," they both admitted.

"She denied any knowledge of seeing a man, a stranger?"

"There's no way Sabin could have gotten anywhere near that house without the dog having him for breakfast," Ellis said impatiently, and Lowell nodded in agreement.

Charles tapped his fingertips together. "Even if she took him into the house herself? What if she found him? She could have tied the dog up, then gone back for Sabin. Isn't this possible?"

"Sure, it's possible," Lowell said, frowning. "But we didn't find any sign of Sabin making it to shore, not even a footprint. The only thing we noticed was where she dragged shells up from the beach on a tarp—" He stopped, his eyes meeting Charles's.

"You fools!" Charles hissed. "Something had been dragged up from the beach and you didn't check it out?"

They looked uncomfortable. "She said it was shells," Ellis muttered. "I noticed that she did have some shells on the windowsills."

"She didn't act like she had anything to hide," Lowell put in, trying to gloss things over. "I ran into her the next day while she was shopping. She stopped to talk, about the heat and things like that…"

"What did she buy? Did you look in her cart?"

"Ah, underwear and, uh, women's things. When she checked out I saw a pair of jogging shoes. I noticed them because—" Suddenly he went a sickly shade.

"Because?" Charles prompted dryly.

"Because they looked too big for her."

Charles glared at them, his eyes cold and deadly. "So. She dragged something up from the beach, something you didn't investigate. Neither of you has been inside the house. She was buying shoes that were too big for her, possibly men's shoes. If Sabin has been under our noses all this time and he's escaped due to your bungling, I personally promise you that your future won't be pleasant! Noelle!" he called.

She appeared immediately in the door. "Yes, Charles?"

"Call everyone in. We may have found Sabin."

Both Lowell and Ellis looked sick, and both fervently hoped that this time they *didn't* find Sabin. "What if you're wrong?" Ellis asked.

"Then the woman may be frightened and upset, but nothing more. If she doesn't know anything, if she hasn't helped Sabin, then we have no reason to harm her."

But Charles smiled when he said it, his eyes cold, and Ellis couldn't believe him.

THE SUN HAD SET, and twilight had brought out a loud chorus of frogs and crickets. Ebenezer Duck and his flock waddled around the yard, reaping the late afternoon harvest of insects, and Joe lay on the porch. Kell and Sullivan were now at the table, drawing diagrams and discussing plans; Rachel tried to work on the manuscript, but her mind kept wandering. Kell would be leaving soon, and dull misery throbbed inside her.

The flock of geese suddenly scattered, honking wildly, and Joe gave a single bark before he lunged off the porch. Kell and Sullivan acted as one, ducking away from the table and running soundlessly, on the balls of their feet, to the living room windows. Rachel bolted out of her office, her face pale, though she tried to be calm. "It's probably just Honey," she said, going to the front door.

"Honey?" Sullivan asked.

"The veterinarian."

A white sedan pulled up in front, and a woman got out. Sullivan peered out the window and all the color washed out of his face. Resting his head on the wall, he swore quietly and at length. "It's Jane," he groaned.

"Hell," Kell muttered.

Rachel opened the door to dart out and catch Joe, who was planted in the middle of the yard. But before Rachel could get out the door, Jane had walked around the car and into the yard. "Nice doggie," she said cheerfully, patting Joe on the head as she passed.

Sullivan and Kell came out on the porch behind Rachel. Jane put her hands on her hips and glared at her husband. "Since you wouldn't bring me with you, I decided to follow you!"

CHAPTER TWELVE

RACHEL LIKED Jane Sullivan on sight. Anyone who calmly petted Joe, then faced Grant Sullivan's fury without blinking an eye, was someone Rachel would like to know. The two women introduced themselves, while Sullivan stood with his arms folded across his chest, his golden eyes shooting fire as he watched his wife from beneath lowered brows. "How did you find me?" he rasped, his voice low and almost soundless. "I made sure I didn't leave a trail."

Jane sniffed at him. "You didn't, so I did the logical thing and went where you weren't, and found you." Turning her back on him, she welcomed Kell with an enthusiastic hug. "I knew it had to be you. No one else could have dragged him away. Are you in trouble?"

"A little," Kell said, his black eyes filled with amusement.

"I thought so. I came to help."

"I'll be damned," Grant snapped.

Jane gave him a cool look. "Yes, you may be. Sneaking out and leaving me with the babies—"

"Where *are* they?"

"With your mother. She thinks I'm doing her a favor. Anyway, that's what took me so long to get here. I had to take the twins to her. Then I had to figure out what you'd do if you were trying to keep anyone from knowing where you were."

"I'm going to turn you over my knee," he said, and he

looked as if the thought gave him immense satisfaction. "You're not getting out of it this time."

"You can't," she said smugly. "I'm pregnant again."

Rachel had been enjoying the spectacle of Grant Sullivan driven to frustration by his pretty, dark-eyed wife, but now she felt almost sorry for him. He went pale.

"You can't be."

"I wouldn't bet on that," Kell put in, enjoying this turn of events as much as Rachel.

"The twins are just six months old," Grant croaked.

"I know that!" Jane replied, her face indignant. "I was there, remember?"

"We weren't going to have any more for a while."

"The thunderstorm," she said succinctly, and Grant closed his eyes. He was really white by now, and Rachel was moved to pity.

"Let's go inside, where it's cooler," she suggested, opening the screen door. She and Kell went inside, but no one followed them. Rachel peeked out the door; Jane was wrapped in her husband's muscular arms, and his blond head was bent down to her dark one.

Oddly, that sight added a little more to Rachel's inner pain. "They made it," she whispered.

Kell's arms slid around her waist, and he pulled her back against him. "He isn't in it now, remember? He was retired before they ever met."

Rachel wanted to ask why he couldn't retire, as well, but kept herself from voicing the question. What had been right for Grant Sullivan wasn't right for Kell Sabin; Kell was one of a kind. Instead she asked, "When do you leave?" She should have been proud that her voice was so steady, but pride didn't mean anything to her at this stage. She would have begged him on her knees if she thought it would work, but his dedication was more than lip service.

He was silent for a moment, and she knew she wouldn't like the answer, even though she was expecting it. "Tomorrow morning."

So she had one more night, unless he and Sullivan planned to spend most of it working out the details of their objective.

"We're turning in early," he said, touching her hair, and she twisted in his arms to meet his midnight eyes. His face was remote, but he wanted her; she could tell it by his touch, by something fleeting in his expression. Oh, God, how could she ever stand to watch him leave and know that she'd never see him again?

Jane and Grant came inside, and Jane's face was radiant. Her eyes widened with delight when she saw Rachel in Kell's arms, but something in their expressions kept her from saying anything. Jane was nothing if not intuitive. "Grant won't tell me what's going on," she announced, and crossed her arms stubbornly. "I'm going to follow you until I find out."

Kell's black brows lifted. "And if I do tell you?"

Jane considered that, looking from Kell to Grant, then back to Kell. "You want to negotiate, don't you? You want me to go back home."

"You *are* going back home," Grant said quietly, steel in his voice. "If Sabin wants to fill you in, that's up to him, but this new baby gives me twice the reason to make sure you're safe on the farm, instead of risking your neck chasing after me."

There was a glint in Jane's eyes that made Rachel think Sullivan would have a fight on his hands, but Kell forestalled that by saying, "All right, I think you deserve to know what's happened, since Grant's involved in it now. Let's sit down, and I'll fill you in."

"On a 'need to know' basis," Jane guessed accurately and Kell gave her his humorless smile.

"Yes. You know there are always details that can't be discussed, but I can tell you most of it."

They sat around the table, and Kell sketched in the main points of what had happened, the implications and why he needed Grant. When he had finished Jane looked at both the men for a long time, then slowly nodded. "You have to do it." Then she leaned forward, planted both hands on the table and bent an uncompromising look on Sabin, who met it squarely. "But let me tell you, Kell Sabin, that if anything happens to Grant, I'll come after you. I didn't go through all that trouble to get him for anything to happen to him now."

Kell didn't respond, but Rachel knew what he was thinking. If anything happened it wasn't likely that he would survive, either. She didn't know how she knew what was in his mind, but she did. Her senses were locked on Kell, and his slightest gesture or change of tone registered on her nerves with the force of an earthquake on the most sensitive seismograph.

Grant stood up, drawing Jane up to stand beside him. "It's time we got some sleep, since we're leaving so early in the morning. And you're going home," he said to his wife. "Give me your word."

Now that she knew what was involved, Jane didn't argue. "All right. I'll go home after I pick up the twins. What I want to know is when I can expect you back."

Grant glanced at Kell. "Three days?"

Kell nodded.

Rachel got to her feet. In three days it would be over, one way or the other, but for her it would end in the morning. In the meantime she had to make sleeping arrangements for the Sullivans, and she was almost grateful to have something that would occupy her time, if not her mind.

She apologized to Jane for the lack of an extra bed, but it didn't seem to bother Jane at all. "Don't worry about us," Jane soothed. "I've slept with Grant in tents, caves and sheds, so a nice living room floor isn't any hardship to us."

With Jane's help Rachel gathered quilts and extra pillows for a pallet, taking them from the top of her closet and stacking them on Jane's arms. Jane eyed her shrewdly. "You're in love with Kell, aren't you?"

"Yes." Rachel said the one word steadily, not even thinking of denying it. It was a fact, as much a part of her as her gray eyes.

"He's a hard, unusual man, but top-quality steel has to be hard to be top quality. It won't be easy. I know. Look at the man I chose."

They looked at each other, two women with a world of knowledge in their eyes. For good or ill, the men they loved were different from other men, and they would never have the security most women could expect.

"When he leaves tomorrow, it's over," Rachel said, her throat tight. "He won't be back."

"He *wants* it to be over," Jane clarified, her brown eyes unusually somber. "But don't say that he won't be back. Grant didn't want to marry me. He said it wouldn't work, that our lives were too different and I'd never fit into his world. Sound familiar?"

"Oh, yes." Her eyes and voice were bleak.

"I had to let him go, but in the end he came after me."

"Grant was already retired. Kell won't retire, and the job is the problem."

"It's a big problem, but not insurmountable. Loving

someone is hard for men like Grant and Kell to accept. They've always been alone."

Yes, Kell had always been alone, and he was determined to keep it that way. Knowing and understanding his reasons didn't make living with them any easier. She left Jane and Grant to bed down in the living room, and Kell followed her into the bedroom, closing the door behind him. She stood in the middle of the room with her hands tightly clenched, her eyes shadowed as she watched him.

"We should have left tonight," he said quietly. "But I wanted one more night with you."

She wouldn't let herself cry, not tonight. No matter what happened she would wait until tomorrow, until he was gone. He turned out the light and came to her in the darkened room, his rough hands closing on her shoulders and pulling her against him. His mouth was hard, hungry, almost hurting her as he kissed her with savage need. His tongue probed at hers, demanding a response that was slow in coming, because the pain was so great inside her. He kept on kissing her, sliding his hands over her back and hips, cradling her against the warmth of his body, until finally she began to relax and yield to him.

"Rachel," he whispered, unbuttoning her shirt to find her naked breasts and cup them in his warm palms. Slowly he circled her nipples with his thumbs and enticed them to hardness; the warmth, the tightening sense of excitement and anticipation began to intensify inside her. Her body knew him and responded, growing heavy and moist, readying her for him because she knew he wouldn't leave her unsatisfied. He slid the shirt off her shoulders, pinning her arms to her sides with the fabric while he lifted her, arching her over his arm and thrusting her breasts up to him. Deliberately he put his mouth over her nipple and sucked at her, the strong motion drawing hot tingles from her sensitive flesh. She made a faint, gasping sound of pleasure as the sensations swept from her breasts into her lower abdomen, where desire was pulling at her.

Her head swam, and she had the sudden sensation of falling, which made her clutch at his waist. It wasn't until she felt the coolness of the bed beneath her that she realized he had been lowering her to its surface. Her shirt was caught beneath her, with the sleeves trapped and twisted midway between her elbows and wrists, effectively pinning her arms while her upper torso lay bare for his marauding lips and tongue to savor. He looked down at her with a tortured, hungry expression in his eyes, then bent and buried his face between her breasts, his hands squeezing them together around his face as if he wanted to lose himself in the scent and feel of her satiny flesh.

She moaned as her body throbbed in need, and tried futilely to wrest her arms free. "Kell." Her voice was high, strained. "Let me get my arms out."

He lifted his head and appraised the situation. "Not yet," he murmured. "Just lie there and let me love you until you're ready for me."

She made a rough sound of frustration, trying to roll to one side so she could free herself, but Kell subdued her, his hard hands holding her flat on her back. "I *am* ready," she insisted before his mouth came down on hers and stifled any further protests.

When he raised his head again it was with hot satisfaction stamped on his taut features. "Not like you will be." Then he bent to her breasts again, not stopping until they were wet and gleaming from his mouth and her nipples were red and achingly tight. Gently he bit the undercurve of her breast, using his teeth just enough to let her feel them but not enough to bring pain.

"Let's get you out of these." The strain was evident in

his voice, too, as he tugged at the fastening of her shorts. It came free, and the zipper rasped quietly as he slid it down. His hand went inside the opened shorts, burrowing under her panties to find the warm, moist, aching flesh he sought. "Ah," he said in quiet satisfaction as his fingers explored her and found her ready, indeed. "You liked that, didn't you?"

"Yes." All she could do was whimper the word.

"You'll like it better when I'm inside you," he promised huskily, and slid her panties and shorts down her hips and thighs, but not off. He left them just above her knees, and her legs were trapped as effectively as her arms. Slowly he ran his hand over her, from her breasts down over her flat belly, to linger at her naked loins.

She writhed under his probing fingers, her heart thundering in her chest and interfering with the rhythm of her breathing. "Don't you even *think* it," she cried, her hands clutching at the sheet beneath her. He was looking at her in a way that told her he liked holding her helpless while he teased her and enjoyed her body. He was more than a little uncivilized, his instincts swift and primeval.

He gave a low, rough laugh. "All right, love. You don't have to wait any longer. I'll give you what you want." Swiftly he stripped her, even of the shirt that bound her arms, and took off his own clothes, then settled his weight onto her. Rachel accepted him with a sigh of painful relief, her arms wrapping around him as he spread her legs and entered her. She reached her peak quickly, convulsing in his arms, and slowly he built her to pleasure again. He couldn't get enough of her that night, returning to her over and over, as if time slowed when they were locked together in love.

It was shortly before dawn when she woke up for the last time, lying on her side with her back to him, snuggled into the warm curve of his chest and thighs, just as they had slept every night since he'd regained consciousness. This was the last time he would hold her like this, and she lay very still, not wanting to wake him.

But he was already awake. His hand moved slowly over her breasts, then down to her thighs. He raised her leg, draping it over his thigh, and slid into her from behind. His hand flattened against her stomach to brace her as he began moving in and out of her. "One last time," he murmured into her hair. Dear God, it was the last time, and he didn't think he could stand it. If he had ever been happy in his life it had been during these too short days with Rachel. This would be the last time her soft body would sheathe his hardness, the last time her breasts would fill his hands, the last time he would ever see the misty look of passion in her lake-gray eyes. She trembled beneath his hands, biting her lips to keep from crying out as the pleasure built within her. When the time came he clasped her to him, holding himself deep within her while she turned her face into the pillow to stifle the sounds she made, then he thrust deep and hard and shuddered with his own release.

The room was growing light now, the sky glowing with the pink pearl of approaching sunrise. He sat up in the bed and looked down at her, her body damp and glowing like the sky. Perhaps this last time had been a mistake, because he hadn't taken his usual precautions, but he couldn't regret it. He couldn't have tolerated any separation of their bodies.

Rachel lay exhausted on the pillows, watching him with her heart in her eyes. Her body still throbbed from his lovemaking, and her pulse was only gradually slowing. "You may never come back," she whispered. "But I'll wait here for you, anyway."

Only the slight jerking of a muscle beside his mouth

revealed his reaction. He shook his head. "No, don't waste your life. Find someone else, get married and have a houseful of kids."

Somehow she managed a smile. "Don't be a fool," she told him with aching tenderness. "As if there could be anyone else after you."

THEY WERE READY to leave, and Rachel was so stiff inside that she thought she would shatter if anyone touched her. She knew there would be no goodbye kisses, no final words to burn into her memory. He would simply leave, and it would be finished. He wasn't even taking the pistol with him, which would give him an excuse to contact her again to return it. The pistol was registered to her; he didn't want anything that could be traced back to her in case things didn't go as planned.

Sullivan had hidden his rental car somewhere down the road; Jane was going to drive them to it, then return to their farm. Rachel would be left alone in a house that echoed with emptiness, and she was already trying to think of ways to fill the time. She would work in the garden, mow the lawn, wash the car, maybe even go swimming. Later she would go out to eat, see a movie, anything to postpone coming back. Perhaps by then she would be so tired she would be able to sleep, though she didn't hold out much hope for that. Still, she'd get by, because she had no choice.

"I'll let you know," Jane whispered, hugging Rachel.

Rachel's eyes burned. "Thank you."

Grant opened the door and walked out onto the porch, which brought Joe to his feet, and snarls filled the air. Calmly Grant surveyed the dog. "Well, hell," he said mildly.

Jane snorted. "Are you afraid of that dog? He's as sweet as can be."

Kell followed them onto the porch. "Joe, sit," he commanded.

There was the peculiar, high-pitched CRACK! of a rifle being fired and the wood exploded on the post not two inches from Kell's head. Kell turned and dove for the open door just as Rachel leaped for him, and he knocked her sprawling. Almost simultaneously Grant literally threw Jane through the door as another shot exploded, then he covered her with his body.

"Are you all right?" Kell asked through clenched teeth, anxiously looking Rachel over even as he lashed out with one foot and kicked the door shut.

She'd banged her head on the floor, but it wasn't anything serious. Her face white, she clutched at him. "Yes, I'm f-f-fine," she stammered.

He rolled to his feet, crouching to stay below the windows. "You and Jane lie down in the hall," he ordered tersely, getting the pistol from the bedroom where he'd left it.

Grant had helped Jane to a sitting position, brushing her hair out of her face and giving her a swift kiss before he pushed her toward Rachel. "Go on, move," he snapped, drawing his own pistol from his belt.

There was another shot, and the window closest to Grant shattered, raining shards of glass all over him. He cursed luridly.

Rachel stared at them, trying to gather her thoughts. They were armed only with pistols, while whoever was shooting at them had a rifle, stacking the deck against Kell and Grant. A rifle had the advantage of accuracy over a greater distance, allowing their assailant to shoot from outside the range of the pistols. Her .22 rifle didn't have much power, but it did have a greater range and accuracy than the pistols, and she crawled into the bedroom to get it, as well as what ammunition she had. Thank God Kell had told her to buy those shells!

"Here," she said, crawling back into the living room and sliding the rifle toward Kell. He glanced around, his fist closing over the weapon. Grant was moving through the house, checking to make certain no one was coming up on them from behind.

"Thanks," Kell said briefly. "Get back in the hall, honey."

Jane was crouched there, staring at her husband with an odd fury in her chocolate eyes. "They shot at you," she growled.

"Yep," he confirmed.

She was fuming like a volcano about to blow, muttering to herself as she dragged the nylon overnighter she'd brought to her, unzipping it and throwing clothing and makeup to one side. "I'm not putting up with this," she said furiously. "Damn it, they shot at him!" She produced a pistol and shoved it into Rachel's hand, then dug back into the bag. She dragged a small case out of it, about the size of a violin case, and threw it at Grant. "Here! I don't know how to put the thing together!"

He opened the case and glared at Jane even as he began snapping the rifle together with swift, practiced movements. "Where the hell did you get this?"

"Never mind!" she barked, tossing a clip of ammunition to him. He fielded it one-handed and snapped it into place.

Kell glanced over his shoulder. "Got any C-4 or grenades in there?"

"No," Jane said regretfully. "I didn't have time to get everything I wanted."

Rachel crawled to the side window, cautiously lifting her head to peek out. Kell swore. "Get down," he snapped. "Stay out of this. Get back in the hall, where it's safer."

She was pale, but calm. "There are only two of you, and four sides to the house. You need us."

Jane grabbed Grant's discarded pistol. "She's right. You need us."

Kell's face was set like granite. This was exactly what he'd wanted most to avoid, one of his worst fears coming true. Rachel's life was being threatened because of him. Damn! Why hadn't he left last night, as he should have? He'd let sexual desire override his common sense, and now she was in danger.

"Sabin!" The voice came from the pine thicket.

He didn't answer, but his eyes narrowed as he surveyed the thicket, trying to find the speaker. He wasn't going to answer and reveal his position; let them find out the hard way.

"Come on, Sabin, don't make it any harder than it has to be!" the voice continued. "If you surrender, I give you my word none of the others will be harmed!"

"Who is that joker?" Grant grunted.

"Charles Dubois, alias Charles Lloyd, alias Kurt Schmidt, alias several other names," Kell murmured.

The names meant nothing to Rachel, but Sullivan's brows lifted. "So he finally decided to come after you himself." He looked around. "We're not in a good position. He's got men all around the house. There aren't that many of them, but we're hemmed in. I checked the phone—it's dead."

Kell didn't have to be told that their situation wasn't good. If Dubois used the rockets on the house, as he had on the boat, they were all as good as dead. But then again, he was trying to take Kell alive. Alive, he was worth a lot

of money to a lot of people who would pay anything to get
their hands on him.

He tried to think, but the cold fact was that there was
no way out of the house. Even if they waited until nightfall
and tried to sneak out, there was little available cover to use
except for the bushes, which were right against the house.
Away from the house, it was open for a good distance in
all directions. That meant it would be difficult for anyone
to catch them unawares, but it also meant the same thing in
reverse. Even if he walked out and surrendered, it wouldn't
save the others. There was no way Dubois would let any
witnesses live. He knew it, and Sullivan knew it; he could
only hope Rachel and Jane didn't realize quite how hope-
less the situation really was.

A glance at Rachel dispelled that idea. She knew, all
right. That had been the problem from the first; she was too
aware, with no veil of ignorance to shield her. He wanted
to take her in his arms and hold her head on his shoulder,
assure her that it would be all right, but with those clear,
level gray eyes on him, he couldn't lie to her, even to give
her momentary comfort. He never wanted any lies between
them.

There was a shot from the bedroom, and all the color
washed out of Grant's face, but before he could move Jane
called him. "Grant! Is the kneecap where I'm supposed to
shoot these people?"

If anything, he went even whiter, swearing long and
low.

"Well, it doesn't matter," she added philosophically. "I
missed, anyway. But I hit his gun, if that counts."

"Sabin!" the man yelled again. "You are testing my
patience! This cannot go on much longer. It would be such
a pity if the woman was harmed."

"Woman," instead of "women." Then Kell realized that

achel hadn't gone out on the porch; they had seen Jane
nd thought she was Rachel. They were both slim and
ad dark hair, though Jane was taller and her hair was a
ttle longer, but at a distance no one would have noticed.
 didn't give him much of an advantage, but it might help
at Dubois would be underestimating the number of armed
eople.

"Sabin!"

"I'm thinking!" Kell yelled, keeping his head away from
e window.

"Time is a luxury you can't afford, my friend. You know
ou can't win. Why not make it easy on yourself? The
oman will go free, I promise you!"

Dubois's promises weren't worth the air it took to make
em, and Kell knew it. Time. Somehow he had to buy a
ttle time. He didn't know what he was going to do, but
very extra second gave chance an opportunity to step in.
iming was always critical, and if he could stall Dubois it
ight throw the man off in some way.

"What about my other friend?" he yelled.

"Of course," Dubois lied smoothly. "I have no quarrel
ith him."

Grant's lips twisted back in a feral grin. "Sure. There's
o way he didn't recognize me."

What a coup it would be for Dubois to capture both
abin and the Tiger, the big tawny warrior with the wild,
olden eyes who had ranged the jungle with Sabin and later
een his prime agent. Each was legendary in his own right;
ogether they had been incredible, so attuned that they
cted as one man. Sullivan had had a run-in with some of
ubois's men a few years back; no, Dubois wouldn't have
orgotten that, considering how Sullivan had made a fool
f him.

A movement in the trees suddenly caught Kell's attention,

and his black eyes narrowed. "See if you can get him to sa
something else," he told Grant, sliding the barrel of the .2
just a fraction of an inch outside the broken window an
keeping his eyes fixed on the spot in the trees.

"Come on, Dubois," Grant yelled. "Don't play game
I know you recognized me."

Kell's finger tightened slightly on the trigger as silenc
reigned; was Dubois really surprised to find out they kne
who he was? It was true that he had always operated fro
the background rather than risk his own safety, but Ke
had been after him for years now, ever since Dubois ha
begun selling his services as a terrorist.

"So it *is* you, Tiger."

There it was again, that slight movement. Kell sighte
down the barrel and gently squeezed the trigger. The repo
of the rifle echoed in the small house, drowning out an
cry of pain, but Kell knew he hadn't missed. He also didn
know if he'd hit Dubois or someone else.

A hail of bullets tore into the house, shattering all th
windows and gouging long splinters out of the walls an
window frames, but the steel-reinforced doors held. "Gue
he didn't like that," Kell muttered.

Grant had ducked to the floor, and now his head cam
up. "You know, I never liked that nickname worth a damn
he drawled, then swung his rifle up. It was an automati
and he fired it in the three-shot bursts of a well-traine
soldier, making good use of his firepower without wastin
his ammunition. Pistol shots came from both the bedroo
and Rachel's office; then all hell broke loose again. The
were tearing the house up, and cold fear filled him, becaus
Rachel was caught in this barrage.

"Rachel!" he yelled. "Are you all right?"

"I'm okay," she answered, and her calm voice mad
him ache.

"Jane!" Grant yelled. No answer. "Jane," he yelled again, is face gray as he started for the bedroom.

"I'm busy!"

Grant looked as if he might explode, and despite every-ing Kell found himself grinning. Better Grant than him. till, Jane's life was in jeopardy, too, and the thought of nything happening to her was almost as hard to bear as he thought of anyone hurting Rachel.

There was another lull, and Grant pulled out his empty lip and slapped another one into place.

"Sabin, my patience is at an end," Dubois called, and Kell grimaced. Damn, it hadn't been Dubois he'd hit.

"You haven't made the right offer yet," he yelled in return. Anything to buy time.

Jane crawled out of the bedroom, her hair all mussed and er eyes big. "I think the cavalry is coming," she said.

The two men ignored her, but Rachel scrambled to her ide. "What?" she asked.

"Men on horseback," Jane said, waving her hand toward he bedroom. "I saw them, coming from that way."

Rachel felt like crying or laughing, but she couldn't nake up her mind which. "It's Rafferty," she said, and now he had their attention. "My neighbor. He must have heard he shots."

Grant crouched low and ran through the kitchen to the ack, where he could see. "How many?" Kell asked.

"Twenty or so," Grant said. "Damn, they're riding right nto automatic fire. Start shooting and draw Dubois's ire!"

They did. Rachel crept up to a window, held the heavy istol out it and fired until it was empty, then reloaded with haking hands before emptying it again. Kell was making udicious use of the .22, and Jane was revealing remarkable kill herself. Had they given Rafferty enough time to get

behind Dubois and his men? If they kept shooting, the
might hit their rescuers.

"Hold it," Kell ordered. They lay flat on the floor wit
their heads covered while the walls were shredded by bu
lets. The light fixture crashed to the floor, sending glas
flying. Grant cursed, and they looked over to see bloo
streaming down his face from a cut on his cheek. Jane gav
a thin, high cry and made a move toward him, despite th
continuing gunfire; Kell grabbed her and wrestled her t
the floor.

"I'm all right," Grant yelled. "It's just a little cut."

"Stay close to the floor," Kell told Jane, then let her g
knowing that she'd fight him like a wildcat if he tried t
keep her from Grant.

Then, suddenly, it was quiet except for a few scattere
shots, and they were abruptly halted, too. Rachel lay on th
floor, hardly daring to breathe, the acrid smell of burne
gunpowder filling her nostrils and even her mouth. Ke
put his hand on her arm, his black eyes drifting over he
pale features as if he would burn her into his memory.

"Hey!" a deep voice roared. "Rachel, are you in there?

Her lips trembled, and tears suddenly blurred her eyes
"It's Rafferty," she whispered, then lifted her head to cal
"John! Is it all right?"

"Depends," the answer came. "These bastards here don
think it's all right."

Kell slowly climbed to his feet and pulled Rachel t
hers. "He sounds like my kind of man."

Rachel felt like the survivor of a shipwreck as sh
walked out on the porch with Kell supporting her. Gran
and Jane followed, with Jane dabbing at the cut on Grant'
cheek, crying a little as she fussed at him. Without the arr
around her waist, Rachel was sure she wouldn't have bee
able to stand.

She gave a ghostly cry when she saw three of the geese lying in the yard, blood on the white of their feathers, but there was no way she could make a sound when she saw Joe lying on his side at the edge of the porch. Kell turned her into his arms, pressing her face into his shoulder.

Big John Rafferty, armed with a hunting rifle and surrounded by his men, who were likewise armed, herded about fifteen men before him. Rafferty's eyes were fierce and narrow under his dark brows as he prodded a slim, gray-haired man before him. "We heard the shooting and came to see what was going on," John drawled. "I don't like riffraff shooting at my neighbor."

Charles Dubois was white with rage, his eyes fastened on Sabin. Beside him was Noelle, her beautiful eyes full of boredom.

"It isn't over, Sabin," Dubois hissed, and Kell gently put Rachel aside, handing her over to Grant. Kell had business to attend to, and explaining it to the law, then keeping it quiet would take some doing.

"It's over as far as you're concerned," he said briefly.

Beside Charles, Noelle smiled her slow, sleepy smile, then suddenly wrenched free; because she was a woman, the cowhand behind her hadn't been holding her securely. And, somehow, she had a gun in her hand, a small, ugly revolver.

Rachel saw it, and everything moved in slow motion. With a cry she tore free of Grant's arm, hurling herself toward Kell. A man grabbed for Noelle's arm, and the pistol exploded just as Rachel hit Kell, knocking him away. She cried out again at the burning pain in her side; then there was only blackness filling the world.

CHAPTER THIRTEEN

SABIN LEANED AGAINST the wall in the hospital waiting room, his nostrils filled with the sharp smell of antiseptic and his dark face cold and remote, even though there was screaming hell in his eyes. Behind him were Jane and Grant, waiting with him. Jane was huddled over, her expressive face pale and full of misery; Grant prowled the confines of the room like some great cat.

No matter how he tried, Kell couldn't get the picture of Rachel, lying on the ground awash in her own blood, out of his mind. She had looked so small and fragile, her eyes closed and her face paper white, crumpled like a child's discarded doll, one slender hand lying palm up. He'd fallen to his knees beside her, oblivious to the scuffle and shots going on behind him, and a low, rough sound had exploded from his chest. Her name had echoed in his mind, but he hadn't been able to voice it.

Then, incredibly, her eyes had opened. She was dazed and in pain, but those clear, clear eyes had fastened on him as if he were her lifeline, and her trembling lips had fashioned his name. It wasn't until then that he'd realized she was alive. Seeing her take the bullet meant for him had been a nightmare come true, and he still hadn't recovered. He didn't expect ever to recover.

Yet he had managed to rip her clothing away from the ugly wound in her side and apply rough first aid, with Jane kneeling beside him and helping. Grant had taken over with the others, doing what was necessary, making certain that no hint of what had happened was leaked.

Dubois was dead, Noelle critically wounded and not expected to survive. Ironically, it had been Tod Ellis who had shot them. During the ensuing scuffle after Noelle had shot Rachel, Ellis had pulled free and grabbed a rifle. His motives were murky. Perhaps he had wanted to get rid of Dubois so no one would know the extent to which Ellis had helped him; perhaps, in the end, he hadn't been able to stomach what he'd done. Or perhaps it had been because of Rachel. Sabin could identify with that last reason; he could gladly have killed Dubois and that treacherous bitch with his bare hands for what they'd done to Rachel.

Honey Mayfield had been fetched to take care of Joe, and she thought he would make it. Rachel would need something, someone to hold on to, even if it was just a dog. Her house had been so badly damaged that it would take weeks to restore it; her pets had been shot, her life turned upside down, she herself wounded, and the man she loved was the cause of it all. Cold, piercing agony filled his chest. He'd nearly cost her her life, when he would have died himself rather than have her suffer this. He'd known the danger, yet he'd stayed, unable to tear himself away from her. This once he'd let his heart overrule his mind, and it had almost killed her. Never again. God in heaven, never again.

He would stay only until she was out of surgery and he knew she would be all right; there was no way he could leave until he knew, until he'd seen her again and touched her. But then he and Grant would have to leave. The situation was critical; he had to get to Washington before the news of this leaked back and the traitor, or traitors, could cover their tracks.

"Jane," he said quietly, not turning around. "Will you stay?"

"Of course," she responded without hesitation. "You know you didn't have to ask."

It had been all he could do to get the local authorities to cooperate; if it hadn't been for one of the deputies, a man named Phelps, who knew Rachel, the whole thing would have blown sky-high. But Phelps had known what to do, and he'd done some long, hard talking to get the lid put on this. Rafferty had guaranteed the silence of his men, and Kell doubted that there was a one of them who would dare cross Rafferty.

The surgeon entered the waiting room, his lined face tired. "Mr. Jones?"

Kell had identified himself as Rachel's husband and signed the release forms for her to be treated to speed things up. Legality be damned. Every minute had meant the loss of more blood for her. He straightened away from the wall, his entire body taut. "Yes?"

"Your wife is doing fine. She's in recovery now. The bullet nicked her right kidney. She lost a lot of blood, but we got some back in her, and her condition is stabilizing. I had doubts about saving the kidney, but there was less damage than I'd anticipated. Barring complications, I don't see any reason she won't be home in about a week."

The relief was so great that all he could do was croak, "When can I see her?"

"Probably in about an hour. I'm going to keep her in ICU overnight, but it's just precautionary. I don't think that kidney's going to start bleeding again, but if it does, I want her there. I'll have a nurse come for you when they get her moved."

Kell nodded and shook the doctor's hand; then he stood rigidly, unable to relax even now. Jane came to stand beside him, slipping her hand into his bigger one and squeezing it comfortingly. "Don't tear yourself apart over this."

"It was my fault."

"Really? When were you put in charge of the world? I must have missed the headlines."

He sighed wearily. "Not now."

"Why not now? If you don't snap out of this you're not going to be in any shape to do what needs doing."

She was right, of course. Jane might not get where she was going by the same route the rest of the world would take, but in the end she was usually right on the money.

When at last they let him see Rachel, he was braced for the shock; he'd seen too many wounded people not to know that the paraphernalia of hospitals often made it seem worse. He knew about the machines that would be hooked up to her, monitoring her vital signs, and he knew there would be tubes running into her body. But nothing could have prepared him for the blow of walking into the room—and then she opened her eyes and looked at him.

Incredibly, a weak smile spread over her bloodless lips, and she tried to hold out her hand to him, but her arm was anchored to the bed with tape, while an IV needle fed a clear liquid into her vein. For a moment Kell was frozen in place, and his eyes closed on the burning sensation that filled them. It was almost more than he could do to walk around the bed and lift her other hand to his cheek.

"It...isn't that bad," she managed, her voice almost soundless. "I heard...the doctor...say so."

God, *she* was trying to reassure *him*! He choked, rubbing her hand against his temple. He'd have given his own life to have spared her this, and he was the cause of it.

"I love you," he muttered hoarsely.

"I know," she whispered, and went to sleep. Sabin hung over her bed for several more minutes, memorizing every line of her face for the last time. Then he straightened, and his face settled into its usual hard, blank mask. Walking briskly from the room and down the hall to where Grant and Jane waited, he said tersely, "Let's go."

RACHEL WALKED THE BEACH as she did every afternoon, her eyes on the sand as she automatically looked for shells. Joe roamed in front of her, periodically coming back as if to check on her, then going off on his own pursuits again. For weeks after she'd collected him from Honey, Joe had been almost paranoid about letting her out of his sight, but that stage had long passed. For Joe, it was as if the events of the summer had never happened.

It was early in December, and she wore a light jacket to protect her from the cool wind. The fall quarter at the college in Gainesville was finished except for the final exams, but she had enough to keep her busy. She'd worked like a Trojan in the months since July, finishing her manuscript well ahead of schedule and immediately diving into another one. There had been the class to teach, and the increasing number of tourists after the slow days of broiling summer heat had kept the two souvenir shops doing a booming business, which meant she had to drive down at least twice a week, sometimes three times.

The scar on her right side was the only reminder of what had happened in July. That, and her memories. The house had been repaired, new Sheetrock hung and painted because the damage had been too great to simply plaster over. The windows had new frames, and she had a new light fixture in the living room, as well as new furniture and new carpeting, because she'd given up hope of ever getting the glass out of the old. The house looked normal, not as if anything had ever happened that had taken weeks to repair.

Her recovery had been uneventful, and relatively short. Within a month she had been going about her normal activities, trying to salvage some of the vegetables in the garden, which had become overgrown from neglect. Still, the pain from her wound had given her some idea of what Kell had gone through exercising his leg and shoulder to regain his mobility, and it staggered her.

She hadn't heard from him, not a word. Jane had stayed with her until she was released from the hospital, and had relayed the information that things had gone well in Washington. Rachel didn't know if Jane knew more but wasn't saying, or if that was all she'd been told. Probably the latter. Then Jane had left, too, to collect the twins and rejoin Grant at the farm. By now she would be round with pregnancy. For a time Rachel had thought she might be pregnant, too, from that last time Kell had taken her, but it had turned out to be a false alarm. Her system had simply gone awry from shock.

She didn't even have that. She had nothing but her memories, and they never left her alone.

She had survived, but it was only that: survival. She had gotten through each day without finding any joy in it, though she hadn't expected joy. At best, she would eventually find peace. Maybe.

It was as if part of her had been torn away. Losing B.B. had been terrible, but this was worse. She had been young then, and perhaps she hadn't been as capable of loving as deeply as she was now. Grief had matured her, had given her the depth of feeling with which she loved Kell. There wasn't a minute of the day that she didn't miss him, that she didn't live with pain because he wasn't there. She couldn't even find out about him from Jane; no information was available on Kell Sabin, ever. He had returned to his gray world of shadows and been swallowed up by them, as if he'd never been. Something could happen to him and she would never know.

That was the worst, the not knowing. He was there, but unreachable.

Sometimes she wondered if she'd dreamed it, that he'd come to her in the hospital and bent over her with his heart in his eyes as she'd never seen him before and whispered that he loved her. When she had awoken again she had expected to see him, because how could a man look like that and then walk away? But he had done exactly that. He'd been gone.

Sometimes she almost hated him. Oh, she knew all his reasons, but when she thought about it, they just didn't seem good enough. What gave him the right to make decisions for her? He was so damn arrogant, so certain that he knew best, that she could have shaken him until his teeth rattled.

The fact was that she had recovered from her wound, but she wasn't recovering from losing Kell. It ate at her day and night, taking away her joy in living and extinguishing the light in her eyes.

She wasn't pining away—she was too proud to let herself do that—but she was merely existing in limbo, without plans or anticipation. Walking the beach, staring out at the incoming waves, Rachel faced the fact that she had to do something. She had two options: she could try to reach Kell, or she could do nothing. To simply give up, to do nothing, went against her grain. He had had time to change his mind and come back, if he'd been going to, so she had to accept that he wasn't going to do it...not without incentive. If he wouldn't come to her, she'd go to him.

Just making that decision made her feel better than she had in months, more alive. She called to Joe, then turned and walked briskly up the beach toward her house.

She had no idea how to reach him, but she had to start somewhere, so she called telephone information to get the number of the agency in Virginia. That was easy enough, though she doubted it would be that simple to get put through to Kell. She called, but the operator who answered the phone denied that anyone by that name worked there. There was no listing for him. Rachel insisted on leaving a message, anyway. If he just knew she had called, perhaps he'd call back. Maybe curiosity wouldn't let him ignore the message.

But days went by and he didn't call, so Rachel tried again and received the same answer. There was no record of a Kell Sabin. She began contacting all the people she had done business with years ago when she was a reporter, asking for advice on how to get through to someone protected by the secrecy of the intelligence network. She sent messages to him through five different people, but had no way of knowing if any of them actually reached him. She continued to call, hoping that eventually the operator would get so frustrated that she'd hand the message on to someone.

For a month she tried. Christmas came and went, as well as the New Year celebrations, but the focus of her life was on somehow contacting Kell. It took a month for her to admit that either there was no way of getting a message to him, or he'd gotten them and still hadn't called.

To give up again, after trying so hard, hurt almost more than she could bear. For a while she'd had hope; now she had nothing.

She hadn't let herself cry much; it had seemed pointless, and she had really tried to pick herself up and keep going. But that night Rachel cried as she hadn't cried in months, lying alone in the bed she'd shared with him, aching with loneliness. She had offered him everything she had and

was, and he'd walked away. The long night hours crawle
by, and she lay there with her eyes wide and burning, sta
ing at the darkness.

When the phone rang the next morning she still hadn
slept, and her voice was dull when she answered.

"Rachel?" Jane asked hesitantly. "Is that you?"

With an effort Rachel roused herself. "Yes. Hello, Jan
how are you?"

"Round," Jane said, summing it up in one word. "Do yo
feel like coming up for a visit? I warn you, I have ulteric
motives. You can chase the boys while I sit with my fe
up."

Rachel didn't know how she could bear to see Jane an
Grant so happy together, surrounded by their children, bu
it would have been small of her to refuse. "Yes, of course
she forced herself to reply.

Jane was silent, and too late Rachel remembered tha
nothing got by Jane. And being Jane, she went right to th
heart of the matter. "It's Kell, isn't it?"

Rachel's hand tightened on the receiver, and she close
her eyes at the pain of just hearing his name spoken. S
many people had denied his existence that it stunned he
for Jane to bring up the subject. She tried to speak, but he
voice broke; then suddenly she was weeping again. "I'v
tried to call him," she said brokenly. "I can't get throug
No one will even admit that they know him. Even if they'
giving him my messages, he hasn't called."

"I thought he'd give in before now," Jane mused.

By that time Rachel had gotten herself under contr
again, and she apologized to Jane for crying all over he
She bit her lip, promising herself that it wouldn't happe
again. She had to accept his loss and stop mourning.

"Look, maybe I can do something," Jane said. "I'll hav
to work on Grant. Talk to you later."

Rachel hung up the phone, but she didn't let herself dwell on what Jane had said. She couldn't. If she got her hopes up again only to have them dashed, it would destroy her.

JANE WENT IN SEARCH of Grant, and found him in the barn, working on the tractor. It was cold, but despite the chill he was working in only his shirt sleeves, and they were rolled up to his elbows. Two chubby little boys with white-blond hair and amber eyes, snugly bundled against the chill, played at his feet. Grant had started taking them out with him, now that she was so big with pregnancy that it was hard for her to chase after two rambunctious toddlers.

When he saw her he straightened, a wrench in his hand. Swiftly his gaze went over her, and despite her bulk a certain gleam entered his eyes.

"How do I get in touch with Kell?" she asked, getting right to the point.

Grant looked wary. "Why do you want to get in touch with Kell?"

"For Rachel."

Considering, Grant eyed his wife. Kell had had his private phone number changed soon after he'd returned home, and Grant had made certain Jane hadn't discovered it since then. It was too dangerous for her to know things like that; she had a positive genius for attracting trouble.

"What about Rachel?"

"I just talked to her. She was crying, and you know Rachel never cries."

Grant looked at her in silence, thinking. Not many women would have done what Rachel had. She and Jane weren't ordinary women, and though they went about things differently, it was the basic truth that they were both strong women. Then he looked down at the little boys playing happily in the hay, crawling over his feet. Slowly a grin cracked his hard face. Kell was a good man; he deserved some of this happiness.

"All right," he said, putting the wrench aside and leaning down to scoop the twins into his arms. "Let's go into the house. I'll put the call through. There's no way in hell I'm letting you get his number."

Jane stuck her tongue out at him, but followed him to the house with a big grin on her face.

Grant didn't take any chances; he made her wait in the next room while he made the call. When he heard the line ringing he called her, and she raced in to grab the receiver from his hand. It took three more rings before the phone was picked up on the other end and a deep voice said, "Sabin."

"Kell," she said cheerfully. "This is Jane."

There was dead silence for a moment, and she stepped into the breach. "It's about Rachel."

"Rachel?" His voice was guarded.

"Rachel Jones," Jane said, rubbing it in. "Don't you remember her? She's the woman in Florida—"

"Damn it, you know I remember. Is something wrong?"

"You need to go see her."

He sighed. "Look, Jane, I know you mean well, but there's no point in talking about it. I did what I had to do."

"You need to go see her," Jane repeated.

Something in her voice got through to him, and she heard the sudden sharpness that edged into his tone. "Why? Is something wrong?"

"She's been trying to get in touch with you," Jane said evasively.

"I know. I got the messages."

"Then why haven't you called her?"

"I have my reasons."

He was the most stubborn, noncommittal man she'd ever met, except for Grant Sullivan; they were two of a kind. Still, even stone could be worn away by dripping water, so she didn't give up. "You should have called her."

"It wouldn't do any good," he said sharply.

"If you say so," Jane returned just as sharply. "But at least Grant married me when he found out I was pregnant!" Then she slammed the phone down with a satisfying bang, and a pleased smile spread over her face.

KELL PACED HIS OFFICE, running his hand through his black hair. Rachel was pregnant, carrying his baby. He counted the months; she would be six months along, so why had she waited so long before trying to contact him? Had something gone wrong? Was she sick? In danger of losing the child? Was something wrong with the baby?

The worry ate at him; it was even worse than what he'd gone through every day since he'd left her in the hospital. The want and need hadn't lessened; if anything, they had grown stronger. But every time the temptation to call her began undermining his common sense, his memory would dredge up the picture of her lying on the yard with her blood soaking her clothing, and he knew he couldn't live if his very presence put her in that sort of danger again. He loved her more than he'd known a human being could love; he'd never loved before, but when he'd fallen, he'd gone over hard. It pervaded his bone and tissue; he was never allowed to forget even for a moment. When he slept it was with the memory of holding her in his arms, but more often he lay awake, his body hard and aching for her softness to surround him.

He couldn't sleep; his appetite had suffered; his temper was shot to hell. He couldn't even have sex with other women, because the simple fact was that other women didn't even tempt him enough to arouse him. When he closed his eyes at night he saw Rachel, with her straight dark hair and clear, lake-gray eyes, and he tasted her on his tongue. He remembered her directness, her honesty, and the games played by women who tried to attract him did nothing other than turn him off.

She was going to have his baby.

The messages he'd been getting had been driving him crazy, and a dozen times he'd reached for the telephone. The messages had all been the same, short and simple. *"Call me. Rachel."* God, how he'd wanted to, just to hear her voice again, but now those messages took on more meaning. Had she just wanted to let him know that he was going to be a father, or was it more urgent than that? *Was something wrong?*

He reached for the telephone and actually dialed the number, but slammed the receiver down before her phone could begin ringing. Sweat broke out on his forehead. He wanted to see her, to make certain that everything was all right. He wanted to see her, just once, heavy and rounded with his child, even if he was never given anything else in this life.

IT WAS RAINING the next day when he drove down the narrow private road that led toward the beach and Rachel's house. The sky was low and gray, sullenly pouring rain as if it would never stop. The temperature was in the forties, but that seemed almost warm after the twenties he had left behind in Virginia, and the weather report on the radio had promised clear skies and a warming trend for the next day.

He had arranged for a flight to Jacksonville, then caught a commuter plane to Gainesville, where he rented a car. It was the first time he'd ever walked out of the office like that, but after what had happened last summer, no one questioned him. It wouldn't have done much good if they had; once Sabin decided to move, he moved.

He stopped the car in front of the house and got out, ducking against the rain. Joe was braced in front of the steps, snarling, and it was so much like before that a tight smile tugged at Kell's mouth. "Joe, heel," he said. The dog's ears perked forward at that voice and the command, and with a small bark he bounded toward Kell, his tail actually wagging.

"That's quite a greeting," Kell murmured, leaning down to rub the dog's head. "I just hope Rachel is as glad to see me." After he'd ignored all of her messages she might well slam the door in his face. Despite the chill he felt himself starting to sweat, and his heart was slamming against his ribs. He was so close to her; she was just on the other side of that door, and he was shaking with anticipation, his loins hardening. Damn, that was just what he needed.

He was getting soaked, so he sprinted across the yard and leaped onto the porch with one bound, disdaining the steps. He knocked on the frame of the screen door, then impatiently did it again, harder.

"Just a minute."

He closed his eyes at her voice, then heard her footsteps approaching the door, and opened them again, not wanting to miss even a second of looking at her. She opened the door, and they faced each other silently through the screen. Her lips moved, but no sound emerged. He tried to see her through the screen, but there were no lights on in the living room, and the dim, gray day didn't help much. All he could really see was the pale oval of her face.

"May I come in?" he finally asked quietly.

Without a word she pushed the screen door open and

moved back for him to enter. He stepped inside, closed
the wooden door behind him and reached to flip the light
switch, flooding the room with light. She stood before him,
small and fragile and very slim. She was wearing tight
jeans and a baggy black sweatshirt; her hair was longer
and pulled back from her face on each side with two big
tortoiseshell clips. She was pale, her face strained.

"You're not pregnant," he said in a tight voice. Had she
lost the baby?

She swallowed, then shook her head. "No. I'd hoped I
would be, but it didn't happen."

Her voice, so low and well remembered, made him shudder inside with pleasure, but her words brought him up
short. "You haven't been pregnant?"

Now she looked confused. "No."

His fists knotted. He didn't know which was worse, the
realization that Jane had lied to him, or disappointment that
Rachel wasn't pregnant, after all. "Jane told me you were
pregnant," he ground out, then abruptly remembered her
exact words, and a bark of laughter burst out even through
his anger. "Hell, no, she didn't. What she said was 'At least
Grant married me when he found out I was pregnant!'" he
told her, mimicking Jane. "Then she hung up on me. She's
so slick that I didn't catch it until now."

Rachel had been watching him, not even blinking as
she drank in his appearance. He was thinner, harder, that
black fire of his even more intense. "You came because
you thought I was pregnant?"

"Yes."

"Why bother now?" she asked, and bit her lip to stop it
from trembling.

Well, he'd asked for that. He looked at her again. She
had lost weight, and her eyes were listless. It startled him,
hit him hard. She didn't look like a happy woman, and

all he'd ever wanted was for her to be safe and happy.
"How are you?" he asked, concern deepening his voice to
a rumble.

She shrugged. "Well enough, I suppose."

"Does your side bother you?"

"No, not at all." She turned away, going toward the
kitchen. "Would you like a cup of hot chocolate? I was
just going to make some."

He took off his coat and tossed it over a chair before
following her. It gave him an overpowering sense of déjà
vu to lean against the cabinets and watch her fiddle with
pots and measuring cups. Abruptly she stopped and bent
her head down to rest it against the refrigerator door.

"It's killing me without you," she said in a muffled
voice. "I try, but I just don't care anymore. One day with
you is worth more to me than a lifetime without you."

His fists clenched again. "Do you think it's easy for
me?" His voice rasped the air like a rusty file. "Don't you
remember what happened?"

"I know what can happen!" she screamed, whirling on
him. "But I'm an adult, Kell Sabin! The risk is mine to take
if I think it's worth it! I accept that every time I get in my
car and drive to town. A lot more people are killed on the
highways every year than by terrorists or assassins. Why
don't you forbid me to drive, if you really want to protect
me?"

His eyes burned on her, but he didn't say anything, and
his remote silence goaded her. "I can live with the risks
you take in your job," she continued. "I don't like it, but
that's your decision to make. If you can't give me the same
right, then why are you here?"

Still he stared at her, frowning. The hunger for her was
growing in him, like an obsession. He wanted her, more
than he wanted his next breath. He could either live with

her, or live without her, and the past six months had shown him just how poor the quality of life was without her. The flat, unvarnished truth was that life wasn't worth living i he couldn't have her. Once he accepted that, his thought moved ahead. He'd have to take steps to make *certain* she was safe; he'd have to make changes and adjust, something he hadn't done before. It was odd how simple it looked all of a sudden, just because he admitted to himself that he had to have her. God bless Jane for getting his attention and giving him an excuse for coming down; she had known that once he saw Rachel again he wouldn't be able to leave.

He faced Rachel across the kitchen. "Can you really take it, the risks I take and the times I'll be gone when yo won't know where I am or when to expect me?"

"I already have," she said, lifting her chin. "What I need to know is that you'll come back to me when you can."

Still he watched her, his eyes narrow and piercing "Then we might as well get married, because God knows I've been a wreck without you."

She looked stunned; then she blinked. "Is that a proposal?"

"No. It was basically an order."

Slowly tears filled her gray eyes, making them glitter like diamonds, and a smile began to brighten her face. "All right," she said simply.

He did what he'd been hungering to do; he crossed the floor to her and took her in his arms, his mouth fastening hungrily on hers while his hands rediscovered the sleek curves of her body. Without another word he lifted her and carried her into the bedroom, tossing her across the bed just as he'd done the first time he'd made love to her. Swiftly he pulled her jeans down and off, then shoved the sweatshirt up to reveal her pretty round breasts. "I can take it slow," he whispered, jerking his pants open.

She didn't need for him to take it slow. She needed *him*, and she held her arms out to him. He spread her thighs and mounted her, controlling himself just long enough to slow his entry so he wouldn't hurt her, and with a low cry of pleasure Rachel took him into her body.

They lay in bed the rest of the day, making love and talking, but mostly just holding each other and reveling in the other's nearness. "What happened when you got back to Washington?" she asked sometime during the afternoon.

He lay on his back with one muscular arm thrown above his head, drowsy after making love, but his eyes opened at her question. "I can't tell you too much," he warned. "I won't ever be able to talk a lot about my work."

"I know."

"Tod Ellis talked, and that helped. Grant and I set a trap, and one of my superiors walked into it. That's about all I can tell you."

"Were there others in your department?"

"Two others."

"They almost had you," she said, shuddering at the thought.

"They would have had me, if it hadn't been for you." He turned his head on the pillow and looked at her; the glow was back in her eyes, the glow that only he could produce. He never wanted to see that light go out. He reached out to touch her cheek. "I was disappointed that you weren't pregnant," he said softly.

She laughed. "I may be after today."

"Just in case," he murmured, rolling onto her.

She caught her breath. "Yes, by all means, just in case."

EPILOGUE

THEY SAT ON THE PORCH of the big farmhouse where Grant and Jane lived, enjoying the warmth of the late summer sunshine. Kell was leaning back in his chair, his booted feet propped on the railing, and Grant was sprawled in a position of total relaxation. Both men looked sleepy after the heavy meal they had just eaten, but nevertheless two pairs of alert eyes monitored the children playing in the yard while Rachel and Jane were in the house. Presently the two women joined their husbands on the porch, sitting down in big rockers.

Kell straightened abruptly as Jamie, who was no more than a toddler, fell down in the yard, but before he could open his mouth the four little boys crowded around her, and Dane—or Daniel?—helped her up, brushing the dirt from her chubby little legs. The five children looked unusual together, with the three Sullivan boys almost white haired, they were so blond, while both Brian and Jamie were dark, with black hair and eyes. Jamie was the queen of that particular crowd, ruling everyone with her big eyes and dimples. She was going to be small, while Brian had his father's build.

The children ran shrieking toward the barn, with Dane and Daniel each holding one of Jamie's hands, and Brian and Craig behind them. The four adults watched them go. "Can you believe," Kell said thoughtfully, "that we're in our forties and have five preschoolers between us?"

"Speak for yourself," Rachel returned. "Jane and I are still young."

Kell looked at her and grinned. He still didn't have any gray in his hair, and neither did Grant. They were both hard and lean, and more content with their lives than they had ever been before.

It had all worked out rather well. Married to Rachel, and quickly aware that there was indeed a baby on the way, Kell had accepted a promotion and was no longer such a prime target. He was still in a position to use his knowledge and expertise, but at much less risk to himself. It had been a trade-off, but one that was worth it. He glanced over at Rachel. Oh, yes, it had definitely been worth it.

"You never did tell me," Jane said idly, rocking in her chair as if she hadn't a care in the world. "Did you forgive me for lying to you about Rachel being pregnant?"

Grant chuckled, and Kell stretched out even more, closing his eyes. "It wasn't much of a lie," Kell said peacefully. "She was before the next day was out. By the way, how did you get my number?"

"I called you for her," Grant confessed, putting his booted feet up on the railing, too. "I thought some of the good life was just what you needed."

Rachel's eyes met Kell's, and they smiled at each other. It was nice to have such good friends.

* * * * *

REQUEST YOUR
FREE BOOKS!

2 FREE NOVELS
FROM THE ROMANCE COLLECTION
PLUS 2 FREE GIFTS!

YES! Please send me 2 FREE novels from the Romance Collection and my 2 FREE gifts (gifts are worth about $10). After receiving them, if I don't wish to receive any more books, I can return the shipping statement marked "cancel." If I don't cancel, I will receive 4 brand-new novels every month and be billed just $5.74 per book in the U.S. or $6.24 per book in Canada. That's a saving of at least 28% off the cover price. It's quite a bargain! Shipping and handling is just 50¢ per book in the U.S. and 75¢ per book in Canada.* I understand that accepting the 2 free books and gifts places me under no obligation to buy anything. I can always return a shipment and cancel at any time. Even if I never buy another book, the two free books and gifts are mine to keep forever.

194/394 MDN FDC5

Name _____ (PLEASE PRINT) _____

Address _____ Apt. #

City _____ State/Prov. _____ Zip/Postal Code

Signature (if under 18, a parent or guardian must sign)

Mail to the **Reader Service:**
IN U.S.A.: P.O. Box 1867, Buffalo, NY 14240-1867
IN CANADA: P.O. Box 609, Fort Erie, Ontario L2A 5X3

Not valid for current subscribers to the Romance Collection
or the Romance/Suspense Collection.

Want to try two free books from another line?
Call 1-800-873-8635 or visit www.ReaderService.com.

* Terms and prices subject to change without notice. Prices do not include applicable taxes. Sales tax applicable in N.Y. Canadian residents will be charged applicable taxes. Offer not valid in Quebec. This offer is limited to one order per household. All orders subject to credit approval. Credit or debit balances in a customer's account(s) may be offset by any other outstanding balance owed by or to the customer. Please allow 4 to 6 weeks for delivery. Offer available while quantities last.

Your Privacy—The Reader Service is committed to protecting your privacy. Our Privacy Policy is available online at www.ReaderService.com or upon request from the Reader Service.

We make a portion of our mailing list available to reputable third parties that offer products we believe may interest you. If you prefer that we not exchange your name with third parties, or if you wish to clarify or modify your communication preferences, please visit us at www.ReaderService.com/consumerschoice or write to us at Reader Service Preference Service, P.O. Box 9062, Buffalo, NY 14269. Include your complete name and address.

MROM11

LINDA HOWARD